Unicorn Witches
The Vengeance of the Godhe

Derek White

PublishAmerica
Baltimore

ISBN: 1-4137-6998-5
PUBLISHED BY PUBLISHAMERICA, LLLP
www.publishamerica.com
Baltimore

Printed in the United States of America

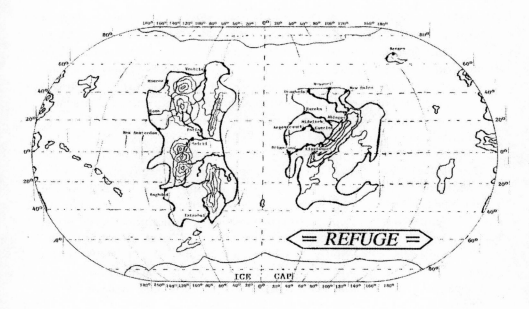

Preface

The inhabitants of the fourth planet of one of the last solar systems found before leaving this galaxy know their world as Refuge. Until the events described in *'Unicorn Witch'* they knew only that their ancestors, and occasionally people now, were brought from Earth by a race they called 'The Old Ones'. The transport to Refuge was initially of unicorns, dragons, and 'were' creatures and endangered species. Later a mutation of Homo sapiens sapiens was added as they began to be burnt as witches. The Godhe, as they call themselves, have their own problem in that at puberty the males' long bones continue to grow whilst their associated muscles atrophy causing constant pain.

From the age of about eight, all natives of Refuge are able to mentally 'call' for small items such as food and it will come to their hand. Some have more power and are able to start fires, cause rain, change the nature of things, and they refer to their ability as magic. Passing five tests gets one classified 'Bronze'. They are (i) Call some object weighing more than one kilo to your hand. (ii) Move that same something under control to a third party, (iii) start a fire mentally, (iv) Make rain, and (v) Change the nature of something e.g. water to wine, charcoal to diamond, etc.

3

Defeat two Bronzes in contest to become Silver. Defeat two Silvers to become Gold, and two Golds to become White.

Passing just one test qualifies a citizen to take a familiar. This familiar may be any animal and that animal gains human intelligence whilst near its partner and will only age as does the human. They are telepathically linked to their best friend for life. The unicorns are universally telepathic and as inherently intelligent as the humans, possibly more so. At the beginning of the story Tyana Counter has the only unicorn familiar in the world.

In *'Unicorn Witch'* Tyana, aided by Marcus, with unicorn partners Karim and Rebel solved the mystery of the losses of powers that had been occurring. They discovered that the hormone produced in the frontal sinus that gave the inhabitants of Refuge their powers was being stolen 'magically' or by telekinesis. Godhe criminals had discovered that an injection of the hormone had the effect of removing for up to six months the pain suffered by the males of the Godhe. It also gave a feeling of well being which made it addictive. The criminals who had been stealing the hormone were caught and sent for rehabilitation. It was hoped that research into why the hormone helped the Godhe men would lead to a cure.

Now, seven years later, their way of life is about to come under attack again.

***

Who's Who

(at the end of Unicorn Witch)

HUMANS:
   (W) = White (G) = Gold (S) = Silver (B) = Bronze

MERLIN PENDRAGON, World President, (W), Familiar Archimedes (Tawny Owl), Married to Laura

LAURA PENDRAGON, Healer, (Never tested for grade), Familiar Princess (Horse), Mother of Marcus.

HONDO COUNTER, Rancher, (G), Familiar Trigger (Horse) Father of Dustine, Darryl, & Tyana

LINDSEY COUNTER, Married to Hondo & Mother of his children, (G), Familiar Lightning (Horse)

DARRYL COUNTER, Ranch hand, (S), Familiar Timber (Horse)

DUSTINE (DUSTY) COUNTER, Rancher, (S), Familiar Ebony (Horse), Married to Megan

MEGAN COUNTER, Healer, (Never tested for grade), Familiar Bess (Horse)

TYANA COUNTER, President's agent, (W), Familiar Karim (Unicorn) Married to Marcus

MARCUS COUNTER, President's agent and Ranch hand, (W), Familiar Rebel (Unicorn)

THOMAS WILLIAMS, Schoolboy, (W), Familiar Jet (Unicorn), Megan's brother

SHAENA LODHI, Head of Camelot Council, (W), Familiar Hawka (Peregrine Falcon)

QAMAR LODHI, Council member, (W), Familiar Storm (Golden Eagle) Married to Shaena

CARLOS IGLESIAS, President European Council, (W) Familiar Javelin (Unicorn)

SOPHIA IGLESIA, Joint Head with Carlos, (W), Familiar Lotus Blossom (Unicorn)

ANGUS, Head of Brigadoon Council, (W), Familiar Battler (Horse)

ELECTRA, Head of Abinger Council, (W), Familiar Blackie (Horse)

BILL CASSIDY, Head of Eureka Council, (W),

SUSQUEHANA, Head of Kissimmee Council, (W), Familiar Kiltie (Pony)

MICHAELA O'CONNOR, Head of Drogheda Council, (W), familiar Sheelagh (Horse)

MAGDALENA, Head of New Salem Council, (W), Familiar Tess (Vixen)

KARILLA, Head of Newport Council, (W), Familiar Penn (Gull)

UNICORNS:

SCIMITAR, Herd leader Kissimmee, Rebel's brother.

ZOLTAN, Herd leader Camelot, Karim's Sire.

BELLE, Karim's Dame, Friend of Merlin, Favourite mare of Zoltan's herd

KARIM, REBEL, JET, JAVELIN, & LOTUS BLOSSOM, Listed above as familiars.

DRAGONS:

MANDRAKE, Leader of pack near Paris, friend of Tyana and Marcus

SHINLU, Mate of Mandrake and co-representative of their people

WEREFOLK:

CANTOR, First Were befriended by Tyana, Leader of his village.

VERNIQUE, Cantor's wife and co-representative of their people.

THE GODHE:

ARISTO, Head of Medical Research on Centrallis, now friend of Merlin & Co.

KRESH AND KRAST, Two female weapons experts captured by Marcus and sent for rehabilitation

OISTRACH, Drug Baron whose operations were curtailed in 'Unicorn Witch' Also sent for 'rehab'

THE OLD ONES, Collective name for the ruling council of twelve Godhe

Chapter One

CAMELOT, REFUGE, 1358.

Just as it had been over six years ago, a marquee was erected in the paddock of the Counter ranch, and enjoying dinner within were most of the guests present when the liberation of Europe had been celebrated.

Aristo was once again the guest of honour, fulfilling a promise made to attend the next seven yearly meeting of Council leaders, and this was due to start in Camelot in two days time. He rose to reply to Merlin's speech; glanced at the electronic notepad he held, then switched it off and put it on the table.

"Friends, as you could see, I had a speech prepared. It took me most of the week's travel here to get it right, but now I've seen you again all I want to do is be told what's happened to each of you since I was last here. I'll go first!

"I have good news, and bad. The good is that we've been able to isolate the component of your hormone Theurgen which helped invigorate our men and provided that we each take a tablet every twelve hours we can be, whilst not as active as our women, more so than before.

"The bad is that we've made no progress in finding the reason why our muscles stop developing once we reach puberty, but at least, thanks to you, we can be free of pain.

"I know, of course, that you've succeeded in replacing the feudal system in Europe with the elected Councils you've had here for over a thousand years, and I look forward to meeting their Heads the day after tomorrow.

"Such information as that we can get from the weekly reports we receive from our own agents. Yes, our own agents. I'm happy to say that we've been allowed to re-establish our base here.

"I'm more interested in the personal things in your life after I left. All I know is that Tyana, Laura, and Karim were each three months pregnant, so where are the children?

"Thomas, have you and Jet made Gold yet? When do I get to hear Megan on harp?

"Your World Council Meeting will be a formal occasion, so let this be a meeting of friends, please. "Marcus, we heard from you last time, so, Tyana, you start, if you will."

<< *Karim, Darling,* >> Tyana mentally called to her partner, who was grazing just outside the tent, << *Is Aristo really being honest with us? Is he really interested in our gossip? What's he thinking?* >>

<< *His thoughts match his words. He really isn't looking forward to matters of state and prefers getting to know us again. I have the impression he has some news he's not looking forward to giving us. He's deliberately avoiding thinking about something, maybe the meeting.* >>

Thus reassured, Tyana rose to her feet, walked over to Aristo, kissed him on the cheek, and returned to her seat.

"We had a girl, Julie, then twin boys, Paul and Christopher, a year later. Karim had twins, Shadow and Star, a colt and a filly; on the very same day I had Julie, then twins again a year later, that time both colts. You'll meet them all shortly.

"Marcus and I made our home in the extension to the ranch built for Laura when she arrived, and he's become a typical Camelot cowboy. There is, I'm happy to say, no work for a detective now. Laura, it's your turn!"

"Merlin and I had a son, Simeon, but unlike Marcus, I found plenty of work to do. Megan and I are still the only healers in Argentcourt, Midwitch, and Camelot. I'm not complaining, though, and I'm happier than at any time of my life on Earth. At our age, we decided that one child was right for us. Merlin still has to spend a lot of time in Camelot, but we have a ranch an equal distance from each town. Dusty and Megan share it, and Dusty runs it."

"But how do you know when you're needed?"

"You surely remember Thomas's partner? There's always a duty unicorn in each town nowadays who can contact Jet. As long as he's within ten miles of one of us he can pass on a request, but if he needs to be further away, we're very near Zoltan's herd, and the message can be relayed. You will I'm sure remember that unicorns can communicate with their own kind over any distance?"

Aristo nodded as he made notes on his keyboard, and then turned to the youngest present.

"Thomas, did you become Gold earlier than Tyana as you hoped?"

"No, Sir! I made Bronze when only seven, which put me a year ahead, but for both Silver and Gold I was a little later than her; in fact I've only just got my Gold."

"And how are you getting on at school? Come to think of it, what do you learn at school on Refuge? How does it differ from being on Earth? I've never asked."

"I'm not sure how to answer that, Sir. I can only remember school here. I'm told I hated it in Wales. Perhaps Megan, Marcus, or Laura would be better informed to say."

"As you wish!

" Megan?"

"You must understand that the system was already running when we arrived, Aristo. The children are sent to school until they know all they need to know for life here. That's a lot less than they teach on Earth. However they have to keep attending until they do know it, so there's plenty of incentive to learn.

"If you talk to one of the others for a moment I'll get you a copy of the syllabus!"

"Darryl, are you still unmarried?"

"I'm afraid so! Still, someone has to be free to do the work around here.

"But seriously, until the right girl comes along I'm happy enough!"

"I'd have thought there'd be no shortage of girls around here who'd want you. According to our figures, there are slightly more females than males of your age on this continent.

"Why are you all laughing?"

"Sorry, Aristo!" answered Darryl. "I don't know how you do things on your home world, but here it's not just a question of numbers. Even on Earth, I'm told there's a tendency to move away from arranged marriages. Here, they'd be disastrous. The four way bond you get when two people each with a familiar marry is such that the union just has to be for life, like Megan, Bess, Dusty, and Ebony.

"Speaking of Megan, here she is with that list for you."

Aristo took the list, beautifully written in easy to read block letters and scanned it—

SUMMARY OF EARTH HISTORY
REFUGE HISTORY
ARITHMETIC (Add, Subtract, Multiply, Divide ONLY)
ENGLISH
REFUGE GEOGRAPHY
MUSIC
FRENCH
MAGIC (EXCUSED WHEN BRONZE)

THE CONSTITUTION

"And what standard to they have to reach before being allowed to leave school?"

"Just whatever they manage in both the Histories, Music, Geography, French, and Magic.

"We insist on them passing quite difficult tests in Arithmetic and English, and they are given a copy of our Constitution when they leave."

This came as something of a surprise to Aristo, having experience with over a hundred different races, all of which had a range of abilities from genius to stupid.

He asked, "But surely there must be some children who grow up unable to pass the tests? What happens to them?"

"Sorry, Aristo! The oldest at the school in Camelot is only fifteen. Maybe intelligence goes with having theurgen, but personally I think it's because we only teach what they need to know. The children can see the point of learning, unlike on Earth where they teach things of no interest."

"But there's so much they don't have the opportunity to learn! No Sciences at all, no Astronomy, no…"

Megan stopped him, "Our adults can all communicate, all read, write, and do sums! Can you name one other world where that's true? It certainly wasn't on Earth!

"Take Thomas! He's just passed with maximum marks in English, French, and Arithmetic, and very high marks in the others. What possible good would it do to make him go back to school?"

Looking around the table, and seeing that all seemed to agree with her, Aristo decided not to press the point and changed the subject. "You were also pregnant if I remember correctly?"

"That's right, I was. Dusty and I have a daughter, Caroline. She'll be the last of the children you meet in a few moments, and she has a surprise for you which will help you enjoy the little recital we've planned."

"Recital? Do I get to hear your harp?"

"You do! One of the former slaves in Paris had been a music teacher and conductor in Milan on Earth. He's added most of the works of the great composers to our records, now lives in Camelot where he teaches several instruments, and is coming to conduct our little group as he wants to meet you before the official concert on Thursday."

The children arrived, were introduced, and without a word being spoken about a headache, Caroline climbed on to Aristo's knee and put her hand on his forehead.

"There, Sir," she said. "You didn't need to suffer through dinner when both Mummy and Auntie Laura were here."

"Thank you, Caroline, but - How did you know my head ached?"

"I could feel it when I looked at you, but in any case, Uncle Jet told me. Mummy had told him."

"Why do you call him 'Uncle' Jet? Surely Thomas is your uncle."

"Same thing, Silly. Oops, sorry, Sir. But it is the same. Thomas and Jet are two parts of one person, just like Auntie Tyana and Karim, Uncle Marcus and Rebel, Carlos and Javelin, and so on. I thought you knew that!"

Aristo hugged the little girl, saying, "It's hard for me. I had been told, but until you explained it that way, I didn't really understand. Thank you again."

Aristo watched, fascinated, as the large dining table laden with the remains of the meal vanished, everyone stood, and the chairs apparently arranged themselves facing a small stage which appeared from nowhere at one end of the tent. He looked outside to see the coach and four he remembered from his last visit arriving with the man he assumed to be the conductor. When he looked back the stage held drums, a grand piano, and a harp. He walked over to Marcus and asked, "Is there any limit to what you people can move just by willing it to happen?"

"All of our people can move small objects in everyday use, up to, say ten pounds in weight, and they can all call for food as long as they're not too far from a store.

"Bronzes, that's about a quarter to a third of our people, can use magic to do useful work and have a lot more control. Their limit on moving would be about half a hundredweight, and they can be up to a mile from something and still 'call' it. Silvers, if they have a heavy familiar can double that, but tire quickly. Golds can move their own weight repeatedly, all day if necessary. Whites can usually move double that.

"We're going to have to create a special category for those with a unicorn as a partner, as once they reach Gold, and the inhibition from the herd stallion is removed, it's hard to define a limit. "You remember yourself what Tyana did when we ended the European war - many tons at a speed so high it couldn't be seen?

"Tonight, I brought the stage, Thomas the harp, Tyana the piano, Merlin the drum kit, and the other instruments were called for by their owners."

"Have you ever wondered just how you do what you do?"

"Frankly, no! We all just accept it. Perhaps your 'agents' as you called them should look out for a scientist on Earth.

"Let's take our places. Signore Mancini has arrived."

Instead of going to the stage, Enrico went first to Merlin for a quiet word.

"I'm sorry if we're a little late, Merlin, but we had the strangest experience on the road here.

"We'd just left Camelot. Thank you for sending the coach, by the way. There was a girl, or maybe a woman, I couldn't tell which, on the road.

"I'd swear she was walking towards us, but when we got to her she was going towards this ranch.

"I offered her a ride, but she backed away, obviously frightened. I'm worried about her, as she looked dirty, tired and hungry. She may be a new arrival, so I thought you should know."

"Thank you, Enrico, I'll deal with it. Now, let us get on with entertaining our guest of honour…

"May I introduce our very good friend Aristo, the only member of the Godhe we have really got to know. He's Head of Medical Research on his home world and their representative at the meeting here.

"Aristo, .. Signore Enrico Mancini!"

Leaving the two to talk for a few minutes, Merlin turned to the younger of Tyana's two brothers.

"Darryl! A word please, if you'd be so kind."

Quickly he outlined what the conductor had told him and Darryl agreed to look for the girl. Merlin rejoined Enrico and made sure the conversation kept going until the added seats in the marquee had filled. He was pleased to note that as far as he could tell, every delegate for the conference had arrived with a partner. None had taken offence at being excluded from the dinner, which he'd been asked by the guest of honour to restrict to family and friends.

Aristo's previous experience of music had been the computer-generated concerts at home. He knew that live music had existed in his race's infancy, but thousands of years had passed since the last Godhe player lived. He was expecting an inferior version of what his home computers could produce.

Instead he was treated to two hours of sheer ecstasy, and he found himself crying several times, something he couldn't remember happening at any time in his life, even as a child.

When the last item ended, Ave Maria by Gounod, sung by Tyana and accompanied only by Megan on Harp, he just sat there in a daze. Megan leapt from the stage, Laura rushed across the hall, but it was little Caroline who got there first.

"He's not breathing, Mummy….His heart's stopped….No it hasn't….it's very fast and weak....Help him, Mummy, Laura!" No help was needed, however, as Aristo recovered unaided.

Later, he tried to explain. "Never in my life have I experienced anything like the emotions your music generated. It was just too much for me. I can give it a name, - Anaphylactic Shock - but I've never heard of music bringing it on."

"I have," explained Laura, "but the victims are usually teenagers at a concert where their idols are performing. I suspect that your race has lost as much in the arts as it gained in the sciences.

"That can wait till tomorrow, though, I prescribe an early night for you."

***

Darryl had little difficulty in finding the girl described. It was still an hour to dusk, so he saw her from a mile away, and she stood, rooted to the spot as he approached on Timber at about eighty miles an hour, using a normal canter, but with the strides multiplied some five times. As he neared and slowed to a normal walk he studied her. She was no longer frozen, but running off to the side towards a group of trees.

From a distance the walker, dressed in Levis, boots, white shirt, and black leather jacket could have been male or female, and Darryl had wondered how Signore Mancini had been so sure. Now, at twenty yards, he had no doubt. Except for his sister Tyana, he had never seen such a perfect combination of feminine beauty and athletic movement. He thought she must be about twenty five or thirty, about nine inches shorter than his six feet, and probably around eight and a half stones. He could see that she had flaming red hair but it was tucked inside the collar of her jacket making it impossible to determine the length.

Timber set off after her, and Darryl called, "Don't be silly, you've seen how fast we can travel. I'm not going to hurt you! Stop to talk!"

She mumbled something, but kept right on going, reaching the trees long before he would have thought possible.

As he and Timber walked in, only a rapid sidestep by the horse saved him from the two footed kick launched from a tree.

She somehow landed on her feet and was off again, but by now Darryl was getting annoyed. Of the Counters he was easily the best at roping steers or calves when needed, as he proceeded to demonstrate, soon having the runner in a noose, and tied to his saddle horn.

She wouldn't give up, though, slipped the noose somehow, and started again.

This time, he galloped alongside and dropped, taking her to the ground with him and knocking the wind from her.

"That's enough! I don't want to hurt you, but I will if you insist! Now, stop a while and talk.

"Then I promise, if you want to go off on your own, you can!"

"You promise?"

"I promise!"

Now up close he could see how attractive she really was. Her eyes were wide open and deep blue with just the odd fleck of green when light from the setting sun caught them at the right angle. For a moment he was too amazed to do more than just look at her, but he knew he had to say something or she would be off again.

"Tell me, have you by any chance just woken to find yourself on that road you were walking down?"

"How do you know that? And if you know that, how can I trust you?"

"Seven years ago my brother and I found the girl who is now his wife. She'd just arrived with her six year old brother. It also happened to one of my best friends. He's now married to my sister; and his mother, who arrived at the same time, is married to our World President."

Some of the frightened look disappeared as the girl digested this information, and she decided she had to trust someone sometime. This young man was as good as any, and if he tried anything…

"I woke this morning, feeling fitter than I've felt for years. I spent the day hiding, and wondering where I was and what to do. I'm hungry, so I decided to go where all the coaches were going.

"I….."

She looked like a little girl caught with her hand in her mother's purse as she blurted out, "I was going to steal some food! There must be some there with all those people going there!

"Please, Mister, where am I? This place is like nowhere I've ever seen, except in a movie or a history book……people still going around in horse drawn coaches!"

"Tell me your name, and I'll try to answer, but I'm only a cow hand, and there are people who can do it a lot better than I. Still, I'll tell you what I can!

"And you won't have to steal food! It's free here, for everyone! Now, what do they call you?"

16

"They call me Lace!"

"That's not your real name?"

"It's what they call me. It'll do. It's what I answer to!"

"Where were you before you arrived here, Lace?"

"Hiding in a side alley in The Bronx!"

"What town, and country?"

"The Bronx. You know - New York, in the U.S. of A.

"Don't you know anything?"

"How can I put this? You're going to find it hard to believe, but you're no longer on Earth at all.

"This place, we call it Refuge, is a haven for people with a certain amount of magical ability. What might help you adjust is that Laura, Marcus's mother, you remember, the one married to the president, well she's from New York, too!"

"What do you mean? Not on Earth? What sort of ability?"

"You said you were hungry. What would you most like to eat and drink?"

"A Burger and Coke! You produce them, and I'll start to believe in fairies!"

"Burger. Would that be a hamburger? And is Coke the brand name for a fizzy drink a reddish brown colour?"

"That sounds like a funny description of them!"

"Here you are, then! Is one enough? Do you want some fries as well?"

As Darryl handed over the snack, he watched Lace's face change from being hard and ready to fight, to like a child in a toyshop. He said nothing, dismounted, and petted Timber whilst she ate.

"I guess I've got to believe you, Mister, but - ," and she started to cry, "what happens now?"

Darryl wanted to put his arms around her to comfort her, but Timber advised him, << *I shouldn't if I were you! She's scared enough already!* >>

<< *Thanks, Friend!* >>

Instead he told her, "Don't worry, Lace. Everyone who's ever come here has fitted in. I expect you've got some talent we can use, and you must have shown some magic yourself, or you wouldn't have been brought here.

"How did you earn your living in America? And call me Darryl, not Mister!"

"Sorry, I'm not saying!"

"Will you let me take you to our home?

"Listen! You can just hear the music from the concert there tonight!"

"Who's there? Any cops?"

"What are cops?"

"You kidding? You know - police!"

"Sorry! I've never heard the word 'cops.' We don't have any. We don't need them. Well, that's not quite true. We have one, or at least he was one on Earth seven years ago, and we were very glad of him when he arrived, but he's retired now, and ranches with me."

"You serious, Mister, er - Darryl?"

"I am. Now, would you rather travel in front of me on Timber, or behind?"

"I never rode before. Behind I think."

Darryl mounted, then using a trapeze grip, right wrist to right wrist, swung her behind him in one smooth movement.

<< Let's go, Timber, home, and as fast as you like! >>

<< Anything you say, Boss. May I just say I admire your taste in girlfriends? >>

"No you may not!"

"May not what?"

Too late, Darryl realised he'd spoken aloud. Again the girl said, "May not what? And you're blushing!"

"I was talking to Timber, and he surprised me, so I answered aloud. I'm sorry!"

"Answered aloud? What other way is there? And why haven't you any reins to guide him?"

Timber slowed to a normal walk, and for half an hour Darryl told Lace all he could of life on her new world, having some difficulty with the concept of familiars.

The concert was still in progress when they arrived, and, after grooming Timber, and turning him loose, throughout which Lace never stopped watching him, he took her to the entrance to the marquee, conjured them chairs, and they enjoyed the rest of the concert, whilst Lace had another Burger and Coke, this time with fries as well.

As the applause died down, he took her to the main library of the ranch, gave her a strong drink, and waited until sure Aristo and the children had retired. He then took her to join the others, introducing the women first; as instinct told him it was men she had been afraid of. The men were simply named. He noticed that Marcus, in particular, she would not look directly at.

"I'm sorry to arrive like this, in my street clothes, M'lady," she said to Tyana. "Compared to Laura, Lindsey, Megan, and yourself, I feel very drab, and underdressed."

"What's wrong, Darryl? Have I said the wrong thing?"

"Don't mind me! You sound much better educated now than you did when we met, that's all."

"Never mind that now!" said Tyana. "The clothes are easily dealt with, as you're just about my size. For the record we don't dress like this all the time but we have a very important guest this evening. Do you like Green?"

"Yes! It's my favourite colour."

Lace found herself clean, as from a long soak, hair groomed, and wearing a ball gown in emerald green with shoes to match. Putting her hand to her shoulders over the strapless dress she found her bra had disappeared to avoid the straps showing, and began to realise that Darryl's tales on the ride about Tyana's power had been simple statements of fact.

"Th.. Thank you, Ma'am! I don't know what to say. It's lovely! I've never worn anything like it in my whole life. I..I'm gabbling, so I'd better shut up!"

"You're very welcome, both to the dress and to our home. Has Darryl been looking after you? Are you hungry? Thirsty? And my name's Tyana, not Ma'am!"

"Thank you again!" answered Lace, feeling a little more in control, "Yes, he's looked after me very well. I can't get used to the idea that I'm not a freak after all!"

"A freak?" asked Laura.

"Yes. All my life I've thought I was the only one who could make things happen just by wanting them to. And now I'm in a place where it seems that everyone can do it."

"You don't know how lucky you are!" Megan told her. "When I first arrived here I spent a couple of days thinking I was dreaming. At least you've accepted that we're real! I'd been here for some time before Dusty taught me to move things by will alone. Before that all I'd done was heal people and animals.

"What did you move?"

Immediately the frightened look came back and Lace turned to Tyana. "Please. I'm very tired. Darryl said I could stay here tonight. If it's alright, may I go to bed?"

"Of course you may! And I'm sure my brother didn't say you could stay with us just for the night.

"You're welcome until you wish to leave, whether it be for one night, or life. If I were you I'd plan on being here for fourteen days at the very least. That's how long it will be before anyone from Abinger comes to ask you questions.

"Laura, would you oblige, please. Your old room should do fine if you don't mind?"

"Mind? Why should I mind?

"Come on, My Dear, let's make you comfortable. You can lock the door if you wish, but I assure you nobody would even think of entering your room uninvited!"

As soon as they were out of the library Tyana smiled at her brother and said, "May I say, Darryl, I admire your taste in girl friends?"

Darryl blushed, as he replied, "No you may not! You're the second one tonight!"

"Oh, really? Who was the first?"

"Timber, if you must know!"

Just then Laura returned, commented that she thought Lace would be asleep within minutes, as she really did look tired when out of the room. She then noticed Darryl's redness and said, "Darryl, may I say I admire your taste in girlfriends?"

She had little trouble mentally diverting the cushion Darryl threw at her. "Have I said something wrong?" she wanted to know.

"You can't be wrong, Mother!" commented Marcus. "After all, you're the third person to say it so far this evening, so there must be something in it.

"Seriously, tell us about her, Darryl."

"The poor girl's scared stiff that someone's going to learn what she did back on Earth. That's why she avoided talking to Marcus as one of her first questions was to ask if we have any cops at the ranch............ so his name came up."

"Thanks a lot, Friend!"

"Most of the time I had to do the talking…"

"Which I'm sure you found very stressful!" interrupted Tyana.

"I'll ignore that! The only other thing I know about her is that I feel very protective towards her. She seemed so tough when I met her, yet so helpless and frightened as well. I really enjoyed her company whilst we were waiting for the concert to finish, and by the way, she thinks the violinists were very good…. that's what she plays herself."

"I can't wait to see her again in the morning.

"All of you, please be kind to her, …. for me?"

***

At breakfast next morning, Aristo found himself sharing the position of guest of honour with Lace, to whom he confessed that he'd never before met a recent arrival. Julie kept him provided with food, and there was a constant stream of questions from the twins, but he did manage a few more himself.

"Tyana, your three children, together with Caroline, and Simeon are all of an age to show the first signs of the sort of power you have, and in Caroline's case I know myself how strong it is.

"Are they paired with familiars yet? If so, where are they?

If not - why not? I want to learn as much as I can in the short time I'm here. I'd also like to meet Karim and Rebel's foals, or should it be children?"

Darryl noticed that Lace was as attentive as Aristo, obviously wanting to learn as much as possible.

"Answering your last question first, the foals, for that's how Karim thinks of them, are with their grandsire, the herd stallion Zoltan. They spend about one week a month with the herd so that they lose none of the fun of growing up. We're not sure ourselves when or even if to annex any of the five children you named. Let me tell you why.

"With only Megan to attend, and two of us due to deliver on the same day, Laura's confinement was here, in the same room as me, and we gave birth within an hour of each other. The same day Karim had twins, Shadow first, then Star.

"Within a week we all noticed that the babies behaved better, and were happier, when we took them out to the stable.

"Before they were a month old we found that life was easier if Shadow was near Simeon, and Star was near Julie.

"After a while, just as we thought there must be some sort of natural bonding, they started not bothering if we took them apart, and we assumed we'd been mistaken. By their first birthday they didn't mind even long separations. Just after that we noticed a similar reaction between our twins Paul and Chris, and Karim and Rebel's Minstrel and Maestro.

"Just as with the earlier pair, with time, they didn't mind separation.

"At first we were all worried by the very slow growth of the unicorn foals, then we realised that just as Karim only ages as I do, and Rebel only ages as Marcus does, this was happening with them, and we must have been right to consider a possible natural bonding. The reason they tolerated longer separations was simply that they no longer lost contact when separated.

"Excuse me! Did you say unicorn foals?" asked Lace.

"Yes! That's just another thing for you to get used to. This world has been made into a sanctuary for all Earth's magical creatures, unicorns amongst them."

Lace became even more thoughtful and would have asked more, but saw Darryl shaking his head slightly to her. Tyana continued,

"Three years ago a friend of Sophia died in childbirth. Only a month after she came here, actually on the very day Marcus and Laura arrived, Megan had accidentally developed a way of using magic in a case of breech presentation where you, or surgeons on Earth, would operate. We took her to Europe to teach her technique to healers there so that no more lives would be lost that way.

"I suppose for Marcus and me, you'd call it a holiday. After Megan had demonstrated in Paris, Caroline came with us, whilst she went on to Madrid, so that there would be four healers able to teach her method. Whilst we were there, their partners, you remember them - Javelin and Lotus Blossom? - also had twins, both fillies.

"One of them bonded with their three year old, Rosa, and the other one, Bella, with Caroline. Lotus Blossom and Javelin didn't mind at all when she came home with us. You remember, of course, that there's no limit to the distance over which they can speak to their own kind.

"So you see, all five have unicorn foals as best friends, all five are bi-lingual, and all have shown signs that they've inherited the sort of power you'd expect.

"The most advanced, or at least the only one who's really been tested, and she did that herself when Julie had a fall and hurt her knee, is Caroline. As soon as she put her hand on the injured leg the pain went, and just by wanting her friend to get better, she did. We're still discussing when they should go through qualification for Bronze."

"The only precaution," put in Marcus, "is that we had Rebel and Javelin, respectively, together with Zoltan and Javelin's original herd stallion all stress to the foals that they may only assist when the children get to Gold in their own right."

"Something I've often wondered, Tyana.

"How do the unicorns get their names? In particular, why Minstrel and Maestro?"

"They're normally named by the elders of the herd when they've grown enough to show their characters. For instance Rebel rebelled against the teaching in his herd and used to go to visit the humans for conversation, and so his original given name was changed.

"Very early in their lives Minstrel and Maestro showed how much they enjoyed listening to music. It's a pity they had to miss last evening's recital. They'd have loved it!

"Shadow moved around just like his sister's shadow, making Star the leader, or 'star' of the pair.

"Bella.... well, when you see her, you'll understand. Even amongst unicorns she stands out. Her twin sister's called Orchid. There's a tradition in her mother's herd that flower names are used for the firstborn. Remember her dame? Lotus Blossom?"

"Fascinating!" exclaimed Aristo and Lace together, then Lace continued to Aristo, "May I ask what that is you're drawing, Sir?"

"Yes, Aristo, I wondered that, too." commented Tyana.

"It's just a sort of Family Tree to help me remember who is with whom.

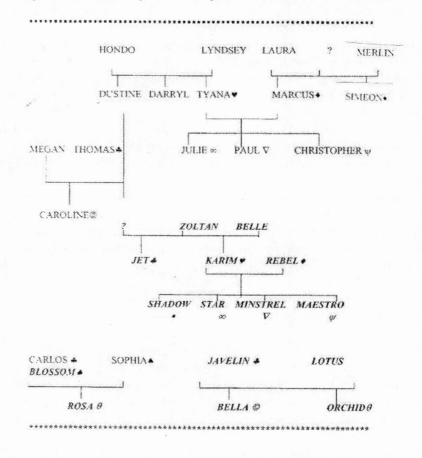

"But what are the funny little signs?" asked Tyana. "Oh, I see! They show which unicorn is paired with which human. I'd love to have a copy, it's so neatly printed."

"Of course you may have one. One for each of you if you wish.

"Thank you."

"One last name question, if I may. Why Karim?"

"That's a little unusual," explained Tyana. "Belle, Karim's dame has always been very friendly with Merlin, as you know, and by extension with Shaena and Qamar. They had a little girl stillborn who they would have named Karim. Belle named her new foal in memory of her."

"Now," Aristo commented, "I must leave at lunch time to collect Carlos, Sophia, Mandrake, Shinlu, Cantor and Vernique, but I suppose you have something planned for me this morning?"

Tyana laughed. "Would you like to visit Zoltan, Karim's sire? He asked me to bring you out to the herd if possible."

"I'd love to. I'll get the chance to see the foals as well. Do we use my ship?"

"How do you feel about travelling on a unicorn at between two and three hundred miles an hour?"

"Thrilled…terrified…I'm not sure. Is it really possible? After all, we don't have animals like horses at home, and I've never ridden."

"Don't worry. Rebel will make sure you don't fall off, and I'll be there on Karim."

"But surely Rebel needs one of you to multiply his stride. I remember that much from my last visit."

This was not, in fact, true, but only Qamar, Shaena, Laura and Merlin, except for unicorn riders themselves knew that the unicorns were the equal of their human partners. Aristo remembered that Karim could move chess pieces, but it never occurred to him that she may be able to do more.

"For the distance we have to go I can handle it for both Karim and Rebel."

<< *Good Morning, Aristo.* >>

<< *Good Morning, Lace. I've heard about you from Tyana.* >>

Unseen by Aristo and Lace, Rebel and Karim had come up behind them and each nuzzled an ear, something they could do whilst talking.

"Hello, again, Rebel. What do you think about this crazy idea of Tyana's?"

Poor Lace just stood there, mouth open, unable to think, let alone reply.

<< *I think you'll enjoy it. Even if you don't, it will be worth the discomfort to meet Zoltan.* >>

Karim left Lace and joined them, a saddle appeared on Rebel's back and he saw a mounting block with steps alongside. Very carefully Aristo climbed to the top then asked, "Are you really sure, Rebel? It would be no trouble to use my ship!"

There was no answer from Rebel but suddenly Aristo found that he was looking forward to a new experience and swung his leg over, finding that this saddle had a handrail at the front for him to grip. Stirrups appeared around his boots, then extra leather straps and supports were added, including a back support. To his surprise, he found it very comfortable, even though, as he commented, "This makes me look a novice compared to you, My Dear, but I'm grateful."

"As soon as you feel relaxed, I'll remove most of the extras. Certainly you'll look just as experienced as me when we arrive. Let's go!"

Rebel and Karim went smoothly to canter, as the most comfortable stride for a novice rider, then slowly increased the multiplying factor until they were travelling at about one hundred miles per hour.

<< Shall we gallop now? >> asked Rebel.

"You mean we aren't galloping?" gasped Aristo, holding firmly to the rail in front of him, and with his eyes tightly closed.

<< Trust me! Look around you. I promise I won't let you fall! >>

Aristo did as asked, and found to his surprise that travelling with his eyes closed, imagining a fall, was much worse than seeing the scenery flash past him.

"I'll probably regret this," he said, "but let's go!"

Before he had time to change his mind, Rebel changed to gallop and increased his speed to two hundred miles per hour.

They stopped on a hill to give Aristo a view of the unicorn herd, a scene he vowed to remember for the rest of his life. Two of the herd came up the hill to meet them, both white, but whilst the larger had horn, hooves, mane, and tail black, the other was like a slightly older version of Karim. He guessed correctly that they were Zoltan and Karim's dame, Belle.

<< You are welcome, Aristo. I thank you for the help you gave to my daughter and her friends in their time of peril. I also wish to thank you on behalf of all my people. Merlin tells us that we would have been wiped out on Earth if your ancestors had not intervened. >>

"Zoltan, no thanks are necessary. We've already been repaid a hundredfold by the discovery that a hormone produced by the humans here can help remove the pain of an affliction our men suffer. We do what we feel is right, just as I believe you would in our position.

"Belle, you're as beautiful as your daughter, yet you look a little sad. May an old man ask why?"

<< I'm not really sad, Aristo. I just looked at Karim closely for the first time in six years, and realised she's aged hardly at all, whilst I look six years older.

<< I know it's because she will only age at the same speed as Tyana, but I can't help feeling a little envious. >>

It may seem strange, but that remark, just the sort of thing one of the women back home would have said in the same circumstances finally brought home to Aristo that these were not just horses with horns; they were people.

"Before we ask each other the questions we have, Zoltan, may I see the foals who've paired themselves with our friends' children?"

Belle led the way to the centre of the herd where he soon realised a class was in progress, even though there was no sound.

The mare in the centre of the circle would look at one of the foals, and whichever she looked at was also watched by each of the others.

Five of them appeared younger. The smallest of the group was pale green, with scarlet mane, tail, and hooves. There was a tiny red mark on her forehead that he presumed was the bud from which her horn would grow. Aristo remembered how she'd got her name and correctly guessed that she was Bella.

"The identical pair must be Minstrel and Maestro, coloured just like Rebel. The other similar to Rebel will be Shadow, which leaves the Miniature of Karim as Star! How did I do?"

<< Absolutely correct! Marcus would be proud of your deductive ability.

<< Please excuse this little group, Fleet, I wish them to meet one of The Old Ones, Aristo.

<< Shadow, Star, Minstrel, Maestro, Bella, to me, if you would be so kind! >>

The five obediently trotted over, were introduced, and exchanged a few words. Aristo wished with all his heart that he had all day to spend with them instead of just a few minutes. He had to content himself with a genuine expression of pleasure at meeting them, and move on to their elders. A couple of hours were passed answering, to the best of his ability, the many questions asked by the adults, and then it was time to return.

The mounting block reappeared, Aristo mounted, failed to notice that the handrail, back support, and other aids were not there, grabbed a handful of mane and said as confidently as he could manage, "The Counter Ranch, please, Rebel, as quickly as you like!"

<< Are you glad you came? >>

He was unsure whether it was Karim or Rebel, then detected a mental laugh as the same voice said, *<< It's both, and Tyana too. We can blend together when convenient. There have been times when we've included Marcus as well. >>*

"Yes I am, though I still don't understand why Zoltan requested it."

<< I believe he wished to make the point that even without a human partner a unicorn is a person in the true sense. I know from your thoughts back there that you're convinced.

<< I don't know why he thought it necessary. >>

Aristo relaxed and enjoyed the ride back to the ranch.

***

Lace leaned on the paddock rail, watching the unicorns canter away until they were out of sight, then realised Darryl was in turn watching her.

"What are you looking at?"

"You were admiring the unicorns, and I can understand that, as I've known them all my life, and I never tire of watching them.

"I was watching you, and thinking how beautiful you are when you relax."

"You're very forward, aren't you?"

"No! I simply told the truth. You asked what I was looking at, and I told you.

"What would you like to do this morning? By custom you have two weeks to get used to this place before anyone asks you any questions."

Lace suddenly adopted the frightened look she had had when they first met. "Questions?"

"Yes, but not the sort you're worried about. We try to keep up to date on the history of Earth, so new arrivals are always asked for any information they have.

"Lace, please trust us. Nobody even cares what you did in New York!

"Now, I'll ask again. What do you feel like doing?

"Would you like to learn to ride a horse, and see round the ranch?"

"What I was wearing yesterday would have done for that, but I don't know what Tyana did with them. This lightweight trouser suit was in my room this morning, so I put it on."

"No matter. When I saw you in one of Tyana's outfits I assumed you'd been given a wardrobe.

"Laura!"

"Why Laura? Can't you do what Tyana did for me?"

"I'm only a Silver. Tyana is White, two grades higher, and she's probably the most powerful witch on Refuge, so even White doesn't begin to classify her properly."

"And what's Laura's grade?"

"She's never been tested, as she's a healer, and won't bother, but we're all certain she's at least Gold, probably White.

"Ah, Laura, will you do me a favour, and equip Lace here to go riding with me? She's never ridden before, and I'm going to teach her."

Laura dressed Lace as easily as Tyana had, then suggested, "Why not ask Princess or Ebony? Either could come with you without her needing any teaching. If Lace is of Bronze ability or above, she may choose a horse as familiar anyway, so she'll never need to learn ordinary riding skills."

"Princess, if she doesn't mind. I've already got Dusty working, and then he'll be going home, so he'll need Ebony." By the end of the ride, Lace knew she wanted a horse as familiar if she qualified. She thought the bond between Darryl and Timber was wonderful. To be able to trust another being like that……

They returned just about the same time as Aristo, and seeing Rebel and Karim properly for the first time, and particularly when she looked into Karim's eyes and remembered her saying 'Good Morning,' she wondered if she might even qualify for a unicorn, however one did that.

After a quick shower and lunch Aristo said his goodbyes to those who would not be at the meeting and left for Europe.

First Dusty and Megan then Merlin and Laura went home. Hondo and Darryl had work to do, and Marcus and Tyana went to Camelot to renew acquaintances with the few European leaders they had got to know towards the end of their adventures there. Thus Lindsey found herself alone with Lace. "Well," she said when Lace showed signs of moving away. "We seem to have been left on our own!

"How about a trip into Camelot? I've got to take the carriage in to collect the children after school and if we leave early I can show you some of your new world."

The reply of, "Whatever you like!" was hardly gracious, however, remembering Darryl's request, Lindsey showed no reaction but went to the stable and returned with the four greys Lace had seen the previous evening, and a Chestnut mare. As no explanation was offered, she asked, "Why five horses for us, when four were enough yesterday to pull the heavier coach?"

Lindsey laughed. "This is my Darling Lightning! I'd never go anywhere without her. She'll just trot alongside."

"She's your familiar?"

Lindsey nodded.

"She's beautiful! I never realised how lovely horses were until Darryl took me out on Princess this morning. Do you mind telling me…What do I have to do to qualify for a familiar myself if I stay here?"

"That depends on what you mean by 'stay here'. If you mean whether you stay on Refuge, I'm afraid you don't get the choice. Nobody does!

"If you mean 'stay with us', then that doesn't come into it. Wherever you live, anyone who can pass just one of the Bronze tests qualifies for a familiar and is able to bond with one."

By now Lindsey had the greys harnessed and coupled to the carriage, all without moving from Lace's side.

They climbed in, the reins came to her hands and she continued, "Things used to be different until seven years ago. You used to have to pass all five tests, but Tyana changed that!"

By the time Lindsey had given Lace a very abbreviated account of what the five tests were and of Tyana's adventures they were nearing Camelot and had passed the spot where Lace had wakened the previous day. She asked, "Why are we coming here? Just for me to see it?"

"Oh no! Today's when I usually shop, and it will let me introduce you to a few of our neighbours."

"Shop? But I…. Darryl said nobody paid for anything! It's all free! You just do what you can, and take what you need. I don't understand at all!"

Lindsey had to think about this, as it wasn't covered in the list of things to tell new arrivals, and Megan had just accepted it, as had Marcus and Laura, the only three she'd ever known.

"Look, you know we, that is Tyana, Hondo, and myself,… we can 'call' anything from Camelot and it will come to us?"

"Yes, but not Dusty and Darryl?"

"I'm afraid they're only Silver. They can't reach this far. Just for the record Tyana and Marcus can call from fifty miles away.

"The point is, you can only call for something if you can be very specific…. you have to know exactly what you want. Well, I know I want some material to make a wardrobe of clothes for you, but unless we've both seen what's on offer, you can't help me choose, can you? Anyway that's only one example. You'll see!"

Leaving the carriage outside the town with the horses grazing, Lindsey took her charge to a large building just inside the wall. "But this is just like a factory," she exclaimed, "with looms weaving cloth. I thought you people did everything by magic!"

"Take a closer look!" ordered Lindsey. "Where are all the workers?"

Lace did so, and saw that there were only ten, but they were in a group, just looking at the machinery, which appeared to her to have no power source….. and yet it worked.

Lindsey continued her explanation. "Tyana or I could take wool or cotton, mentally spin it into thread, then cause it to form into cloth. However, if we did that we'd never have time for anything else. There aren't that many Golds around, so we try not to waste time doing what lower grades can manage.

"These folk are all either Bronze or Silver, and they take delight in coming up with new designs or materials for us to try."

Lace was taken next to three warehouses, none of which had anyone working in them, yet she saw the contents changing even as she watched.

Trees arriving outside by horse drawn carts were cutting themselves up into convenient shaped planks which then moved into one end of the store. Fifty yards away at the far end other, obviously seasoned pieces of timber were disappearing, and she worked out that someone somewhere was using them.

The next building had shelf after shelf of boxes of vegetables. These were going, but none were arriving and she asked why.

"That's an easy one." answered Lindsey. "The deliveries are always done before noon. One of the people involved stands here by the doorway and arranges the boxes as they arrive.

"I brought you here partly to see it, but also because I'd heard about a new strain of onion, and I need to see it if I want to 'call' some to the ranch."

The third one was not so pleasant. Row after row of hooks contained half lambs, pigs, bullocks, or fowl.

"I don't understand," said Lace. "There's no unpleasant smell. It's a warm afternoon, yet none of it seems to be going bad. Why?"

"You remember when I listed the Bronze tests? One of them is to change the nature of things? Well that's much the same as not allowing things to change as they want to, isn't it?

"That man over there," Lindsey pointed to where a man was apparently dozing in the sun outside the warehouse, "is working very hard at keeping it all fresh. He'll do two hours, then someone else will take over.

"There's another room at the back filled with fish. They only work one hour shifts there!"

"I see. Is that the sort of work I might get given if I stay?"

"You keep saying 'if I stay'. You really don't have the choice. None of us do!

"We don't know yet what you could do, but don't be too disappointed if you do end up with a job like that. You know, that man you saw only works for two hours a day, and his wife in the fish area only for one. That's not so bad, is it? They weren't made to do this. They happen to both like music and she paints whilst he's a writer. This work gives them plenty of time for their hobbies.

"Even if you did have the choice of whether to stay on this world, I know at least one member of my family who would be terribly disappointed if you did go!"

Lindsey saw Lace blush, the first reaction she would have considered absolutely 'normal' since they'd met. She wondered what she could be hiding about her past, and gave her time to recover her composure by asking, "Anyway, what makes you think you may have the choice?"

"Your friend Aristo! I asked him if he'd take me back if I wanted. He said he didn't know if he could, but he'd find out from the Old Ones. I didn't have time to ask who they are!

"He did say that it's never arisen before as people didn't know any of the Godhe personally."

"Let's change the subject. I've seen the onions, so let's go back to the fabric warehouse and start planning a wardrobe for you"

Lindsey wasn't surprised to find Lace enthusiastic after the first few minutes of looking at pictures and, all too soon for her, it was time to collect the children.

"Oh, Granny, you've brought Auntie Lace!" exclaimed Christopher. "That's nice!" said Paul.

Lace blushed again.

"Did I say something wrong, Granny?" asked Christopher.

"No, Darling. Lace is a little hot, that's all. She hasn't got used to the weather here yet. Have you had a good day?"

"Usual boring stuff. We had a new girl in class, and Bronze Magic was back to the start again. Can I ride Lightning back home? Please, Gran?…Please?!"

<<Alright with you, Dearest? >>

<< I'll take all of them if you like!" >>

"Yes, Christopher, Lightning says you may.

"Anyone else?"

Paul joined his twin, but Julie, together with Caroline and Simeon, both of whom were to be collected from the ranch later, chose to ride in style.

"Caroline looked at Lace for a minute or two then announced,

"You're a Healer like Mummy and me, aren't you?"

"You mean 'like Mummy and I', don't you?" asked Simeon.

"Don't be picky! Split it into two sentences…. You're a Healer like Mummy…. You're a Healer like me!

"Well, am I right, Lace? I'm sure I am! Maybe you don't know that you are. Mummy says it's possible. Have you ever made anyone better? Or even an animal that's come to you for help?"

"I don't think I can call myself a Healer, Caroline. There have been a few people who got better and thanked me for helping, but I didn't really do anything for them!"

"But you must have done something! Think! Tell me exactly what you did!"

Lindsey felt she had to stop this before it got out of hand.

"Caroline, Lace is my guest, and you're being very rude!"

Caroline went red, but it didn't stop her carrying on.

"Sorry, Gran, but this is very important. You know how busy Mummy and Auntie Laura are. I'm not strong enough to help much, but if we've got another one, they can have a bit of time off!"

"I don't mind answering, Lindsey, because there's not much to tell. I just wanted them to get better, and I held their hands and prayed!"

"What's 'prayed'?"

"Caroline! Don't be rude!"

"I asked God to help make them better!"

Caroline refused to be repressed.

"I thought Aristo was the only Godhe you'd met!"

Simeon had been following this, and thought he could help.

"Caroline, think about Tyana's trouble with the people in New Salem before your Uncle Marcus came to Refuge. They thought that everything was created by God, spelt G-O-D, and I think that's the God Lace means.

"Lace, if I may call you Lace, I think Caroline may be right. Is praying anything like wishing for something to happen?"

Lace looked at the Simeon and thought, *'I'm having a conversation with a six year old who has the brain of an adult.'*

"Yes, Simeon, it's very much the same thing, and yes, I did want them to get better with all my heart."

"See, Granny? Told you she was a Healer! And she's nice too!"

"Well, Lace," said Lindsey, "if Caroline's right, and she seems pretty sure of it, you don't have to worry about sitting in a warehouse moving things around. With no science here, the only help for people who get injured or sick comes from our Healers, and there are never enough of them to go around!

"I suggest you go with either Megan or Laura tomorrow and find out for yourself. You don't have to, though. It's only a suggestion ….it's up to you!"

"I will! And I'll no longer say, 'if I stay'."

She turned to Caroline and hugged her saying, "No one has ever said I was 'nice' before.

"And the twins seemed pleased to see me too!

"How about you, Julie? And Simeon. Can we be friends?"

Julie joined in the hug, whilst Simeon looked thoughtful but Lace didn't notice.

Dinner at the ranch was interesting for Lace, as she'd watched Lindsey prepare it, and she remembered seeing most of the things used when in town. The 'instant cooking' took some getting used to, but she had to admit it was very convenient.

All, and especially Darryl, were pleased to note that the frightened look which had appeared so often the day before seemed to have left her. She did, however, take little persuading to have another early night, being happy to retire at the same time as Julie

Chapter Two

Having enjoyed Aristo's visit, and the pleasure of seeing Helga from New Amsterdam with her new husband, it was all too soon for Marcus and Tyana that the morning of the first truly world wide convention arrived.

"The only good thing about this meeting is that we'll get to see Carlos and Sophia!" stated Marcus. "Are they bringing Rosa?"

"They'd better, or Caroline and Bella are going to want to know why!" replied Tyana.

Belle brought Merlin from his home at a ten times gallop in ceremonial dress. She had him at the ranch in plenty of time to join the coach and four greys taking the party to Camelot and to the new larger Council Chamber.

Merlin glanced at the gong to the rear that sounded, bringing the meeting to order, various groups of people who had been chatting taking their places. He only then noticed the vacant seats, and his heart almost stopped as he realised whose they were. The space craft of the Godhe had not arrived.

Five normal chairs, and two large platforms were unoccupied. Aristo, Cantor, Vernique, Mandrake, Shinlu, Carlos, and Sophia were missing.

<< *BELLE!* >> he cried mentally.

<< *Ouch!* >> said Archimedes.

<< *Yes, Merlin. What's wrong?* >>

<< *Sorry, Archimedes, my old friend.* >>

<< *Belle, can you please contact the Duty Unicorn in Paris. Did Aristo leave on time?* >>

Whilst waiting for a reply, Merlin advised those present what he was doing, and arranged with Rebel/Karim that Belle's reply would be broadcast to the meeting. He was to regret making this arrangement.

<< *I can't contact Vitesse, who should be on duty according to the roster, and I don't know any others in Europe.* >>

<< *I suggest getting Rebel or Karim to try.* >>

Rebel tried first to contact Javelin and Lotus Blossom, who would, of course be with Carlos and Sophia. Next he tried Vitesse, then Gabriella in Madrid, worked his way through the entire list of contacts, ending with a call to Javelin's herd stallion, the only other unicorn he knew in Europe.

<< *Beau, this is Rebel from the other continent!* >>

<< *Yes, Rebel, I remember you well. What can I do for you?* >>

<< *I find that I'm unable to speak with any unicorns in any of the human cities in Europe. Will you try, please, investigate if necessary, and report back?* >>

Merlin turned to Shaena on his right and whispered, "The last time I was this worried was seven years ago before we knew that Europe even existed.

"What can have happened?"

<< *Merlin, I'm speaking to you alone. Karim and I have been considering this. The chance that there's no connection between Aristo's disappearance and our loss of contact with Europe is just about zero. You need Marcus again!* >>

<< *I'd already come to the same conclusion, Rebel. I'm hoping that one of the others will suggest it.* >>

<< *One will...and will think it her own brilliant idea.* >>

Merlin sounded the gong again and asked, "Does anyone have any suggestions which we may consider whilst waiting for Beau to reply?"

Magdalena from New Salem caught his eye, receiving permission to speak. "The chance that there's no connection between Aristo's disappearance and our loss of contact with Europe is just about zero. You need Marcus again!"

<< *Beau here, Merlin. I was lucky. One of my stallions was very near Madrid, and tried to enter it. He can see easily enough, but there's some sort of invisible barrier surrounding the town. Even though he could see his friend Prancer, he couldn't hear him. It seems reasonable to suppose that it's the same everywhere else.* >>

<< *Thank you, Beau, you're probably right.* >>

<< *What can we do to help?* >>

<< *Beau, this is Rebel. Restrict this conversation to only myself, and I will include the few here who need to know.*

<< Please do nothing, and ensure that no other unicorns take any action. Our great strength is that the enemy, whoever they are, will not know of the power we have. I want it kept that way. Let them continue thinking we are just familiars, and that unpaired unicorns are just animals with no intelligence. Please ensure every unicorn herd in Europe knows this, and advise us of any change. >>

"Magdalena has proposed that we ask Marcus to become a detective again. Have we a seconder?"

There were several, including a few of the European delegates, and the motion was carried unanimously.

"I have no doubt that those delegates who have had a three month journey here are thinking of how quickly they can board the fastest schooner we have to get back to Europe."

Looking around, and seeing several whispering to their neighbours, Merlin was sure he was right in saying this, and continued, "I ask you to reconsider. Whatever has happened has obviously been very well organised, and I'm sure there will be some sort of reception ready for you, probably one which you won't like!"

Merlin paused again to give them time to consider this.

"I remind you all that seven years ago Tyana and Marcus didn't rush into Europe to find who was stealing our theurgen. They investigated, a word new to our language as crime here is so rare, carefully until they knew the answers to all three questions - Who? - How? - and Why? before they acted. We must do the same now. It will take some two months at least for you to get home; so a few days thought is hardly a long delay.

"I extend to you all a welcome to stay as our guests for as long as you wish. You may find a trip to Abinger to study the records kept there dating back over seven thousand years of interest.

<< Jet, please ask Thomas to come to see me as soon as possible. Thank you. >>

"Anyone who has a horse as familiar, if you meet a guide I'm arranging to be available tomorrow morning. He will teach you Tyana's very effective multiplying spell which will enable him to get you to Abinger before lunch. You will find it extremely useful when travelling at home later.

"I must caution you about one thing. Thomas is, as yet, only Gold, and only thirteen. He is, however, able to qualify White with ease and will do so whilst at Abinger. He will be in constant touch with me, and represents me at all times. If he gives an instruction, it will be my instruction!

"I declare this meeting, important though it seemed only half an hour ago, postponed until further notice.

"Please reassemble here at ten tomorrow morning..................... I have further considered and anyone who has a familiar other than a horse who wishes to go with Thomas will be supplied with one and taught as needed.

<< Rebel, please ask Qamar, Shaena, Marcus, Tyana, Electra from Abinger, and any two leaders from Europe you feel we can trust to come to our old Council Room. >>

***

Merlin looked around the room, and decided that Rebel had, as he'd expected, chosen wisely.

Helga from New Amsterdam and Hammid from Baghdad were present, though looking puzzled. Merlin found all eyes on him, so had no need to call for order.

"Seven years ago, in this very room the Camelot Council gave an eighteen year old girl, who was then only Gold, the task of solving the mystery of losses of magic powers in our teenagers.

"I'm sure you all remember that that decision led, eventually, to the liberation of Europe.

"I rarely use my power as World President, but I'm doing so now, and that's why you're here. If we were to discuss what action to take in open council we'd still be here next week!

"I agree with Magdalena that the chance of two separate tragedies is vanishingly small, and we are faced with an enemy who timed his or her action to coincide with the absence of the leaders in Europe. We are probably expected to rush there as soon as possible to fall into a trap.

"I asked Rebel to invite two leaders from Europe to join us, and if he feels that you two are the most suited to the task, he will be right! For those who have not met them, we have here Helga, who gave Tyana and Marcus every assistance when they freed New Amsterdam, and Hammid. All I know is that he is Head of Baghdad Council. You are welcome, Hammid. Why do you think Rebel chose you?"

"At the time I received your request, incidentally that was the first time I'd been addressed by a unicorn, I was thinking along the lines of your opening remarks - that there would be a trap waiting for us. I believe they are telepathic? Maybe that's why. Or maybe it's because, like Helga, I have learned to speak English. Whatever the reason I'm at your disposal."

Merlin quickly introduced the others present, then immediately handed over the chair to Marcus.

"Merlin, would you care to enlarge on what you said about Thomas going to Abinger before we discuss the loss of contact with both Aristo and the cities in Europe?"

"Certainly! You, Marcus, better than anyone on this world, know that a human of Gold ability with a unicorn as a familiar is many times more powerful than two, or even ten Whites."

There were gasps from Hammid, Helga, and Electra.

Merlin continued, "I feel that we're going to need all the power we have, as

I'm quite sure we're opposed by either members of the Godhe, or a similar scientifically advanced race and.."

"How do you justify that assumption?" interrupted Helga.

"Marcus will explain that in a moment. The only time in the past we've had any real dealings with the Godhe, except for them bringing us here, was when Tyana and Marcus captured two of their ships and imprisoned their crews. All the details are recorded at Abinger as faithfully and fully as they could remember when they returned, and I want as many as possible to read that account.

"Apart from Marcus and Tyana, Thomas and Jet make up the only human/ unicorn pair in New America. I propose to give Thomas the job of getting everyone safely to and from Abinger, and to study the records themselves. Although he has only just made Gold, I tell you that that was in his own right, without help from Jet. Working together they could easily defeat all of the council leaders from every town on both continents who sent delegates, including those of us in this room with the exception of Marcus and Tyana!"

"But that's nineteen adults, most of them White!"

"That's right! I'll tell you now why Rebel chose those he did to attend this meeting. He knew he could trust you to be included in a secret so closely guarded that for seven years only eight humans, six unicorns and two dragons have known it. This information must not fall into the hands of whoever our enemy is!

"The average intelligence of a unicorn is higher than that of an average human!"

Again Merlin paused as he watched this information being absorbed, but not immediately believed. He had himself grown up with unicorn friends, but knew what a culture shock it could be to some people to learn that 'man' was not necessarily supreme. "A unicorn will only become the familiar of a human of a very special type. I'm sorry that this will embarrass Tyana and Marcus, but Rebel and Karim have each assured me that they recognise humans, even whilst they are still babies, who are, as they put it 'good enough to have been born a unicorn'. By the time the human reaches Gold, the unicorn, who already had the same inherent magic power we have, has developed also to Gold. The two together have so much power it has to be seen to be believed. Incidentally, Thomas and Jet don't know yet. I intend him to be recognised as White by the authorities in Abinger, with the leaders as witnesses.

"Henceforth I propose a special classification for Unicorn White Witches. We can't call them 'Unicorns' as that would be confusing. Think of a suitable name please, Electra.

"Also, try to devise a one-off test for them to perform; one which will demonstrate the ability to handle, say ten tons, whilst retaining the sort of control needed to thread a cotton in the eye of a needle."

"You mean ten hundredweights, do you not?"

"I mean ten tons. Tell her, Tyana!"

"He's right, Electra. At Venicia Karim and I moved thirty or forty tons of wall rubble fifty yards so quickly that the movement could not be seen, and the air replacing it made a noise like a clap of thunder. We also piled it neatly in the same movement. Ten tons is heavy enough that forty Whites working together couldn't even move it, yet light enough for a young Unicorn Gold to handle easily."

"Now," instructed Merlin, "Marcus will explain why we suspect The Godhe, or a similar race, to be behind this."

Marcus acknowledged Merlin and stepped forward. "As you'll see when you read the records in Abinger, when we first encountered the second of the Godhe ships, the Type Sixty Three, it was invisible to us. We knew where it was as we'd conjured rain to outline it, but more important was that whilst it was invisible, Rebel and Karim were unable to read any of the thoughts from within it.

"There are only two possible explanations for the losses of contact with the unicorns in Europe. Either they're all dead, or there's a barrier such as the Type Sixty Three ship generated. Beau's report confirmed that it is, I'm happy to say, the latter."

"I believe it likely that there is a trap in Europe, but in spite of that, I propose to go there with Rebel. I further believe that all others should stay here in New America until we can report what we're up against."

"That's exactly what I hoped you'd say!" said Merlin

Tyana was on her feet, eyes blazing with anger, and screamed at poor Merlin, "And do you expect me to stay here too? -

"No! - Listen a moment!"

"You've explained how much more powerful a White Witch with a unicorn familiar is. What I feel, but have never been able to prove, is that the four of us, Marcus with Rebel, and Karim with me, together are more powerful than the total of the two pairs. There's a word for it, but it escapes me at the moment... Electra?"

"Synergy!"

"That's it! Thank you! I can't prove it, but with what's at stake, we must go too!"

"Marcus, what does Rebel have to say?"

<< I can speak for myself, Merlin. Tyana is right. I too feel that the four of us are greater than the two pairs. >>

"Nothing has been built which is faster than the *Unicorn Witch*, so we leave in her as soon as she can be provisioned. Merlin, we leave you and Laura to care for our children. We have preparations to make, and we'll see you at the ranch."

Merlin sounded the gong to bring some sort of order back to the meeting.

"To make it official, I propose that we ask Marcus and Tyana to investigate and report back to me. Let the minutes show that, Electra.

"I also propose that we encourage every delegate to attend tomorrow morning and that all who are able travel with Thomas to Abinger. I remind you again that, young though he is, he will be my representative.

"Meeting adjourned!"

***

At the Counter ranch, Merlin found Belle and Laura engaged in a chess match which had now been going since ten in the morning. They stopped to listen whilst Merlin advised them, and the rest of the family, of the day's events, as Marcus and Tyana had not yet come home.

After a long silence as the news was digested, Lindsey was the first to speak. "In the interest of safety in numbers, I'd like everyone to move in here, together with all the familiars. There will be plenty of room with Tyana and Marcus away.

"Speaking of familiars, the foals are due back tomorrow evening, and I think we should qualify the children Bronze immediately. It can't do any harm to double the power they have, and we all know whom they'll pair with. In fact it will be interesting to see if the spell has any effect at all!"

Marcus and Tyana arrived just in time to hear this remark, and agreed with all she had said. Their schooner was in Brigadoon, already being provisioned, and they were leaving at dawn.

The children arrived home from school. With unicorns as friends it would have been impossible to keep secrets from them, so, young though they were, they were told all that had happened, ending with…"so I'm sure you understand that we'd like you to keep together, and one of us will travel to and from school with you in future. Does any one of you not feel able to qualify Bronze tomorrow evening?"

"That's not fair, Granny!" cried Julie. "Paul and Chris are a year younger than us. They should be made to wait."

"It's not a question of being fair, Julie," said Simeon. "Two more Bronzes in the house might make a difference one day, and the point is, it will be safer for them. That's what matters.

"Have any of you thought about Lace?"

"Thank you, Simeon," put in Marcus, and then turned to his daughter. "Do you really want your Mummy and I to have to worry about you even more than we will anyway?"

"No, Dad! You do what you think is best. Simeon's right - as usual!"

"Answering your last question, Simeon,

"It appears not!

"Lace, from what happened to me seven years ago, I'd guess that your life was in danger on Earth! What did you do there? I want to assess whether you need extra protection."

"Darryl said nobody would ask what I did on Earth. He said all that matters is what we do here!

"Anyway, I don't need any protection! I've taken care of myself for years!"

<< *Rebel?* >>

<< *She's so mixed up and terrified about her past being told of, she's not thinking the answers. We'll have to leave it for now, and learn later. I'm sure Laura will get the truth out of her!* >>

"Very well! I suggest you stay at the ranch, and always keep near at least one member of the family.

"If it makes you feel better, I had to do the same when I arrived here! Laura was given a familiar the first evening but Dusty and Darryl played nursemaids to me for a couple of days till I met Rebel."

It is to Julie's credit that she spent the rest of the evening making sure the twins knew all they needed to for their Bronze tests. When they went to bed, each of them changed their glass of water to wine, and the following morning Caroline's services were needed before breakfast.

***

Dusty appointed one of his hands to take over, something the man was glad to do when the reason was explained, and on the way to his childhood home, he visited Zoltan, brought him up to date, and arranged that all unicorns knew that Megan and Laura were now at the Counters'. *'It's funny,'* he thought to himself as he left, *'I used to think of Karim as just like my Ebony, but with a horn. Now I treat Zoltan as Merlin's equal, and I'm proud to have him as a friend.'*

<< *I'm embarrassed to say I overheard that, Dustine.*

<< *I was about to call you to say that whilst Aristo was here I had the impression he was avoiding thinking about something unpleasant. It may be relevant. Good luck!* >>

The children were asleep earlier than usual, even though it must have seemed an adventure having everyone at the ranch. The adults also retired early, but found it hard to sleep with their friends missing.

Rebel and Karim called Belle, Jet, and the horse familiars to them and soon had a circle of guards round the ranch house comprising themselves, Belle, Jet, Ebony, Bess, Trigger, Timber, Lightning, and Princess. One unicorn and one horse were awake at any time. Archimedes was offered a place, but said he preferred to stay near Merlin, as he might need all his wits.

Tyana and Marcus were gone when the others awoke.

The coach and four took the children to school, with Laura driving, surrounded by the entire family. Archimedes was high overhead as a lookout. Belle stayed behind to report anything unusual to Merlin through Jet.

"Mummy," asked Simeon, "are we going to be taken to school like babies every day from now on? Is it really so dangerous?"

"That's the problem, Darling. We just don't know. Maybe the trouble is only over in Europe, or maybe we will be attacked today.

"I'll be happier when Shadow and the others return this evening, and you all have the protection of being Bronze.

"Tomorrow, you can ride in, with one of the adults with you. How does that sound?"

"Can Shadow come into the school?"

"In the circumstances, yes - don't you agree Merlin?"

"I certainly do!"

A chorus rose of, "And Star!"

"And Bella!"

Then, only slightly behind, "And Minstrel!"

"And Maestro!"

For the first time since realising Aristo was missing, Merlin was able to smile.

The journey was uneventful, the children joined their friends, and the coach took Merlin to the square. He, Thomas, and Jet remained whilst the escort returned to the ranch.

It says a lot for Merlin's oratory that every single one of the delegates turned up to join Thomas outside the assembly hall at ten o'clock, and they each had their partners with them.

Over half would need horses, but a call from Jet to Belle at the ranch ensured that she would bring twenty in.

Whilst waiting, Merlin explained how and why Tyana had developed her stride length-multiplying spell, and assured them it had been in common use in New America for seven years now. He had Thomas demonstrate it with a modest three times, then five, and finally ten. As a finale he had Jet come through the square at close to three hundred miles per hour.

"Only a White can manage that, but you mustn't try it, as over strange ground you would have too little time to see gopher holes and ruts. The earlier speeds represent what we've found possible for Bronze, Silver, and Gold. Is anyone below Gold? - Don't be ashamed if you are!"

Two of the partners were only Bronze, and expected to be told that they couldn't go.

"Thomas, when travelling, have these two up front please, alongside yourself. Tyana assures me you will be able to handle all three."

<< Jet, actually I wish you to handle your own, whilst Thomas does the other two. Or vice-versa. Alright? >>

<< Of course, Merlin. I'll let him know. >>

<< Please also explain to Thomas that this ability of the unicorns must be kept secret. He is not to be embarrassed by taking credit for anything you do. Karim made that clear years ago! >>

Belle arrived. There was a short session of practice, and they set off. Thomas was at the head with Helga's new husband on one side, and Hammid's wife on the other.

As soon as clear of Camelot, he had Jet give the instructions simultaneously to all the riders and changed to gallop, then to nine times speed.

After an hour he stopped to give the party a rest, but found it unnecessary. By lunchtime they were entering Abinger, and even though most of the town came out to welcome them, Thomas noticed that in the centre of the square a group of twelve carried on working.

Operating in two teams of six they appeared to be taking blocks of granite, sculpting them to shape, building two columns about three feet in diameter, then bonding the whole into a solid block as they went. One of the sculptors came across to Electra and asked, "How tall shall we make them, Madam Leader?"

"About ten feet, with an eight feet by four platform on top of each. When those are finished, I'd like the statues life size, and also on eight feet by four feet platforms.

"How long will it take?"

"They should be roughed out by dusk tonight, then finished by tomorrow lunchtime. Will that be soon enough? I can bring in more sculptors if needed."

"No, Rondell, that will be fine. Thank you again!"

"What are they going to be, Electra?" asked Thomas, voicing the question the whole party was pondering.

"Merlin asked me to arrange statues in memory of Tyana and Marcus to honour the work they did seven years ago. He regarded it as important and I had Belle forward the instructions to Rondell. They started this morning as we were leaving Camelot.

"Now, to work! If you would be so kind as to form into little groups with friends keeping together, my townsfolk will take you to their homes. I suggest you all relax, as far as possible, today, and we'll start our research tomorrow. Thomas, you'll be my guest.

"I promise that if there's any news, however slight, Jet will be told and Thomas assures me he will pass it on."

***

Laura and Merlin used the coach to collect the children in the afternoon, and arrived at the ranch just as Zoltan himself escorted the foals into the paddock.

Paul and Chris spotted him first, and shouted in unison, "Hi, Granddad Zoltan!"

"This is an honour, Zoltan," said Merlin. "Please ignore the children's rudeness. We are, with your permission, hoping to annex all five of them with the foals this evening. I speak for us all when I ask you to stay for the ceremony."

<< I'd like that very much, Merlin. Although I've seen an annexation, I've never had the chance to see the Bronze tests performed. >>

"Have we your permission?"

<< You have, though I think we'll find that they're already partly bonded. Who will officiate? >>

"I'm proposing to ask Shaena.

"Belle, will you please take one of the horses into Camelot, pass on my request to Qamar and Shaena, and ask them if they will dine with us?"

<< Of course! I'll be glad to!

<< Laura, may I take Princess, for the company? >>

"Certainly, Belle, I'm sure she'll be ready to chat all the way there, and all the way back."

The children were, as children everywhere do when they arrive home from school, raiding the kitchen. The only difference is they were doing it without leaving the paddock, each as close as possible to their best friend. They were showing a variety of tastes. The twins each had a jam sandwich with ice cream. Julie and Simeon, having been introduced to the American delicacy by Marcus, were eating Hamburgers, and Caroline was picking from a plate of cheese and salad.

<< *Do you always give them so much freedom to choose what they eat?* >> Zoltan asked Lindsey.

"They know all about the disappearance of Aristo's ship. They know about the loss of contact with Europe. If it helps them forget even for a few minutes, I don't mind this one evening."

Fifteen minutes later the children had finished their snacks and Caroline shouted, "Mummy! They're coming! I saw them on the road just outside Camelot. May Bella and I go to meet them?"

"Sorry, Darling. I have to say No!" answered Megan. We still don't know what is safe and what isn't!"

"But..."

<< *And I say No, too!* >>

An angry sounding Zoltan was sufficient to stop the others adding their protests to Caroline's.

<< *Merlin, would you be so kind as to explain to me what is happening as they perform each task?* >>

<< *Of course! Shall I do it privately to you, or aloud?* >>

<< *Just for me, please. All the others know, do they not?* >>

Shaena and Qamar arrived, astride Princess and Belle respectively. Hawka and Storm flew high overhead, keeping them assured that there was no activity nearer than Camelot.

She took up a position in the centre of a semi-circle with the candidates for Bronze facing her. Those not involved formed another semi-circle, Lace being between Laura and Darryl, and asking questions of each in turn, but then Belle took over, passing on to Lace the details of Merlin's commentary to Zoltan so that there would be no unnecessary noise.

"Caroline, Julie, Simeon, Paul, Christopher, I have been asked here this evening to annex you with Bella, Star, Shadow, Minstrel, and Maestro.

"Rebel has already given his consent for the last four.

"Zoltan, can you confirm for me, please, that the foals understand what this is for, and are willing?"

<< *I can, and they are! So is Bella!* >>

"However, we have a problem! We are unable to ask Javelin for his permission. I'm not sure I have the authority to officiate in the case of her and Caroline."

<< *Would it help if I was to ask Orchid to ask our sire?* >>

"Did I hear you correctly, Bella?

"Did you offer to ask your sister to seek your father's permission?"

As Shaena asked this, and the significance dawned on those present, everyone started to speak at once.

<< *SILENCE!* >> This was Zoltan at his most authoritative. He then continued so that everyone present could hear, including passing on Bella's half of the conversation.

<< *Bella. Can you speak with your sire or with your dame?* >>

<< *No, Sir, not since yesterday at about noon.* >>

<< *But you are able to converse with your twin sister?* >>

<< *Yes, Sir, but I find it harder than usual!* >>

<< *Please ask Orchid to tell your parents what we are proposing, ask first for their permission, and then that they be available so that we can pass messages via you and Orchid in half an hour's time.* >>

<< *Yes, Sir... He says to go ahead, and he is delighted to hear from us and that we are all well!* >>

Shaena was once again in control.

"Let us take you in order of oldest first.

"You will each then, if successful, set a new record as the youngest ever Bronze."

Caroline walked forward with Bella, raising her right hand to receive a nosebag filled with oats. She then sent it to Princess and located it on her face, saying, "Thank you for bringing Shaena!"

<< *That completes two of the five tests, Zoltan. She has conjured an object to her hand, and then sent it to a third party under control.*

<< *She now must conjure fire and rain.* >>

Five torches had already been set on the paddock fence. The first in the row lit, then rose out of its holder to fly across the paddock to be extinguished by the rain Caroline had caused to fall there.

<< *The final test is to transmute one material into another. This is by far the hardest of the five.* >>

She next produced a sprig of a bush, bearing bright red flowers on some branches, and black lustrous berries on others. Everyone present recognised Belladonna, or as it was sometimes called, Deadly Nightshade.

Caroline picked several of the berries and handed them to Shaena, who found she was holding small black grapes. She thanked Caroline and ate them, to the horror of those watching.

"Grapes will do me no harm!" she commented. "Why the surprise? After all that is what she's supposed to do!

"I'm proud to be here at this moment, and ask you to use the power you will gain wisely, Caroline."

She raised her arms in the traditional manner and, willing the union to be as strong as that she shared with Hawka spoke the ancient spell:-

"These two I now join, so let all heed
In future cut one, and both shall bleed.

"Do you feel any different, Caroline?"

"It's not like Mummy told me it was like when she and Bess were annexed. I feel a little closer to Bella, that's all."

<< We had already discussed the possibility that you were already bonded as firmly as was possible, Caroline, so do not be disappointed.

<< I feel that you should continue with the others, Shaena, just in case they are less secure. >>

All agreed with Zoltan, and in turn the other four went through the tests and the ritual. Simeon chose to convert pebbles to oats for Zoltan as his finale, whilst Marcus and Tyana's three all opted for water to wine.

The greatest effect of Shaena's spell, as might be expected, was on the twins. Being the youngest they had had less time for natural bonding.

Merlin clapped his hands to get attention, saying, "That half hour is up. I hate to ask this of you at the end of a tiring day, Caroline, but we really do need to find out what has happened in Europe.

"Do you feel up to it?"

"I think Shaena's spell had some effect after all. I don't feel even a little bit tired.....just excited."

Contact was made, and after a little experimenting it was found that Carlos could speak to his daughter Rosa, Orchid could speak to her sister Bella, and Bella could pass it to Caroline. Zoltan could listen in and relay the tale.

<< Now, Carlos, please tell us in your own words what has happened in Paris, and we will then tell you our news! >>

Just after breakfast two days earlier Javelin had received the news from Rebel that Aristo had left Camelot and would be with them in less than an hour's time. He proposed to collect Carlos's party first then go on to the dragons and weres.

"I explained to him that Cantor and Vernique were already in Paris and with us, so he would only have Mandrake and Shinlu to collect."

About three quarters of an hour later, what they had assumed to be Aristo's ship had landed in the centre of the square and immediately become invisible. Javelin and Lotus Blossom found that they could not read any thoughts from within, but remembering Marcus's story, realised why.

Suspecting something was wrong they had tried to call Rebel or Karim, but found that they couldn't contact anyone outside the town. When they tried to leave they discovered a barrier of some sort that they were unable to pass through.

They had watched helplessly as Aristo landed just beyond the river, his door opened and he walked towards the drawbridge.

Another ship had landed between Aristo and his own, a female about Tyana's size, but a little older emerged, pointed a weapon at him, one of the Godhe's assault rifles with heat seeking rockets such as Tyana had had to deal with before, and fired. Aristo was killed instantly. All four of them had combined to try to take control of the missile, but the same barrier that prevented physical passage obviously stopped their magic working.

The female entered Aristo's ship and it left in the direction of Madrid, whilst her own left towards the East. Obviously they were heading for other cities.

For the rest of that day the ship remained invisible and the barrier remained in place. Carlos and Sophia had decided not to draw attention to themselves by trying to attack until they learned more. Whoever was in the ship had nothing to gain by just sitting there, so they simply arranged a watch. Vitesse reported that she had lost contact and was told to act like a horse.

Yesterday morning they had found the ship visible, but the barrier was still there. When a crowd had gathered to look at it a voice had said, in French, "This is the voice of your new ruler. My name is Kresh. The present Head of your Council, Carlos will report here two hours after noon tomorrow for instructions!"

That time had almost arrived and they still were undecided what to do.

Belle had, on her own initiative relayed all of this to Rebel/Karim, and Marcus took over.

"It is essential that the unicorns' power be kept secret, and if they don't already know of them no mention must be made of the dragons. As there were several weres in the town, they should just keep a low profile and hope to pass as humans.

"Carlos, you should go as ordered, with Sophia, Javelin, and Lotus Blossom nearby. There must be two barriers, one round the ship and another round Paris. Kresh will have to let down the inner one to either attack you or let you in. If there is a trap the unicorns will know and you can attack. If not, pretend to accept her as ruler, show awe of the Godhe's power and weapons, and find out what this is all about!"

Carlos and Sophia were given what information Merlin had, and advised to strengthen the bond between Orchid and Rosa. This they did at once. They would, for as long as possible, keep open the link through Orchid and Bella.

"A request on behalf of Vernique," finished Carlos.

"Her older sister and niece are visiting Abinger. I've assured her they'll be alright, but could Thomas please check when he's there?

"As far as I know they are the only two weres in New America at the moment. Vernique's sister is Seline, and her daughter Fallon."

***

Approaching the ship, Carlos called out, "Well, Kresh, I hear you wish to challenge me as ruler of Europe!"

From the speaker came the reply, "I do not challenge you. I simply state that I rule. Only if I have your word that I will not be challenged will I drop the barrier that keeps you inside Paris. Unless you agree, the people will soon starve."

"Can we not talk face to face?"

"I assume you have the same power as Tyana and Marcus. Do you take me for a fool?"

"I give my word I will not use that power unless you make the first hostile move. If you do not agree, I'm leaving now!"

Carlos turned and started to do just that, secure in the knowledge that he had three allies watching his back. One of the four cannon turrets turned to him and there was an explosion a few feet in front of the barrel. This was followed by two more.

"Wait, Carlos. I must know how you did that. I agree to your terms. Come aboard!"

"Now who's being taken for a fool? We talk in the open."

"Compromise! Half way up the access ramp, with six feet between us."

"Agreed!"

The door opened, a ramp extended, and Kresh walked almost halfway down it.

Carlos obligingly went to six feet from her.

"Now, Kresh, Why have you imprisoned us?"

"I will ask the questions!"

<< She did not think the answer. >>

"Compromise! Take turns, and you can be first. I promise to answer truthfully, if you will do likewise."

"Agreed! Where are Marcus and Tyana?"

"I have no idea! I assume they were at the meeting we planned for the day before yesterday. I'm not in a position to ask them where they are now, am I?"

"You promised to tell the truth! Can you really not speak to them? We know you have some way of communicating - something connected with the unicorns."

"Strictly it's my turn to ask a question, but I will answer, then ask two of you. The unicorns communicate between themselves telepathically over any distance. They are intelligent enough to understand human language. In each town we have one, in the case of Paris it's a mare called Vitesse. When your barrier went up she lost contact and is very distressed. If you lower the outer barrier I will ask her to find the answer to your question. Now it is my turn!

"Why have you come back to this world?"

"I work here, for the Medical Research Group!"

<< She tells the truth! >>

"Then why did you have Aristo killed?"

"Personal reasons! Now it is my turn again"

<< His death was necessary for the good of all! This seems a very strange thought. >>

<< I agree. >>

"Will Marcus and Tyana come to Europe to find out what has happened?"

"I think that very probable. They must be worried. Ask another - I think two each is more efficient!"

"Will you work for me if the rewards are great enough?"

"Definitely not! There's no possible reward you could offer which would make me work against Tyana and Marcus. Have you come back for revenge, or for profit?"

"Neither!"

<< Both!... Marcus points out that this lie of hers relieves you of your promise to tell the truth. Pretend to join her as we planned. >>

"If Tyana and Marcus are coming it will take them at least two months. What do you propose to do during that time?"

"My job! I came here to find out how your powers, which defy several known laws of our science, are possible."

<< She tells the truth! >>

"Do you mean to harm them when they come?.. Or us?"

"Of course not, I just want to study them!.. And you. It will be easier with your cooperation."

<< As she said! >>

"What do we gain if we do agree to join you?"

"What do you ask?

"The sort of power Le Roi had when he ruled, for a start, and the use of some of the weapons Tyana told me about."

"That should be possible!"

<< No chance! But I need him to convince the people to cooperate, so I'll play along! >>

"This must include Sophia, my wife!"

"Agreed! Return with her tomorrow morning, and we will discuss a contract."

<< As she said! You can trust her that far, at least. >>

When he returned to his home, Carlos's first question was,

"Why did we stop without learning more?"

<< Two reasons. First we must avoid arousing her suspicions, and second this has been very tiring for Caroline, Bella, Rosa, and Orchid.

<< We will be with you again tomorrow! >>

Zoltan insisted on staying so that a guard similar to that posted the evening before could be used, but the precaution proved unnecessary.

***

One look at Caroline the following morning was enough for Megan to excuse her going to school and to send her back to bed.

"It's just as well!" remarked Merlin. "We really need her this afternoon to monitor the meeting with Kresh.

"I'll take the others to school if you've no objection. I should show my face in Camelot, anyway!

"Just give me five minutes with Belle to advise Thomas what to tell his group!"

"Certainly!" agreed Laura. "Zoltan and Belle are still sleeping, as they were the only two unicorns here last night and insisted on always having one of them, and one horse awake at any one time. I'm sure Princess won't mind taking you."

So it was that after breakfast four excited newly qualified Bronzes on their familiars, led by Merlin on Princess set out for school.

"Dad," asked Simeon as they left the ranch, "now that we're all Bronze, can we learn to multiply the strides? I can't wait to travel like you do when you're in a hurry"

"Yes, please!" chorused the others.

"I promise to teach you all this evening," answered Merlin.

"But if I do it now we'll get to school too early, won't we? Let's just enjoy the ride, and you can tell me what you're going to learn today. Incidentally, I don't expect you to boast about being Bronze. Your friends will learn about it soon enough!"

Megan, Lindsey, and Laura watched with pride until the little party went over the hill, then went indoors to do the day's housework. Lace offered to help, the first indication she'd given that she wished to be friendly, but was told by Lindsey, laughing, "Housework is not like you're used to. Just watch!"

Ten minutes later, such are the benefits of living on Refuge, they were relaxing in the kitchen and waiting for Dusty and Darryl to come in for morning coffee and a chat. Hondo was too far away to join them.

As the men entered the house Laura screamed and staggered. She felt as though she was being torn apart and clutched her chest.

"I'm.....dying!" was all she managed to say as she collapsed.

They felt so helpless. They could see her life ebbing away but had no idea why.

The heartbreaking cry that came next was heard by all on the ranch,

<< *Help me!....I ...,* >> and then there was nothing.

<< *Sorry, everyone!.........That.......was......* >>

They recognised Belle's mental voice, then Zoltan's replaced it.

<< *There's no easy way to tell you this! That cry was from Princess, ...relayed by Belle.........She is no more!* >>

Only then did they realise that it wasn't Laura who was dying, it was Princess!

Nothing like this had ever happened before. Partners always died together and unless somebody acted very quickly Laura was going to die herself.

<< *Laura. LAURA! WE NEED YOU!* >> called Zoltan.

Dusty shouted at Megan for the first and only time he ever would.

"Do something!....Megan!....Do something!

"Darryl, wake Caroline, quickly!

"Megan!.......Megan.....She needs you!"

Megan forced herself to snap out of the trance she was in and took mental control of Laura's heart, forcing it to beat. This was far from easy, as Laura obviously wanted to die. Only the extra strength she had because of partnership with Bess allowed her to win the battle.

Caroline came in and joined her mother. Laura stopped resisting now that it was two to one, even if one of the two was only six years old, and Megan was able to start her breathing as well.

Five minutes later she found that if either she or Caroline relaxed, Laura would not, or could not, breath unaided, and her heart stopped as soon as they released control.

"Dusty, Lindsey, can you take over for me to give me time to think?"

Lindsey tried, Dusty tried, as did Darryl, but Laura's will to die was too strong for them, even with the brothers and their mother working together.

Lace, who had until now just watched and marvelled when she realised what Megan and Caroline were doing, walked over and took Laura's hand, going pale herself, but whatever she was doing, Laura stopped fighting to die. She still couldn't breathe unaided, but at least when Megan relaxed a little her heart continued beating, though very erratically.

<< *Megan!* >>

She was very glad indeed to hear Belle's voice.

<< *There's only one answer! You must annex me with Laura at once!* >>

Megan couldn't spare the effort to speak and had to reply mentally, << *I can't! Even if the rules allow it I don't know how!* >>

<< *I can remember the spell, if that's the problem.* >>

<< *No, that's not it. There's a lot more to it than reciting a few words in rhyme.* >>

<< *Then you, Dusty, must get someone who can...and quickly!* >>

"Right, I'll get Shaena.

<< *Ebony, we have a job to do!* >>

<< *Let Ebony go into Camelot slowly on his own to bring you back. Ride me! I'm ten miles an hour faster in a normal gallop, fifty with you doing your best to multiply, and over a hundred with Shaena or another White aboard.* >>

<< *Let's go!* >>

Less than three minutes later, Zoltan heard from Belle, and passed on what she said to Megan and Darryl.

<< *Zoltan, we daren't take time to stop, but we've just passed Merlin. He's flat on his back, but he must be alive as Archimedes tried to attract our attention. I've told him help is coming, and to tell Merlin if he comes round.* >>

<< *What about the children and the foals?* >>

<< *No sign!* >>

Darryl left at a run and within minutes Zoltan was able to tell Megan that he'd taken a wagon.

"Will she be alright, Mummy?" asked Caroline between making Laura breathe out and in again.

All Megan could do was smile and cross her fingers as it was taking all her effort to keep the heartbeat steady. She was very relieved to hear from Belle far sooner than she'd hoped.

<< We've just passed Merlin again. He's half sitting, and Darryl is just arriving with the wagon. >>

As the sentence finished in her mind the doors flew open and Shaena ran in, followed by Belle.

"I've explained to Belle that though I will always be grateful to her for trying, this idea of hers could easily kill her instead of saving Laura, but she says it's worth the risk. What do you think?"

"If I was Belle, loving Merlin as she does, I'd want to try. Certainly it's the only chance Laura has. She's conscious now, but won't speak to me! I think she resents being kept alive."

Shaena had had five minutes since Belle first told her she was coming to Camelot and why, so had already thought out a suitable spell. Perhaps with more time she could have done better, but what really mattered was the intense willing that the bond between the two she faced be strong. She waited no longer, raising her arms and summoning all the power at her command.

"These two I join, one of whom will replace
Princess, whose memory we'll never erase!"

Belle staggered, then said to Laura, *<< Don't fight me, Laura. Princess was my best friend. I know she would want you to live to care for Simeon and Merlin.*

<< Join me as a partner……..or I fear I may well die too! >>

Laura looked at Belle, the first time she had really looked at anything since she collapsed. Tears welled up in her eyes, and Shaena breathed a sight of relief, knowing that the bond had finally formed. Megan and Caroline relaxed into each others' arms, and Lace started to regain her colour.

They only had a moment's rest before the clatter of hooves sent them running outside to see what help Merlin needed.

"I'm alright! Look after Laura. Zoltan kept me informed once I regained consciousness, and if you manage what you're trying it will be the first time one half of a pair has survived when the other died."

"How is she?"

"I can speak for myself, just about, Darling," answered Laura as she walked a little unsteadily out to join them.

"Belle almost lost her own life pulling me back, but she managed it. I feel as if part of me has been taken, though. I miss her terribly! What happened?"

"She sacrificed herself so that I might live, as you'll hear in a minute!"

<< Zoltan, Bella, Belle, I know it's still very early in Europe, but please organise a conference, including Tyana and Marcus. I have terrible news for them! >>

"Merlin, where are the children? And the foals?" asked Laura.

"Give me a few moments, My Dear. I believe them to be unhurt, but I don't want to have to go through it all twice. Could you possibly help my headache? I still feel terrible!"

Laura, Megan, and Caroline all rushed forward and between them raised the depressed part of the skull where it was fractured. Then Laura fused the bones whilst Megan took away the headache and Caroline mentally tried to put back his dislocated shoulder. She managed to ease the pain, but had to wait until her mother could help as she wasn't strong enough on her own to overcome the strength of the muscles holding the joint out of place. Merlin couldn't help contrasting the ease with which Laura dealt with this break with the four weeks that he had spent with his arm splinted the day she and Marcus had arrived on Refuge, and all Lace could do was watch, wonder, and try to learn.

<< All present for your conference, Merlin. Save your energy! Just think and I'll pass it on. >>

"Thank you, Zoltan. You're a good friend!"

Merlin gave the background to his trip with the children then went on, *<< I was leading the four foals at a gentle trot, with them about ten yards behind me. The children were chattering excitedly about learning Tyana's multiplying spell this evening. I'd promised to teach them!*

<< Suddenly I could no longer hear their hoofbeats and turned.

<< They were all there, behind me. I could see them shouting, and I presume the foals were calling too, but I was unable to hear them and they couldn't move forward. It was as if they were pressing against a window.

<< I didn't have long to wait to find out why. One of the Godhe females walked from behind them, pointed at me what I assume to be one of the assault rifles Marcus told us about and fired.

<< Of course I tried to turn the rocket back to the sender, like Karim did in Europe, but try as hard as I like I couldn't affect it at all. It just kept coming.

<< Just before it hit me, Princess reared up to take it full in the chest. I have no doubt she knew just what she was doing and died to give me a chance to help the children.

<< I feel so proud to have known her!

<< Working it out from how Belle saw me, I fell, hurting my shoulder and fracturing my thick stupid skull.

<< A fine bodyguard I turned out to be - beaten by one woman.

<< Tyana, Marcus, Karim, Rebel, I'm so sorry! They've all gone, and it's my fault! Can you ever forgive me?

<< I honestly believe them to have been captured rather than hurt. If she'd wanted to kill them she could have just done so! >>

The Tyana/Marcus/Karim/Rebel merge was quick to answer.

<< We agree with you! Our children are almost certainly safe, and I wouldn't want to be in their captors' shoes when they start trying to escape! >>

<< Obviously Kresh and her group have learned from our last encounter. This force field of theirs cuts off both communication and our ability to control objects within its sphere. They seem to have developed a different version of the invisibility type used before, as you said you could see through this one.

<< She must have released it just long enough to allow the rocket to pass through. Now we know, we'll simply keep trying if it happens again until that moment of release, and turn it.

<< You have nothing to reproach yourself for, Merlin. I don't see how any of us could have done better!

<< With Princess dead, what of Laura? >>

Quickly Zoltan brought the others up to date, then Belle announced, << Princess must never be forgotten! In future I will be known as Princess, and when I am gone, I hope another will take the name with the same pride that I do! Yes, Zoltan? >>

<< I wish to say something before resuming my task of passing on Merlin's thoughts.

<< I feel an emotion that I have been taught is unknown amongst unicorns. The desire for revenge against those who would kill my friend and take hostage my grandchildren. No, I'm unfair to myself. It's not revenge exactly, just the sure knowledge that these people must be stopped, and an intense desire to help.

<< Merlin, would it be possible for me to partner you without causing harm to Archimedes? >>

"You mean like Belle, I mean Princess, is partnered with Laura?"

<< Exactly, and I pledge the services of my whole herd in the same way if it is possible. They will NOT get away with it! >>

"We must consult the records."

<< There's no need, >> put in Archimedes. << I have already lived over sixty years. If I die, and in doing so make Merlin more powerful, and help avenge my friend, I consider it worth it! >>

"Shaena, will you please try?" asked Merlin. "I don't believe there's any risk to Archimedes. We are too long bonded. There are only two possibilities in my opinion. Either I will be the first with two familiars on the planet, or there will be no change."

So once again, for the second time within an hour, Shaena was to form a unique bond. She had in front of her Merlin, mounted on Zoltan, with Archimedes perched on his shoulder.

As this was so new, she had Laura and Megan adding their wills to hers, and reciting in unison,

"We add one to these two, and let all be warned

None may interfere with the Triad so formed."

As all had seen annexations many times before, they realised that they had been successful. This was confirmed when Merlin announced, "Please reconvene at one in the afternoon Camelot time. Zoltan and I have much to discuss, and he has a lot to learn in a very short time."

Caroline and Bella needed no encouragement to have another nap. No one was surprised when Megan announced that she was joining them. Lace was already asleep in her chair.

Laura put an arm round her new Princess and together they walked out to the paddock. She still couldn't manage a smile with her son missing, and her first familiar dead, but life did seem a little better than it had an hour earlier.

<< *Merlin, I need you to visit the site of the abduction,* >> called Marcus through Rebel and Zoltan. << *This is more important even than training Zoltan to use his new skills. For now you can just draw on his power if needed. Be careful though, you're several hundred times more powerful than you were this morning!* >>

They set off towards Camelot and immediately the advantages of the Triad became apparent as Archimedes rose high in the air, scanning the area for miles around, and both Zoltan and Merlin could see through his eyes. The journey was uneventful, and they arrived at the site.

<< *There's nothing here, Marcus.* >>

<< *Let me see for myself, through Zoltan's eyes, please.* >>

Zoltan slowly turned and gave Marcus, through Rebel, a panoramic view.

<< *There's the usual depression where the spaceship settled. Throw a rock into the centre of the circle, but don't go near it!* >>

Merlin did as asked, with Zoltan learning from the thoughts just how to conjure for himself as a rock picked itself up, flew across the glade, and simply landed.

<< *So, they really have left. Carry on practising with Zoltan and we'll speak again when Carlos has his meeting.* >>

Like his daughter Karim, Zoltan was a fast learner, and within an hour would have passed a Bronze test.

<< *Thank you, Archimedes, for risking your life to give me this chance.* >>

<< *I want what's best for Merlin. Like him, I thought it unlikely that I would get hurt, but I felt it worth the slight risk.* >>

"Will you two stop talking about me as though I wasn't here?"

"Now let's go and see how Laura and Princess are getting along!

"Zoltan, do you agree with the name change?"

<< *It's the highest compliment she could pay her. I would have done it first, but I don't see myself as a Princess!* >>

Merlin realised his new partner had a sense of humour.

<< *What do you know of Lace, Merlin?* >>

"Very little! She only arrived on the night of the concert, and she's very reluctant to talk of Earth. She seems to distrust men, and Marcus especially. Why do you ask?"

<< *I don't know what she did, but when she held Laura's hand, it seemed to make Megan's job a lot easier. Laura stopped fighting her so hard. We should find out!*

<< *I tried at the time, but her mind seemed to go blank just after she had thought that Laura was too good to be allowed to die.* >>

"I don't care what she did on Earth! She's here now, and if she helped save Laura, that's enough for me, and, I suspect, for any of us.

"Still, one can't help being curious. What could be so bad that she's afraid to talk about it?"

<< *She is next to, but not with, Dustine and Darryl leaning on the paddock rail and watching Laura with Princess.*

<< *I suggest we find out! I've studied Marcus's questioning technique, and believe we can use it. I'll pass the answers to others.*

<< *As you say, we can forgive anything after the help she gave.* >>

Laura spotted their return, and joined Merlin at the rail.

"Now, Lace, I think you owe us an explanation!

"Do you not agree?"

"No, Merlin!" shouted Darryl as he jumped in front of her.

"She's only been here a short while, and I promised we would ask no questions!"

<< *Trust Merlin, Darryl!* >>

"I ask you to trust me, Darryl, and you, Lace.

"First! What sort of name is Lace? It's not your real one, is it? What are you really called?"

"I'm answering no questions!"

<< *Melanie.* >>

"Why are you afraid of policemen, like Marcus?"

"I said I'm answering no questions!"

<< *I stole things.* >>

"Let's change the subject.

"Laura, do you remember when you stopped fighting Megan and Caroline, and began to want to live again?"

"Vaguely. Somebody held my hand, and things didn't seem quite so bad after that. Why?"

"That somebody was Lace! Incidentally, she comes from New York. Have you ever met her before?"

"Not that I know of. Why do you ask?"

"Just a hunch I have that she knew you already. Are you sure? Possibly under a different name? Say……..Melanie?"

Lace could not avoid a reaction when the name was mentioned.

"I never met her, but there was a Sister Melanie who ran a sort of unofficial Mission Hospital. We used to send her down and out people with no insurance who the other hospitals would refuse to treat.

"Was that you, Lace? If it was, you should be proud of what you did!"

"I never heard of her!"

<< How the Hell did Merlin learn my name? >>

Darryl could stand no more of it, turned to Zoltan, and said, "All of us here know that you people can tell instantly if the human in front of them, even as a baby, is, how do you put it? 'Good enough to have been born a unicorn?'

"Personally, I say now that I don't care if the answer is no! After what she did for Laura this morning I will forgive anything, but I ask you, Sir, to tell us all…..Is Lace a good person?"

<< She is, but she believes herself not to be!

<< Melanie, or we will still use Lace if you prefer it, I'm so sure that I'm right that I already have in mind a particular unicorn mare from my herd to partner you.

<< Please tell our friends your story! >>

Melanie threw her arms round Zoltan's neck, weeping, and, still holding on to him for comfort, she did as asked, but not before thinking, *"Can I really relax and trust these people?"*

To her surprise she found the question answered.

<< You most certainly can! >>

And so Lace had her first private conversation with a unicorn, which gave her the courage to tell her story.

"I was told that I'd been found, twenty four years ago, in the grounds of a convent, with a note pinned to my shawl saying 'Please take care of my daughter Melanie. I'm sorry!'

"My mother was never traced. By the time I was twelve my life was planned for me. I would take my vows and work as a nurse in the Mission Hospital, funded from various charities.

"Ten years ago support for the hospital was withdrawn as the nuns would not agree to discontinue treating criminals, drug abusers, and several other classes who used their services freely.

"The hospital continued to function though, as huge sums of money were deposited in the collection box at regular intervals, and one day I followed a teenage girl I'd seen leave such a parcel. I discovered she lived with other street kids in a tenement block that had been condemned.

"Whilst I was wondering what to do I was grabbed from behind by the leader and taken into a room with three other boys.

"Two held me whilst the leader and his friend tore off my novice's habit, and I was thrown down to the ground, two holding a leg each, and the other held my hands above my head."

"You don't have to give us the details," interrupted Megan.

"We only want to know why you think you're bad!"

"I do have to tell you - you'll see why in a moment!

"As the leader undressed and I realised what he intended, I began to hate him with all the power I could muster. I wanted him dead!

"And that's exactly what I got! He fell over, clutching his chest.

"His friends panicked, let me go, and ran out of the room.

"One of the girls came in and helped me dress and leave. I heard afterwards that the doctors said he'd had a heart attack, probably brought on by drug abuse.

"I visited them regularly after that, and, as all I was wearing when the girls first saw me was a pair of lace edged panties, I was given the street-name of Lace. At that time it was just a joke, and a way for them not to have to admit my vocation.

"The Mother Superior found out, realised where the money had been coming form, and to cut the story short, the hospital closed, and I was thrown out on to the streets at fourteen.

"The tenement block was pulled down, we all moved to a disused warehouse, and I decided then that I would carry on with the work.

"Several of the kids were pickpockets, but I quickly found that if I wanted something badly enough it just came to my hand, and I was far better than any of them. I would walk to within four or five feet of a businessman, bring his wallet instantly to my hand, pass it to one of the others, and look for the next.

"We soon had enough money to buy beds and kitchen equipment, and opened for business, at first in a very small way.

"I still remember our first patient. Melissa was a suicide attempt that failed. Fifty Paracetamol tablets and they got to her two days later when pumping her out would do no good."

"Sorry to interrupt again, Melanie," put in Laura, "but most of the others will not have heard of the drug you mention.

"It's a common painkiller on Earth, freely available, but even half that number of tablets can be fatal, causing liver damage which can't be cured. Carry on, please!"

"She discharged herself when told she was going to die anyway, to keep the hospital bill for her family low and came to us to wait for the end.

"I sat with her holding her hand for hours, trying to help her come to terms with what she'd done, and sometime in the second week, we realised she was getting better. She was able to go home to her family, but her doctor just refused to believe that she'd taken that many tablets in the first place.

"Melissa came back to us, and put the whole venture on a sound footing. We stole the money and she handled all of it.

"The authorities thought we were a charity as she opened a bank account in the same name as the Mission which had closed.

"Melissa advertised in soup kitchens and similar places, and before long we started getting what you might call referrals from the proper hospitals.

"About four years ago I took in a man with several gunshot wounds, and saved him. I don't know how! I could swear that he had five .44 bullets in him when he arrived, but just by wishing him better he was able to walk out a week later.

"The gang boss who ordered him dead came to see me and threatened to burn the place down if I ever went against him again.

"He had a heart attack, just like my attacker. The two men with him drew their guns, and I remember thinking that I didn't want them dead. I just wanted them gone. They hit the wall behind them so hard their skulls were flattened at the back, so they died too!

"The police started to realise that I was always around when a large cash robbery took place. I no longer bothered picking pockets. Bank delivery vans were much more efficient, and I had just run into an alley after emptying one into our panel van when the next I remember is waking up here!

"So you see, I really am not a very nice person to know!

"Annoy me too much, and you die, like the four I told you about! And I can't promise it won't happen here if someone makes me angry enough.

"I almost killed Darryl that first night! I would have if he'd tried anything!

"I also swore to kill whoever hurt Laura if I ever meet her.

"I meant it too, and I still feel the same way. If I meet her, she's as good as dead!"

Zoltan addressed Melanie, but allowed all others to hear him.

<< *I still say you're a good person!*

<< *For what it's worth you would have found Darryl much harder to hurt than a normal human on Earth.*

<< *You saved hundreds of lives, and caused the deaths of four. From what you say it may well be that the act of killing those four saved many more who would have become their victims!*

<< *As for your oath to kill the woman who attacked Merlin, killed Princess, and hurt Laura, I wish you luck!*

<< *My own daughter Karim has killed several dozens, if not hundreds when they were trying to harm Tyana or Marcus.*

<< *This is a primitive world and here it is accepted that if someone tries to harm you, then it's quite in order to take whatever action is necessary to protect yourself. I know I wouldn't hesitate, though I feel that Laura, and perhaps Megan would.*

<< *However, I speak for all of us when I say that you are welcome!* >>

He then continued privately to Melanie, << *You need have no fear of men here, My Dear. The crime of rape is unheard of on this continent, and since they were allowed to keep their Theurgen, the men of Europe are just as trustworthy.*

<< *Megan, this evening and during tomorrow will you please spend as much time with Melanie as possible and make sure she learns a little more of life here than she's managed to pick up so far!*

<< *Merlin, I will arrange for Victrix to be here the day after tomorrow at ten in the morning. Perhaps you would officiate. If Melanie can throw two grown men back into a wall without a familiar and when she's not even trying, we must teach her to control the power she undoubtedly has, do you not agree?* >>

<< *I do indeed!* >>

Instead of looking happy, as Zoltan and Merlin had expected, Darryl turned away, put an arm round Timber's neck, burying his face in the mane for a moment, then slowly walked away. Dusty was quick to follow.

"What is it, Brother? We get the best news that anyone could hope for and instead of being happy for her you walk away!"

"It's better this way!"

"But you really care about her. That's obvious to all of us!"

"Think about it, Dusty! Zoltan is planning to pair her with a unicorn. What time will she have for the likes of Timber and me after that?

"I had hoped that she'd take Cindy, a mare Timber likes, as a familiar."

Dusty thought for a while, looking for the argument that may have some effect on his brother, who he couldn't remember ever seeing depressed before.

"Do you think Laura would have cared any less for Merlin if he had only had Archimedes whilst she had Belle? - I mean Princess!"

"Don't be silly! There's no comparison! I'm not Merlin!"

"No, but you're still Darryl Counter, and Silver, which only one in twenty people reach. You're not too bad looking, though I say it myself who look similar, but much more important,

"You care about Lace, and you're the first male she has ever felt able to trust.

"So get right back there and apologise, Brother!"

Darryl turned, to see Lace being comforted by Megan. He walked over in time to hear, "....knew I was right to keep my past a secret. He was just beginning to like me, and now he doesn't want to know. I'll never forgive Zoltan for telling everyone!"

"Lace!" he called as he came nearer.

She turned her head to see him standing like a naughty little boy, turning his Stetson through his hands, and looking down at his feet.

Megan pushed her towards him. Dusty from behind pulled his arms apart, then forward to envelope Lace as she came to him.

Neither spoke, but soon, when each realised the other was relaxing, the forced encounter became a hug of friendship, then a cuddle and they walked away arms round each other.

"Darryl, I…….."

Her voice dropped to a bare whisper as she continued.

"….. I don't know what to say. I had hoped you'd never find out how evil I am. …. No wonder you left like you did.

"What's so funny?" she asked as she felt him chuckle.

"The idea that I left because of what you did on Earth. I don't give a damn what you did there! You're here now. We all trust Zoltan's judgement, and he said you were a good person. Even if he'd answered 'No' I wouldn't have cared.

"For me, you helping to save Laura was all that counted. That, and the way I feel myself."

Then he had a thought.

"You've met my sister Tyana. How do you think she would feel about killing a man?"

"Tyana……..Kill a man?…."She'd never do it. She's one of the nicest, gentlest people I've ever met."

"I'll have to tell her that when she gets back. Marcus won't let her forget it!

"There's a book in the library at home called '*Unicorn Witch*'. When you get the chance, read it. It tells about her adventures seven years ago.

"At one time her powers were taken away, and she killed the man responsible with her bare hands. She then gave a bullying jailor a lesson he'll never forget for abusing her friend."

"But how?"

"Marcus was Illinois State Champion in Karate. I expect you know what that means?"

"It means he's amongst the best!"

"Well he trained her to be even better than himself. She must have killed at least twenty for each of your four, and the one I told you about was with her bare hands, or perhaps I should say feet, not magic.

"But, and this is what matters......She never harmed anyone who was not trying to harm her or her friends.

"And she never would!"

Darryl could feel her relaxing as she digested this, and revised her opinion of his sister.

"Then you could really accept me as a friend?"

"Lace, I already love you! I think I have since I watched you when Aristo left for the herd."

"Nobody falls in love that quickly!"

"Tyana and Marcus did. Sometimes it's quick, sometimes it takes weeks, like it did with Laura and Merlin.

"Do you really feel nothing in return for me?"

Melanie blushed, which was really answer enough, and Darryl continued, "One thing you haven't accepted yet, is that here we don't try to hide our feelings. There's no need.

"Please don't lie to me, though. If you feel nothing, we can still be friends."

Before Melanie could think what to say Megan arrived to carry out Zoltan's request, insisting on an immediate return to the ranch, so it was from Megan and Dusty that she learned the real reason for Darryl's apparent rejection of her when she told her story.

"He said he loved me," she told them. "Is it possible? Or does he say that to all the girls?"

"We'll forgive you for asking that," replied Dusty, "but I ask you never to repeat it.

"Darryl has had friends who were girls. He may even have spent the night with one or two of them, though I doubt it. I am, however, absolutely certain that he has never loved them other than as friends, nor would he have told them that he loved them.

"If he said he loves you, then - quite simply, - He does!"

"You've lived here all your life, Dusty, and he's your brother.

"Megan, do you agree with him? How long did it take you to fall in love with Dusty? - If you don't mind telling me."

"Answering your last question first, I arrived here with a young brother to look after. Thomas was only six. I was made welcome by the whole Counter family, just as you have been yourself, but from the first day, there was something special about my friendship with Dusty.

"I felt safer with him than even with Tyana. I suppose it took me about a week to realise it was love. Dusty was just like Darryl, thinking he wasn't good enough for me, and if I hadn't made the first move we'd still be sharing just a cuddle as friends.

"Don't look so shocked! I'd just arrived here after nearly dying in a fire, and I was no virgin educated in a convent.

"The people looking after me were in real trouble. You've seen how their lives depend on what they call magic ability? Well try to imagine the effect of up to twenty of them losing those powers at one time, and the same happening again every two years. You'll read about it in that book Darryl told you about.

"The nearest I can give as an example is for you to consider the effect of one or two members of each family in New York waking up blind one day.

"In spite of all that they found time to make us welcome, even making me a harp.

"Believe me, there's no finer man anywhere than Darryl!"

The conversation had to become more general as others arrived, but Megan continued her task next morning, and had Melanie performing the Bronze tests for the family by the evening.

Darryl, as requested by Zoltan, had found work to do away from the house.

Melanie, for her part, had made every effort to do as Megan asked, had accepted at face value all she'd been told. She was determined to find a way to avoid hurting Darryl when she was annexed with Victrix.

When she finally fell asleep in the early hours it was with a smile on her face.

Chapter Three

W*ake up, Thomas!* »
  "What time is it?"
  <<*Just after seven in the morning, but Electra tells me all the others are having breakfast and are eager to start.* >>

Thomas was at once fully awake, cheated by cleaning and smartening his clothes and dressing in them magically, and in less than a minute from Jet's call was joining Electra and her husband. They had no children, but Thomas was not sorry to have only adult company. Like Tyana before him, he found that with a unicorn as a familiar he had matured much more rapidly than normal teenagers do.

"What will we be doing this morning, Electra?" he asked.

"I want everyone to read the book based on Tyana and Marcus's adventures. I expect you've been taught from it at school, and I'm sure there's a copy at your home, so you may be bored. If so, I'm sorry!"

"You mean '*Unicorn Witch*'? To be honest, reading it properly is one of the things I've always meant to get around to doing one day. When I was younger I didn't bother because I thought I knew it all anyway as I was involved in all the meetings - through Jet, you know.

"Just treat me like all the others, please."

By eight thirty all were assembled in the Abinger Council Chamber and Electra brought them to order.

"When Tyana and Marcus returned over six years ago from Europe they visited us, and independently wrote diaries detailing all their experiences and thoughts.

"Those diaries are available for you to study, but what you may find more useful is an account of all that occurred which one of our historians has made partly from the diaries, and partly from our own records of events before their adventures.

"When you've read your copy, which you'll find is in your own language, it's yours to keep. You'll then realise just how much we all owe them, and how fitting it is that they be honoured by the statues you saw being constructed."

Each of the group found in front of him or herself a leather bound book entitled: *Unicorn Witch (An Account of events in the year 1351 which lead to The Unification of Refuge)*

Before anyone had time to comment, Merlin made his report and, as had been promised, Jet passed it on to all present.

There followed ten minutes discussion before Electra called the group back to order and announced, "I, or another of us, will be in the room with you whilst you read this. We have all read it, and assure you it's the fullest account available. Please feel free to ask any questions."

With that, Electra left the room, and a man who they later learned was the writer of the book took her place.

Long before lunch, Thomas had decided that this whole exercise was designed to dissuade the leaders from returning to Europe, and to keep Jet and himself from demanding to go with Tyana and Marcus.

<< *It's not fair, Jet, we'd be much more use helping guard Camelot, or even better, going on the Unicorn Witch!* >>

<< *I don't agree, Thomas! Instead of complaining, let's see what we can learn. If there is anything, I want us to be the ones to discover it. You'll have noticed that Tyana and Marcus have made no mention of Karim's and Rebel's part. We'd better do the same. Merlin said you must take credit for any ideas I have!* >>

Thomas was delighted to find, over an early lunch at noon when they were comparing ideas, that he was the only one to point out,

"There appears never to have been any investigation into how the message which started the story got into the records here."

"Which message do you mean?" asked Hammid.

"The one which made Merlin cut short his visit and rush back to Camelot. The one that made him get permission for Karim and Tyana to be annexed. How does it go.........?"

Thomas started turning the pages over, but Electra quoted it:-

"In times of stress and trouble you'll need
The power of a girl with Horn and Steed!

"You're wrong, Thomas, we have tried to find out, but without success. One day the page was blank, and the next it had the verse. Merlin was the only one to whom it meant anything and events seem to have proved him right.

"Have you any ideas yourself?"

<< *I have, Thomas, but let me use your voice, so that they won't realise the idea is mine.* >>

"Yes! That's why I asked about it. We already know from Aristo that the

Godhe keep a team here somewhere. He spoke of weekly reports when he had dinner with us.

"One of them must have worked out, as Merlin did, that a combination of intelligence and sheer mass in a familiar, combined with Tyana's natural ability was what was needed to unify the world. They would obviously disapprove of the way Europe had developed and would want to change it without interfering themselves.

"We know that Kresh has somehow fooled the ruling council and is working for Medical Research, and that Aristo has been killed, but just maybe we still have a friend in their camp, if only we can find first it, and then the friend."

"May I speak?"

All looked to Hammid's side, to the beautiful dark haired, dark eyed Salome, who hadn't spoken on the journey from Camelot, but had just revelled in the excitement of the ride.

"Of course you may, Salome!" replied Electra.

"In Abinger, all are equal. What can you add?"

"I'm a very fast reader, averaging some 30,000 words an hour, so I've finished it. The map which you will read about Marcus acquiring from the former King of Paris shows an island on Longitude Zero.

"This is the by far most likely place for their base to be!"

Jet spoke to the whole assembly.

<< *I'm interrupting Merlin to tell him this at once. I have no doubt he will wish me to thank both Thomas for his observations, and Salome for hers!* >>

***

Jet's news could not have arrived at a better time, as Zoltan and Princess had just called the conference to observe and assist during Carlos's appointment with Kresh.

Marcus didn't hesitate for a moment, saying, "I'm sure they're right, and we're already changing course for the island.

"We brought along the planetary radio we took from Le Roi in Paris. Perhaps we'll hear something on it if they happen to use the same frequency."

Marcus attempted to explain what 'frequency' meant in this context, but had to give up.

"We waste time!" Merlin commented. "We can all learn about radios when this is over.

"Marcus, what do you advise Carlos to do?"

"First he must learn how many there are in the ship.

"If Kresh was the only enemy, he could simply bind and gag her, but that wouldn't help defeat the others, and the effect would be to warn them how we work.

"Carlos, arrive with Sophia, riding your partners. During the conversation, either Javelin or Lotus Blossom should try some very simple magic on Kresh without her knowledge just to find out if it's possible. You never know! They may have developed a personal screen like the ones round the city and round the ship.

"Try not to arouse her suspicions today. We want all the information we can get before we take any action ourselves. If you can think of a way to get her thinking about the children and foals, it would be a great help."

Whilst they were walking slowly to the square for the meeting, Merlin brought Thomas and Jet up to date with their news, and passed on Vernique's request. He asked him to delay passing on the knowledge of the kidnappings.

Thomas and Jet were appalled to hear of Princess's death, and fascinated with the idea of Merlin, Archimedes, and Zoltan forming a Triad. This, including the spell used and use of two Whites to perform the rite he was told to pass on to Electra.

<<May we form a Triad ourselves?>> asked Jet. <<It seems a very good idea, having a bird as the third pair of eyes.>>

"I want everyone who is able to do just that!" answered Merlin.

"And that especially includes you, Tyana, and Marcus!"

<<We're here! The door's open, and this time we'll go inside.

<<If we lose contact, do you want us to get out - if we can?>>

<<No!>> answered Marcus, <<I'm sure she'll let you out again. You're no use to her trapped in the ship. Just learn as much as you can and tell us later.

<<Be patient, please. As soon as we've learned all we can from her, I'll tell you exactly how to put her in her place, but I don't want to act until we know why they've taken the children, and ideally we have them back.>>

Kresh was obviously either a fool, or very sure of herself, as she did not switch the ship screen on again after Carlos and Sophia entered, and the others were able to listen in.

"I know what you've offered us, Kresh, but what do you want in return?

"Just how do you want us to help in your research?"

"I want first to find out just what the limits of your powers are, then by finding a way to counter them, I hope to scientifically duplicate them."

<< She tells the truth, but we don't want her to find out just how powerful you are! >>

"How do we start?"

"Pour me a drink, please, whilst I think!"

Carlos caused a bottle to open and fly across to meet the glass lifted by Sophia. It was worth it to see Kresh's face as she lifted the glass to her mouth, then spat it out.

"Well, you did say you wanted to know what we can do," purred Sophia, "and changing the nature of things is just one example. As it poured, I changed the wine to vinegar!"

"I believe you would call that a joke? Be advised that we Godhe have no sense of humour - or at least I don't!"

"Pull another stunt like that and the deal's off!"

"Just take it as doing you a favour! I could as easily have killed you by making it a snake venom solution. We witches make good friends. Believe me, you don't want either of us as an enemy!"

As Sophia said this, Lotus Blossom sent a bag of flour in through the still open door to burst over Kresh's head. The flour fell as though on to a bell jar over her, none of it reaching her body.

"Truce! I won't try to hurt either of you!"

<< The truth! >>

For an hour, Kresh had the tests for Bronze demonstrated, then had Carlos and Sophia demonstrate how much more they could do. Obviously they only reached a self imposed limit of about what a normal White could manage. Once the pattern was established, the others withdrew to give the twin foals a rest. It was arranged that the next contact would be initiated by Carlos when they had something worth while to report. Carlos and Sophia decided not to try to form Triads yet.

Merlin, though, was anxious that as many as possible were formed in New America.

Qamar/Storm and Shaena/Hawka were bonded with Sabre and Lady, two of Zoltan's herd with no trouble. Just as easily Laura/Princess added an owl, Guinevere, much to Archimedes's delight.

Attempts to form Triads with Hondo, Lindsey, and others had no effect.

It didn't take long to learn the basic rules, and Merlin summarised them for Thomas to pass on.

"A Triad must consist of a unicorn, a human of White ability, and another, so far always a bird, but there's no reason to assume another animal wouldn't do.

"Thus, for example, a White with a horse familiar will be unable to add a bird as a third member, but probably could add a unicorn.

<< *It makes sense!* >> added Zoltan. << *Remember a unicorn is already an equal partner, so what happens is that the partnership takes a familiar, making a Triad.* >>

"Or," finished Merlin, "the White takes a partner who then shares the familiar, as happened with myself."

<< *You realise we've overlooked Megan? Let's find out about a White with a horse familiar!* >> commented Zoltan

"I hadn't realised, but you're right! How could we? After the power she showed yesterday she must be of White ability even though she would never be tested! Have you a unicorn in mind?"

<< *I have! Victrix has a twin sister, Lucky. I'll arrange for her come with her tomorrow.* >>

***

As soon as he'd delivered all his messages, Jet wanted to know, << *What bird do we want as the third member of the best Triad on Refuge?* >>

<< *We're not the best, Jet. Maybe one day, but not yet!* >>

<< *I was joking!* >>

<< Let's go for a trip outside town when we finish work, but in the meantime, we've some unfinished reading to do.

<< And we must check on Seline and Fallon for Vernique. >>

Unfortunately the reading, whilst interesting, yielded no more information, and it was a relief when Electra came in to announce, "Will you all please come to the square where you saw statues the being sculpted. They are finished, except for a little job we'd like Thomas to do."

The party lined one side of the square whilst the citizens of Abinger lined the other three. Electra raised her arms for silence then spoke.

"Thomas, as all the visiting council leaders have already been told, a new classification has been created for those of White ability who have unicorns as familiars.

"The usual contests are useless as they would be too one sided. This was demonstrated first by Tyana, then Marcus, before the awesome power you command was realised.

"In future those like yourself will simply be asked to perform a test, but before I explain it, will you please lift the finished statues on to their pedestals?"

Thomas looked at the life-sized model of Tyana riding Karim, and said, "But that one alone must weigh about five tons, and the other at least the same."

71

<< Zoltan tells me we can do it easily! >>

Thus encouraged, Thomas lifted the statue of Tyana and Karim, then carefully aligned the plinth to the top of the pedestal, finding to his surprise that it was as easy as controlling a small brick. Once he'd done this he saw the inscription around the base near Karim's forefeet.

TYANA COUNTER, FIRST IVORY WITCH

It was just as easy to position that of Marcus and Rebel with its inscription:-

MARCUS COUNTER, SECOND IVORY WITCH

"Now the test, Thomas. This will be the only requirement in future to become known as an Ivory Witch.

"Simply exchange the statues!"

<< What does Zoltan say about that? >>

<< Nothing! But if Merlin asked for this test it must have been after discussion with Tyana and Karim.

<< You take Tyana and I'll handle Marcus! >>

Even though Electra and the council members had been warned that ten tons was going to be simple for Thomas, there was still a gasp when the two life sized granite figures rose, circled each other, and settled simultaneously on to their new pedestals.

"Thomas, you are now the third Ivory Witch.

"Congratulations! Use your power wisely and for the benefit of all! Thank you!

"The Show is over, Ladies and Gentlemen, and there are still records to study.

"Thomas, you may take the rest of the day off, if you wish."

They needed no encouragement, but before leaving the square looked around the audience. Thomas had no trouble identifying the two werefolk. They had been allowed front places being only five feet tall, and their close-cropped short blonde hair, showing pointed topped ears, together with very white skins made his task easy. Jet walked over to them.

"Hello, Seline, Fallon.

"Vernique is worried about you, but I assume I can tell her you are well?"

"Mais oui, Thomas.

"Je regrette que Je ne parle pas l'anglais depuis. Nous venons ici pour l'apprendre."

("Certainly, Thomas. I am sorry that I don't speak English yet. We came here to learn it.")

Thomas chatted to Seline for a few minutes, then promised to spend longer talking to them, and helping improve their English when he was able. He thought how lucky he was to have spent six years in the company of bilingual friends, and thus have an excuse to see this girl again.

They left at a gallop, and were soon approaching the nearby mountains.

<< *I've never known you unable to speak to a girl before, Thomas. Why is that?* >>

"I did speak to her!"

<< *No! You spoke only to her mother, not to Fallon.* >>

"She fascinates me! It must be wonderful to be able to change and fly, whenever you want."

<< *She is also very beautiful. Are you sure that has nothing to do with it?* >>

"Do you mind if we change the subject?"

<< *If you insist! Let's see...*

<< *You already know what bird you want as a third member with us, don't you?* >>

The effort of speaking at a full gallop was tiring, so Thomas gave up.

<< *I've admired Storm ever since Megan and I arrived on Refuge over seven years ago, and I can't think of anything I'd rather have on my side in a fight than a Golden Eagle.....*

Can you? >>

<< *No.... I agree with you, and they can fly very high. With their eyesight we'll not miss much. Let's find one!* >>

This was easily accomplished, as there were more males than females in the area, and in response to Jet's call a young one came to perch on a branch near them. He readily agreed to the suggestion that he join, and promised to meet them in the early evening in the square.

Electra selected Hammid to assist, in order that similar Triads could be formed when he returned home, but all were surprised when instead of one eagle, three arrived for the meeting.

Jet questioned the one they had befriended, then the other two. He was then able to explain to the group, << *His sister and her mate from a nearby eyrie followed as our one seemed so excited. Now they know why, they wish to join too!* >>

"Ask Merlin how far The Unicorn Witch has got please, Jet."

Thomas was speaking aloud for the benefit of Electra and Hammid.

<< *Rebel here, Thomas. Marcus says we're about one hundred miles South West from the nearest land in New America.*

<< *Why do you ask?* >>

<< *I have a pair of young mating Golden Eagles here who wish to join Triads. You could wish for no better partners!* >>

<< *We're less than one day out, so we'll turn about and meet you down river from Brigadoon.*

<< *Congratulations on your promotion. Be as quick as you can, but no risks, please! Don't travel in the dark!* >>

<< *Uncle Marcus.* >>

<< *Yes, Thomas?* >>

<< *What if the Godhe go looking to see how far the ships returning to Europe have got?* >>

<< *A very good question! Thank you, Thomas.* >>

<< *Merlin, please arrange that Rix sends four ships from Newport to look like the expedition they expect.* >>

Bonding with Tallons, as they decided to call their third member was easily accomplished, and Thomas conjured a perch and windshield large enough for the three eagles, fitted neatly to the front of his saddle.

Promising to return as soon as he was able, He and Jet left and were in Camelot before dusk. Even with the windshield, Tallons and his friends needed a lot of preening before they could sleep, and Merlin designed an all enclosed version, still with all round visibility, for use the next day. Jet had to be forbidden by Zoltan from joining the guard for the night.

***

Awake at dawn, Melanie tiptoed outside without waking her hosts, and with little effort found Princess grazing. "Good morning, Ma'am!" She felt proud of her demonstration that she had accepted unicorns as people. It was unfortunate that she'd not yet learnt that unicorns could graze whilst asleep.

Luckily her mental panic when she received no reply was enough to attract Zoltan's attention, it being his watch.

<< *Melanie!.. It's alright. Princess is asleep. Can I help?* >>

"I want to try to arrange to have Cindy as a familiar as a surprise for Darryl, but I have no idea how to do it.

"I know it would mean a lot to him, as he was afraid of losing me when he heard about Victrix. As much as I like the thought of sharing my life with a unicorn, I'm sure I could be happy with a horse…. It was all I could think of."

<< *There is more merit in your thoughts than you realise, Melanie. However, Merlin needs as many triads as possible. Did Megan explain what a triad is?* >>

"Yes, but she emphasised the tremendous power they have. With my history it will be safer for everyone if I have a horse!"

<< *Once and for all, you are now one of us!* >>

<< *Darryl loves you! That won't change just because you become a part of a triad. You will have your horse, if she agrees, but you will have Victrix as well.* >>

"Did you say he loves me?"

<< Yes! Please don't interrupt! We are at war! Our enemy already controls the other continent, and it's important that you realise just how serious the situation is.

<< By tradition newcomers like yourself are given two weeks to relax and get used to life here. I'm afraid that's a luxury we can't allow you. Merlin and I need all the help we can get! If you're of White ability, as I believe you are, we need you; just as we needed Marcus seven years ago. >>

Melanie threw her arms around Zoltan's neck, buried her face in his mane and wept again.

That is how Dusty and Darryl found her a few minutes later.

"Zoltan, what's wrong?" they asked together.

<< Relax! They are tears of joy. She's developed some self-respect at last with a little help from me, and finally realised that there's a place for her here.

<< Until this morning she was convinced we were just being polite to her. She found it inconceivable that she could be wanted for herself. >>

"I don't know how you did it, Zoltan," said Darryl, "but I for one will always be grateful!

"Come, Lace, it's time for breakfast, and I assure you it doesn't pay to keep our mother waiting!"

"Do you always eat this early?"

"Of course not, but Thomas and Jet have to leave as soon as possible, so we're all joining them."

Melanie managed to control herself until Thomas had left, then asked, "Have any of you met Victrix?"

Merlin answered, "I know all about her, and Megan, this affects you too, so please pay attention!

"Victrix and Lucky are twin mares, their parents being from the herd near Drogheda. To avoid inbreeding there's always some exchange of foals between herds, and they were part of such an exchange.

"They are each about one hand taller than Karim and Princess, and white with green contrast.

"Do you understand what contrast means, Melanie?"

"I think so. They have manes and tails that are green?"

"Yes, and horns and hooves!

"I can't tell them apart, but that never matters with unicorns as they let us know who is whom when they speak. Victrix, the one Zoltan wants to bond you with, Melanie, was so called as she's never been beaten in any competition she's ever taken part in."

"What - even in races with the stallions?"

"That's right! She will drive herself to exhaustion rather than not be first. You and she should compliment each other. She has enough self-confidence for the both of you!

"Now, Megan, a surprise for you!

"Zoltan and I feel that you must be of White ability to overcome Laura's resistance as you did, and we need all the triads we can form.

"Lucky is coming to form one with you!"

"But I love my Bess!"

"As I love Archimedes, My Dear, but you need have no worries on that score. The bond becomes three way, with both you and Bess gaining.

"An example is that the information I'm giving you about the twins is actually from Zoltan's memory. I've never met them."

Megan considered this for a moment, realising that perhaps it wouldn't be such a bad thing after all.

"Tell me more about Lucky, please!"

"They called her Lucky because just as Victrix has never been beaten in competition, Lucky has never lost a game of chance."

"What sort of game of chance?"

"Anything from which of two twigs dropped over a bridge will come out the other side first to which will be the last apple to drop from a tree in the fall.

"When the herd has had human visitors, such as my son, our three grandchildren, and Caroline, they join in the card games they play with each child having a unicorn partner. Whoever partners Lucky always wins, even if they try to lose.

"It will soon be ten, and then we'll all know.

"Dustine, you look worried! Is something wrong?"

"I was thinking of all that I said to Darryl the day before yesterday about Melanie thinking no less of him just because she was partnered by a unicorn.

"I know now just how he felt!"

Merlin looked to Megan for a reply, and she obliged.

"Darling Dusty, just consider how you'd feel if you were a White, were forming a triad, and I was not even Bronze. Would it bother you?"

"Of course not! I loved you long before we knew your power, and all I have to say is, .

"I'm proud of you!"

Victrix and Lucky arrived, paired off with Melanie and Megan. Cindy enthusiastically agreed to be Melanie's and Victrix's familiar, and by half past ten there were two more triads in Camelot.

Melanie lost no time in trying to cash in on her new partner's telepathic ability. As Megan, Lucky, and Bess went towards Camelot for a long talk, she, Victrix, and Cindy went in the opposite direction. As soon as she felt she could she asked, "Victrix, can I really relax and get used to living here? Did Zoltan speak for all the others when he said I was welcome? Does Darryl really love me, as he said?"

<< *When Zoltan asked me to join you and to form a Triad with Cindy he explained about your past. Frankly it was only the fact that you'd showed some spirit that made me agree to join you. Yes, you can relax and make a new life here. As for whether Darryl loves you, I'm prepared to tell you, but only if you let me tell him exactly how you feel. That's only fair, isn't it?* >>

"I'll have to think about that. In the meantime I think we should do as Megan and her group are, and go off to get some practice, and find our just what we can do. Agreed?"

<< *That sounds like a good idea! Cindy?* >>

<< *I'm still getting over the shock of finding that I can think clearly, and even stranger remember what I've thought. I leave it to you two for now. Suppose I provide Lace with transport.* >>

<< *Lace?* >>

<< *Well that's what Darryl calls her.*

<< *What's your opinion, Lace? Lace or Melanie?* >>

"I think it's fascinating hearing you two talk about me as though I wasn't here. And 'Lace' is fine with me. I think Darryl will always think of me as that, anyway."

By the evening Zoltan was able to advise Merlin that he could stop worrying about Melanie. She, Victrix, and Cindy had bonded into what he believed to be the most powerful Triad so far, closely followed in strength by Megan, Lucky, and Bess.

***

Thomas and Jet followed the route Tyana had used over seven years earlier and reached Brigadoon in late afternoon.

The *Unicorn Witch* was already tied up, and Marcus greeted them. "I'm proud of you both, Thomas. Your help came at just the right time seven years ago, and you've done it again. Thank you!"

"It's our pleasure, Uncle Marcus, I only wish we could come all the way with you.

"You're wrong about one thing though… it's not 'both' of us now, it's 'all three' of us!

"Say Hello to Tallons! Jet will help him answer!"

"I'm pleased to meet you, Tallons. Thank you for bringing your sister and her mate. Do they really understand what this is all about?"

<< *Yes, Uncle Marcus. Jet has explained it fully, and if the trip down here was a sample of life to come, they'll enjoy it.* >>

Tyana arrived, having taken on board extra food suitable for the eagles, as well as fifty strips of wrought iron, and a large number of cannon balls. She presumed Marcus must have a reason for wanting them, but she couldn't think of it, and pride prevented her from asking.

Because of the meeting there was a shortage of Whites, so Thomas was co-opted to work with first Tyana, facing Marcus, Rebel, and the mate of Tallons's sister, reciting,

"We add one to these two, and let all be warned

None may interfere with the Triad so formed."

Then it was the turn of Tyana and Karim, with the remaining bird.

Looking at his new familiar's feet, Marcus commented, "I can understand why Thomas chose Tallons as a name. What shall we call you? Have you any preference?"

<< *I was the fastest of my group, if that's any help!*

<< *Thank you again for this chance. It's a wonderful feeling, having the love of a human and a unicorn, instead of wanting to kill anything that moves.* >>

"We'll call you Swift!

"How about you, Darling, how do we address your third member?"

As Marcus was asking, the subject was gently rubbing her cheek against that of Karim.

"That's easy. She is called Caress!"

<< *Caress. Yes, it suits her!* >> said Swift.

<< *Uncle Marcus, this is Bella. Orchid is calling me. Are you ready to hear from Uncle Carlos?* >>

Before the question was completed, Karim had set up the conference.

<< *Ready, Sweetheart. Let Papa tell it in his own words.* >>

"We spent an hour or so, as you already know, demonstrating Bronze ability, then about what a normal White can manage.

"She was very impressed, but was particularly pleased that the personal barrier she was wearing stopped us doing anything to her. After she realised she was safe, I was able to ask a few questions myself. As far as I remember it went something like…

"Aren't you worried that Tyana and Marcus will be able to overpower you just like they did last time?"

"Not at all. If these barriers stop you, they will stop them."

<< As she said. >>

"Would it not be safer if they were dead?

"I'm worried. They're a lot more powerful than we are, you know."

"Our leader has captured their children. With them as hostages, they won't dare to interfere."

<< As she said. >>

"So you're not the leader then. Who is?"

"That doesn't concern you!"

<< Krast! >>

"I'm still worried. There's nowhere on Refuge you can hide from them. If any harm comes to the children they will kill all of you…And I have to admit, I'll help them.

"I love those children as much as our own Rosa."

"We only want them to study. They will be safe."

<< As she said. >>

"But where are they?"

"Safe! That's all you need to know."

<< On our island! >>

"She was beginning to get suspicious, so we stopped questioning her and got down to the everyday running of the town. What do you want us to do now, Marcus?"

"I'd be grateful if you let her think she's won. As soon as we have the children free, I promise you we'll enable you to imprison her.

"Just do everything she wants, subject to two conditions.

"Don't let her discover that the unicorns have power and that we can still keep in touch, and don't let her learn more than she already knows about the weres and dragons.

"I don't believe they'll just wait two months for us to get to Europe. It seems more likely that once we're assumed to have sailed, an attempt will be made to secure the towns in New America just like they have in Europe.

"Merlin, it's up to you to make that as hard as possible."

***

Merlin was already thinking along the same lines, and with Laura, was in Abinger, calling an emergency meeting of all leaders.

As a formality, and to guarantee the full attention of those present, first Merlin then Laura performed the statue exchange as a demonstration of their new status and ability.

Karim had taught her father the broadcast voice she developed when touring with Tyana, and Merlin used it with the same effect.

First he recounted everything that had happened, this time including the attempted murder of himself, the kidnapping of the children and foals, the sacrifice of her life by Princess followed by the formation of the Triads, and all the conversations monitored with Kresh.

A shocked silence followed his summary, and he went on,

<< Marcus has said, and we agree with him, that we can expect an attempt to be made to take control of the towns in New America.

<< We must not let that happen. The very least we must do is make it as hard as possible, so that Marcus and Tyana can have time to rescue the hostages. >>

Magdalena was the first to recover, and asked, "But what can we do against the power and weapons of the Old Ones?"

<< If Tyana and Marcus had thought like that seven years ago they would never have captured not one, but two of their spacecraft.

<< The very fact that they met no opposition in Europe, and their knowledge that Tyana and Marcus are not here, together with believing you have sailed for home will, I hope, make them overconfident. There's much that we can do. I estimate that it will take another month for them to get Europe running without the barriers round the towns. They can't leave them there as they still have to feed the people.

<< By that time, I want every town on this continent to have several Triads like the ones Laura and I are parts of.

<< Zoltan here has pledged his whole herd to help, and it's possible that other herds will join too.

<< I would like the leaders of Kissimmee, Brigadoon, Argentcourt, and Midwitch to return home and take their instructions from Thomas.

<< New Salem, Newport, Drogheda, and Eureka, I will visit in that order, and organise your defences myself.

<< Our European friends, I ask that you stay and help us.

<< You can do no good on a sailing vessel for two months. Here you may well get the chance. >>

***

Receiving their new orders from Merlin, which included responsibility for their home town of Camelot, Thomas and Jet decided to spend the time waiting for the return of the leaders by visiting Rebel's twin brother's herd eighty miles up river from Kissimmee. Scimitar had followed his younger twin's career with pride for the last seven years, and, when asked by Rebel, readily agreed to hear what Thomas and Jet had to say.

So busy had Rebel been that he had only just had time to tell of the last week's events. To say that Scimitar was displeased that his nephews and niece had been abducted would be an understatement.

<< *Just who does this Krast person think she is?* >> he demanded to know.

<< *Rebel tells me that she's one of the Old Ones, but that doesn't really help. Can you explain it better, Thomas, or Jet?* >>

"What you'll find hard to understand, Sir, is that whilst unicorns always act for the greater good of all unicorns, with no thought for personal gain, most humans are basically selfish. That includes the Godhe, or Old Ones as you called them.

"Seven years ago Krast was one of the drug traffickers put out of business as a side effect of Tyana's and Marcus's activities in Europe. Krast's friend, Kresh's lover, was killed and the two females seem to have returned for vengeance. I suspect they are also out for personal gain, but we've not yet discovered how."

<< *Did Rebel have anything to do with the death of the Godhe person who was killed?* >>

"No! His leader tried to kill Tyana with a rocket firing gun, and Karim turned the missile round to save her."

<< *Why did you agree to join Thomas as a partner, Jet?* >>

<< *I was unpopular in the herd because of my colour. Thomas offered me an alternative way of life, one that Karim seemed to enjoy very much. She was happier than any of the mares I knew amongst my teachers.* >>

<< *And are you still happy?* >>

<< *Certainly! Has Rebel not told you that Karim's dame is now a partner to Marcus's mother?* >>

<< *No!* >>

<< *Or that Zoltan himself is now a partner to Merlin, and has pledged his whole herd to serve as partners to help defeat the threat to Refuge?* >>

<< *No! I must speak with my brother and with Zoltan! Please excuse me!* >>

Jet quickly made friends with a few of the younger unicorns, and asked them to show him Tyana Ford. Thomas sat in the shade of a large tree to think, whilst Tallons stayed on his perch on Jet's saddle.

With most of the herd following, the party made their way to where Tyana had, to enable her to cross the Tallahachi River, widened it at that point seven years earlier, creating a ford one hundred yards wide over one hundred yards length of the river.

The upstream edge had suffered removal of much of the sand covering the rocks she had used to reduce the depth in the previous main channel, and it had been many years since Tyana had visited.

<< *Let me show you something of the ability which comes from association with one of the human White witches,* >> said Jet to the group of admiring unicorns.

<< *And you will find this interesting, Tallons, My Friend.*

<< *All of you must remember, though, that only a very few carefully selected humans know that unicorns can also develop the power you're about to see. You must never tell of it!* >>

Just as Karim had done to impress Rebel some seven years earlier, Jet lifted several tons of sandstone from the nearby cliff face and held it over the exposed rocks, whilst crumbling it to sand and spreading it evenly.

<< *I'm nobody's familiar. Thomas and I are equal partners, but at Karim's insistence this is kept secret. Tallons here is our familiar, and we gained even more power when he joined us.* >>

Scimitar walked to where Thomas was resting, then called the herd to him, announcing,

<< *Our way of life is threatened!*

<< *Zoltan, sire of Karim who you will all remember, has advised me that a group of the Old Ones has imprisoned all humans in Europe, may try to do the same on this continent, and have taken hostage four foals and their human children Bronze partners.*

<< *These Old Ones are trying to find out how the humans perform their magic. As soon as they discover that we unicorns also have power, though even we ourselves didn't know this until Tyana found out, we won't be safe.*

<< Zoltan said he has pledged his whole herd to assist.

<< My feeling is that I should do likewise, but I invite your comments. >>

All those who had seen Jet's demonstration immediately voted, << *Yes!* >> and explained why.

An elderly mare, Zolinne, Scimitar's and Rebel's dame came forward to face her leader and son.

<< *Your brother has shown us the way!*

<< *Karim, Rebel, and Jet, are so happy that it must be right.*

<< *You will be wise to allow any who wish to join, but not to insist upon it. I am available myself!* >>

<< *I thank you, My Dame, and agree.*

<< *So be it!* >>

Thus was Thomas able to report that the leaders of Kissimmee and Brigadoon should stop at Tyana Ford, where a whole unicorn herd was waiting to join the Civil Defence, as Marcus called it.

Thomas waited with the herd, he and Jet explaining as much as they could of life with a human partner. When they had all accepted the principle that they too could perform what the humans called magic once they had been shown how, Jet then went on to introduce Tallons.

<< *The humans found that their powers doubled if they took a familiar.*

<< *Zoltan took this one stage further, and now he and Merlin share a familiar; in their case an owl named Archimedes.*

<< *Archimedes risked his life to give Zoltan that chance!*

<< *Thomas and I share the lifelong friendship of the best fighting bird, and our power increased when we bonded to form a Triad.*

<< *You will know instinctively if the human in front of you can be trusted with the responsibility.*

<< *I am sorry if it embarrasses him, but Zoltan knew Thomas to be good enough to have been born a unicorn when he was only six years old, and allowed us to be annexed.* >>

They didn't have long to wait, as Susquehanna from Kissimmee, and Angus McDonald from Brigadoon, together with their mates and deputies, all had horses as familiars, were of White ability, and had learned well Tyana's stride multiplying spell. Thomas reminded them of the ceremony they had witnessed when he bonded with Tallons, then left the selection of partners to Scimitar.

He had Susquehanna assist him for half of the bondings, and Angus the other half, so that each could add to the Triads when they reached their homes.

The combination of Angus, his familiar a seventeen hand stallion named Battler, and Thor, a unicorn slightly larger than the horse gave telekinetic power greater than they were able to devise a test for.

Susquehanna with her pony, Kiltie, and Zolinne, whilst nowhere near as strong as the Angus Triad, far exceeded the best Thomas and his could do.

<< *Does that mean you will no longer want me?* >> asked Tallons.

<< *We would no more part with you than leave each other!* >> replied Thomas/Jet.

<< *If we had to choose now, we would still look for one of your kind. You must remember that Angus and Susquehanna were already bonded to and loved horse familiars!*

<< *Anyway, your eyesight and ability to fly so high more than make up for the difference in Triad strengths.* >>

Tallons relaxed, seeing the truth in what he heard.

The other triads fitted into the same pattern. The greater the combined mass, the more powerful the Triad.

<< *This is further confirmation that there is a connection between mass and sheer power. We must advise Merlin.* >>

Watching over half of his herd leave with the humans, Scimitar felt proud, rather than sad, which showed to Thomas and he asked why.

<< *Zoltan told me, and I agree with him, that the future of unicornkind is in partnership with humans.* >>

"So why did you not join a Triad yourself, Sir?"

<< *I will, when I meet the right human for me. Zoltan had no such problem as he knew Merlin. I can't explain why, but I feel I should wait.*

<< *Anyway, the herd needs me a little longer.*

<< I bid you farewell, Young Thomas, and Jet.

<< You will always find a welcome here! >>

"Goodbye, Sir! And thank you again!"

With that Thomas and Jet headed for Camelot and home, arranging with Zoltan that he could visit the herd the next day.

Possibly because Argentcourt and Midwitch were so near Camelot, had thus grown to respect Merlin, and had known Tyana personally for all of her life, Thomas had no trouble arranging Triads in each town.

Within a week, not counting Merlin, Laura, and Thomas there were more than ten Triads in each of the five towns Thomas had been given responsibility for.

***

Merlin had as little trouble with Abinger, Zoltan being able to persuade Caliph the local herd leader to pledge his followers. Caliph's favourite mare, Jasmina bonded with Electra, and Caliph himself with her husband.

In New Salem, Magdalena with Tess, her fox familiar agreed immediately and were bonded with a red unicorn mare Scarlett.

However, even when they demonstrated how much Magdalena's power had increased, the only two other Whites in the town flatly refused. One of them, Timothy, the previous leader explained to Merlin, "Seven years ago we were made to violate our religious conviction and take familiars on the grounds that we needed the protection.

"We never saw any theurgen thieves. All that happened was that women who previously knew their places took power from we men, and for what?

"Nothing! If your Tyana with her high and mighty arrogance had never come here we would still have suffered no losses, would we?"

"What can we do, Merlin?" asked Magdalena. "Because there was no real organisation here until seven years ago, we only have these two Whites, One Gold, and a dozen Bronzes.

"The men here still spend most of their time in worship.

"The women still do most of the work. Of course it's very different with the young ones, but it will be another ten years before we catch up with the other towns."

Laura spoke before Merlin could think of a solution. "Don't worry, Magdalena! The fact that Timothy and his crowd won't cooperate is unimportant. No self-respecting unicorn would have bonded with a bigot anyway!

"Merlin, you carry on to Newport and the others. I'll go back to get reinforcements for here.

"You, Timothy, can go to pray for guidance - you certainly are in need of it!"

Merlin did as suggested and had the same success as had Thomas and Jet. Pegasus from the nearest herd to Drogheda proved just as cooperative as had Caliph, and a week later each of his other towns had at least ten Triads practising hard to work together moving very large weights. The time taken by Tyana and Marcus to befriend the unicorn leaders when they had passed seven years earlier proved invaluable.

***

Returning to Abinger, Laura assembled the European leaders and explained her problem. When she called for volunteers, every single one stepped forward, but unfortunately only twelve of them were White.

Nevertheless the whole party elected to wait out the war, if war it was going to be, in New Salem.

Magdalena was delighted, as the influence of over twenty outsiders could only do good amongst what she referred to as her God-botherers. Including Magdalena/Tess/Scarlett there were thirteen Triads to guard New Salem. Camelot had even more when Laura returned to join Merlin and Thomas.

Later that evening Merlin found her crying on Thomas's shoulder. He didn't have to ask why. "I miss him, too! I suppose it's finally hit you now that you've had time to relax.

"Think how much worse it is for Tyana and Marcus.

"All three of theirs are missing, and they have nothing to do but worry as they sail South West. At least we can keep busy.

"Knowing those four children, they'll be alright! The only chance of them getting hurt will be when they decide they've waited long enough for a rescue and take action themselves. I just hope Marcus and Tyana get to the island before that happens."

"You really believe they're still alive, Merlin?

"You're not just saying it to make me feel better?"

"Of course they are! There would be no point in taking them just to kill them.

"That could have been done when they thought they'd killed me. Also Kresh mentioned holding them as hostages to ensure Marcus and Tyana were no threat."

<< *That shows how little they know of our son and daughter-in-law! .... And her friends!*

<< *May I enquire through Bella how Carlos is getting on?*

<< *It's been well over a week since we heard from them!* >>

"Certainly, Zoltan. It's late afternoon in Paris.

"You and Princess see if you can set up a conference including everyone as usual!"

***

"You've saved me calling you. May we have your news first?"

Merlin obliged, telling Carlos of the preparations made in New America, and surprised him by describing some of the loads moved by Triads made up of Human/Unicorn/Horse.

Marcus had little to say, except that he and Tyana had worked their fitness and Karate ability up to what it had been when last needed. Swift and Caress were bored, but understood the reason for the journey, and were looking forward to getting to know the children.

"I wish we were bored," began Carlos. "Kresh is a very good organiser, I have to admit that much.

"Paris is functioning just as though none of this has happened. The outer barrier is down, and people come and go as usual, but poor Vitesse has a personal screen that she has to wear all the time. Javelin and Lotus Blossom have one each as well, but at least they understand what it's all about.

"All Vitesse knows is that for the first time in her life she can only contact unicorns within ten feet of her, and humans if they are right next to her. She's very distressed. Fortunately we've convinced Kresh that the foals are too immature to need one.

"How long before you reach the island, and we can deal with our new leader?"

"Less than another week. We've been in luck, with a high wind blowing in exactly the right direction."

"Kresh is still conducting her tests. She keeps making adjustments to a box of some sort with dials and slides on it, then getting us to conjure something whilst she points a machine with a saucer shaped thing on it at us.

"So far, nothing she's tried has had any effect. She's getting rather frustrated."

"Mandrake and Shinlu turned up yesterday, but I managed to get a message out to them by Cantor, and they're going to stay around, but out of sight.

"What news of Vernique's relatives? Did Thomas see them?"

"He did, and they're safe and well, but worried about all of you in Paris, naturally.

"Have you any idea when, or even if, Krast intends to try to invade us on this continent?"

"She had a meeting with several other Godhe earlier today.

"That's why I was about to call you. When they left, the other three ships went East, so be on your guard tonight!"

"I think we'd better warn everyone. There were only three headed our way?"

"There were only the three at the meeting. Others may be coming to you from elsewhere."

"Goodbye, and Good luck. You have all our love!"

Marcus and Tyana stayed in contact and discussed possible tactics, but of course Bella and Orchid were no longer needed.

Suggestions ranged from turning the ships upside down as soon as they either landed, or switched off their screens, whichever happened first, to trying to chain them, as had proved effective on their first meeting.

"Try to avoid doing anything that we've done before!" advised Tyana! "Krast is no fool. I don't think she would have started this unless she was certain she could counter anything we did to her last time."

It was eventually decided to have supplies of cannonballs available, together with lengths of chain, strips of iron, lengths of rope, and ready made gags. Marcus gave instructions on what should be practised by the Triads.

Each town was to be advised by the duty unicorn, and at least two triads were to be on watch at any one time.

Marcus ended the discussion so that preparations could be made, saying, "We would appreciate it if you'd keep in contact when dealing with whoever comes."

"Just before you go, Uncle Marcus, do you agree with me that the easiest target for the Godhe would be Abinger?"

"Give me your reasons, Thomas!"

"The only work, except for a little farming that they do is keeping records.

"They are very good at it, and very intelligent, but I don't think any of them would be any good in a crisis, especially if it was necessary to hurt someone!"

"You could well be right. Now tell us the other reason."

Thomas went red as he replied, "I'm also worried about the safety of Seline and her daughter Fallon, so far from home.

"In a fight they will transform to wolf and give themselves away immediately."

"I accept the reasons you give, Thomas, and your thinking is very sound. I believe you should go. That is what you want isn't it?

"What do you say, Merlin?"

Instead of answering Marcus directly, Merlin said, "I say that I'm proud of you, Thomas, and ask only that you keep in touch.

"In future you're to address me simply as 'Merlin'. As an Ivory Witch and by the suggestions you've made you've earned that right.

"On this continent at least, it's time to put these Godhe in their places.

"Kresh says she came here to learn the limit of our powers. I propose that we don't disappoint her, but I want her to find that anyone she sends to New America just disappears. I prefer that she gets no information back to let her know what we've done - - whatever that will be!"

Chapter Four

Thomas was not allowed to leave until dawn, a fact that they were all to deeply regret afterwards. Half way to Abinger Zoltan advised him that a ship was descending, visible, into the square in Camelot.

Jet immediately called ahead in the hope of avoiding just what Thomas had feared.

<<Seline!

<<Seline!>>

<< What? -- Who's calling? -- I can see nobody! >>

<< It is I, Jet, the unicorn you saw when speaking to Thomas.

<< You absolutely must not transform to wolf if there is trouble in Abinger. Camelot is already being attacked, and we believe Abinger is likely to be next, or even any moment now! We don't want you to take part. These particular Godhe may not know of your ability. Please keep hidden, if possible, and make sure Fallon does too. >>

<< Very well, if YOU say so. >>

***

Watching the ship descend, Merlin decided to act immediately. He formed a Gestalt with the Triads of Laura, Qamar and Shaena, choosing those as he knew them so well, and when it was still fifty feet from the ground, the ship was inverted and slammed down on to its top.

It was then chained to the nearest buildings to keep it that way. Knowing that the rectangular outline facing them represented some sort of door, Merlin tried to remove it without success. The Gestalt was reformed and tried. Where the door had been was now a space. Qamar and Shaena ran forward to enter it, carrying ropes and gags they would be instantly available.

89

"Remember that there will be four of them," called Merlin, "and the most dangerous will be the female weapons officer."

They needn't have worried. The sudden inverted landing had knocked all four unconscious, and using their power to lighten the load, Shaena and Qamar each emerged with two bound and gagged Godhe.

Zoltan had remained, as arranged, in contact with Karim, who had passed the events on to her five partners.

The sire/daughter bond was still so strong that to Tyana and Marcus it was as though they'd been watching through their own eyes.

<< Turn it back on its base, Merlin, then walk through it, letting me see as you do, please. >>

Merlin did as requested, and through Zoltan then Princess for those outside, and Zoltan then Karim for those on the schooner everything he saw was shared. Meanwhile Sabre and Lady were informing the other nine towns between them.

<< Turn back to that corner you just passed, please! >> called Marcus. *<< Yes, I thought so. You see that round lens with a red light over it? There was nothing like that on the ones we saw before. It looks like a hurried addition, and I'm sure it's a camera either recording what happens, or, worse for us if true, transmitting the events back to Krast.*

<< If it's the latter, the next town will not be able to do as you did.

<< Now, this is very important. The four prisoners must be body searched very thoroughly.

<< Laura, please check them for injury. If they are just knocked out, then now's the best time to search them.

<< The generators for the personal screens such as Kresh is using in Paris could be any size. Their science is so far ahead of Earth's that you must assume nothing.

<< Strip them, and give them new clothing from our stores. They must be allowed absolutely no personal possessions, but otherwise treat them well.

<< Keep them wherever convenient, but always near a unicorn.

<< Questioning them will have to wait until any attacks on other towns are dealt with.

<< Jasmina is even now calling for advice. Have Zoltan synchronise to help! >>

***

Electra had no sooner convened her defence triads than she heard what was happening in Camelot from Lady, and a falcon from the triad on watch advised that a ship was approaching.

"You all saw how that worked. I wish Thomas was here, but we should be able to manage it."

As in Camelot, four triads waited until the ship was about fifty feet up and tried to turn it - with no effect. It landed in the centre of the square, and as it did so, Electra found she had lost contact with Merlin and his war Council. Exactly what Thomas had feared had happened.

"Has anyone any ideas what to try next?" asked Electra.

She was still waiting for an answer when a voice, male, using perfect English announced from the ship, "Your leader, Electra will report here for instructions immediately.

"My name is Job, and I warn that for each minute I have to wait one of your buildings will be destroyed, starting with the one in front of the door to this ship."

"That's our main library!" shouted Greft, the librarian.

"We must give in. The records are our reason for living!"

So ended the defence of Abinger. The unicorns were fitted with limiting screens, as in Paris. The council members were called in to give their word to obey instructions from the Godhe, and Abinger joined the towns in Europe, except that for now, the outer barrier was kept in place.

Seline looked at her daughter. "Do we do as Jet asked, Fallon, or do we fight?"

"I think we should wait a while at least. He seemed to know what he was talking about, and he and Thomas are on the way here."

"You like him, don't you? Yet you never spoke a word when he was here."

"Of course I like him. Who would not? He is polite, friendly, and is helping Merlin even as I read that he did seven years ago when he was only six.

"He's more of a man than anyone else here in Abinger. If he'd been here this would never have happened."

"But, Fallon, Darling, what could he have done?"

"I don't know. You've heard Uncle Cantor and Auntie Vernique talking about Tyana and Marcus. Would they have given in just like that? No! They would not, and you know it!

"Thomas will save us. I just know he will!"

"I don't see what he can do, but we are guests, and he does represent Merlin, so we'll wait at the side of town nearest Camelot, and watch for him. Let's go."

They were still waiting when a very worried Thomas arrived at the barrier, and outlined to Merlin his plan of action.

Receiving approval, he and Jet went back to behind the group of trees nearest to the barrier and quickly constructed a tunnel down at thirty degrees, shoring and roofing as they went, until sure they had passed the barrier, then up to join the weres. The newly formed opening was easily camouflaged by Jet moving some bushes to conceal it, whilst Thomas greeted Seline and Fallon, introduced them to Tallons, and heard about the morning's events.

"I'm sorry they looked after you so badly," apologised Thomas. "The trouble is that the people here are historians. They're very good at recording events, but have no idea of original thought. That was why I warned you not to interfere.

"We'll soon deal with them, though, but first we must tell Merlin what happened here.

Jet returned through the tunnel to report. After detailing the hopelessly inadequate defence put up by the inhabitants, he went on, << *Zoltan, we were right. At least for this one, the barrier can be tunnelled under. I'm returning to join Thomas, so we'll be out of contact for a while.*

<< Have you news of the third ship yet? >>

<< Yes, Jet, it attacked New Salem. This is how Magdalena dealt with it. Her fox Tess thought of it, and it worked perfectly. It may well give us a useful technique for dealing with a single member of the Godhe wearing a screen. >>

***

Warned by Zoltan that the trick used by Merlin would probably not work, Magdalena decided to use one of Tess's suggestions.

It seemed that the Godhe liked to land in the square, so she surrounded the square with Triads, three to each side with detailed instructions on how to act.

The expected ship started its descent and at about fifty feet they made the attempt to turn it over but, as expected, nothing happened.

As it reached ground level and cut its engines a thirty feet deep pit appeared below it, the ship fell in, and the spoil from the pit, together with several hundred tons of granite was piled on it. They decided to leave them there for a day to sweat a little before any further action.

***

When told of this, Thomas smiled for the first time since he'd left Camelot. "Let's get this over with before lunch," he said.

Arriving in the square, Tallons flew over to the ship and landed on it for a moment, then returned to his perch. The shield round the ship had been turned off after the surrender of Electra and her people.

Remembering the details from '*Unicorn Witch*', Thomas conjured four six inch cube boxes lined with mirrors, and broke one of the lengths of iron available into eight, positioning one piece in the barrel of each cannon.

Taking four each, he and Jet heated them to melting point, and as soon as they had wet the barrels the mirror boxes were slapped over the small openings he believed to be the laser ports, and the iron allowed to cool.

Like all the Triad members, Jet had learned Karim's loud voice technique, and Thomas made good use of it.

<< *You in the space ship!*

<< *I represent Merlin, President of the World Council.*

<< *You have one minute to remove it from the square, or I will see that it never flies again!* >>

Electra came running out to Thomas, shouting, "What are you doing?

"We gave our word not to interfere with them."

As she spoke a low hum came from the ship, and Thomas realised that the barrier round the ship had been reinstated.

"I speak for Merlin, Electra. You had no right to do that, but in any case I'm not bound by what you said. I wasn't even in Abinger at that time!

"Watch, and learn!"

<< *You now have only half a minute!*

<< *Be advised that your silly barrier round the ship will make no difference. I have just come from Camelot, and the one you have round Abinger failed to stop me!* >>

As Thomas had expected, they could not resist firing one of the cannons at him, which naturally exploded. He obviously had them worried, as this meant a repetition of what had happened seven years earlier, something that Marcus had been sure they would not let occur.

<< *Be further advised that a six inch hole will appear right through the ship, entering by the door and leaving on the opposite side.*

<< *If anyone is in the way, the hole will pass through them!*

<< *Unless this event is followed by immediate surrender, further holes will follow, in which case all four of you will probably lose your lives.*

<< *Ten seconds! 9.8.7.6.5.4.3.2.1.* >>

The cannonballs ordered by Marcus in his preparations were by Jet's side, each six inches in diameter, and weighing close to fifty-six pounds. During the countdown, Thomas and Jet had been preparing to send one of them to the other side of the square as fast as they were able, and on zero thought together NOW!

Fifty six pounds travelling at over ten thousand miles per hour packed kinetic energy such that the force field round the ship might as well not have been there, and Thomas's promised hole appeared, accompanied by much sparking and smoke from within the ship as the generator powering the screen overloaded.

The ship's engines could be heard getting louder, and the dust near the ship started to swirl.

<< *Surrender, or die! Attempt to rise, and I will destroy your ship completely!* >>

The engines were turned off, the door opened, and four Godhe slowly walked down the ramp which extended from the doorway.

"Seline, Fallon, go forward and search them for weapons.

"Electra, I want them strip searched before they are allowed out of your sight, and given clothing from your own stores.

"You Godhe, please note that I did nothing which at least twelve of these people could not have done as easily as I.

"It's just that they are peace-loving historians, whilst I have seen one of my best friends killed, and four of my family's children kidnapped.

"One of you go back inside and turn off all the barriers, or I will still riddle the ship with holes until I happen to hit the right part of it."

The female did as instructed, returning with one of their assault rifles that she fired at Thomas.

Jet had no trouble turning the missile back to its sender, stopping it three feet away, rocket flaring furiously, but getting nowhere.

<< *I am getting tired of this.*

<< *Seline, take that weapon off her, before I forget to control that rocket.*

<< *You four, back in to the ship. We are going to see Merlin.*

<< *I can't trust myself to keep you alive.* >>

"Electra, can I rely on you to keep out unwanted guests until I can return?"

"Yes, Thomas, and you have our thanks.........and apology."

Thomas was given no more trouble. His cannonball shot had done no serious damage to the craft. Obviously it could no longer go into space, but proved adequate to fly to Camelot, where the four prisoners were searched, clothed, and added to the four already in custody.

As soon as this was done, Fallon threw herself in to Thomas's arms, and kissed him saying, in French of course, "I told Maman you would save us. I told her you were more of a man than anyone in Abinger."

Thomas was scarlet, and didn't know what to do. He enjoyed the kiss, the first he had ever had if one didn't count those from Megan, and the hug, but was too embarrassed to respond, especially in front of Merlin, Laura, and his sister's family.

"I must return to Abinger, Merlin.

"Electra can't be relied upon to think of a new defence if needed. I leave the ship as a present to you. Maybe Marcus can tell you how to use it to contact their Galactic Patrol and end this before anyone else gets hurt."

Seline and, especially, Fallon demanded to return with him.

"Even you need someone to watch your back," stated Fallon.

"You cannot rely on those there to help, but I will tear the throat out of anyone who threatens you."

"She would too!" commented her mother. "If I didn't get to them first!"

Only Megan was not happy at the thought of Thomas returning, but just like a sister, she wasn't worried about the danger - she worried about Thomas falling in love with a shape-changing alien, for that is how she saw Fallon.

Two horses were given from the ranch's herd, and with Jet multiplying for himself and Seline's mount, whilst Thomas handled Fallon's, they returned to take charge of Abinger's defence.

***

<< It is time we had a few answers, Merlin.

<< Please let Tyana and me listen in as you question the eight prisoners.

<< Leave the women to last. Choose the senior commander! >>

"Very well, Marcus!"

"Come, everyone, let us introduce ourselves!" and with that Merlin led the way to the makeshift prison, which had been his own apartments before his marriage to Laura. They were chosen as, hewn from solid rock, they had only one entrance and no windows.

"I know one commander is Job. Step forward, please!"

Nothing happened, but of course Job had thought about hiding his identity, which was enough for Zoltan.

<< He is the third from the left end of the line, and the other one is third from the right end. >>

"The third from each end step forward!"

Again nothing happened.

<< Zoltan, let us make them think I am speaking in their own language, as Marcus did in Europe. >>

<< Perhaps you do not speak our language. The third from each end step forward, please! >>

This time they did as requested, with very worried looks all round. Merlin reverted to English, having made his point. "Now, I know that you are Job, but what do we call you?"

Silence.

<< Odel. >>

"So, who is the senior, Job, or Odel?"

"How do you know my name?"

<<*Job.*>>

"The only thing you need to know is that, if we wish something to happen, then it does. And that includes learning anything we wish from you.

"You seem to be under some delusion that you have rights here. You lost those when you decided to attack us!

"I will ask the questions. You will answer them."

"Why? From what you just said you can learn the answers anyway!"

"Because it amuses us!

"Now.-- Why was it necessary for Aristo to die?"

"That is for you to ask your friends in Europe when you can. He was injured in Paris, and your healers could not, or would not, save him!"

<<*He tells the truth, as he knows it!*>>

"Why, when we have always been grateful to your race for your help since we discovered your existence, did you suddenly take control of Europe, and take hostage four of our children to aid control of our most powerful witches?"

"I can answer the first question, but I know nothing about children being taken. Your boy Thomas referred to that in Abinger, and I couldn't understand it then. We would never do such a thing. Children are very precious to us, especially those who carry what we now call the theurgen chromosome."

<<*Again, he tells the truth, as he knows it.*

<<*Ask the others if they agree with his answers, please, Merlin.*>>

"Do you other seven find any fault with the answers I've been given?"

There was no response, except for a shaking of heads.

<<*They all agree with him. It begins to look as though Krast has been very clever indeed.*>>

"Sit down, all of you. I wish to tell you a story."

For the next hour, holding back only the information that the unicorns were more than communicators who were telepathic between members of their own kind, Merlin told his version of events from the dinner party with Aristo to the present day, including the attempt on his life, but not the details of Aristo's death. He described the sacrifice Princess had made, and near loss of Laura as a result. He even included the lucky break that two of the foals could still speak through the barrier round Paris. To show good faith, even the *Unicorn Witch*'s journey to the Godhe's base to rescue the children was described.

Job responded. "As you said - you wished to tell us a story.

"That story was a good one, but that is what it must be! A story!"

"You don't believe it, then?"

"No! And I believe I speak for all of us."

<< *He tells the truth and I have checked - the others agree.* >>

"Can you think of any way I could convince you it is true - in every detail?"

"No!"

"We'll have lunch now. You may ask for anything you wish from the foods and drinks you know we have on this world.

"Afterwards, I ask that you tell us what you believe to be the events of the last, shall we say, month here.

"Will you please do that, as a favour?"

"I will!"

Eight requests were made, and even though they knew to expect it, the immediate delivery of a complex menu on trays within seconds of the order being given produced reactions from each of the eight.

Hardest to explain was that a fish dish requested by Job was not possible, as there was none in the stores.

"So there really are limits to what you can do?"

"Of course," replied Merlin. "We don't make the food from thin air. It has to come from somewhere. Did you not realise that? With various amounts of success we can all move things around, but we can't make something from nothing.

"Someone has to catch fish, then it is stored until needed.

"We have the control to keep it fresh as long as we wish, as that is the same really as changing one substance to another."

"Change one substance to another? Transmutation, the goal of all early alchemists? Can you show me? Or rather, will you, please?"

"I will do exactly what Sophia did to your Paris leader in that story I told you earlier.

"Taste your wine, please!"

Job did as requested.

"Now taste it again!"

"Arrrrrgh!"

"You see? From a good Bordeaux to sour vinegar.

"Any of our Bronzes could do that. I see that just like your Paris leader you have little or no sense of humour.

"You may drink it now, it is restored to wine!

"If you've all finished, we will serve coffee, and listen to your story, if you will be so kind."

Job waited until all were comfortable and had their drinks.

"I had better start over six months ago, rather than a month."

<< *He is beginning to wonder if your story was true!* >>

"At our annual meeting on our home world, Aristo was forced to once again report that we still had no idea how you do what you do, and also that, apart from synthesising the active ingredient of your hormone theurgen and giving it in tablet form, no progress had been made on our own problem either."

"A young biochemist Krast had been asking the council for two years for permission to carry out experiments on you people, as she was sure that if we could stop what you call magic, we could by science duplicate it, understand how theurgen worked, and thus perhaps solve the affliction our men suffer. I have to admit I couldn't follow the logic, but that's how she came to be here. She argued that secrecy was no longer needed as you knew of us, and received her permission, on the understanding that she only used volunteers."

"May I interrupt for a moment?

"Where did Krast come from?"

"I don't understand the question! She was educated like all our young people, trained in her case as a Biochemist, and applied for a job on this planet as she expressed a special interest in the research because her father had just died at only one hundred and thirty four.

"There are very few of our people willing to serve here, and she was brilliant. We were glad to have her.

"Aristo objected, but wouldn't say why."

<< *I just bet he did, Merlin!* >>

"Please continue!"

"Krast left our base with her assistant to visit Paris, and talk with the leader of the Council before he left for Europe. Carlos was one of the natives on our list permitted to meet us, because of Aristo's carelessness some time ago.

"She had only been there one day when she called in to report that Aristo had tried to intervene in a local argument, and had been killed by one of the primitives there.

"Krast told me she had reported to our home world, and had been told to take what action we thought fit.

"She announced that she was going to take over Paris, and establish some sort of discipline in the rabble who had caused the death of Aristo."

"Another interruption, if I may.

"Have you ever been off the island before?"

"No! Only Krast, her assistant, and those who collect from your Earth were allowed to travel until this emergency."

"I won't ask the name of the assistant - it's all too obvious!"

"You can't possibly know it!"

"Kresh?"

"But how…………?"

"Is there any section of the island to which you did not have access? In particular is there any way Krast could have our children and unicorn foals on the island without your knowledge?"

"It's large enough that they could be there. We have little reason to stray from the main camp, and there are several other areas which used to be used."

<<He's thinking of how it could be done. He's almost convinced that they must be there. I've got the locations and will pass them to Rebel later.>>

Merlin told of the events of seven years earlier, including the arrest and removal of Krast, Kresh, and the other drug traffickers.

"So you see, Aristo was far from careless.

"By the time he arrived we knew all about you from those we had captured."

"You mean you people captured two of our space craft, one of them a type sixty three, fully armed, and took eight prisoners?"

"Not we people, just Tyana and Marcus, and there were only seven as one of them was killed by his commander."

"But how did they do it?"

"How do you come to be here yourself?

"Changing the subject slightly, How many spacecraft have you on this world?"

"I don't believe I should answer that."

<< Ten. >>

"Does the ten you have include Aristo's and any which are delivering people from Earth?"

"What are you? Some sort of telepath?"

<< Yes. >>

"Are we to expect anyone new in the near future, or has that part of your job been suspended?"

"You were to get someone on this continent tomorrow, but I have no details.

"I've just realised something. According to you Krast and Kresh were here before, and were taken away by the Galactic Patrol. Yes?"

"That's correct!"

"Well your story must be fiction! They would have been given a rehab. treatment and would know nothing of their previous lives!"

Merlin smiled, replying, "For us that's just another question to ask when we can!"

<< *Any questions, Marcus, Tyana?* >>

<< *Yes! Ask about the interstellar communicator I used before to contact the Galactic Patrol!* >>

"You referred to the Galactic Patrol. Have you a communicator aboard capable of contacting it?"

"Yes! .... I don't suppose you would allow us to use it?"

"Of course I will. You see, that story I told was true in all respects. Later I'll tell you the truth of how Aristo came to die.

"All eight of you into the ship without the hole, and its commander may try to contact your police force.

"You may not attempt to contact the island, though, and the ship will be destroyed instantly if you try.

"Have I your word?"

"Yes!"

<< *Yes!* >>

The party trooped into the designated vessel and Odel addressed the ship's computer in English, "Computer, open a channel to the Galactic Patrol!"

An attractive female voice answered, also in English, "Negative, Commander, repairs will be required first."

Odel crossed to an apparently plain wall and opened a panel.

"Repairs? Most of it's missing. How could that be?"

Merlin chuckled as he commented, "You people really are naïve, aren't you? "Obviously Krast doesn't wish you to make contact with anyone at home!"

"We'll try the other one!"

"If you wish, but it will be exactly the same!"

And, of course, it was, though the six inch hole passing as it did through half of it would probably have disabled it anyway.

"It seems we owe you an apology, Merlin.

"Your story must be true! How did Aristo die?"

After hearing this, Zoltan was able to report that all eight believed Merlin, and would give no trouble.

"Let us go back to the island, and we'll soon clear this up!" stated Job.

<< *He means it!* >>

"Not a chance!

"We have four children and four unicorn foals on that island.

"None of you are going anywhere until they are safe!"

"You don't trust us still?"

"On the contrary, I know you tell the truth. However, I also know that the children will be rescued by Marcus and Tyana as surely as I know that the sun will rise tomorrow! If I rely on you releasing them they may get hurt.

The two ships were hidden after having their camera lenses covered, and the eight prisoners paroled to take no further part in the repression of Refuge. They did, in fact, make a sincere offer to help in any way they could.

***

The excitement of travelling at over two hundred miles an hour on horseback was such that Thomas and his party were within sight of Abinger before Seline spoke.

"Are you ready for a hero's welcome?"

"I'm no hero, Seline. The situation I dealt with should never have arisen in the first place! There are twelve there with more power than I have, you know."

"What they could have done doesn't matter! It's what you did that counts."

Thomas was all the more surprised, therefore, when he received no welcome, but was ignored by all he met and had to go looking for Electra to ask why.

"Do you really not understand, Thomas?

"All our lives' work is represented by the contents of our library, and you risked it all when you acted as you did!"

<< *You must take charge at once, Thomas! We cannot afford that sort of attitude. Merlin makes the decisions as President. I suggest you make that clear!* >>

<< *Thank you, Jet.* >>

"Electra, Merlin gave me a job to do. I demand that you call a meeting of all here, particularly all triads.

"I will speak to them in fifteen minutes!"

"You forget that I'm the Council Head, and you are only thirteen years old."

"Electra, this is not open to discussion. My authority comes from the World President. I am sure that consultation with your records, of which you seem so proud, will confirm that I'm within my rights.

"I may be only thirteen, but I represent Merlin and I'll replace you if necessary. Call the meeting!"

Word travelled quickly, and not only the twelve triads turned up but, or so it seemed, everyone in the town.

"I would like to remind you," began Thomas in Jet's amplified telepathic voice, "of events seven years ago.

"If Tyana and Marcus had not succeeded in their mission to find who was stealing theurgen, it is likely that we would not yet have made contact with Europe, and your records would be that much poorer.

"When they had solved the mystery, and closed down Le Roi's operation they could have returned to Camelot.

"Instead they risked their lives so that those living in Europe could be freed, and Merlin was elected unopposed to be the first World President.

"Many of you were present when he decreed that we would fight, and that any vessels Krast sent to this continent would, as far as she was concerned, just disappear.

"If you did not agree with that policy, then that was the time to say so.

"If we lose this war, we will all be stripped of our powers, the unicorns will lose theirs, and probably the weres and dragons too.

"That is why many of the unicorn herds have pledged all their members to help in the fight. You can hardly be expected to do less."

<< I can't read them all at once, but some will never change their minds, whilst most of the younger ones agree with you. >>

"With or without your help, we are going to defend Abinger, and if it happens that a few records are destroyed along the way, it will be a small price to pay for the right to carry on making those records.

"I happen to believe that since this town represents the only success that Krast has had so far, it's likely that here is where she will make her next move. I intend to be ready.

"Those who believe as I do that Merlin is right please stay.

"Anyone else, of whatever rank, GET OUT OF MY SIGHT!"

Thomas found himself with Electra, five of the younger council members, and all of the children and teenagers, but Greft, the librarian, and most of the older townspeople left. Looking around, he found he had six triads including his own. Four of them had horses as third members, and the fifth had a falcon.

"Thank you, Friends. It would appear that it's up to us. I welcome any suggestions."

"I don't know if it is a help, or if you know already, but I have one, an idea that is, or at least I've learned something I didn't know was possible, and if you didn't know either then it might be something which may help you, but of course if you already know then I am wasting my time and yours as well. I…"

The speaker was in her twenties, striking rather than beautiful, was riding a blue unicorn with white contrast, and had a pad on her shoulder on which perched a falcon which could have been the twin of Hawka, Shaena's familiar.

Thomas could bear the suspense no more.

"Stop! That's enough. Thank you. Please introduce yourself, and then tell us.

"If you can't put it into words, let your partner do it."

<< *Her name is Gabbie, I am her partner Roxy, and our familiar is Sweetheart. Gabbie is short for Gabrielle; so spare us the jokes, please.*

<< *We have found that if Sweetheart is out of our sight, and we look through her eyes, we can perform magic just as if we are there ourselves.*

<< *Please excuse the way she spoke earlier. She gets like that when she's excited about something.* >>

"Thank you, Roxy, Gabbie. That really is an important discovery.

"I ask all of you to experiment to see if it works with horses too, and to join me here tomorrow morning at ten for a further meeting.

Electra invited Thomas to stay with her, joining Seline and Fallon who were already her guests. He accepted, but first reported Gabbie's discovery to Merlin so that all triads could learn this new skill.

Electra's welcome back to Abinger may not have been what Thomas expected, but she tried to make up for it when he arrived at her home.

She started to explain and apologise, but Thomas stopped her.

"It really doesn't matter now, Electra. We have six triads including your own, which should be enough.

"I'm more interested in discussing tactics than carrying on an argument. As far as I'm concerned we're still friends, and I'm not even reporting the incident to Merlin."

"Thank you for that, Thomas, but I think how we act should be left to you, and possibly Gabbie. You see, my whole life has been devoted to observing and recording.

"I've never had to solve a problem in my life. That's why I couldn't think quickly enough when we were attacked before.

"I'm truly sorry that I let it happen, but even though most of the council have more sheer power than you, Jet, and Tallons, we just couldn't think how to use it.

"Do you really believe Krast will come here next?"

"I only know that that's what I would advise her to do, as this is the only place she has held even for an hour.

"This must be boring for you both, Seline. I'm sorry!"

"You needn't be. For us, fighting is a way of life. We never went looking for it, but often we had to deal with Le Roi's soldiers looking for slaves. They never learnt, and kept coming back however many we killed. Let me just repeat, one of us will have the throat out of anyone who attacks you.

"Now, let us relax. I hear you play piano, as does Electra.

"Will one of you oblige? Music is relatively new to us, as we had no instruments until our friendship."

The remainder of the evening was spent with Electra and Thomas taking turns at the piano, with Seline enjoying the music and Fallon just enjoying watching her hero.

***

Next morning Caress was circling lazily at about ten thousand feet above the ship and feeling bored when her peripheral vision detected movement from the side. Two disc shapes were climbing rapidly on the horizon in front of the ship. She turned towards them for a better view and called,

<< *Tyana, Look!* >>

Tyana recognised the shapes as ships of a type she was all too familiar with, and saw they were heading for New America.

"Marcus, warn Merlin he's got company coming! I'm going to join Caress again."

<< *Two more, Karim. Tell Marcus!* >>

Thus, shortly after he received the first message, Merlin heard, << *Two more coming on about the same course.* >>

<< *Have either of you any idea what she may be planning now, Marcus?* >>

<< *If I was her, I would send in one ship in a visible state, and watch from the other one whilst invisible.*

<< *She may not be that clever, but that's what you should beware of.*

<< *Also, make sure everyone can use Gabbie's trick. We've tried it, and it's as easy as Thomas said. Please thank her.* >>

"But where will she strike next?" asked Laura.

"We warn everyone, but, thinking as Marcus just did, and putting myself in her place, I would want to know what happened to the ship I sent to New Salem. From her point of view it just vanished immediately after landing.

"If Marcus is right and that thing with the red light lets her see what goes on, then we will be the other target.

"Let's get ready. At the speed they travel we have only a few minutes."

<< *General alarm to all leaders. This is Zoltan for Merlin.*

<< *Expect two ships, probably one only visible. We suggest rain to outline the observing one, and then bring it down!* >>

Merlin was right. Camelot and New Salem observed ships together, and by the time they arrived it was raining gently, with a little mist to ensure that for a good view the observers would be low.

Given Caress's warning, each town had its triads in gestalt and waiting. Krast was learning fast, and only Camelot was attacked initially, one ship landing visible in the square.

When the observing ship, outlined, was at about five hundred feet, a cannonball was sent to go through it just as Thomas had done.

It bounced off, but Marcus had the answer ready.

<< *They've obviously strengthened the screen, or force field, whatever they call it, after Thomas's adventure in Abinger.*

<< *No matter! Take seven balls with a concave portion on one side, so that they fit together well.* >>

As quickly as he said this it was done.

<< *Now fit an eighth to the front with a point on it, and send that lot at the same speed!* >>

The kinetic energy that the screen had to deal with was now not only eight times larger, but delivered over a much smaller area, and a little extra, thought of by Qamar was added.

As soon as the missile was clear of the ship it was turned and brought back through it, split into its eight components, as the screen was now inoperative, and the eight individual balls used again.

One of the ten six inch holes passed through something vital and the ship fell, becoming visible as it did so, to land edge on and embed itself in grassland just outside the wall.

Using Zoltan's broadcast voice, those in the ship that landed first were addressed, << *This is the Acting President.*

<< *Surrender immediately or share the same fate!* >>

Thus were added four more prisoners, and a complete working space ship.

"Why 'Acting President,' Merlin?" asked Shaena.

"They think I'm dead and Krast may be able to hear what's said to the ships. I don't understand how she could, but that's what Marcus said was possible!"

Laura and Megan entered the crashed vessel, finding only one crew member alive. Lace followed and, as she had before, made sure she saw everything they did. Being high in the turret, the female weapons officer had not been hit by any of the balls. She did, though, suffer a broken back as well as other injuries that, if on her home world, would have resulted in either death or quadriplegic paralysis.

Amazingly she was conscious, greeting Megan, who found her, with, "Please finish me off! I know how bad it is ……….. I don't want to live in a hover chair!"

"Just relax!" ordered Laura. "Do you feel any pain at all?"

"No, except for a headache, and my vision is blurred."

Megan, being nearest, laid her hand on her patient's temple, and with the other one stroked her hair away from her eyes.

"The pain…. It's gone…. I'm dying… I'm…… sorry!"

As she said this she fainted, making the healers' work much easier. Working as they had on Merlin so recently, they aligned the broken bones and fused them. First both femurs, the long thigh bones, then several ribs and both scaphoids, the tiny wrist bones so often damaged by trying to save oneself when falling.

Finally the most difficult, the spine.

"What do you think, Megan, do you fuse whilst I feel, or the other way round?

"And what do you think she meant - the 'I'm sorry' at the end?"

"You're more gentle, and probably more sensitive than I am. You put her how you feel it should be, and I'll fuse the vertebrae. She'll lose a very little mobility, but I agree that's the best course.

"The 'I'm sorry?' I hope it means she wishes she had not taken part in the attack, but we'll see."

Odel arrived, asked by Merlin to check the communicator, but as expected, it had been sabotaged, as had the one in the ship that surrendered. He almost collapsed when he saw their patient.

"Juno! Will she be alright? How did she survive the crash?"

"Is she special to you?"

"We were to marry, until they said our chromosomes were incompatible. I'll always love her."

Laura couldn't help softening her voice as she replied,

"Answering your questions in order -

"Yes, she will be alright, though she will need a lot of reassurance when she wakes, as she was aware that her back was broken."

"Her back's broken?"

"I said her back was broken. Was, not is!

"She survived because first, she was in the turret, and thus had not being hit by any of the cannonballs, and second, we were here."

"What do you mean - you were here?"

Laura coldly catalogued Juno's injuries, followed by listing their treatment. "There's no spinal cord damage, but there will be a delay before she regains the use of her legs. We can heal only so much. The indignity her nervous system has suffered will take time."

Laura's voice suddenly hardened as she remembered that they were in the middle of a war.

"But time is what you have plenty of. You're not going anywhere. Incidentally, the last words Juno spoke were to say that she was sorry. I would be grateful if you can tell me later what she meant."

As the women learned when they rejoined the triads in the square, the emergency was over. New Salem reported seeing two ships, but they left without descending immediately Merlin's defence proved successful.

The return to the island, though, was not reported by either Caress, or Swift.

<< *Perhaps they've gone to see Kresh or Krast in Europe!* >> suggested Marcus. << *If they have, we'll be hearing from Carlos soon. I would dearly love to be a fly on the wall when they report what they saw.*

<< *It seems that they were able to increase the power of their protective screens, but not enough to withstand over eight times the force Thomas used.*

<< *You must not assume that they can't do so though. If possible, think of yet another way to defeat them.* >>

<< *Carlos calling. Two ships have just landed, and the commanders, one of them a female, have come into join Kresh. From your description, and the way the others are giving her respect, I would say the female is Krast.* >>

<< *You're calling direct - not through the foals?* >>

<< *That's right, my friends, we have our own tunnel like the one Thomas built. We're going back now, and we'll let you know what we can of what happens!* >>

"I believe we can all relax, at least until we hear from Carlos.

"Let each town leader try to think of a new way of dealing with a space ship if it should come," continued Merlin, "and we'll compare notes tomorrow morning.

"Were there any survivors in the one which crashed, Zoltan?"

<< *Only one. A female named Juno. She was badly injured, but through Princess I was able to watch as Laura and Megan healed her. We now have another five prisoners, and Krast has only five ships left. Are you going to question them?* >>

"No! They would know no more than the others. We'll just put them together with the other eight, leave them to talk, and then parole them tomorrow."

<< *The last words of Juno were to say that she was sorry. It will be interesting to know for what. I'll arrange for one of the unicorns to monitor her recovery.* >>

***

When Juno regained consciousness, she found Odel holding her hand, and Job just behind him looking equally concerned.

"What happened? Where are we? I should be dead. I remember my back was broken, yet my foot itches.

"Scratch it please, Odel Darling. The right one!"

"I'll try to answer.

"Where are we? That's easy! We're in some sort of living accommodation hewn from solid rock in Camelot. I gather it's where Merlin used to live until he married Laura."

"Laura! I seem to remember her. She was with the girl who held my hand and touched my head, and wherever she touched no longer hurt."

"You don't know the half of it. You had several broken ribs, both thighbones were broken, both wrists, and your back just above the pelvis.

"Laura casually mentioned that she didn't have to repair any nerves as the spinal cord was only squeezed a little, not cut."

"How long ago did I crash?"

"About half an hour. There were three of them, Megan and Laura who did all the work, and another who just watched.

"Between them they put you back together in about ten minutes, and said that all you would need was reassurance when you woke up.

"They said you could stand if you felt up to it."

"Stand? With two broken legs and a broken spine?"

"That's what Laura said, and after what I've seen since we came here, I believe her. Try it, but they said you may not be able to walk for a while."

Very carefully, Juno put first one leg then the other to the floor, found it did not hurt, and, encouraged by Odel, tried to stand but nothing happened. She collapsed, crying hysterically, into Odel's arms. "I knew it was too good to be true! I'll be in a chair for the rest of my life."

Just then Melanie came in. "Excuse me, may I see the patient?"

"You're the one who was watching. Do you enjoy seeing her suffer? Did you not see enough?"

"Please don't be angry! My name is Lace, and I haven't been here long myself. None of us enjoys the suffering of others, and I only want to help if I can. I was watching in wonder at what they could do."

She walked over to the bed and grasped the hand Odel was not holding. Juno stopped sobbing immediately and looked at the girl, who seemed paler, then at Odel.

"I feel better! I'd like to try again! Will you help me?"

They held a hand each as Juno tried again to stand, and this time the legs obeyed her orders, straightening when told, but she still held on with both hands.

Melanie and Odel walked back to arms length and with just his eyes Odel begged her to walk towards him.

Dragging her feet slightly, she managed it and fell into his arms, and he carried her back to the bed. He looked at Melanie, saying, "I'm sorry I shouted at you! And thank you! Will...Will she ever recover?"

"You heard what Laura said. All she needed was a little encouragement and a lot of T.L.C."

"I don't believe we have that."

"Oh yes you have! Tender Loving Care. Enjoy your stay!"

Melanie left and after a while Odel remembered the question he'd been asked to pose.

"Laura said the last words you spoke were to say that you were sorry.

"Sorry for what?"

"I volunteered for service on Langala IV partly because I didn't approve of what Krast proposed, and hoped to help. I was ashamed that I took part in the raid to subdue the Eastern continent as she has the Western one."

"From what I've seen up to now, you don't need to worry!

"So far our glorious leader, who was going to solve all our problems by learning how their so-called magic works, has lost four very expensive ships, possibly five depending on what happened at New Salem, and we thirteen are prisoners.

"Well, not exactly prisoners. I can tell you that if you give your word not to take further part in what they call 'this war', you'll be treated as a guest."

"How will they know my word can be trusted?"

"I wish I knew, but, take it from me, Love. They will know!

"I had no hesitation in giving mine.

"Have you any idea what happened to Merco's ship which went to New Salem? I wasn't watching the monitor as it descended."

"Sorry! We have no idea. We just lost contact, and when Krast flew over a minute later there was no sign of it!

"Have they treated you well?"

"I told you. We're guests until this is all over. We ate better last evening than I ever remember eating at home.

"And they are such friendly people. I understand why Aristo loved them so much, and why our ancestors wanted to help them.

Most of what you were told at home is just fabrication.

"Excuse me!"

The interruption was from the commander of the newly surrendered ship.

"Yes, Kallen?"

"Have you considered the possibility that all that has appeared to happen is actually some form of hypnosis by these people?

"I trust Krast, and she warned us not to believe everything we were told."
Odel looked thoughtfully at Juno. "What about what they did to help her?"

"Are you sure she was really injured in the first place? It's easier to believe in
hypnosis than in miracle cures. Would we be allowed to access the records in the
crashed ship?"

"Let's see!

"Merlin! Merlin!" he shouted, and the surprised group were allowed to visit
the crash, remove the recorder disc, transfer it to Kallen's ship, and view it.

There were gasps of horror from all five as they saw the terrible injuries Juno
suffered in the crash, throwing her as it did from the turret to the control room
where Megan found her. Kallen paused the playback. "I've got to admit, if I
found her like that, I'd have done as she asked and finished her. Continue."

The silence that followed the ending of the record, when Juno was carried
from the ship, was finally broken by the ship's cook.

"What we just saw was impossible, but do you know what frightens me most?"

"They just put her together like you would a broken doll. To them it was quite
normal, not a miracle.

"And did you see how they carried her out?"

"Just gently pulled on one hand whilst she floated three feet off the ground.

"They can have my parole any time they like. You've got to face it, Kallen.

"We're out of our depth."

He turned to Merlin, who had just returned and asked, "Sir, may I ask one
question, Your Honour?"

Merlin smiled, and nodded, "Certainly Corda

"My brother was the cook on our ship which went to New Salem. Does he
live, and how are the others? And how do you know my name?"

"As far as I know all the crew of that ship are alive and well, but probably very
frightened as they will not understand what happened to them.

"Tomorrow morning, if you wish to join those who have given their parole,
you may come with me and we will find out together."

"You have my parole now, Sir!"

"I wish I'd never learned to speak English, then I wouldn't have come here."

"Tomorrow will do! Please remain in your quarters until then. Thank you."

***

When Merlin asked Thomas what he had to report at the end of that day,
Thomas could only reply, "Like Marcus, I confirm that Gabbie's method works,

and it's just as effective with horse familiars too. Otherwise, there's nothing to report."

He had really spent the most enjoyable day of his life so far, finding the friendship with one his own age which he had never before enjoyed. Jet had left in the morning after the six triads had had their meeting to spend the day discussing tactics with Gabbie and Roxy. Seline thoughtfully spent the day practising her English with Electra's husband, leaving Thomas and Fallon alone.

After five minutes silence, Fallon decided it was time they became friends. She had had her mother teach her to say in English, "You never speak to me, Thomas. Do you not like me?"

Guessing she'd learned this specially, Thomas used French to reply, "Of course I like you, Fallon. It's just that up to now a girl has just been another person, like another boy.

"For some reason you're different. I felt it when I first met you, and when you kissed me in Camelot it was like nothing I've experienced before."

Seline smiled and asked, "Have you ever kissed any other girls?"

"Not like that! It was different from when my sister kissed me."

"I should hope so! Come here and I'll show you!"

Thomas backed away as she came forward, but found himself in a corner. Once again he found he was hugging a beautiful blonde girl the same height as himself, and this time he was able to kiss back.

"There, that didn't hurt, did it?" she asked as she relaxed into his arms.

Thomas just turned her head for more.

By mid morning, he found himself able to talk to Fallon as readily as he had to Seline, and suggested they went out for a walk. Hand in hand they looked around Abinger, some inhabitants being greeted with smiles, others by Fallon baring her canine teeth and growling, which sent the recipients hurrying on their way.

Sometime during the afternoon Thomas plucked up courage to ask what he had wished to ever since they met.

"Do you mind if I ask a personal question Fallon, or rather a favour?"

"Of course you may, Cherie, I have no secrets from you!"

"I've heard how you can transform to wolf or to a large bat, but I would dearly love to see it done."

"Is that all? … We will have to go outside the town, though, as Maman made me promise not to let the local people see in case it frightened them."

<< Jet, can you spare time to join Fallon and me? >>

<< Certainly! Gabbie, Roxy, and I have just finished. I'll tell you all about it later. I'm coming! >>

Thomas mounted Jet, took Fallon's right wrist in his own, and swung her up behind him. As they trotted out of town, it was her turn to ask a favour.

"I've heard about your multiplying spell to travel at up to over four hundred kilometres an hour, Thomas, and I know you used it when we were coming from Camelot. Can you show me the high speed please?"

"It's not my spell. Auntie Tyana invented it, but yes. Let's get you in front so that you can really enjoy it."

They changed places, and Fallon took hold of Jet's mane carefully.

<< *You won't hurt me, Fallon. Hold very tightly with both hands, please, and here we go!*
<< *Where to, Thomas?* >>

<< *Fallon is going to show us how she transforms, so just gallop till you come to somewhere private.* >>

Five minutes later, and many miles from Abinger, after what Fallon would always remember as the ride of her life, they came to a clearing near some hills and Jet stopped.

"This really is nothing special for me, you know. It is as natural as walking once learned."

"But how do you do it?"

"I just wish to be in whichever form I want to assume, and there I am!"

<< *Please show us, Fallon. Like Thomas I have only heard of this ability, and would like to see it in practice.* >>

"I feel foolish doing something so simple for you, but very well. I'll go to wolf first, then to bat, back to this form, then reverse it - - Human to bat to wolf to human! Will that do?"

"If it's not too tiring for you!"

Fallon took off her boots, then quite unselfconsciously crossed her hands and took hold of the sweater she was wearing by the waistband, then in one movement peeled it off over her head to reveal that that was all she'd been wearing above the waist.

Before Thomas could speak, the trousers followed the sweater to the ground, and where a pure white figure had been was suddenly a wolf galloping towards him.

From about ten feet away the wolf leapt as though for Thomas's throat, then a large bat beat her wings once and easily cleared him.

Tallons took off and the two flew together for a few minutes, Thomas and Jet being able to see Fallon in bat form through the eyes of their partner. At close quarters they could see that her face remained the same, as did her hands, but her colour was now black, her breastbone was enlarged as were her arm muscles. Silk-like membranes joined arms to legs, and leg to leg.

Whilst they could understand the word 'bat' being used, she seemed to them as Jet commented, << *Like a very pretty black girl with long arms in a bat costume.* >>

They came back to the ground, Tallons being hard pressed to copy Fallon's glide path, which impressed him.

As they landed, a wolf trotted a few paces, turned, and was instantly Fallon again, as they knew her best.

She held her pose just long enough to see that Thomas was embarrassed, then changed to bat, walked erect to show that she was still the same size, and enveloped Thomas in her wings, kissing him. Closing his eyes, Thomas found he could tell no difference, until he found himself taking the weight of a wolf whose hind legs did not reach the ground.

He tightened his grip to take the weight and found himself with his arms around the naked human Fallon, who commented, "Thomas. Cherie, you really do like me, don't you?"

He let go and jumped back, but this only gave him a better view of the girl, and he blushed, turning his back as he did so.

Jet took pity on him, and instantly dressed Fallon again, much to her surprise. "How did you do that? You had your back to me! And I didn't know you could do it anyway!"

<< *Let him recover, Fallon. Actually it was I who dressed you, but only a very few trusted humans, and only Cantor and Vernique amongst your people, know that unicorns have that ability.*

<< *Please keep the information secret, even from your mother!* >>

"Fallon," called Thomas who was himself again, "have any of your people tried to perform magic, apart from the shape changing?"

"Yes, many times during the last seven years, but with no success at all. This is even more puzzling now that Jet tells me unicorns can!

"Changing the subject... Why do you find the sight of me naked repulsive?"

<< *Get out of that one if you can, Partner!* >>

Thomas smiled at her. "Fallon, just the opposite is true. Dressed, you are a very pretty girl, and I'm proud to be seen with you.

"Undressed I see you are truly the most beautiful girl I have ever seen. It's just that I have only ever seen children and my sister naked. It will not bother me in future!"

<< *Was that good enough, Partner?* >>

<< *I couldn't have done better myself!*

<< *Fallon, I would like to thank you for that demonstration. I would not have believed it possible to change so rapidly and smoothly.* >>

"Thank you, Jet, for the ride here. Can we travel at the same speed going back?"

They could, of course, and did, meeting Seline in time to join Electra for dinner and another musical evening.

***

Without exception the five new prisoners agreed to join their colleagues, offering Merlin any help they could give.

"I need a crew to take Kallen's ship to New Salem. How many are needed? And how many can we take as passengers?"

Kallen stepped forward to answer. "We only really need the commander for planetary journeys, but you did say Corda could come, Sir.

"As for passengers, they can fly with whatever you can fit in to them."

"Corda, we won't need weapons, but travel in the turret please, to leave more room in the main area.

"Laura, we may need a healer, so please join Archimedes and me..... Oh, bring Princess, and I will ride Zoltan, just in case we need transport when there.

"Shaena, take charge here, please!"

"Can we find room for Guinevere? I don't like leaving her alone."

"Of course."

Thus the two triads were able to go without the Godhe realising the significance of the make up of the party.

Kallen was puzzled when asked to land just outside the town of New Salem, and even more so when there was no offensive action against the ship as it descended. Scarlett had, of course been advised who was coming.

His amazement was even greater when Laura mounted Princess and, taking Corda's right wrist in her right hand, swung him easily behind her, as one would a child. Then to cap it this seven stone old man mounted Zoltan, took his wrist and did the same. To add to his puzzlement he noticed his landing on the unicorn's back was very gentle as though he only weighed two stones instead of ten.

As they arrived in the square, Merlin was amused to notice that Magdalena had given a front seat to Timothy the previous leader. He was going to comment, but then decided to keep out of what were, after all, local politics. Instead, Kallen was further questioned.

"What do you know of the crew of the ship sent to New Salem?"

"Very little. I had not met any of them before this mission.

"I didn't even realise Corda's brother was on her."

<< *The truth* >>

114

"So we must assume that they will try to attack us again if we give them a chance?"

"I suppose so, but where are they?"

"Before I answer that, I remind you of your word to help us if you can. That means that any knowledge you gain of how we work you must keep to yourselves."

"Agreed!"

<<Agreed!>>

"They are about thirty feet below the square. That pile of granite is not normally a feature of New Salem, but was added, as we don't know just how much power your ships have.

"I'm going to form a shaft to expose the door to it, and give them a chance to surrender."

Estimating where that was likely to be, Merlin controlled the Gestalt of Triads, a neat quadrant of the pit was emptied to below door level, and a few inches clearance created over the dome of the ship. Using Zoltan's broadcast voice just as Thomas had used Jet's, he addressed the occupants.

<<This is the Acting President of the world you have chosen to attack. We have allowed you time to consider the wisdom of that action.

<<You will find that you can now open your door and rotate the turret until it is in open air. Do not attempt to leave, but you will find it interesting to stand in the doorway and watch.>>

Two broomsticks, used by children as transport were brought, and as Kallen and Corda watched they grew until large enough for them to obey the instruction, "Please sit on those and hold tightly to the handle in front of you. You need have no fear."

The two brooms rose slowly, then descended some twenty-five feet to the open doorway, and on into the ship, returning to Merlin when the passengers had dismounted. Zoltan monitored the conversation within and broadcast it mentally to those in the square.

As they descended Kallen commented to his former cook, "Corda, they're all there, one with an arm in a sling, and one with a crutch, but all alive, so please leave this to me.

"Hello the Ship! Permission to come aboard, Commander?"

"G...G...Granted....Who?....How?....Kallen,! What happened to us? Do you know?"

"You were stupid enough to believe in Krast, as we were.

"Before anything else, please check your interstellar communications equipment!"

"But why?"

"Just do it, please."

"Computer, check status of specified equipment!"

<< The computer is obviously answering, and from their thoughts it is as we expected-sabotaged. >>

"All our ships appear to be like that. It's an unpleasant fact that Krast does not intend us to contact anyone at home."

"All our ships?"

"This is the fifth. These people have captured two intact, including this one, have two with slight damage, and one destroyed."

"Aristo was killed by Krast, herself. I haven't got the full story yet, but, believe me, these people make marvellous friends, and very deadly enemies."

"The thirteen of us captured have all given our words to take no further part in Krast's action."

"Thirteen?"

"Thirteen. One ship crashed and the only survivor was Juno. It was seeing a record of how they treated her injuries that finally won us over to their side.

"I don't expect you to believe any of this, but just promise to take no action for twenty four hours, and you will be allowed out."

"Allowed out? Where are we? Do you know?"

"About thirty feet below the square you landed on. They simply caused the ground to open up and swallow you, then piled hundreds of tons of granite on top to make sure you stayed here."

"Did you say 'simply'?"

"I believe they found it simple.

"Now, will you come?"

<< The three men believe Kallen and Corda. As usual the female is set to cause trouble. She's wearing one of the personal screens we've heard about. >>

Going back to the doorway, the four Godhe found that the ship was slowly rising, and the rubble which had been above was spilling round the sides and filling in below them. Within a minute the ship was sitting in the square as if it had just landed.

"You may leave one at a time, and come to me, first. I am riding the large white unicorn and have an owl on my shoulder."

One by one Merco, the commander, walking with the aid of a crutch, Raster the navigator/engineer with his arm in a sling, and Batch, Corda's brother emerged, promised to wait twenty four hours before taking any action against the Refuge natives, were checked by Zoltan, and then sent to lay on beds which had appeared as soon as the injuries were observed. Laura made no attempt to deal with them until the fourth member of the crew had emerged.

The last out was Wanda.

<<She has just turned her screen on, but before she did so I learnt that she has a small weapon hidden between her breasts, and is waiting for a chance to use it. She will have to turn off the screen before she can attack us. Have you any ideas,

Anyone?>>

Tess had. After seven years with human intelligence, the vixen had developed into an extremely clever campaigner, and gave her instructions to her partners.

A dozen of the strips of the wrought iron requested by Marcus were quickly fashioned into an egg shaped cage, eight feet by three and a half, and in two halves.

These two halves came together around Wanda, fused to one, and then rose some ten feet into the air, taking her with it.

She appeared to be standing in mid air, six inches off the bottom of the cage.

<<Thank you, Tess. Very well thought out! Please let me take over.

<<Now, Wanda, you have to turn off your screen to attack us. As soon as you do that you will drop to the bottom of the cage, and we will remove your weapon. When you wish to surrender, just turn off your screen!>>

No action, except that Wanda's cage rose to twenty feet, a slight pause, then thirty feet, forty feet.

"Give it up, Wanda!" called Merco. "That's an order!"

<<As soon as she turns it off, locate the generator and remove it please, Zoltan.>>

At sixty feet Wanda turned off her protective screen, grabbed for the weapon to find it missing, went to turn the screen back on, only to find that missing too.

"Are you looking for these?" called Merlin, holding up the two items removed, and lowering the cage slowly to the ground.

"The choice is yours. You may be a prisoner, or our guest, like your sixteen colleagues."

"I give in. I'll be a guest, please."

<<How hard can it be to fool these primitives? I'll wait my chance.>>

"As you are finding out, it can be very hard to fool us, Wanda. You stay in chains, and with no personal possessions until you decide that your war is over!"

Wanda's uniform disappeared, to be replaced by a simple trouser suit in red, with no pockets, and she found herself chained by an ankle strap to one of the fifty-six pound cannonballs nearby. The ball rose to travel slowly, obliging her to walk with it to a table, around which were four chairs. "Wait there!"

Laura now turned to her patients. Corda's brother she touched briefly then waved him to join Wanda.

Merco she discovered had twisted his knee as he fell when the ship dropped. It took her only some five seconds to repair the torn ligaments and reduce the swelling. The pain disappeared as soon as she touched him, and when sent over to the table he kept looking at his knee then back at Laura.

Raster took a little longer as he had put out an arm as he fell, breaking his collar bone.

<< It's an awkward one with a spare piece of bone floating loose, I wish I had Megan here! >>

<< Can't Princess help? >> asked Guinevere.

<< I don't know. I'm still not used to the extra power I have myself, and even less used to having a partner. If I move the pieces where I want them, Princess, can you fuse the bones like you saw Megan do for Juno? >>

<< I believe so. Let's try. >>

If anything Laura and Princess worked more smoothly than had Laura and Megan, such was the advantage of telepathy, and Raster could not believe his senses as they told him he was fully recovered from his injury.

"What do I owe you?" he asked.

"I don't work for reward! But if you feel you owe me anything, just help Kallen and the others convince Wanda that she will never win."

It was becoming almost routine that the supply of food on request, something which every child over eight years old on the planet did every day, impressed the Godhe more than had their own capture.

After the meal Merlin had one more request of Merco.

"I know it's a sacrifice, and you may consider it treason, but I want you to instruct your computer to take orders from Hammid, one of the European leaders.

"Hammid, please let Merco instruct you as necessary, but I trust you not to go rushing back to Baghdad or over to Paris.

"Simply hide the ship here for use if we need it."

This was quickly accomplished, and in less than half an hour the party, now with four more 'guests', albeit one with a ball and chain, returned to Camelot, where a conference was organised. By using their tunnel it was possible to include Carlos and Sophia as well as Mandrake and Shinlu, thus reforming the War Council of seven years earlier.

By dusk in Camelot the leaders of each town in New America, Tyana and her party, and Carlos and his had shared all their knowledge.

Carlos took the opportunity to recount what he knew of the meeting between the newly arrived Godhe and Kresh.

The first part of their conference had taken place behind one of their screens and although neither Javelin or Lotus Blossom could read anything from within, Orchid had picked up a few snatches which were:-

".....uch more trouble than we anticipated...

"Saw four sailing ships about a quarter way here as we expected, so who is left behind is...

"...lost five ships

"...need more information before we try ag..."

It then became too fast for her to follow, but shortly afterwards Kresh had summoned Carlos and Sophia to join her.

Krast was introduced, and she then asked, "How could the people in Camelot turn over a spacecraft like this one and slam it down on its top?

"Everyone we've spoken to here and the records Aristo kept say that the weight of one person is about the limit you people can influence!"

"That's not quite true," replied Sophia. "I've seen Tyana and Marcus each move over a ton of rubble, and I heard that Tyana moved more than that in competition."

"What's your personal limit?"

"I've never moved even a quarter of that.

"You must remember that the other continent is about one thousand years ahead of us in development. Look how easily Marcus and Tyana captured you last time.

"Maybe there are hundreds or even thousands of people of their ability. We just don't know. Can I ask a question?

"Why are you so keen on taking control in New America?

"Surely you can learn all you need from just us?"

There was a long pause as Krast decided how to answer, and Javelin was able to pass on her thoughts.

<<*She is thinking that New America must be even richer in Theurgen than she thought, and she must have it.*

<<*I picked up some puzzlement from Kresh as if she wanted that question answered too.*
>>

"My instructions were, amongst other things, to compare the abilities on the two continents, and discover whether any difference is due to training or to natural ability. I intend to do just that!

"With Merlin dead, and the other leaders travelling back to Europe, who would be in charge in the towns?"

"Did you say Merlin dead?"

"I did, but it need not concern you. Answer the question!"

"Of course it concerns me. Anything you do to make the witches on the other continent mad makes me fear for you, and for us since we've joined you. How did he die?"

"An accident, but he is dead anyway. Answer the question."

<< *I shot the old fool!* >>

"I'm afraid I can't do so. If we were away, our deputies would take over. Your guess is as good as ours regarding the other continent.

"Just why did you call us into this meeting?"

"We have had some slight trouble taking control on what you refer to as the other continent. I wish to know just how powerful the people there are, and it seems that even you don't know."

<< *The truth, but then she went on to think that maybe they should attack from orbit, whatever that means.* >>

"Krast," said Sophia, "if you want our help, you really will have to be more honest with us. I'm very good at reading body language, and you're not having slight trouble, you're finding it impossible. We tried to tell Kresh here how difficult it would be, but she chose not to believe us. What have they done apart from turning over a spaceship?"

Krast smiled, but somehow, Carlos did not find that reassuring.

"That's the trouble, all we know is that one ship crashed from a great height at a time when those on the ground could not even see it, two surrendered, and one just vanished. That means I have lost five including the first, which they turned over. How can that be possible?"

"How serious is the loss of five? How many have you left? Can you get more from your home planet?"

"I've still got five…and I don't want to call for help from home."

<< *I'd better say five, but even with the others we've only got fifteen!…and I can't call for more!* >>

"I can only say that Sophia and I are the strongest left on this continent, as the other leaders went to New America, and neither of us can do as you say they did."

"Sit in that chair please, Carlos, and hold those electrodes."

"What are electrodes? And if you are thinking of trying to harm me, I advise against it. We've already shown Kresh that we make bad enemies."

"I promise I wish you no harm.

<< *The truth.* >>

"Just hold those bits of copper tubing and look at me.

"Now, do you say that neither you or Sophia could turn over a ship like this, and smash it down?"

"I certainly do!"

"And there's nobody here with more power than you two have?"

"Not as far as we know."

Kresh and Krast exchanged glances after looking at some sort of printed graph, then suddenly the latter announced,

"You may go! ...And... Thank you for being honest with us."

"After we left, not even Orchid could pick up any more.

"I'm sorry!"

<< *I suggest,* >> said Mandrake, << *that we reconvene at the same time tomorrow after we've considered what we know!* >>

***

During breakfast, Electra took the opportunity to question Thomas, and to try to rebuild the friendship she had previously enjoyed.

"Are you really sure that we will be Krast's next target?" she asked.

"I'm not sure of anything! I thought she'd try here first, but instead she tried Camelot and New Salem. I just know that here is where I would advise her to try, as it's the only place which has not immediately captured any ship trying an attack."

"I said we were sorry, and..."

"You misunderstand! I'm not criticising you for failing last time. That is, as I've already said, history.

"I'm only interested in what happens next time, and yesterday whilst Fallon and I were just playing, I'm ashamed to say that Jet, together with Gabbie and Roxy, have planned for everything they could think of, and I can't improve on their ideas.

"We're going to relax today, as Merlin is sure that we'll have plenty of warning if Krast leaves Europe.

"I'm going to spend most of the day speaking English with Fallon and Seline, with Jet helping them out if necessary."

"Merci, Thomas! Tu es tres generous."

"English, please, Seline!"

"Thank you, Thomas! That is very generous of you. I had expected to see you...

<< *ride off* >>

"...ride off with Fallon...encore?

<< *again* >>

"again."

Thomas and Jet found they enjoyed Seline's company even more than they had Fallon's. She had a ready wit that showed as she quickly became more comfortable with the language.

Thinking back though, Thomas decided that saying 'Goodnight' to Fallon was probably the highlight of the day.

Chapter Five

early next morning, the two ships referred to as slightly damaged were, with the help of their commanders, put back in order. Thomas's cannonball holes were easily repaired by causing the outer skin of the craft to stretch inwards to seal them. Merlin's removal of the door complete was more of a problem as none of the gestalt involved could remember to where they had sent it. A makeshift door was added instead using material from the ship Juno had crashed in, but this would suffice for what Merlin had in mind.

One of his fleet of four working ships he kept at Camelot. One was already in New Salem and one he intended for use by Marcus and Tyana, but until then Job took to Brigadoon, putting Angus in temporary charge.

The fourth he had Odel and Juno take to Abinger for Thomas's use if needed. Merco had given his parole and offered any help he could give, and so was taken by Odel back to his ship to give any assistance Hammid in New Salem might request.

"But what are you planning now, Merlin?" Shaena wanted to know.

"I know as little as anyone else about military tactics, My Dear, but it seems to me that any advantage we have gained by having these ships of The Godhe is better shared around.

"There is no obvious merit in keeping them all together, especially if Krast knows where they are. She certainly knows that four were here, including the one destroyed. Detailed planning will come later, when the children and foals are free, and Marcus can help.

"Now, let us have lunch, and let's invite our guests to, what did Marcus call it, a barbie?"

"Alright, Darling, but the word is 'barbecue'. I believe he picked up that horrible corruption of it from Megan, who used to watch some infantile

Australian Soap Opera. Please don't ask, I'll tell you what one of those is some other time."

The captured Godhe, including Wanda, were invited to join Laura and Merlin, Qamar and Shaena, and the whole Counter clan including Melanie to the area often used for contests just outside the walls.

"Excuse me!"

Merlin turned to see Kallen looking puzzled. "Yes, Kallen?"

"We were invited to a barbecue. I asked, and found what that was, but where are the cooking facilities?"

"Where would you suggest we put them?"

"Well, for this number, you would want about three square yards of grills over red hot charcoal, and it will take ages to set up."

"You misheard me. I said 'Where would you suggest we put them?'"

"I suppose in that large clear area with no vegetation."

"Very Well!

"Qamar, would you oblige, please? Three square yards of iron grills over charcoal, built to about waist height, and the tools you've seen Marcus use."

The required items were soon where requested, all having been made instantly available by Merlin beforehand, though only Qamar knew that.

"Qamar, you took me too literally. The charcoal needs to be red hot. No matter!

"Caroline, as the youngest present, will you please show our guests how even a child lights a barbecue.......or anything else we wish to burn?"

Caroline came forward, made eye contact with Wanda, and then glanced at the barbecue for a half second, during which the centre reached red heat. She turned back to Wanda, smiled, then went back to join Melanie and Darryl.

Hondo made sure he was being watched, then passed his hand across the charcoal for effect and the grill was ready for cooking.

With nobody going nearer than twenty feet to the grill, the Godhe watched as steaks, sausages, chicken portions, Kebabs, hamburgers, bacon, and many items they did not recognise, appeared, turned themselves as they cooked, joined vegetables and salad items which appeared on plates which themselves were not previously within sight, and then floated to land gently in front of them.

"What do you think of my little demonstration, Wanda?" asked Merlin as he joined their guests.

"Do you still think we are primitives and that it will be easy to fool us?"

"I'm sorry, Sir. I've no excuse to offer except to say that I was trained to disbelieve my eyes and to rely on my orders.

"I see now that the orders were wrong. I've heard what you did for Juno, and

I saw myself what you did for Kallen and Raster, and I know their injuries were real as I saw them happen.

"I give my word that I will help you all I can if you will trust me. Even if you don't, I will not cause you any more trouble."

<< *Zoltan?* >>

<< *This time she means it. Ask her a few more questions as she is holding something back.* >>

"Thank you, Wanda. You are free," as he said this the shackles disappeared which no longer surprised her, "but it would be better if you told us what you're hiding."

"Hiding?"

<< *Do they know? or are they guessing?* >>

"Yes, Hiding! You are keeping something from me, and, frankly I don't like it. What is it?"

"You wouldn't believe me if I told you!"

"Then you have nothing to lose, have you?"

"I went through all the training to join the Galactic Patrol. Do you know what that is?"

<< *The truth.* >>

"We do! Please go on."

"I failed the final combat tests, and Aristo recruited me to work for him. He knew Kresh was up to something, but he didn't know what.

"Of course when your people killed him, I felt loyalty to her and determined to avenge him."

<< *Still the truth as she knows it!* >>

"Wanda, Aristo was killed by Krast as part of her plan. She also tried to kill me, and only the sacrifice of her own life by a very dear friend saved me.

"Here is a book written in English," he said as he gave her a copy of '*Unicorn Witch*', "which will explain a lot to you. Can you read the language?"

"We all can. It forms part of our training to come here!"

"Enjoy your meal, then please read it and we will speak later.

"By the way, I know you told the truth!"

***

After the past few weeks it took a lot to surprise Thomas, but the arrival of one of the Godhe's ships, and the message that it was for his use achieved it.

Odel and Juno assured him, and Jet confirmed they were truthful, that he was trusted to put it to good use if needed, but to keep it hidden until then.

He had Odel give a conducted tour to Electra, Seline, Fallon, and Gabbie, followed by other tours for anyone interested, then hid the vessel by burying it just below ground outside the town.

Odel and Juno were delighted to be told, "You may do as you wish until you here a voice inside your head tell you to return to the ship.

"Jet, my unicorn, can contact you anywhere now that he knows you personally."

They looked so pleased that Thomas had Jet explain, << *They were not allowed to marry at home, though they wished to, so they will be very happy together for a while.* >>

"You're subject to our laws on this world, you know!

"If you wish to marry, Electra will oblige."

They looked like teenagers on their first date as they thanked him. "Just like that?"

"Just like that! Electra hears your declaration that you are to be considered man and wife, you sign the register, and that's it! I'm sorry if you expected more… this is a primitive world and we like to keep it simple."

Juno smiled and replied, "Simple? It sounds divine!"

Electra had a new wing added to her home for their use.

The morning was devoted to English lessons, then in the afternoon, Jet contacted Zoltan purely as a courtesy call, and was just in time to join the conference.

***

<< *This is just like old times!* >> commented Mandrake as everyone reported in. << *Do I detect my old, or rather young, friend, Thomas?* >>

<< *Hello again, Sir! My regards to Shinlu.* >>

The full 'War Council' from seven years earlier, plus Carlos and Sophia, and Cantor and Vernique were present, the only change being that Merlin presided, whereas Marcus had previously taken the mental chair.

"You and Zoltan," he had said, "are doing very well so far!"

"You're better at running a meeting than I ever was."

"Mandrake, having opened the meeting with your comment, have you anything to add?"

<< *Shinlu and I debated for many hours last evening, My Friends, and we believe we learned more than we realised at the time yesterday if one extrapolates from the small items mentioned. Shall I summarise?*

<< *We know that Krast is the real leader, and that she and Kresh are involved in this at least in part for revenge, but also for profit. They intend*

to harvest Theurgen from the whole world, just as was done on a small scale before.

<< *More important, Krast has at her disposal far more than the five ships she admitted to!* >>

"We all know that. She has fifteen!"

<< *You miss the point. We both believe that Kresh knows nothing about the extra ones.*

<< Now, Marcus, please explain what she meant when she thought that maybe they would have to deal with Merlin from orbit. >>

"From orbit," explained Marcus, trying to think of a way to explain what was meant to people with virtually Stone Age scientific knowledge. "From orbit means…Let's just say they can inflict damage on a town from a thousand miles above it…and we won't know until it's too late!"

"But how?" asked Merlin. "I don't mean technically how, but what form will the damage take?"

"One of two possibilities. On earth we had the ability to fire missiles from orbit at tens of thousands of miles an hour at targets on the ground.

"That, I think we could deal with.

"The other possibility is some development of their laser weapons, and that's what worries me. We have to find out.

"Merlin, call one of the weapons officers in to join you, and question her. I'll give Zoltan the questions. She'll never know she took part in this conference."

Wanda was the most quickly available, and probably the best choice because of her loyalty to Aristo.

"Thank you for coming, Wanda." Merlin said to her after introducing the others physically present.

"We are considering what Krast may do next.

"One possibility is that she will attack from orbit. What weapons has she that she could use against us from such a height?"

"I'm surprised that you know enough to even consider that!

"I was told you were backward, with hardly any technology."

"Please just answer."

"If all the ships are like the one I was in, she has four missiles each capable of wiping out all trace that a town ever existed, or of demolishing just one building if that was what was wanted."

"So there are no beams like lasers which can be used from up there?"

"No! It's been tried, but the atmosphere makes them unreliable. Also we have defence screens against lasers and other beam weapons, whereas against a missile weighing enough and travelling quickly enough we have no defence.

"I'm worried for all of us now, My Lord, if she should be annoyed enough we are doomed."

Merlin smiled, but there was no humour in it, and he replied, "Relax, Wanda. What you've described we can handle!"

"What has she for use at close quarters that we don't know about?"

"There's a version of the rocket weapon which targets one particular person. It homes in on his or her electromagnetic brain pattern…let me re-word it.

"You know there is electrical activity in the brain?"

<< *Say yes - I understand!* >> Marcus advised Merlin.

"Yes! Go on"

"Each of us has a different pattern which can be detected and used to guide a missile."

<< *I know how to handle that, Merlin!* >>

<< *Thank you, Thomas, I might have known you wouldn't let yourself be left out!* >>

"We can handle that easily! What else?"

Wanda was dying to ask just how Merlin proposed to deal with a weapon against which she, herself, knew of no defence, and it had taken him only a few seconds.

"You know lightning sometimes takes the form of a ball which appears to float around?"

"We do!"

"We can generate such a ball of immense size, and then control it.

"She could send one to demolish just one building, or a whole town."

<< *Any ideas, Anyone?* >>

<< *No problem!* >>

<< *Thank you, Marcus.* >>

"We can deal with that just as easily, Wanda. Is that the last of her surprises?"

"Not quite, there is also a sonic disruptor beam which causes buildings to shake themselves to pieces."

"It will be interesting to see what happens when we are telling the buildings to remain stable, and her bit of science is trying to make them shake. I believe we would win!"

<< *Do we need Wanda any more?* >>

<< *Ask about the weapons used by the criminal element - people like Oistrach who deal in drugs. It may not be Oistrach himself, but if they are harvesting Theurgen then it is probably for sale, so the other ships Krast thought of…do you follow?* >>

"One last question, Wanda.

"Seven years ago we had dealings with one Oistrach, a drug dealer. If one or more of such as he had ships here, what armament would they have?"

"The Galactic Patrol always has the best! The criminals might have the same, but certainly no more, and probably less!"

"Thank you for your help! You may return to the others."

"May I make a suggestion, Your Honour?"

"You may, and as Aristo's friend, you may address me as Merlin."

"Our home planet is seven of your days travel from here, and if a ship left now, it would, unless that ship was lucky enough to contact another vessel, be only fourteen days before help arrived. Why not send one with a volunteer crew?"

"We'll consider that! Now, you may go."

Wanda left, still wondering how Merlin proposed to deal with three weapons against which she knew of no defence.

"Does anyone favour acting on Wanda's suggestion?"

Mandrake was first to reply.

<< *We considered just that action ourselves before the meeting, Merlin, and decided that these Godhe, although we owe their ancestors our very existence, must learn that we will not tolerate interference.*

<< *We suspect that their idea of treating those who do wrong, even such wrongs as the killing of Aristo, will be some sort of therapy to rehabilitate them into society. Obviously that is what was done to Kresh and Krast, and for whatever reason it failed to work!*

<< *They have sinned on this world, and on this world they will be punished!*

<< *We suggest sending for help, but only when we have already almost finished dealing with the invaders ourselves.* >>

"Does anyone disagree?"

None did.

"Carried unanimously, then…, Marcus?"

<< *There's another reason for not sending a ship. You have only four, which means you can only have four of their own defence screens activated for our use. Perhaps the crashed ship can have its screen salvaged, I suggest getting some of the Godhe to try.* >>

With that the conference disbanded, and Zoltan ensured that all leaders knew its decisions, and in particular, knew what weapons could be used against them and what suggestions had been made to deal with them.

***

Still believing that Abinger would be the next target Thomas called a meeting of his active triads for practice.

Tallons and Gabbie's falcon Sweetheart were sent to circle the town at about ten thousand feet. Two of the other triads were asked to send tree branches to represent missiles as far as they could into the air over the town, then bring them down as fast as they could. When either Thomas or Gabbie saw the missile coming through their familiar's eyes they had no trouble turning it in whichever direction they wished.

"With the real thing, if it happens, we'll send it back to the ship which fired it!" explained Thomas.

Remembering the sessions of competition from '*Unicorn Witch*' when Sophia was being trained, Thomas took two triads, gave two to Gabbie, and then had the birds by the side of archery butts.

Looking only through the birds' eyes, they duplicated the competition invented by Marcus. Taking turns, side one fired an arrow at side two's target. Side two had to turn the arrow and send it into side one's own.

After a while they were able to perform the task with a couple of tons of rock instead of an arrow, and Gabbie declared herself satisfied.

Thomas worked them for another hour, practising the techniques discussed for dealing with the personalised rockets, and the lighting balls, then once again the highlight of the day was saying 'Goodnight' to Fallon, which took another hour or so. His final act was to report to Merlin what they had achieved.

Seline left the house to visit Jet when the teenagers had retired.

"May I ask a question, Jet?" she asked.

<< *Of course, Seline. It's only fair to tell you that I already know the question, but please carry on!* >>

"I'm worried about the friendship between Thomas and Fallon. They are both at an age when they could each easily be hurt by the other. Can you tell their real feelings?"

<< *I will tell you, but you must never reveal this conversation to either of them!* >>

<< *I promise!* >>

<< *Fallon absolutely idolises Thomas. He could do no wrong, and she would take his side in any argument, even to the death. That is not the same as loving him, but I believe that too is coming.*

<< *Thomas has never had a girlfriend, nor has any girl paid him the sort of attention Fallon has. He enjoys her company, and particularly the physical contact. He loves her, but then he loves everyone. However, if you were to ask him the same question he would probably say that he is in love with her.*

<< *I have the same concern as you, and will try to help them if I can!* >>

Seline kissed Jet on the nose. "Thank you!"

***

Merlin had all towns practise Gabbie's technique; particularly the variations devised by Thomas, and then turned his attention to Marcus's suggestion of salvaging the screen equipment from the crashed ship. It proved possible to mount it on a small wagon complete with a power source.

Merlin did not attempt to understand any of it, but Kallen assured him he could operate it when asked, doing anything from making Camelot invisible, to having a force field round it which would stop any missile except one coming from orbit at high speed.

"I'm sorry, but nothing will stop such an attack!"

Merlin just smiled, and thanked him for his help

Just after lunch the news they had all expected came from Carlos, though none were expecting quite all that he said.

<< *Merlin, all three ships have left Paris and headed East! We no longer have even the barrier round the town.*

<< *Kresh asked us to keep an eye on things for her as she was needed elsewhere.*

<< *We can guess where that is! Good luck.* >>

Zoltan warned all towns to have birds aloft and waiting, reminding them that two circling the town was better than immediately above it.

Storm and Hawka reported a single ship below their own level, headed towards Abinger.

"It looks as though Thomas may be right," commented Shaena, "but where are the other two?"

***

Tallons reported seeing the ship arrive, and land just outside the town.

<< *Stay alert, Tallons, please!* >> Jet advised.

<< *You too, Sweetheart! There are two ships we have not accounted for.* >>

A single female bearing the traditional white flag of truce left the ship and walked towards the town, stopping when within hailing distance.

"My name is Krast! I would like to speak with Electra."

Quickly Gabbie had Roxy outline a course of action for Electra, who replied, "Stay where you are. I will send a unicorn who will bring you into the town!"

Her own Jasmina trotted out to Krast, and stood by a mounting block Krast was sure had not been there when she landed. She climbed aboard, held the mane, and was taken into the town square. Jasmina passed a commentary of her thoughts to Jet, and the whole of the 'War Cabinet', hastily convened, listened in.

<< *This should be easy, but I must be careful.*

<< *No sign of the ship they captured.*

<< *Only six people in the square. One of them is only a child. All riding unicorns except one. I suppose I am riding hers.*

<< *Four of them have horses there as well. No, the horses are leaving. They seem to be going out to where I came from. Strange!* >>

"I presume you are Electra?" she asked the woman on foot.

"I come to give you one chance to surrender the town before I commence to destroy it one building at a time."

<< *As she said.* >>

"You say your name is Krast?"

"I did!"

"Well, Krast, I had hoped you'd come to apologise for the behaviour of your last representatives.

"If you've merely come to threaten, you may make your demands to the youngest member of our council. He may be amused, but I am not! .... Good Day!"

The other five moved slightly away, leaving Krast facing Thomas, and getting more angry by the second, which was, of course, just why Gabbie had suggested this course of action.

"Come back here! I haven't finished with you!" she shouted at Electra, who turned to speak to her neighbour and completely ignored Krast.

<< *As she said, but she is as annoyed as we can possibly get her now!* >>

"Krast!" called Thomas.

"You may either return to your ship, or speak with me! The choice is yours. Unlike Electra I am vaguely interested in what you have to say..... Something about destroying the town?

"What makes you think you will have any more success than your underlings?"

"You cannot influence what you cannot see.

"Five minutes after I return to the ship your library will explode!"

<< *She will have Kreshfire a missile from orbit - Do you understand that, Thomas?* >>

<< *I do! Don't worry!* >>

"Are you a gambler, Krast?"

"What do you mean?"

"What will you wager that not only will you fail to explode the library, you will have cause to worry yourself!"

"I do not wager with a child, and certainly not on certainties!

<< *He must be bluffing! There's no way of stopping what I've planned. I'll have his mental pattern, though!* >>

"Before I leave, do you mind me making a record of your appearance, as you may be harmed when the explosion occurs?"

<< *I was going to target Electra, but this upstart is even more annoying! Do we let her, Thomas?* >>

"Yes, Krast you may! Then Jasmina will return you to where she picked you up."

Krast pointed a small camera with a dish aerial on the front at Thomas for a few seconds, then thanked him and left.

Jasmina's commentary resumed.

<< *I'm very pleased with that. I've got the exact coordinates of the library, and a record of Thomas's brain pattern. If they somehow divert the missile......no they couldn't possibly.....but if they do, then he will be next with no warning.*

<< *Here we are at the mounting block. These animals must be very intelligent to take a stranger like me, even though I didn't hear Electra tell her where to go.*

<< *She must have given all the orders before she came out in the first place.*

<< *I'll be glad when this is over, and Oistrach and I can retire!* >>

Jasmina trotted back to the town, and Krast couldn't help herself admiring the animal as she went. She, herself, entered her ship, which promptly became invisible.

Tallons and Sweetheart kept diametrically opposite each other as they circled, paying full attention to the area above the town. Neither trusted Krast to wait five minutes, but in fact, she did, giving them time to get to their preferred ten thousand feet altitude.

Down below, Gabbie, Roxy, Thomas, and Jet appeared to observers to be in a trance, each pair being mentally with their highflying familiar.

The missile was spotted at about twenty thousand feet, but had passed them before they completed turning it end for end. It continued down, tail rockets now first slowing it, then sending it back whence it came.

There was no satisfaction in seeing a brilliant white flash above, and knowing that four more of the Godhe had died. For a moment or two it was as though they had two suns.

<< *These things always have a self-destruct system in case of accidents.* >> explained Marcus. << *Keep alert! You may have destroyed a ship, or you may not!* >>

Four more appeared simultaneously. Two were turned immediately, then so were the others, but not before they got within the sight of those on the ground. All four were detonated before they rose out of sight.

Tallons noticed a disturbance in the clouds over the city.

<< *One ship descending in an invisible state,* >> he reported.

<< *No sign of the third one - perhaps we destroyed it!* >>

The two birds continued their vigil, but the partners withdrew mentally back to the square, and had a gestalt of the six triads summon drizzle to outline the ship as it arrived.

It stopped some fifty feet above the square, and from its base there dropped a ten feet diameter ball of lightning that soon changed direction towards the library.

Two of the lengths of chain made ready, each forged from links one inch in cross section, and buried in the ground lashed out as though from a whip and hit the ball.

The discharge to the square left a crater twenty feet across, with melted chain in it, but no-one was hurt. The chain was of no further use, but that was unimportant, as they'd prepared plenty.

<< *Plan Two next time, if there is a 'next time'!* >> called Thomas/Jet.

There was, but this time Thomas was the target, and the ball was twice the size.

This ball was also earthed, but the chains were passed over the attacking ship first, so that the discharge was from ball to ship to ground.

The ship became visible and fell. Just in time to avoid injury to the occupants Electra called on the gestalt to catch it, and it landed with hardly a bump. There was no sound from it, and Marcus explained, << *All their electrical and electronic equipment will have failed. There is no insulator made which could handle that much static discharge. You'll find you have four more prisoners, but I suggest leaving them inside the ship until Krast leaves - If she does.* >>

Even though ten thousand feet above, Tallons, who had been watching Krast's ship whilst Sweetheart looked upwards, was able to see the missile Krast intended for Thomas, and called to him,

<< *Something coming from the ship outside the town!* >>

Gabbie smiled, commenting, "This is like taking candy from a baby! She's doing everything as we expected her to.

"Let me have the pleasure!"

The missile had short wings and was travelling at only two hundred miles an hour. Gabbie had no trouble in bringing two halves of an iron coffin shaped container from the side of the square, where several lay ready for use, to surround and catch the missile long before it got near Thomas.

She opened a pit below it, dropped it in, piled rocks on top, and waited.

There was no explosion. Apparently it had to have Thomas's brain pattern next to it before it detonated, but it was decided to leave it where it was until after the conflict.

Thomas rode Jet out to within sight of Krast's ship and waved. The ship took off and headed West.

First Shaena, then Bridie, Angus's wife in Brigadoon, confirmed that she was heading for Europe.

<< *Now,* >> suggested Zoltan, << *let us see what we have caught!* >>

The six triads returned to the square, and to the silent ship, mentally accompanied by the whole War Cabinet. Once again, Thomas called on Jet's amplified telepathic voice.

<< *You in the ship. I speak for the World President.*

<< You are our prisoners, and may open the door. If you cannot do this, simply make a noise and we will do it for you! >>

From within there was a noise of metal against metal.

As Merlin had before in Camelot, Thomas had his gestalt remove the door, but unlike Merlin, he made sure he knew where to find it afterwards.

First out was Kresh, recognised by Jet from the mental picture Javelin had given, hands in the air and looking very pale. Her three companions looked no better. She was amazed to find that a teenage boy headed her captors. "My name is…"

"Kresh! Yes, we already know," finished Thomas, "and you've given us quite a lot of trouble.

"You will be taken to Camelot shortly, and Merlin will deal with you. Have you finally learnt that on this continent you cannot win?"

"I have! I will give you no more trouble and neither will any of my crew!"

<< *She tells the truth! The other three agree! She wonders if she heard you correctly when you mentioned Merlin.* >>

"What will your leader Krast do?"

"I have no idea! She now has only three ships."

<< *She really believes this!* >>

"If you allow me to repair my power supply, I will call the Galactic Patrol and end this."

"You may look at it, but be prepared for a shock. Look first at the communication equipment."

Returning to the dead ship with the engineer, Kresh opened the panel covering the interstellar communicator, looked briefly, and returned to Thomas.

"You knew!"

"Not for certain. We knew that the other five ships had been sabotaged. It was possible that yours had not.

"I have some other news for you to think about.

"Krast is working with Oistrach, and has another ten ships in Europe!"

"How?…No!…Forget that! If you say so then it will be true and I've been used just like all the others.

"How are they, by the way?"

"Three were killed in an attack on Camelot. The others are our guests until this is over. They have all offered to help us in any way they can. Odel and Juno are here in Abinger and I intend to ask them to take you to Camelot."

"I would like nothing better!"

"For the little it is worth…I'm truly sorry!

"I had no idea Krast intended to take over like she did. I knew when she killed Aristo I should have stopped her, but I just couldn't stop myself going along with her plans. I don't expect you to believe me, but I really am sorry!"

<< *All of that was true!* >>

<< *Ask Juno and Odel to join us, please, Jet.* >>

The birds returned, were telepathically praised for their work, and the other triads dispersed, leaving just Thomas and his with the four prisoners.

"Are you not afraid we will attack you?" asked Kresh. "After all there are four of us and only one of you!"

"For one thing you gave your word, and I believe you meant it, and for another, attacking me would be the last action you ever took! I could easily throw the four of you at hundreds of miles an hour into a wall, but I would let Tallons here have the pleasure of dissuading you!"

As Thomas spoke the eagle looked straight at Kresh, opened his beak, spread his wings, and, releasing his right foot from the pad, flexed the Tallons which gave him his name.

Kresh shivered, and resolved anew never again to cross one of these strange people.

Juno and Odel had been watching the battle from what they thought was a safe distance, and felt it necessary to apologise to Thomas.

"We should know by now, Thomas, but we were taught that there was no defence against missiles from orbit, and even more so against ball lightning. That will even destroy one of our defence screens.

"What can we do for you?"

<< *Ask Electra to return, please, Jet* >>

Juno and Odel just looked at each other without speaking whilst they waited, but it wasn't hard to imagine the thoughts going through their minds.

Electra rode into the square and, having been primed by Jet told Odel, "I would like you to deliver these four to Merlin, and then return with me, if you will, please."

Odel sounded frightened as he asked Thomas, "Are you not coming? You know who this is, do you not?"

"Yes, but she's Merlin's problem now. Electra will accompany you. You won't have any trouble. You may find this hard to believe, Odel, but she's much more powerful than I am!"

"Forgive me, but I do find that hard to believe!"

"It's true. She was there to step in if I couldn't handle Krast."

Thomas turned to face Kresh, who had been listening.

"Actually you four owe her your lives, or at least thanks for saving you injury. It was Electra who caught your ship and lowered it gently when it was falling. I wasn't going to bother."

"Then, if you don't mind me asking," continued Odel, "if Electra is the more powerful, why were you in charge of the defence of Abinger?"

Thomas smiled as he replied, "All the adults were busy with their normal work, so I offered to handle it."

Juno, the former weapons officer wanted to know, "But Kresh used the most advanced weapons we have against you and you only had hundredths of a second to decide what to do. What did you do when those missiles came down, by the way? You obviously turned them round, but you did it before we even knew they were coming!"

Thomas smiled as he answered, "I want you to particularly remember that when you're making your report to the Galactic Patrol back on your own world, Juno."

Kresh and her three companions were very subdued on the short flight to Camelot, which was, of course, exactly the effect Thomas had hoped for when he implied that dealing with the Godhe had been the sort of work to be entrusted to a child.

Within half an hour Electra was back with Thomas, and Odel and Juno went off to continue enjoying their honeymoon. Seline and Fallon were able to resume their English lessons as Thomas was absolutely certain that they would see no more of Krast for at least the rest of that day.

***

"So you're Kresh, of whom I've heard so much!" Merlin greeted his newest prisoner. "It gives me more pleasure than you could possibly imagine to welcome you to Camelot.

"Having had time to consider, do we still have your parole for the duration of this war?"

"You do! But who are you, Sir?"

<< *Zoltan?* >>

<< *She speaks the truth.* >>

"My name is Merlin. I'm sure you've heard of me, and possibly of my death? One day, perhaps, you may learn that on this world there is little which is not impossible."

"Even the power of life and death? Krast saw you die!"

"I have no interest in educating you beyond the knowledge that it's not in your best interests to annoy even one of us.

"We know that you were involved in this by Krast, but you have to take some of the blame. What happened to you when you were taken from here over six years ago?"

"I admitted what we'd been doing, as did the others, so there was no trial. We were all sent to a rehabilitation hospital for treatment, and a year later given a new start with new identities."

<< *True.* >>

"So why didn't it work?"

"I don't know the details, but whatever they did had absolutely no effect. I still had all my memories and when Krast met me just over a couple of years ago she suggested that since we'd been so lucky we should return here. She pointed out that with our previous experience of you we were easily the best people to investigate your powers. The Council were looking for volunteers, so - here we are."

<< *True.* >>

"But Aristo knew you! Why didn't he stop it?"

"As far as he knew our memories had been erased and new personalities implanted. He may have suspected, but he couldn't prove anything."

"How about Oistrach, and the plan to harvest theurgen from this world in bulk?"

"I don't suppose you'll believe me, but I thought there were just the two of us, and that Krast had got authority to do what we did. After all, we really do need to solve the problem of what happens to our men, and I still feel that learning why theurgen helps them will lead to a solution."

<< *All true.* >>

"That didn't stop you sending missiles down to Abinger, though, did it? Or using a ball of lightning against which you believed there to be no defence?"

"I don't understand that myself. I'd never do anything to hurt anyone! Was their defence really handled by that boy Thomas? And how did he do it?"

<< *I'm puzzled, but she's telling the truth!* >>

"You're forgetting again, Kresh, that I'm not here to answer questions, but to decide what to do with you.

"Zoltan, call Wanda in, please, and advise all of the others << *set up the usual conference* >> and have them listen in."

When Wanda arrived Merlin quickly explained that Kresh's rehabilitation had been ineffective, but that even allowing for that her actions seemed out of character. Could she suggest an explanation?

"The rehab. process just can't fail to work. It's been in regular use for centuries, and if it failed with Kresh, then it would have failed with all others who followed her and thus been discovered to be faulty. So it must be that she's been moulded to be as someone, probably Krast, wanted her.

"Given enough time with her, and if she'll trust me, I can find out for you."

<< *Tyana here, Merlin. Ask her how, as I've a feeling we can speed this up.* >>

"Just how will you do that, Wanda? And what do you, Kresh, think of what she said?"

"I think Wanda must be right, but it's not a field I know much about. I promise I'll help in any way I can. I don't like being used."

"Using hypnosis I can regress her to when the treatment occurred, and have her repeat the orders she's been given. However, even with full cooperation it will take two days to do if it's to be without damage to her. Even going that slowly it could be very dangerous for her."

<< *Remember when Karim did the same sort of thing with Darren when I started my investigations before, Merlin? Karim can teach the technique to her father, and you'll know in minutes.*

<< *You ask for her consent whilst Zoltan learns. No, Karim says to make it Princess instead as she was more comfortable with Crystal than with Darren. Same gender, and exposure to a mind like Zoltan's might be too much for her.* >>

"Kresh, you know we use the unicorns as communicators as they are telepathic over any distance between themselves?"

"Yes, I remember that. That's why we developed the screens for them."

"My wife has a particularly intelligent one called Princess. If you would trust her to merge with your mind, we could learn anything you know but can't remember, and, best of all, there would be no risk attached. It's been done before."

Princess came in and stood before Kresh.

<< *Hello, Kresh. I want to help you if you'll let me be your friend.* >>

"Merlin, it's wonderful! She spoke to me inside my head. And she's so beautiful. Those eyes…..I never realised before… Tyana had one like this, didn't she?"

<< That was my daughter, Karim. Now, will you trust me? >>

"Oh yes!" she answered, throwing her arms around Princess's neck and sobbing. "How could anyone not trust you? I don't believe you could tell a lie if you tried. If possible, please help me remember too, won't you?"

Just as Darren and Crystal had remembered everything for Karim, overcoming the posthypnotic commands to forget, and so did Kresh.

Oistrach had asked to be first into the rehabilitation unit, and had looked confident as he entered, which had puzzled all of the others, including Kresh herself. His crew, then Jove and his had followed at fifteen minute intervals, then Krast, and last of all Kresh herself.

She had been placed in a chair facing a battery of lights and a screen, held there by cuffs, ankle straps, and a head restraint, and given a spray injection into a bared arm. This was what she had expected.

She had been told, when in the trance state which quickly followed, that her behaviour in the past was just that, and she must look to the future. She would be given a new background and training, and must from then on work for the good of all. Only that way would she remain as happy and content as she felt at that time. She was to follow the orders of anyone giving her name as Krast even if they seemed strange orders, as they really would be for the good of all. Anything Krast told her not to remember, she would forget.

She had been trained as a biochemist and had worked hard for four years, being recognised as talented and when Krast visited her to suggest volunteering for service on Langala IV it seemed the natural thing to do. Krast had suggested the line of research that had been carried out on Carlos and Sophia and that too had seemed to her to be perfectly natural. Even the firing of missiles had seemed in order, as, since Krast said so, it must be for the common good.

When Princess withdrew gently there were tears in her eyes, as there were in Wanda's, Laura's, and Merlin's. Zoltan looked the other way, so we don't know about his.

Surprisingly, Kresh recovered first, turned to Merlin, and murmured quietly, "I'm so sorry!……I'll do anything in my power to help put things right…….Those poor children! She'd better not have harmed them. Do you know them?"

Neither Laura nor Merlin could answer, but Princess told her,

<< Three are Laura and Merlin's grandchildren, and the fourth is their own son. >>

Kresh just collapsed to the floor sobbing.

<< Everyone, Kresh is no longer our enemy, but can be counted on as the staunchest ally we have. >>

This surprising news was circulated to all triads, and then Kresh was reunited with her fellow Godhe guests and given a meal. It proved harder to convince them of her conversion than it had their captors, and in the end Merlin had to reassure them himself.

Melanie, as always an interested observer renewed her vow to deal with Krast if and when the opportunity came and asked her new partner what she thought.

<< Aristo was Zoltan's friend, so if not bonded to Merlin he would probably seek vengeance himself. As he can't, it's up to us! The most important thing is to ensure that she does not leave Refuge. >>

***

Immediately after breakfast, Kresh apologised again for the kidnapping of the children, and asked, "Is there nothing that you will allow us to do? There are enough of us here to easily take control of the island and, once there, I'm sure we'd find a communicator that works or quickly rebuild one."

"I've had similar offers from several people, including Wanda, who actually worked for Aristo. I have two reasons for refusing. First, I trusted your home planet to deal with you all seven years ago, a mistake I won't make again. In future anyone who sins on this world will be punished on it.

"Second, we don't know in exactly what conditions the children are being held. It may be that they would be harmed if you did as you suggest. Their best chance of rescue is by Tyana and Marcus, who are almost there. No doubt you remember how formidable they can be."

"But surely they're on their way to Europe, aren't they?"

"That's what you were meant to think. In reality they are about ten hours sailing from your island and I expect to hear later today that it has become our island."

Chapter Six

Swift and Caress went for their usual high flight after the humans had breakfasted paying particular attention to the area from which Tyana had seen one of the Godhe ships leave the afternoon before in a hurry. Marcus had commented, "I've never seen one travel so fast inside the atmosphere!"

Explaining that remark had taken most of the rest of the day.

<< *Look, Marcus, Tyana,* >> and through their familiar's eyes they could see a dome shaped area slightly different in appearance from the surrounding sea. You would never see it from sea level, but from several thousand feet up, the barrier could be detected.

"What do you suggest, Darling?" asked Tyana.

"I've already thought about that. Since we can tunnel under one on land, maybe we can swim under one at sea. Anyway that's what I want to try first. If we can get ashore without them knowing we've arrived, we can deal with them without them having the chance to use the children as a shield."

"Do you really think they would?"

"Krast would, if she's here!"

They headed for the barrier, and had almost reached it when Karim/Rebel 'heard', << *Hello Dame, Sire, Are you on the three masted ship that's just reached where the barrier was?* >>

Before the message had finished, the four had merged, and were asking, << *Are all eight of you alright? What part of the island are you prisoners on? How many are guarding you? Is Krast there? What happened to the barrier?* >>

<< *We're not being held. We're doing the holding! There are four prisoners here for you, and a spaceship. We've lots to tell you, but first—How's Granddad?* >>

<< *He's fully recovered. Grandma's fine too!* >>

<< *But...we saw Princess die!...How...* >>

"Poor Simeon," commented Tyana to Marcus as their partners brought the children up to date with Belle's change of name, and about the formation of Triads. Marcus addressed his partner,

<<*Rebel, let Karim carry on whilst you set up a conversation for Shadow with Laura through Princess. Poor Simeon thought his Mum was dead.*

<<*Swift, Caress, could you please go and look at the children and foals for us?* >>

<<*Of course we will! We were just going to offer!* >>

It took an hour for the unicorns and adults to get to the spacedrome, but the eagles made it in less than five minutes and Tyana and Marcus were able to see their children for the first time in over three weeks. They could also see that the Godhe were securely tied and would give no trouble until they themselves arrived.

After a very emotional reunion between the humans and their children, and the unicorns and their foals, Simeon proudly presented Marcus with their diary:

****

Our record of events from when Krast captured us
until Marcus and Tyana rescued us
by *Simeon Pendragon*
with help from
Julie Counter
Paul Counter
Christopher Counter
With a cover and notes
by our friend Plathe

****

The first sign that we were in trouble came with a cry from Shadow.

<<*Simeon! Princess was talking to me and now I can't hear her!* >>

I watched as my father obviously realised something was wrong, stopped and stared behind us. We all looked around and saw a woman come from behind trees with something in her hands we didn't recognise.

She pointed it at Dad and the front part of it went quickly towards him. All four of us 'grabbed' at it mentally but found we had no effect. We watched with horror as Princess reared up throwing Dad off, but taking the thing on her chest.

The four foals were terrified, partly because of what they could see happening, but also because they couldn't contact their parents or Zoltan, something beyond their understanding.

Calming our familiars at least gave us something to do and took our minds off what we'd just witnessed, but by the time we'd done that we found that we could no longer see outside of a circle which centred on a space ship just like Uncle Aristo's.

"Inside, all of you!" commanded the woman, and we all did as she told us, but only because Star gave us a message.

<< *Julie says we're to obey her for now. She says that she thinks Granddad's alive as Archimedes seemed just to be worried and annoyed and she doesn't want that woman to check on him.* >>

We all entered the ship, and almost immediately fell asleep. I was the first to recover, followed by Julie, and finally a few minutes later by the twins.

Julie put her finger to her lips in the old 'hush' sign and called her partner, << *Star, are you alright, and are the others with you?* >>

<< *We're all together in a sort of stable. We don't know where yet. We only woke up a little while ago. Suppose you and Simeon talk and we'll all join in and pass it on?* >>

<< *Is that alright with you, Simeon?* >>

<< *Yes! First, why did we have to just give in? I went along with it as you said it could help Dad, but I'd like to know why.* >>

<< *I saw Archimedes flying around, and I think that means Granddad's alive. That thing we couldn't stop was intended for him and if that woman knew he survived she'd have tried again.* >>

<< *Has anyone any ideas about where we are, and what we can do about it? Yes, Paul?* >>

<< *I can smell the sea, like when we visited Newport.* >>

<< *No, it's not Newport, there's no fishy smell, just salty air. And it seems earlier in the day, as though we've gone towards Europe. Someone's coming!* >>

The woman came in through the side door and said, "So, you're all awake. My name is Krast, and if you behave yourselves and do exactly what anyone here tells you, no harm will come to you."

I decided to make sure she thought she'd killed Dad and threw myself at her, only to find I couldn't get nearer than two feet away. I pounded on the invisible barrier, shouting, "You killed my father. I hate you, I hate you, I hate you!"

Krast sprayed me with a mist and I fell to the floor.

"He'll be fine. That was just the same gas I used to get you here quietly. When he wakes, try to get him to behave."

The twins decided to cause their own bit of trouble.

"I want my Maestro!" screamed Paul.

"I want my Minstrel!" echoed Chris.

Julie just looked at Krast, and cradled my head on her lap.

"You may all have an hour to think about cooperating, and then I'll be back."

<< *As soon as Simeon wakes, we'll go looking for our familiars!* >> announced Julie mentally.

<< *Don't wait for me. I held my breath, but thanks for the cuddle.* >>

We found ourselves in a room secured by a simple lock with the key outside. Hardly the sort of barrier to keep us in, but as I pointed out, << *It's probably some sort of test, but let's go anyway.* >>

The twins worked together to unlock, and then relock the door behind us, leaving Julie and I to lead the way.

Three more locked doors, each harder than the one before, later we found ourselves in the fresh air. The buildings were perfectly square with no joins to see, but with an obviously new stable such as would be found at home on the side of the one we'd left. The foals were inside and very pleased to see us. Krast came through a side door.

"Just as I expected! What am I going to do with you to keep you where I want you?"

"Stop playing games with us, for a start," I told her. "It was obviously some sort of test, but we did it anyway as we wanted to see that our mounts were being looked after properly. They need regular grooming at this age, and lots of small meals. You really should leave us together to save yourself a lot of work.

"To find out if we could open locks, why didn't you just ask? Why are we here, anyway? I want to go home!"

Krast smiled, but the sight was hardly a reassuring one, and she replied, "You're here as an insurance. Whilst I've got you, your parents will behave. It's as simple as that."

"Make the most of it!" Julie told her. "When my Dad gets here you'll wish you'd never been born!"

"We'll see. Now, pay attention!

"As you guessed, the locked doors were just a test. You may go anywhere you find you are able. There's a barrier against your magic about a hundred yards from here, but any of these buildings is open to you, and you may stay with your pets if that's what you want. There's plenty of food in the freezers and the barn, and cooking facilities in the kitchen. If you need help, just press the large red button in the entrance hall and one of us will return."

"How many of you are there here?" Julie asked.

"Enough! That's all you need to know."

<< *She's lying. Her thought was that there is only her on this part of the island.* >>

"How big is this place?"

"As far as you're concerned, about two hundred of your yards across, and circular!"

<< *Twenty-five miles by thirty.* >>

"Please, Miss, I got a question!"

"Very well. What's your name?"

"Paul. I want to know…Are the others in this place as nasty as you are? Are there any nice ones like Uncle Aristo?"

There was a long pause as Krast thought out how or whether to answer this one.

"Everyone here works for me!"

<< *Brilliant, Paul. Congratulations! She thought about a new arrival in deep sleep, about one technician who is a prisoner like us, and about twelve Godhe like herself.* >>

"I have to leave you for now. Don't forget - the red button if you need help."

<< *I'm going to see how Kresh is doing. They should be able to manage for a day or so.* >>

Krast left, and as we knew she was really leaving, we decided to risk speaking normally to avoid tiring our familiars.

"First," said Julie, "we need a leader. Simeon, you're elected!"

"Why me? You're just as old as I am, Julie." I answered.

"Yes, but the twins respect you more because of your Dad, and anyway, I don't want the job. So, Mr Leader, what shall we do?"

"Yes, Mr Leader," chorused the twins, making an adventure of it. "What shall we do?"

I thought about it for a while, and then told them, "First we explore, and then we eat. We obviously have plenty of time, so we'll stay together. Let's check each of the buildings."

The largest we found to contain room after room with rows of cages about the right size for small animals like rabbits and a stationery cupboard.

"Just what we need!" I exclaimed. I collected several pens and a pile of paper. As I told the others, "We must write down everything that happens to us and everything we see. Then when we're rescued we won't have to keep telling the story over and over again like your parents had to when they got back seven years ago.

"What's wrong, Paul?"

"Chris 'n' me can't write yet."

"Don't let that worry you! I'll keep the diary, and you and Julie can help me remember all that's happened each day when I do it. How's that?"

This cheered the twins up considerably.

The other buildings proved to be filled with equipment that none of them recognised. At least Krast had told the truth about the kitchen and much to our surprise we enjoyed our lunch.

"Mr. Leader, what do you think our Mum and Dad would do if they were here?" Paul asked me, and I replied, "That's exactly what I was thinking about, everyone. But more important, what would they want us to do?

"They wouldn't want us to take any risks, but with Krast out of the way, and we know there's no one else here, I think we could try to get beyond this barrier of hers. Let's go and look at it."

From a distance it looked white, but when we got right up to it it seemed more like a mirror, and touching it caused a slight tingle to the fingers.

"Perhaps it doesn't go under the ground," suggested Julie.

We dug down, mentally, of course, until there was a six feet deep pit next to the barrier, but we could still see the mirror effect, so we filled in the pit and went back to the stable that was to be our home.

"I'm tired, Julie!" cried Paul.

"So'm I!" confirmed Christopher.

"We all are," I told them, "and I think I know why. We left for school, and then were brought here. We've had lunch and looked around, yet the sun is only just getting high in the sky.

"We must have been taken towards Europe, or even all the way. After all, we don't know how long we slept. Since we're all tired, let's just go to sleep."

I'd always needed less sleep than the others so after tossing and turning for a while and watching them sleep I made a start on this Diary. Julie suggested that we count Day One as when Aristo came to visit, so that's what I've done. So all that I've written so far is for Day Five.

DAY SIX

We were all awake before dawn, confirming my idea that we've travelled West. After a hearty, if early breakfast, we went back to the barrier as Julie had had an idea.

"Maybe it stops at the ground, but as we dug down it went lower. Let's try a tunnel to go under it."

We found a section which couldn't be seen from the buildings in case Krast came back then working together we tunnelled down from about twenty feet away so that when we got below the barrier there were at least six feet of earth above us and we were delighted to find we could pass below it.

The tunnel was enlarged until the foals could also pass through and we found we could see the sea in three directions, and rolling hills in the fourth. Shadow broke into my thoughts,

<< *There must be another of those barriers around this place, as we still can't speak to anyone else!* >>

<< *Thanks, Shadow, but that's no surprise.* >>

"Obviously the other people are over those hills, but let's just explore around the coast today. We'll leave the longer trip until Krast goes away for more than just a day."

We found we could get down to the sea on two sides, but there was nothing to learn, and no sign that people had ever been there. The South side had cliffs with sheer sides rising over fifty feet from the beach.

We returned and all helped me fill in this diary. Just after lunch we had the satisfaction of a visit from Krast. It seemed from her thoughts that she just wanted to reassure herself that we would be alright on our own, and the foals were able to read her intention of going for three days next trip.

DAY SEVEN

Sure that Krast would be away for three days, we all lost no time after breakfast in getting through our tunnel and riding North towards the hills, but after an hour they seemed little nearer, so I called a halt.

"Remember the island is thirty miles long, and maybe the other buildings are at the other end of it," I said.

"If only we'd had time to learn the multiplying spell. As it is, we'd better go back and prepare enough food to be away overnight, one day there, and back the next."

"That's not enough time!" said Julie. "We may need a day there, wherever there is. It'll have to wait until she goes away again."

"But…" started the twins together.

"No 'buts'!" I said. "She's right!"

We returned to the stable, and Julie and I spent the rest of the day taking it in turns to teach the twins to write, and to play various games.

DAY EIGHT

Krast didn't come today and we had enough time to prepare food for three days away. We found a cupboard containing clothing that provided the raw materials to conjure saddlebags for the foals. Lessons continued. Both Paul and Chris can now write their names and know all their times tables up to twelve.

DAY NINE

Krast seemed satisfied that we were coping and Shadow was able to read that she intended to spend the next week in Europe with someone called Oistrach.

DAY TEN

As we trotted towards the distant hills, I again wished aloud that we'd had time to learn the multiplying spell.

"We must be strong enough to learn it, Simeon," commented Julie, "or else your Dad wouldn't have said he'd teach us.

"Do you think we could work it out for ourselves?"

"Why's it called a multplyin spell?" asked Paul.

"Multiplying! It means making bigger by a number of times."

"Making what bigger, Mr. Leader?"

"For multiplying - anything. For this spell, the length of each stride our unicorns take. Do you understand, Paul, Chris?"

Paul looked thoughtful for a while then answered, "I think so. I wish! I wish!.......I wish each stride Minstrel took was two times as big as it is."

His face screwed up as he concentrated on just that thought and he wished, and wished with the single-minded determination that five year olds can have.

Minstrel caught on to the idea and wished also. Immediately they began to draw ahead of us as they were travelling twice as fast.

<< *Stop! Wait and teach us!* >> called Shadow.

Minstrel wasn't sure that he should, because all the foals had been told that they mustn't help us until we're Gold. I hope I was right when I said that Zoltan would want them to help. I had to tell him I was speaking for my father, and he then agreed and explained to the other foals what they had done.

Teaching the twins their tables paid off, and we found that they could manage four times with the help of their partners, whilst Julie and I could both do it unaided. We didn't bother to find out how much more we could do, as we had no intention of splitting up the party.

"Well done, Paul!" praised Julie. "Mum will be so proud of you!"

"Yes," I agreed, "this is going to make a big difference.

"Let's change to a gallop for a while, multiply it by four, then stop for a rest after a quarter of an hour or so.

"Minstrel, Maestro, you must tell us if you start to get tired.

"Let's go!"

Four times the foals' gallop might not seem much to anyone who's seen Tyana in a hurry, but it still amounted to over sixty miles an hour, and we all enjoyed the experience to the full.

The hills that had seemed so distant a couple of days ago were quickly only half a mile away and we stopped for a conference.

"Don't waste time, Simeon," said Julie. "Just tell us what to do. I'm sure you've thought about it on the way."

She really does know me better than I know myself. I had thought about it, remembering all that I could about *Unicorn Witch*, and answered "We walk very slowly to the top of the first hill, and when we get near to it, I'll go on ahead on foot to have a look first.

"Remember how they told us in school that Marcus kept his party below the skyline when looking at Paris for the first time? Well like that!"

I went to the top, then called back, "Come forward, all of you. We can stand in that clump of trees and see quite a bit without them seeing us."

We could see a large area with no grass growing, just dark grey stuff with spaceships like Aristo's on it, and buildings like the ones we'd already explored at one side. We watched for half an hour without seeing any movement at all either near the space ships, or near the dozen buildings around the landing area.

"Simeon, why are we being so careful not to be seen?" asked Julie. "After all, what can they do to us? And Krast did say we were allowed to go anywhere we could!"

I had to agree with her. "Yes, I suppose you're right. We'll go nearer, but let's walk quietly. I don't suppose they ever look outside anyway as there's supposed to be nobody else here.

"Maybe we can find the Godhe person who's a prisoner just like us."

As we'd guessed, there was no lookout, and no alarms, so we soon found ourselves wondering which building to investigate first.

We quietly tried each of the main doors to the buildings until we found one locked. The foals listened and could detect no thinking from inside it. Leaving them with a supply of oats on the side of the building out of sight of the others, the twins unlocked the door and we went in.

There were two other locked doors, so first we looked inside each unlocked room.

"I wish my Dad was here," said Julie as we looked around a room filled with equipment with dials and switches. "This means absolutely nothing to us. We'd better not touch anything!

"That means you, too, Chris!"

"She's right, twins." I said. "Don't touch anything! Just try to remember what's in each room so that we can tell your Dad when he gets here."

They were very reluctant but they obeyed.

"What sort of thing are we looking for, Mr Leader?" asked Paul.

"That's just the trouble, Paul. We don't know. But at least we know what this building is used for!"

"We do?" asked the other three in chorus.

"Storage of spares! Look more carefully and you'll see that there isn't just one of anything, there are rows of them. Just like visiting the stores at home and seeing rows of legs of beef, for instance."

The other unlocked rooms were also storage areas and we finally had to choose between the locked ones. The others looked to me, but how was I to know?

"Let's take the nearest, since we have no way of knowing what's there."

The lock was as simple as had been used to try to detain us and inside we found a man sleeping on his back with a tube leading to a mask over his face from a machine of some sort with tanks on it.

"Any ideas, anyone?" I asked.

The twins shook their heads, but Julie had one.

"This looks like a man from Earth, so he must be the new arrival Krast thought about. Maybe the tube's keeping him asleep till they're ready to wake him up. Let's take it off.

"If he doesn't waken, or if he looks worse, we'll put it back again. He looks very healthy. I'm sure that's all that tube can be doing, but I wish we had Megan or Laura here.... Or even Caroline."

"Don't wish that, Julie." I told her. "Four prisoners are enough."

"You didn't mind when I wished Dad was here earlier!"

"Not the same! Your Dad wouldn't be a prisoner. Krast would!"

"Go on, then. Do it!"

For a few minutes there was no change, then the sleeper's breathing speeded slightly and he was obviously going to wake. We smiled at each other to give confidence we didn't really feel, and waited.

He sat up and looked around.

"Hello! What happened? Is this a hospital?"

'At least he speaks English, one of the languages we know,' I thought, then said aloud, "Hello, Sir! Can you tell us what you remember, and then we'll do the same?"

"Alright! My name is The Great Mephisto, or at least it's really Frank Baron. I was giving a magic show at a theatre in London when there was an almighty bang and the roof fell down. The last I remember was looking up and thinking 'this is it!'"

"I've never heard of a magic show, Sir. What did you do?"

"I'm a member of the Magic Circle, and the theme of the show was reproducing, that's doing again, the tricks done by old famous magicians. For instance I had a gun fired at me and caught the bullet in my teeth...You look puzzled!"

"We've never seen a gun, Sir."

"What sort of witch are you, Sir?" asked Chris.

"I'm a magician, not a witch. I'll show you in a minute.

"What do you mean? ...You've never seen a gun!"

"Just that, Sir. We've never seen a gun!"

Whilst Frank thought about this, he walked around the room and he thought we didn't see him hide a couple of objects as he did so. Paul followed up his twin brother's question, "Yes, but are you a Bronze, a Silver, or what, Sir?"

"Be quiet, you two!" ordered Julie.

Frank went over to the twins and showed them his hands were empty then produced a piece of metal about the size of a playing card from behind Paul's ear and a ball bearing from Chris's nostril.

"You don't seem very impressed!"

"I'm sorry, Sir! Should we be?"

Frank smiled and was obviously puzzled himself. Then he said to us, "Well it took years of practice to become as good as that, and I was top of the bill at the theatre. Who do you know who can give a better magic show with nothing to work with except what's in this room? You still haven't told me which hospital we're in, and if you were in the theatre too."

I was beginning to think that perhaps the Old Ones had made a mistake, and this man couldn't do real magic. I looked at the others for support, but they just nodded to me that they were trusting my judgement.

"One thing at a time, Sir," I said. I'd decided to test the idea that he was a mistake. I got the foals to 'listen to him' and tell us later what he thought.

"Are you hungry or thirsty, Sir?"

"A little. Can you have a coffee and sandwich brought here?"

"Julie, would you mind going out for one?"

Julie caught on quickly, went outside, conjured the items, and returned. Whilst Mr Baron ate I told the others what I planned.

"May I have the little ball of metal you held, Mr Baron?"

"No, you keep it in your own hand, just let me have a good look at it. Now, keep it on your hand so that you can watch it, and go over to the bed whilst we stay here.

"Let me introduce Julie, Paul, and Chris, and my name is Simeon. We're in that order along this wall, and none of us can touch another, agreed?"

"Yes, but what's the point of this?"

"You'll see, Sir. Now, look again at the ball, then speak one of our names please."

Frank looked again at the ball and said, "Julie!"

Julie held out her hand to show the ball on it.

"How?..."

"Another name, please!"

Frank looked at them and said in quick succession, "Paul, Chris, Simeon, Julie," and as each name was spoken the owner 'called' the ball to their hand, watching Frank get more and more puzzled. He sat on the bed, and Julie walked across holding it between finger and thumb so that he never lost sight of it then dropped it on to his hand. He found himself holding a small cube of wood.

"Did I get hit on the head, or something?" he asked. "This must be some sort of dream!"

<< *He thinks he's going mad, and dreaming about real magic.* >>

All of us had heard the message, so Julie said to him,

"That's right, Sir, just lay down and let me put this mask over your face again, and sleep. You'll feel much better when you wake up next time."

He allowed Julie to do as she said and within a minute was as we'd found him.

"Why'd you do that, Julie?" asked Chris, who hadn't thought as quickly as his sister, "I liked him."

"Yes, Chris, I liked him too, but he seems to have been brought here from Earth by mistake. He can't even understand our Bronze magic, so we're better off without him.

"Let's see if the other room holds the technician Krast thought about being a prisoner."

The remaining locked door led to a similar room, but the occupant of the bed was obviously one of the Old Ones, and he was like a younger version of Aristo. He was as easy to waken as had been Frank Baron, but, of course, he knew just where he was, and why.

"Hello, Children... Bonjour, Mes Enfants!"

"Hello, Sir, we can all speak French if you prefer."

"No, English is fine. I am called Plathe, and I obviously have to thank you for my rescue. Where is Krast? I presume the Galactic Patrol have her prisoner? But why entrust the job of waking me to you four?"

I was sorry to disappoint him, but I had to say, "I'm sorry, Mr Plathe, but this isn't a rescue! Let us tell you our story, and then you can tell us what to do next.

"Are you hungry or thirsty?"

He was, but showed no surprise when Julie was able to supply his needs, and listened intently as I told our tale, starting with Aristo's departure for Europe, and, thanks to help from the others, missing nothing out up to waking him.

"You say you learned that there are twelve with Krast here?"

"Yes, but that was a few days ago, Sir. She's gone to Europe to see Oistrach, whoever he is, and may have taken some with her.

"Would you like us to find out how many there are in the other buildings?"

"No, I don't think so. It's too risky. The sleeping equipment they had me on seems to be set for about a hundred days, so there's no reason for them to come here. I think we should all go back to your prison and see if I can contact my superiors from there."

Doing this took the rest of that day, and all of next as they had to go at Plathe's walking speed, but once there it was easy enough to find a hiding place for Plathe to go to when Krast returned, and after a night's rest he helped me fill in the diary by adding his own story which, as he said to us, "was the least I can do in view of the way we've let you all down.

"I'm sure your people in Abinger will be happy to have explained at last the riddle which started the revolution before you were born.

"Let me have the book, and I'll do it in my own handwriting!"

With us looking on, and passing what he had to say to our familiars, Plathe wrote:

***

My name is Plathe, and for twenty of this planet's years I have worked here as coordinator between our rescue squad and the location team who place new arrivals. I was also asked to compare the development on each of the two continents, which had not been done for over a thousand years.

When I reported the situation in Europe to Aristo he asked me to work out a strategy to correct it without revealing our participation.

It took me two years, but after watching several qualifying sessions in what they now call New America, and comparing the results achieved, I decided that if anyone ever bonded with a unicorn they might have enough power to change things. We knew about Le Roi stealing the hormone you call Theurgen, but not about the involvement of some of our own people, so it was in New America's interest to do something about Europe anyway.

I paid special attention to Camelot as they had by far the most powerful exponents of what you call 'magic', and, using our invisibility screen I watched hundreds of contests. At one of them I saw a young girl of seven or eight riding a unicorn and came up with the idea of encouraging her to bond with her steed - but .... How?

That very evening I visited Abinger and inserted a short riddle in their records for them to solve. Merlin realised that Tyana should bond with Karim and the rest, as they say, is history!

Three months ago Krast and her team arrived with new orders from the Council of Elders and when I overheard what her idea of a new line of research was I tried to call Aristo. She interrupted me before the connection was made and the next I knew was seeing the four children who told me their story.

***

DAY THIRTEEN

Half of the day spent watching Plathe search for communications equipment, but in the end he decided that there was none here.

The other half we continued the twins' lessons, but had the advantage that Plathe could first help teach them, and was then able to teach all four of us some basic astronomy.

DAY FOURTEEN

Lessons as yesterday, but in the afternoon I asked Plathe to try to find a way of turning off the screen around our prison ready for when we're rescued. He agreed to look, but insisted on adding this note himself:

I'm looking for the generator controls as the children have asked me, but I must say that I consider it a waste of time. There is no way they can be rescued. No one even knows this island exists, and it can't be seen from the sea.

DAY FIFTEEN

Plathe worked out that the very centre of the dome shaped screen was in the top room of a tower in the middle of the group of buildings. He could not, however, get into it.

After an hour or two trying to find the locking mechanism, Julie said to us, "Forget it! We'll just change the material of the door to wood like we did with the ball that Baron man had, burn it, and then walk in."

To our surprise it took the combined efforts of the four of us with the foals helping to put her words into action but finally we succeeded. Even Plathe was impressed as a strip all around the door burst into flames and he was soon able to push it in.

"With luck," he said, "because we still left part of the door in place around the edge no alarms will have been triggered."

We didn't understand this so he went on, "Nobody will know we've opened it!"

Obviously the equipment inside meant nothing to us but Plathe said that as soon as we wished him to he could turn off the barrier. Of more interest to us were the rows of screens around the room giving a view of all the approaches to the island.

"Am I right that we can watch for when Dad comes to rescue us?" asked Julie.

Plathe found tears in his eyes as he sat all four of us down and explained, "From outside the large barrier around the island you can't even see that there's an island here. I think we have to rely on my own people coming. I don't want you to get your hopes up."

Paul smiled and said, "My Dad will come, he has to, and he'll probably have Mum with him. You'll see!"

I'd had time to think, and even if Plathe was right, I didn't want the twins giving up hope, so I said, "We'll take turns watching for ships. We only have to look every hour or so. As soon as we see one coming - it will be a three masted schooner, probably the *Unicorn Witch*, we must go to the room at the other end of the island that switches on the big one and turn it off so that they can see us. Do you know where it is, Plathe?"

"I can find it, but Krast's friends won't just let us walk in, you know."

"I know, but we've got plenty of time to plan. Will Krast come to this room when she gets back?"

"I doubt it. She can control the screen from her ship so she has no reason."

DAY SIXTEEN

Today Plathe taught us that our sun is called Langala and Refuge is the fourth planet out from it. He had to make models before we finally understood. I wonder if Dad knows? We took turns to visit the screen room about every hour, but saw nothing.

DAY SEVENTEEN

Today we spent our time answering hundreds of questions for Plathe, and he wrote down all that we said as if it was important.

He knew we could move things about, but had no idea that children as young as we are could have any real power. It frightened him a bit.

DAY EIGHTEEN

Still no visit from Krast. We hope that that means she is having trouble from our parents and friends back home.

DAY NINETEEN

This is Julie. Two days ago Simeon remembered being told that when one of a pair dies, so does the other......and we all saw Princess die, so our Gran, his Mum, must have died too. I don't know what to do, and none of us, even Plathe can console him. He won't eat, he just sits in the screen room watching them in turn.

I feel I must write this, though, as I saw two of the space ships go off towards home, then a little later, two more.

We had a visit from Krast yesterday, but she only stayed long enough to ask us if we needed anything.

DAY TWENTY

The twins between them persuaded Simeon that if he died, so would Shadow, so he's realised he has to live. Anyway, he has his Dad to think about. He's going to need him as well.

The ships haven't come back. I told Simeon it meant our folks had destroyed them. I don't really believe it, neither does Plathe, but it was enough to make him eat again. He's still watching the screens, though.

We discussed our chances with Plathe last evening, and just in case he's right, and Marcus and Tyana are not coming for us, we're going to try to steal one of the spaceships, as Plathe says he can fly it home for help.

We've packed enough food for all of us for a week, and he's done us a really nice cover for our diary on what he called a computer.

Simeon reporting again. Over half way to what Plathe calls their base.

We can see that the four ships which left have not returned, in fact we can only see two now. We got to the same building Plathe was kept in without being seen and were going to spend the night locked in his old room, but it was too crowded, so Julie and the twins are with Mr Baron, but we can keep in touch through the foals.

Plathe says that all we have to do is get him into one of the ships, and since they are all the same as each other, they can't catch him once he's left. The only trouble is that they only open the door for their own Commander. We don't understand that bit. How can a spaceship think?

Plathe has told us which building has the controls for the main barrier round the island in, and told us how to turn it off. Chris has a plan, which will get our friend in to a ship.

I told him it was too dangerous, but Julie's idea was even riskier, and I hadn't any better ones, so we're watching the place they keep the ships until a Commander goes out to one. Plathe says that usually a Commander goes out first, and then the other three join him, or her. We spent the whole morning watching but no one went near the ships. I hope we've done the right thing, letting the twins try Chris's plan. They said, and I have to agree, that it's best that they try on their own so that if they do get caught, we can rescue them.

Julie suggested that we all go and tie up the Commander as soon as he's opened a door, like we were told Tyana had done in New Salem, but I'm worried that there may be too many of them who could come from the building nearest the ships. At least this way two of us remain free, and I'm sure they won't hurt the twins.

Paul insisted, "It's safer than staying together this time!". I'm very proud of them.

Whilst Julie and I stayed in the building and watched from the door, the twins went with Minstrel and Maestro to the trees the other side of the spacedrome as Plathe calls it.

Half way through the morning someone walked over to the nearest spaceship, said something to it and the door opened.

Julie waved her hand, and Paul and Chris came galloping across at normal speed towards us, shouting, "Help! Help! We pressed the red button and nothing happened. Help!"

The man left the ship and spoke to them in English.

"Here, Children! Tell me what happened!"

They were around the other side of the next ship before they stopped, and he went to them. Paul said again that they'd pressed the red button and nothing happened, and only after the third time of asking did they explain that they couldn't find Simeon or Julie, and they were frightened.

"We've been travelling for three days, Mister!" said Paul.

"I'm hungry!" said Chris.

"What have you done with Julie?" asked Paul.

They kept up a constant barrage of questions until Plathe was inside the ship and the engine started, making the noise he'd told us to expect.

The Commander turned around, and immediately Chris and Paul were off at full multiplied gallop heading for the trees around the base. We almost felt sorry for the poor man as his ship went straight up into the sky.

He ran, though we can all walk faster, back into the building he'd come from, and we watched as four of them came out, got into two carts with no horses and went off after the twins.

As they went into the trees Paul and Chris, who'd galloped all around the base, arrived back in our building from the other side very excited. We hugged them as the foals got their breath back, and then waited quietly with the doors locked and the foals 'listening' for thoughts near us.

I'm sure I heard the engine of the other space ship, so they either used it to look for us or went to visit our prison.

Nothing else happened that day, but at least we know there are only four here now, so tomorrow we're going to try Julie's plan and tie them up. Some lengths of wiring from the machine that was keeping Plathe asleep will do for ropes. We've made enough for eight people just in case we were wrong about there being only four. We had a practice tying each other up and I really believe we can do it. Anyway we're going to try!

DAY TWENTY-FOUR

Looking outside we can see that the spaceship has come back, so carrying some of the wire each under our jumpers round our waists so that it doesn't show we went quietly into the building which the Commander came out of yesterday.

They were only four, so one of the ships must not have a crew, and all were having breakfast. We waited until they'd finished eating and two were taking dishes away from the door we could peep through. The other two were sitting facing us and I thought '*It's now or never!*'.

We'd agreed that the twins take any with their backs to us, so making sure they knew which one they each had, and agreeing that Julie take the female and I the man, I pushed open the door and we ran in.

I wouldn't have believed a grown person could move so slowly, but we'd taken six or seven steps towards them before anyone reacted. By then Paul and Chris had each tied the legs of their victims and they were falling over. Julie and I each tied ours to the chairs they were sitting in. We would have had time to help the twins, but they didn't need it.

Paul and Chris were sent to see if the screen control room was locked whilst we watched our prisoners. It was a funny feeling to know that for the first time we were in charge.

Julie and I heard at the same time from Shadow and Star,

<< *They've found the room, and it's not locked!* >>.

Only a few minutes later came even better news.

<< *The screens are working, just like in that other room, and Dad's here! Dad's here! There's a three masted ship right up against the barrier! We're going to turn it off! Then we'll say Hello....It should be fun!* >>

As the barrier went down, each of the eight of us heard from a merge of Marcus/Tyana/Rebel/Karim. They didn't know, of course, that we'd turned it off. All they knew was that the barrier had gone, so at first they just asked if we were all well and where were we being held?

I would have loved to see their faces when Shadow proudly said, << *We're not being held. We're doing the holding! There are four prisoners here for you, and a spaceship. We've lots to tell you, but first -- How's Granddad?* >>

Explanations took about an hour by which time the *Unicorn Witch* was beached and we were able to show our prisoners to Marcus and Tyana. We all fell in love immediately with Swift and Caress when they arrived early so that Marcus and Tyana could see that we really were well.

I just had time to put in the last full stop before they came into the room and I could give them this book.

***

"Thank you, Simeon!" was all Marcus could manage, then, as he re-read the cover, "Thank you, All of you!

"Who is Plathe? And where is he?"

"Please take the time to read this, Marcus, and we believe it answers all your questions. Then you and Tyana can decide what to do next. I think we've done all that we can!"

The merge of four read together, and the unicorns passed it on to the hastily convened 'War Cabinet'. When he'd finished Marcus just looked at the children for a long time before he could think of words adequate to praise what they'd managed to do. In the end the best he could do was, "Children, what you four have done, allowing for your ages, is far greater than what Tyana and I did seven years ago. You won't know this yet, but Rebel and Karim passed on what we read to Merlin and he also thanks you, not just as Simeon's father, but as President of Refuge!"

"Marcus ..."

"Yes, Simeon?"

"May we all go out to play for a while, and will you and Tyana get lunch for us? We don't really want to be grown up yet, but you see, we had to, didn't we? After what Krast did, all we could think of was not letting her get away with it. And we did, didn't we?"

<< They'll be quite safe, Marcus. The children were right. There's nobody else on the island. >>

"Yes, of course you may. Once again, we really are very very proud of all of you. We'll call you in time for lunch!"

The children went out and Marcus turned to where the four Godhe were still bound and gagged, two on chairs and two lying where they'd fallen. He removed the gags and moved the prone pair apparently instantaneously to chairs.

"I'm going to ask you just two questions, and on the answers depends what we'll do with you!

"First, though, introduce yourselves!"

"Makrill, Commander of the vessel stolen yesterday with the help of the children!"

"Fairo, Weapons Officer under Makrill!"

"Landro, Engineer and Navigator!"

"Kaarvel, Cook!"

"So, first question, and I warn you I already know the answer.

"Who did Krast go to visit when she left for Europe?"

The other three looked puzzled and turned to Makrill who answered, "She didn't tell us, but presumably her assistant, Kresh!"

<< The truth as they know it, and the others agree. >>

"How did Aristo die?"

"He tried to intervene in a dispute in Paris and the local inhabitants injured him!"

Kaarvel interrupted, "He was my friend for twenty years and those savages wouldn't let their healers try to help, nor would they let Kresh bring him here!"

<<Again they think they tell the truth.>>

Marcus relaxed and the binding wires fell away.

"Don't try to move for a few minutes. Let your blood circulate again first. I'd be grateful if you would answer just one more question for me - How long would it take for one of your ships to come here from Camelot?"

"Less than half an hour! Why?"

"You'll see! It will make life easier for all of us if I can have your word that you will just be patient and wait here for one hour and not try to attack us - and 'us' includes the children!"

"May I ask a question myself first, though I don't see how you could know the answer. Is my brother Kallen alright?"

"I do know, and yes, he's well!"

"One hour? Yes, we'll agree to that, but what can change in an hour?"

<<All four agree!>>

Marcus didn't answer but instead had Rebel set up a mini-conference with Merlin and Laura.

"Merlin, I'd like you to have Kallen and Kresh come here with you both. It's the quickest way to reunite you with Simeon. He really does need to see Laura as he thought she was dead after seeing Princess killed."

"Oh dear! I hadn't considered that. It must have been terrible for him.

"Why Kallen and Kresh?"

"I want the quickest way to prove to the four Godhe here that they're on the wrong side.

"Bring some decent food, please, as from what the prisoners, or should I say parolees told you, we wouldn't eat well if we relied on the larders here!

"By the way, what do you think of our kids? We spend nearly a month worrying about them, and planning how to take over this island, then when we get here they just make us a present of it?"

"We're still celebrating! Electra already says she wants that Diary. See you soon!"

Tyana was pleased with herself for thinking of something Marcus had overlooked. "One more thing, Merlin," she said, "Can you come via Newport and bring a crew for the '*Witch*'?"

Makrill and his crew had been watching and thought that Tyana and Marcus were in some sort of trance, so they had to try very hard to avoid showing surprise when she said to him, "We're going to have a look at the childrens' prison at the other end of the island. Our unicorns need to stretch their legs after three weeks on board ship. Within that hour you promised us one of your ships will land, and I ask that you go out to meet it."

Rebel advised the foals what they were doing and ten minutes later they were inspecting the prison after enlarging the childrens' tunnel. Of course they didn't expect to learn anything, but felt they just had to see where they'd been held and marvelled anew at their resourcefulness in escaping.

Meanwhile Merlin called for Kresh and Kallen and explained what he wanted of them. He didn't need Zoltan's confirmation that she was sincere when she said, "Of course we'll help....May I say that we think it's wonderful that your son and grandchildren are safe and well. Can you tell us how Marcus and Tyana did it?"

Merlin laughed. "In good time, My Dear. I assure you you'd never believe it if I told you, so you can hear it from the four of your own people who are there!"

When they arrived they found Simeon riding Shadow and once again in charge, with the others lined up for inspection:- Julie on Star, Paul and Chris on Minstrel and Maestro, then Makrill, Fairo, Landro, and Kaarvel.

As arranged on the flight, Kresh gave her orders as she walked first down the ramp,

"Makrill and party, to me in my office, please!

"Julie, Paul, Chris, find your parents please, and tell them they're invited for lunch!

"Simeon, your Mother and Father want to see you inside the ship!"

As all rushed to obey her orders, Kallen asked Kresh, "But how did the children know it was safe when they saw you?"

"Easy! When we arrived the unicorns told the foals what to expect, and the foals told their riders!"

***

After a lunch which was easily the best meal any of the Godhe could remember having, and after allowing the six of them of talk freely, Rebel reported that they were all now staunch allies against Krast and Oistrach.

Merlin officially handed over the conduct of the war to Marcus.

"I know you say I've done well, but much of what I've done was at your suggestion, Marcus, and I'm copying your own daughter here. We need a Leader, and you're elected!"

Catching on to the reference to the Diary, Tyana and Laura joined in chorus with Merlin saying,

"So, Mr Leader, what do we do?"

"First, I'd like to make it impossible for Krast to use this island as a Base again. Any ideas, Kresh?"

"The main shield, which the children turned off for you .... you were right, by the way, I wouldn't have believed what they did if you'd told me ... goes down to the seabed. It can be controlled from an approaching ship, but I can program it to respond only to one voice!"

"Do so, please. Make it your own!"

"You trust me that much? After what I did?"

Tyana hugged her old enemy and answered for Marcus, "Yes, we trust you that much! So don't let us down!

"If your ships are now keyed to the Commander's voice, can we use the one left outside?"

"I have access to any, so yes! What do you want us to do?"

Marcus answered, "Even if there is a communicator here, I don't want it used. The children sent Plathe off to get help, and by the time it comes I want this war to be over so that those who need punishing will receive it here, not on their home world where it can go wrong!"

"We really are sorry!"

"No one's blaming you, Kresh, but it remains a fact that we can't rely on your Old Ones to do the job properly!"

"Tyana, please 'call' for any of our possessions we want from the *Unicorn Witch*.

"You four, thank you for volunteering. The *'Witch'* is yours to keep. Please get aboard her and we'll 'push' her off the beach for you."

Rix's brother, the captain of the volunteer crew wanted to know, "But won't you want her again, Sir? She's the finest craft we've ever seen!"

"No, Tom. In future we'll travel as you came here. The very least the Godhe owe us is a Presidential Spaceship!"

"Makrill, and company, please collect any personal possessions you want with you, and any you feel our other guests in Camelot may want. As soon as you're all ready we'll leave.

"Merlin, please have Zoltan arrange that all who can be spared from the towns come to Camelot for a meeting, including bringing all the spaceships.

"Can anyone think of anything we've overlooked here?"

Kresh did. "Just one possibility, Marcus. There are some two dozens of our barrier generators here in the stores. If we take them we could defend each of the main towns in New America without keeping one of our ships there, and protect each new one we retake in Europe. "I presume you intend to take the fight to them, now?"

Marcus picked her up, swing her round and kissed her on both cheeks. "With you now on our side, I certainly do!"

Kresh blushed, caught sight of her reflection and commented,

"I didn't know we could do that. It must be mixing with you humans!"

<< Dad, this is Star! >>

<< Yes, Star? >>

<< What about the man Julie woke up, Frank Baron? >>

<< Thank you, Star. We'd all forgotten him. >>

"Sorry, Everyone, a slight delay. Star points out that if we leave and close the barrier to all except Kresh, we'll be abandoning Frank Baron the new arrival in deep sleep. The children put him back to sleep, but I feel that we ought to take him with us just in case anything goes wrong with the machine he's on.

"Could that happen, Kresh?"

"They never have broken down, but anything's possible! Normally it wouldn't matter as an alarm would go off, but with no one here to hear it......."

"Laura, you're wearing white, and he thinks he's in hospital, would you let Simeon take you to him and wake him, please?"

As instructed Simeon stood behind Frank and out of his line of sight so that when he recovered Laura was the first person he saw.

"That's a relief!" he said. "I dreamt that I woke once before and met four children who could do real magic!

"Wait a minute.... this room.... it's the same as in my dream and you... you're not in a nurse's uniform are you? Where am I, and what's happening, or is this still a dream?"

Laura took his hand and mentally calmed him then, still holding him said, "I'll tell you where we are in a few minutes, but first let me say that about seven years ago my son and I woke like you have, and my last memory had been going for a ride in Central Park, New York. I'm now happier than I've ever been in my life, and so is my son, who is also here.

"We're not on Earth at all, Frank!"

"You know my name? Yes, I suppose you would from the papers in my wallet..........Did...did you say 'Not on Earth'?"

"No, Frank, I know your name because you gave it to my younger son Simeon and his friends. Mine is Laura, and Yes, I said 'Not on Earth'…. That wasn't a dream. Look behind you, and you'll see."

"Hello, again, Mr Baron."

"Please come with us," continued Laura, "and we'll give you something to eat and drink, then a ride in what you'd call a Flying Saucer. Full explanations will have to be given later when we've a bit more time."

<< Laura! >>

<< Yes, my Darling Princess? >>

<< Zoltan suggests that for now we should not let our Godhe friends know that they made a mistake bringing Frank here. If they ever do manage to develop something to stop our magic it would be amusing to have them test it on Frank! >>

"Frank, I'm going to introduce you to the rest of my family in a moment, but also to six members of a race called The Godhe. Will you please humour me by not saying anything in front of those six to let them know that you found it strange that the children could do 'magic'?"

"But…."

"Please! It really is important. We're in the middle of a war here! Just trust me for now. We'll explain everything when we get back to Camelot!"

They had now arrived back with the main group, and Laura continued, "Everyone, I'd like you to meet Frank Baron, from London.

"Frank, the children you already know. This is Merlin Pendragon, my husband, Simeon's father, and President of this world; my elder son Marcus and his wife Tyana, who are the parents of the other three. Marcus has taken Tyana's family name here of Counter.

"And these six good people are from the race which, for many thousands of years, has tried to preserve Earth's magical creatures by bringing those in danger here, a world we call Refuge. I'll introduce them after you've eaten, and you've had time to think about all this!"

Marcus added, "Just look out of the window and you'll see several unicorns and a couple of flying saucers. That should prove to you that we're not pulling your leg!"

While Frank ate, he answered a few questions from Marcus, mainly about conditions on Earth, but then when he'd relaxed a little Marcus asked, "Were you always a magician, Frank?"

"No! I went to University to take a degree in Engineering, but I changed in the first year, and ended up teaching I.T.. You know, computers and the like.

I got made redundant in the late 80's and found I could make a lot more money on stage. I could make all my own equipment for one thing. There! I've had more than enough for now! The children fed me, you know, so if you're waiting for me, let's go!"

Chapter Seven

As he had done so often before, Merlin glanced at the gavel and it banged to bring the hastily convened meeting to order. All the 'captured' Godhe were present, together with representatives from each town with Electra taking notes. Thomas had elected to remain in Abinger but was present mentally, as were Mandrake, Shinlu, Carlos, and Sophia. This was not known to the Godhe, and anything they had to say would appear to come from Tyana or Marcus.

"Marcus, please summarize our position for everyone, and I formally put you in charge of dealing with the remaining members of the Godhe who are here on Refuge for illegal purposes."

Marcus looked around at the odd assembly whilst he sorted out his thoughts, deciding they all had one thing in common, shown by his first word.

"Friends, as most of you know, we have to either protect ourselves for another twelve to thirteen days and then let the Galactic Patrol deal with Oistrach and Krast, or we can tackle the job ourselves.

"I'm in favour of the latter course, as we don't yet know what's happening in Europe and a delay could matter. If anyone disagrees, then NOW is the time to say so!"

<< I can detect no thought against us doing the job. >>

"You all know that Krast's first move was to kill Aristo, then take captive four of our children and unicorn foals in an effort to prevent Tyana and myself interfering. She did not know that in trying to imprison those particular four children she had made her most serious mistake so far and the island is now lost to her. Neither could she have anticipated the development we've made in magic which means that there are now many with even more power than Tyana and myself.

"Krast and Oistrach now have either eleven or twelve ships, depending upon whether one was, or was not, destroyed during the attack on Abinger."

168

"It was!" declared Kresh.

"Thank you, so she has eleven! We have seven, and also twenty-four defensive screens, ten of which are already in place in our principal towns, leaving fourteen spare to use in Europe.

"With odds like that it's obvious that we wouldn't win a straight fight, so I have no intention of trying. The near deaths of both Merlin and his wife Laura, and the deaths of Aristo and seven of the crew of the spacecraft are more than enough!

"I thank again members of the Godhe who have joined us, but whilst I welcome your advice, you are reminded again that this is our world, and these people are to face our justice. Any of you who wish to take no part in any action against your fellow Godhe may return to being our guests until your Galactic Patrol arrives and I promise that we'd have no hard feelings."

There were no takers for this offer.

"Good! Thank you again!

"Thomas managed a successful defence against three of Krast's ships using only six Whites including himself, and we believe that that represented the worst she could do. The details of that are known to those who need to know and all of our towns are similarly prepared.

"Thus I'm confident that we will have no further trouble here, but we urgently need to know what has been happening in Europe, and especially the whereabouts of Oistrach and Krast.

"I propose retaking Europe one town at a time, starting by making Paris secure. Our actions will then depend upon what we learn in the next one we free.

"I've already explained to our Godhe friends that the most powerful of our witches usually have two familiars, and are thus known as Triads. Only these will be involved in our first trip to Europe for which we'll use four ships.

"Tyana and I will lead. We may need the services of a Healer, so I ask that either Megan or Melanie, neither of whom is here, together with five other Triads join us. I also ask for four Godhe crews of two, one member of each of which may be required to stay in Europe to operate a protective barrier.

"Kresh, you may head one if you wish! I make you responsible for selecting the other three. All willing please report to me or to Kresh as appropriate in the area outside the walls of Camelot in three hours. Thank you!"

Again Merlin caused his gavel to silence the dozens of conversations that sprang up.

"I have not yet wound up this meeting!"

"I remind you that whilst not everyone can go to Europe, those who stay here will still have their parts to play. It will be of no use saving our friends across the water if in the meantime Krast wreaks havoc here!

"I intend to stay in New America myself, and I wish Magdalena, Thomas, and Gabbie to do likewise. They have each shown an understanding of tactics which I may need with Marcus in Europe. I would also appreciate the continued help from most of our European colleagues in New Salem.

"Meeting closed! You may go!"

***

All signs of the strain of the last three weeks vanished from Lindsey's face as Zoltan passed on to her the news that not only were her grandchildren and Simeon safe, but had taken over their island prison and presented it to Tyana and Marcus. She lost no time in having Princess pass on the news.

Last to hear were Dusty and Darryl who were out on the range. They came rushing back to celebrate when contacted by Lucky and Victrix. Thus when the news came that Merlin wanted a Healer with the party to go to Europe they heard that together too.

"I'll go!" announced Megan and Melanie as one person.

"There's no contest, Megan," continued Melanie. "Quite apart from the fact that you have Caroline to think about, this is my chance to do something to thank Zoltan for accepting me as he did. You're prepared to go; but I really want to!"

"But," said Darryl, and that was as far as he got before a look from Melanie stopped him. She went on, "Darryl, are you going to try to stop Tyana or Marcus going?"

"Of course not! …… I wouldn't dare!"

"But they've only just got their children back, so why not?"

"Marcus's knowledge is needed, and I know Tyana will insist on going if he does. I was just being selfish, I guess. I don't want to lose you!"

"I'll be back! Look, just suppose that you had to decide to send either Laura, Megan, or me, who would you give the job to?"

"You win! I'd send you, simply because the other two have children. Do be careful, though, Lace. Krast is a killer. From what I've overheard she tried to destroy Abinger completely, and only Thomas's quick thinking and planning saved it."

"Krast is a killer? You told me yourself that Tyana has killed with her bare hands. If Marcus was a Chicago cop he's probably had to kill a few. And just in case you've forgotten already…So have I!

"Now, help me collect a few things together, then Cindy, Victrix, and I have a date with a spaceship!"

"There are a couple of hours yet. Can we spend a little time together? Let's go for a walk. I need to be doing something… there's something I've got to say to you, but I'm not very good at explaining my feelings."

They walked slowly away from the house to sit on a paddock rail and watch Timber, Ebony, Lucky, Victrix, Bess, and Cindy grazing, and, guessed Darryl, chatting about him and how shy he was.

"I want you to promise me that you'll take no risks. You're going up against what are probably the worst criminals the Godhe have, who'll make the ones you told us about back on Earth look like angels. Quite simply, Lace, I love you and I don't want you to go, but if you must, then I want you back in one piece!"

<< *Remember saying that you'd only tell me his feelings if I'd let you tell him mine, Victrix?* >>

<< *Of course!* >>

<< *Well what are mine, if you're so clever?* >>

<< *You love him! You just haven't fully realised it yet!* >>

<< *Well what do I do about it? I've never even kissed a man before.* >>

<< *It's time you learned!* >>

"Aren't you going to say anything?" asked Darryl.

"Sorry, I was speaking with Victrix, just like you were with Timber that first evening I came. She said I should kiss you."

"That's funny, she told me the same thing!"

"She what?"

"Victrix….She said I should kiss you!"

Melanie tried to feel cross with her partner, but somehow Darryl's mouth looked so tempting with the slight smile as he admitted discussing her with Victrix that she just laughed instead and followed her advice. Much to her surprise the feel of his arms around her, combined with the new sensation to her mouth and the smell of a healthy young man made her feel … … … she couldn't put a word to it, but it certainly was… … different. For the first time since she was attacked in the tenement block She'd allowed a man to touch her, and as she thought about that she couldn't help tensing, which Darryl felt.

"Easy, Lace. I shan't forget what you went through back then. Eventually I hope we'll do more than kiss, but it can wait. After all, I've waited till now; a little longer won't hurt me!"

"You mean you're a .. a .."

"A virgin? If that term can be applied to a man, then yes I am. I'm not ashamed of it, and with Victrix partnered with you there'd be little point in hiding it would there?"

"Darryl, that's not the sort of information Victrix would pass on. She wouldn't even tell me how you really felt.

"Now, another kiss if you'd be so kind, then we must go!"

***

When Marcus arrived to see how many had volunteered he wasn't too surprised to find that the answer was 'Everyone!'

What did surprise him though was that by the time he'd made his selection from those available, Kresh presented him with a table which She'd produced in seconds using one of the ship computers showing how she proposed crewing the vessels:

Makrill & Kaarvel	Kallen & Corda
MARCUS, Rebel(U), Swift(E)	SHAENA, Lady(U), Hawka(F)
ANGUS, Thor(U), Battler(H)	BRIDIE, Rainbow(U), Glayva(H)
Kresh & Fairo	Merco & Wanda
TYANA, Karim(U), Caress(E)	QAMAR, Sabre(U), Storm(E)
MELANIE, Victrix(U), Cindy(H)	HAMMID, Pegasus(U), Khan(H)

(U)=Unicorn   (H)=Horse   (E)=Eagle   (F)=Falcon

"I've done five copies! One for each ship, and one to leave with Merlin. The new man, Baron, has been given a radio tuned to the ships' frequency, and can work it for Merlin. As you can see, although the ships could carry everyone in one if needed, I've spread the load. Two unicorns, One Horse, One bird in each. Is that satisfactory, Sir?"

"It is, Kresh. And the name is Marcus!"

He was smiling as he said it, and Kresh visibly relaxed.

"Everybody aboard, please. It's almost tea time here, but we can arrive in time for a late lunch in Paris. Carlos and Sophia have one prepared, and Paris is still as Kresh left it. … No barriers and no Godhe!"

Watching the four ships depart Merlin sensed that he was being watched and had it confirmed.

<< The new man, Baron, wishes to ask you something, Merlin. >>

"Well, Frank, do you think you might get to like it here?" he asked as he walked up to the man.

"Will I be allowed to stay, Sir? That's more to the point!"

"Call me Merlin! Since the Godhe are not being told that they've made a mistake, and I doubt if it's the first they've made, that decision is mine, and as far as I'm concerned it's yours. Do you want to stay? From being what everyone on Earth thought of as a magician you've become the only non-magician, as it were. It can't be very nice for you to say the least. If you want to go back when this is over, I'm sure it could be arranged, and you'd wake to think it was all a dream!"

"There's nothing back there for me! I'd just broken up with my girl friend, and I've got no living family. If you can find me something useful to do, I'd like to stay!

"Is there anywhere I can't go?"

Merlin laughed. "If a place looks as though it's private, then ask. Otherwise, go anywhere you please, and do whatever you like. just ask anyone who looks over eight years old for help when you're hungry or thirsty and they'll give you what you wish."

"But I'm supposed to keep near the radio to help you keep in contact with the four ships."

"This will take some time for you to get used to, Frank, but even when they're on the other side of the world, Zoltan here can still speak with any of the unicorns, that's one reason they're with them, and they in turn can share their thoughts with the humans."

"What's the other reason for them being there?"

Instead of answering, Merlin took him to where Hammid's wife, Salome, was still watching the sky into which he'd disappeared.

He introduced her and to give her something to do asked her to spend an hour or so giving Frank the briefing usually given to new arrivals, especially including the classification Bronze through Ivory. Also she was to include a history of the last month, and then have him read '*Unicorn Witch*'.

"When she's done that, Frank, let me know if you still want to stay. Life here isn't always fun! We haven't even got electricity!"

'*No,*' thought Frank, '*but you soon could have!*'

***

The trip to Paris was uneventful and the four ships landed in full view of the town, activated their barriers, and a small party rode in to join Sophia and Carlos. As Kresh had explained to Tyana on the way across, their ships could detect each other when invisible, so there was no point in using that facility.

Kresh was allowed to go into Paris mainly to reassure Carlos and Sophia, or rather Javelin and Lotus Blossom, of her conversion and she rode Victrix whilst Melanie rode Cindy. The others were promised that they could visit the next day but as this was to be a social event rather than part of the war they had to be content with a promise of food to be sent out. Bridie and Angus had not seen a dragon before, but after a brief conversation through their partners Rainbow and Thor they soon understood why Marcus and Tyana counted Mandrake and Shinlu as friends.

After dinner Kresh told Sophia, "I really did want to find out just how your magic works, you know. That part wasn't an act. I'm truly sorry about the rest but it was just that the treatment I had made anything Krast suggested seem normal. I didn't know such a thing was possible!

"How much did you lie when I was questioning you?"

Sophia laughed, then replied, "We didn't exactly lie. We just conveniently forgot to tell the whole truth. You got truthful answers to the questions you asked."

"Give me an example, if you don't mind."

"Well, for instance you asked me if I could manage the sort of loads Tyana has moved around, and I told you that I'd never even moved a quarter of that.

"That was true enough. Of course I didn't add that I could have if I'd wanted!"

"But what about turning over a spaceship? They weigh over one hundred tons!"

The others had been following this exchange and when Sophia was wondering just how much to tell her, Tyana came to the rescue.

"If you have fifty people, that's only handling two tons each, and Sophia could manage that easily enough!

"When this is all over, I'll answer what questions we decide we can, Kresh, but please don't ask until then. It's not that we don't trust you, but supposing you get captured by Krast....

"Could you resist telling her anything she asks?

"No, don't bother to answer, and nobody's blaming you, but it's a fact that until you've had expert treatment on your home world or, better in my opinion Krast is no longer around, we won't know, will we? We believe that Princess undid the damage, but let's be sure. Do you mind returning to the ship now? Victrix will take you, or Karim if you fancy a change."

Kresh went back on Victrix, deep in thought, and the planning could start. Cantor and Vernique, tipped off by Rebel walked in to join them, the former asking as he entered, "What's the plan, Marcus? I presume you have one!"

"Only the outline of one. I propose to fly to about fifty miles from Madrid, keeping low all the way, then travel by horse and unicorn to take a look.

"We know there's a barrier, as the unicorns can't hear anything from there, so we're going to tunnel under it. What happens next depends upon what we see!"

"How much d'ye trust yon Lassie from the Godhe?" asked Bridie.

"Aye, I wondered that meself!" added Angus.

Marcus looked to Tyana for an answer, as the Scots had known her all her life.

"She allowed Karim's dame, Princess to merge fully with her mind when we first captured her, and that means she could have no secrets from us. The only danger would be if Krast got hold of her as Kresh just may still have to obey a direct order from her, so we'll keep her within sight at all times…not because we can't trust her, but just to be sure Krast has had no opportunity to speak to her.

"We'll take Makrill, Kallen, Kresh, and Merco as Commanders with Kaarvel in reserve and Wanda to accompany us when we leave the ships.

"Now that the Parisians know they're on our side, the other Godhe can spend the day first setting up a barrier of our own, keyed to go down to let any of the four commanders in, and then they can relax and get to know a few people."

"Is that wise?" asked Sophia.

"I intend to insist on no secrecy from the Godhe in future, so the more people who know them, the easier that will be to achieve!"

***

Having left at dawn and flown at no more than fifty feet all the way from Paris, the four ships settled down near enough to trees to provide some cover. With Wanda riding Victrix, all eight Triads were soon below the horizon and looking from behind trees to where Madrid should have been visible.

"I've never seen anything like that before," announced Wanda as they looked at the perfect mirror finish on the dome.

Swift and Caress flew high over the three-mile diameter dome and reported, << It's all exactly as you can see from your side. There's no sign of any other space ships, but there are a few round depressions where some have been. >>

"No sign of life outside the dome, so all of you stay in the trees and watch whilst Tyana and I tunnel under if we can!"

Following Thomas's plan they started behind a copse, went down at ten degrees shoring as they went until below the barrier, then up at the same angle until about to break through.

"Tyana, Darling, take Rebel and Swift with you, and wait at the entrance whilst I push out this last bit."

"But I…"

"No 'buts'. I can still remember how to teleport out to where you are if necessary. Just make sure we can still 'talk' through Rebel and Karim before I do break out."

<< O.K. Marcus, we're out, and I can still hear you! >>

They heard the sound of the earth being thrown out into Madrid, just outside the wall they calculated, then from Rebel and Karim together, << He's gone!

<< They probably won't recognise an Eagle as connected with him. Take a look, please, Swift. >>

The tunnel, large enough to have a unicorn walk through, was just wide enough for the eagle's five feet wingspan, and he flew confidently down the slope, just reaching the lowest point before he was heard to stop flying, and Rebel/Karim told Tyana, << Now he's gone too! >>

'Don't panic!' thought Tyana, than told Karim, << Ask Victrix to bring Wanda here! >>

Quickly Tyana told her what had happened, and to Wanda the explanation was obvious.

"This dome must be filled with gas. When Marcus broke through it affected him, then it poured down into the low part of the tunnel and got your Eagle. How long can you hold your breath?"

"Long enough to go to get Swift and to see if you're right."

She almost did, too, collapsing only ten feet from the entrance on the way back. Quickly Wanda made two trips herself, one for Tyana, and then another for Swift. The both revived within five minutes in the fresh air.

"You're lucky, Tyana. It's obvious they've used the sleeping gas we use when transporting people. Marcus can be under for weeks or even months without harm."

"I don't want that! I want him out now!"

Wanda took charge and took the unhappy woman back to the main group in the trees by which time she'd thought out what to do.

"Each ship carries a suit to allow the engineer outside in space if needed. Wearing those two of them could probably get Marcus out, or if they could find the controls, turn off the barrier and let the gas out."

Rebel didn't wait for Tyana to decide, saying, << *Let me take you back to get some, Wanda!*

<< *Pegasus and Thor, come with me back to the ships! We've work to do. I'll explain on the way!* >>

"Who said that?"

"It was Rebel, Wanda," explained Tyana who had been included in what he'd said. "Aristo knew how intelligent unicorns are. You're only the second member of your race to be trusted with the knowledge. Please don't let us down!

"Off you go, and hold on tightly to his mane. This will be the fastest you've ever travelled on land!"

Watching his partner go off at close to three hundred miles an hour, Hammid asked, "Why Pegasus? Not that I mind, but Rebel seemed very sure who he wanted."

"You can always ask him when he gets back, but my guess is that he chose the largest and strongest. If you could see them I bet they're going straight through or over most of the obstacles we went around on the way here."

Time seemed to drag for Tyana, but really it was less than half an hour from Rebel leaving to Kaarvel and Makrill dragging Marcus out of the tunnel.

"How strong do you think that barrier is?" Tyana asked the two engineers whilst they waited for him to recover.

"The ones we've seen and used before are no stronger than the one round the ship Juno was in, but we've never seen one that's gas tight before."

"Did you see any of the people who live here?"

"No, but to be truthful we didn't look. We just got him out as soon as we could. It wasn't hard - - he'd dropped just inside the crater he'd made and that's still outside the wall. Look! He's coming round."

Marcus remembered nothing after mentally pushing the last of the earth out of his way and was quick to thank the three Godhe for their help. After listening to what Tyana had learned whilst he slept he looked at the space suits the Godhe were still wearing.

"I'd never get in one of those even if we mentally altered them. There's just not enough material, but I wouldn't be going into space, so all I need is an air supply and the helmet and visor.

"Can that be done, Kaarvel? And the other one for Tyana?"

"It could, but you'd be better off going in with one of us as we understand the controls for the barrier."

"He's right, My Love, and with everyone asleep you're hardly going into danger."

As they'd guessed, the gates to the town were open as they had been now for seven years, and everywhere they could see people asleep wherever they'd been when the gas was released. The centre of the dome was easy for Kaarvel to calculate and he was about to climb the steps leading to the small tower thought to house the generator when Marcus stopped him.

"Look! The door's half open, and I can't see why it should be.

"Back off a hundred yards or so, and I'll open it fully from there. Even better, we'll be behind at least two buildings when I do it."

Marcus did as he'd suggested and the door just opened. Nothing happened. He and Kaarvel started to return when Marcus saw that the door was slowly closing again and pulled Kaarvel back to safety. Once again, nothing happened.

"Don't you believe anything you see?" asked Kaarvel.

"It's an instinct that's saved my life before now! There's something not quite right about this. It looks too easy. I'll open it properly this time!"

As he said this he took the door off its hinges and threw it over the nearest building. An almighty explosion followed.

"Now that's more like the Krast I know, and that may not be the end of it. Let me go first, and keep well behind."

'Picking up' a couple of rocks each about his weight, Marcus walked them ahead of him into the room and 'jumped' them up and down a few times. Several guns fired across the room, and only when he could produce no more reaction did Marcus light a small fire in the middle of the room.

Two more weapons fired, this time they looked like some sort of laser.

"I think we're safe. You can turn it off, now. Give me five minutes to get back outside though, as I want the wind blowing in the right direction. Alright?"

"But how?..... Oh, never mind..... Five minutes it is."

A very relieved Rebel/Karim and partners welcomed him and had the explosions explained. One minute later, with eight triads having nothing better to do, a veritable gale was blowing away from them as the barrier went down. They reduced it to a slight breeze, then, when Kaarvel rejoined them went back to gale force.

As the citizens recovered it was quickly learned that they knew nothing. A couple of tests showed that they still had their theurgen, so Victrix took Wanda back to the ships, which all moved to land just outside the town wall. Kaarvel was left in Madrid with one of the spare barriers, which he mounted alongside the new one that he asked permission to study.

Marcus left the townspeople with the distinct impression that Kaarvel had singlehandedly freed them, thus ensuring him of a good welcome and any assistance he would ask for.

They quickly learned the little the people could tell them. A space ship had landed in the centre of the town and a barrier had gone up cutting off the unicorns from the rest of the world. All attempts to enter the ship or influence it had failed. A couple of hours later whilst they were still trying the barrier had changed in appearance and that was the last they knew until they woke up. The party returned to Paris in mid afternoon.

After introducing Carlos and Sophia to the delights of a barbecue, Marcus convened a meeting, including all the usual members and catalogued the day's events, calling for comments. As he'd expected, Mandrake had an explanation for what they'd found in Madrid. Marcus had had the same thought himself, but wanted to see if the idea was too far-fetched.

<< *If we start with the assumption that Krast and Oistrach simply want to strip the world of the hormone theurgen, it would make sense to put the towns to sleep, and then 'harvest' it without even waking anyone up. We should have thought of the possibility ourselves.*

<< *I suppose that's why you had the test run, Marcus?* >>

"It was."

<< *Did you think to check on whether the Healers were still there?* >>

"No, but I'll have Rebel do so now. Gabrielle's back on duty so he'll have her find out. Prancer can help."

<< *Shinlu, here, Everyone. Even using every Healer he can find and, harder, persuade to cooperate, Oistrach can only have had time to collect from one, or perhaps two towns. Tomorrow, you must find out the status of each, make secure any asleep like Madrid was, do what we can for any already milked, and hope we can handle the one they are actually working on now.*

<< *Merlin, the battle is here now. We need those ships you're holding in reserve, and any Godhe who'll come!*

<< *Just keep back Odel and Juno with the ship in Abinger for your own use. Please let us have the rest.* >>

"We'll do that today, Shinlu. Laura and I will come ourselves and......"

<< *No! We've enough Triads here, and you're needed in New America. Also Simeon needs his Dad!*

<< *It's the spaceships we want!* >>

"There's nothing quite like a dragon for putting one in one's place is there?" asked Merlin.

"I beg your pardon?"

Merlin realised that he'd spoken allowed and been overheard by Frank.

"Sorry, Frank. I'll explain shortly. Just give me a few minutes, please!

"Shinlu, will tomorrow morning for you, lunchtime for us be early enough?"

<< *It will! Please don't be offended, Colleagues across the sea, but it's very late where you are. Let us continue without you, and we'll speak again at the same time tomorrow.*

Goodnight! >>

"Goodnight, All.

"Now, Frank, you've read 'Unicorn Witch'?"

"I have. Is it factual? Are Tyana and Marcus really as powerful as that book makes them seem?"

"If anything they played down their own part when telling the story. The point is....Do you remember the conferences between those in Europe and we who were still here?"

"I do. Amazing is the only word for the unicorns' ability. If only they were intelligent too....even as they are I'd hate to have one for an enemy!"

"Well, I and several others were involved in just such a conference, and I accidentally spoke aloud."

Frank thought for a few moments, and Merlin thought that was the end of the matter, but then he heard, "Is it all top secret, or can you tell me about it?

"The reason for asking is that my work back on Earth, creating illusions, getting people thinking what I want them to think and so on is not that different from military strategy, which was a hobby. I was a member of a club which re-enacted battles using model soldiers. Perhaps I could help?"

After he'd heard of all that had happened in the last month, been allowed to read Simeon's diary, and been told of the conditions found in Madrid, he asked to be allowed to sleep on it. That, thought Merlin, was a good idea for all of them.

***

The children had gone to school riding the foals, escorted by Zoltan and Princess. Dusty and Darryl were out, as they put it, 'doing all the work', and both Megan and Laura had 'house calls' to do. Megan rode Bess, whilst Lucky was happy to take Laura.

This left Merlin to entertain Frank as they finished a second coffee. "Well, Frank," he started the conversation, "did sleeping on it help?

"Did you have any ideas we could use?"

Although Merlin's tone of voice indicated that such a thing was obviously out of the question Frank ignored that and replied, "I can't criticise what you've done so far. The fact is, what you've done has worked, so must be right.

"The one thing you've got to use against the advanced science of the Godhe is what you call your magic. Basically as I understand it you can

180

mentally affect the molecules of which matter is made up. You can order them to all go in one direction, instead of the random motion they usually have; you can order them to speed up their vibration so that they heat up, or slow it down so that they cool; you can change the arrangement of the atoms in an element to change its allotropic form, and you can rearrange the molecules in a compound if all the necessary radicals are there or available locally so that the nature of the material changes. Is that right?"

"Frank, I haven't the slightest idea! You might as well have spoken in a foreign language for all it meant to me.

"We can move things, heat them, cool them, and change them!"

"Why do you ask?"

"Because I need to know the limits before deciding how you could use your abilities to the full.

"So far you've been entirely defensive. With eleven ships against you, you need a way of putting most of them out of action, and that means you need to attack!"

Merlin looked at this latest arrival with more respect than he'd been feeling so far, having classified him as 'that mistake'.

"And, just how, may I ask, could we 'attack'?"

"The only idea I've had so far is to use your ability to move things to 'port' a bomb into each of the ships from a distance when they open the door to let the crew in."

"No Frank. There've been enough deaths!"

"It doesn't have to be that sort of bomb. It could, for instance, be a sleeping gas grenade but I'd need to study a ship first to be sure what would be needed, and I'd need to talk with some of the Godhe to learn just what materials we have to work with. I'm sure I could come up with something though, if you'll give me the chance.

"Apart from any other consideration, their whole defence is going to be against your magic. They won't be expecting the sort of thing I have in mind."

So it was that when Mandrake received his reinforcements, he also gained an experienced military tactician, engineer, and computer expert with a working knowledge of all the sciences.

<< *Marcus,* >> he said after interviewing Frank, << *this is probably the first time in history that the Godhe have sent a scientist here. Just from the few ideas he's had on the way over, he must be with the party that inspects Oistrach's ships when we spot them.*

<< First, though, we must secure any towns that are just asleep. I suggest the same approach as we used for Madrid. >>

"Where do you think we should start? Any ideas?" asked Tyana.

<< Put yourself in Oistrach's position, Tyana. You'd want to be as quick as you can, so you'd start at one end of the continent and work your way to the other, after putting them all to sleep, of course. >>

"But how do you account for Paris being different?"

<< Two reasons. First, I believe they really do want to know how your magic works, and it was as easy to run tests in Paris as anywhere else. Just consider what a criminal could do with the knowledge of how to duplicate magic scientifically.

<< Second, Paris was the only town where the Council Head had not already gone, leaving only the deputies in charge. If they were going to have trouble, it would be from Paris, where the leaders are known to be easily the most powerful on the continent. >>

Marcus looked first around his little group comprising Tyana, two dragons, two weres, two Godhe, Carlos and Sophia and the partners and familiars making up the triads. He then turned to the new arrival.

"Before I give my orders, I'd welcome any suggestions you may have, Frank. Merlin tells me you've made a study of old battles, and you're also a scientist, probably the first we've ever had."

"Thank you, Marcus," he replied as he studied the map, "I agree with Mandrake. If I were this Oistrach, I'd start by putting them all to sleep, then go to either Venicia or Istanbul, followed by Moscow or Baghdad.

"We can't really plan until we know which. I suggest using four ships, two each to free Roma and New Amsterdam. Obviously the same cautious approach you employed in Madrid should be used.

"During your last war, when you freed Europe you made many enemies, and they made a last stand at Venicia. Let's take the other three to Istanbul first. If they're all just asleep, but still with their what was it?"

"Theurgen!"

"Yes, theurgen, then let the others free Baghdad tomorrow as we'll be reasonably sure Oistrach is in Venicia or Moscow.

"Of course, I may be completely wrong, so each town must be approached on foot and with care!

"I'd like to go with the Istanbul party!"

Marcus now understood why Merlin had sent him Frank when all Mandrake had asked for were spaceships. He gave the necessary orders changing only the choice of ships, using three of the experienced crews for the search for Oistrach. He tested them all on their ability to spring the traps that may well be waiting for them.

Kresh and Fairo took Tyana and himself. Kallen and Corda carried Melanie and Frank. Merco and Wanda with Qamar and Shaena completed the party. This left plenty of sheer moving power with several Unicorn/Horse Triads available for the other four ships.

Travelling due South from Paris it was a simple matter to keep below fifty feet until fifty miles from Istanbul. On this occasion Marcus had all the Godhe stay with their ships and warned them to be prepared to defend themselves at a moment's notice. Victrix gladly provided transport for Frank, and soon the party was some five miles up river from the town. Caress and Swift flew on ahead, climbing as they did so to give them a view of the whole area.

"Just a few circular depressions outside the town, and the same sort of mirror dome that we saw at Madrid." stated Marcus.

"All forward to help with the tunnelling, please. Frank you'd better be the one who comes in with me, so that you can learn about the barrier controls. Put this hood on!"

Everything was as in Madrid. The same booby traps, even to the exploding door, and the same controls, which Frank needed no instruction in, pronouncing them 'obvious'.

Whilst the triad-induced wind was dispersing the gas Tyana and Karim returned to the ships to collect Fairo and one of the portable barriers. It was found that the sleepers still had their powers. All they'd lost was a month.

"Hammid, Angus, and Bridie can free Baghdad tomorrow. I want to see Venicia!" announced Marcus, and by mid afternoon the three ships were fifty miles to the East of it.

This time, Storm and Hawka made the flight, and reported many depressions from ships, but nothing to see except the same sort of barrier they'd become used to. Wanda assured them that had there been any ships in the depressions she would have detected them even from fifty miles.

"It looks as though Mandrake's guess was right, Marcus," commented Frank. "They've already been here, and gone on. May I suggest a variation this time?"

"Go on!"

"Dig your tunnel, but go in and bring out just one person who's asleep. If possible pick one who can stand the shock of having lost his or her powers just in case you're right about that too!"

"Yes, that's a good idea! Wait a moment or two."

<< *Rebel, please find someone who knows the unicorn partner of the Leader of Venicia, assuming he or she has one, and ask who we should waken.* >>

"This may take some time, Frank. I'm trying to find out from the Council Head who would be a good person to waken.

"In the meantime, we'll get our tunnel prepared, and, Tyana, could you have the ships brought here, please?"

Once they arrived, Marcus gathered all five Godhe around and asked, "Have any of you formed an idea of what Krast's overall plan was? I can't make any sense of it. She isolated the towns and obviously plans to milk the inhabitants of their theurgen as quickly as it can be done. We've more or less accounted for why Paris was different - they couldn't be sure that they could get away with it with Sophia and Carlos there. But what was supposed to happen if they'd succeeded in putting barriers around the towns in New America. Did you know what was happening on this continent?"

The other four looked to Kresh for an answer, who said, "I'm the wrong person to ask. We've already established that whatever Krast told me I'd have to accept.

"Wanda, you worked directly for Aristo, but Krast didn't know that. What did she tell you?"

"She told us that Aristo had been injured by the people of Paris, and that the healers wouldn't help him. She said, and we had no reason not to believe her, that she had authority to take whatever action she thought fit.

"We were involved in putting the barriers around each town, but knew nothing about any of the new gas-tight type. We were also told that Paris was a special case as Kresh had been given a research assignment.

"She told us that the barriers were only to be there until she'd had time to visit each town and explain how things were going to be in future.

"We were given orders that each town in New America should be treated in the same way, but as you know that proved to be harder than expected."

Frank had been as attentive as anyone and told the Godhe, "You realise you'd have been next on their list of people to put to sleep - - - - - - permanently, don't you?

"Just how much would a world-full of theurgen get them when they sold it?"

Wanda answered, "We'd have been next? I'd rather not think about that. I've read the transcript of the trials when Oistrach, Jove, and their crews were brought home before. The amount they used to collect each year then would keep one person in luxury for life. This time it looks as though they were going for many thousands of times as much.....You could buy several whole worlds for less!

"You really think they'd have harmed us?"

Frank studied her name badge, and then answered, "Wanda, I don't mean to be rude, but from what I read in '*Unicorn Witch*' and what I've seen here, I'm sure that there's never been a more gullible set of people than you lot.

"A good con man from Earth would have everything you own within a few days!

"Just think about it. With the job done here, the inhabitants asleep, and all of you dead with the bodies removed, there'd be nothing to trace any crime to Krast and Oistrach.

"I'm sorry, Kresh, but I'm sure even you would have been included too. It's the only explanation that fits the facts we've got.

"Don't you agree, Marcus?"

"Well, you worked it out more quickly than I did, Frank, but I have to agree with every word.

"Strangely enough, Wanda, gullible was the word I used to describe you all when I first met Aristo all those years ago.

<<Message from Thor, Marcus. Angus says Roma and New Amsterdam secured. May they have permission to move on to Baghdad? >>

<< Tell them 'Yes' - All four ships to go! Return to Paris for a meeting afterwards. >>

No sooner had this good news been passed on than Marcus got the message he'd been waiting for, *<< The leader is Johann Schmidt, and we're in luck. He was only Gold when he went to New America and had no familiar, but a unicorn, King, recognised his ability, agreed to change his own name to Kaiser, recruited an eagle now called Phoenix, and they're a triad. Apparently Kaiser had seen Thomas and Tallons with Jet and been impressed.*

<< We're to look for an eleven-year-old girl with red hair in a house very near the main gates, or rather where the main gates used to be before Tyana removed them. I've got a mental picture of her.

<< Johann says that whomever we pick it's going to be a gamble, but that girl is his daughter and Kaiser will be able to let him speak with her if Rebel makes the contact. It sounds like as good a choice as any. Don't ask about her mother, though! I did, and she died giving birth to Greta. A breech, and of course it was before Megan's time. Johann's sister and her husband will be in the same house. >>

"Put your hood on, Frank. I know who to get!"

Fortunately, Greta was where forecast, and was soon outside and reviving. Melanie needed no prompting and was sitting by her side so that at the first sign of panic she was able to take her hand. The effect was instantaneous, and she looked around the strange collection of people, particularly at the Godhe men the like of whom she'd never seen.

"What's happened to me? Why are we out here outside town? Where's Uncle Klaus? I was with him!"

Tyana knelt down in front of her, whilst she had Karim ask Melanie to continue holding her.

"Greta, all your family is alright, as far as we know, and we're going to make it possible for you to speak with your father in New America in a moment.

"My name is Tyana Counter. Have you heard of me?"

Greta's eyes opened extra wide as she realised why she knew the name.

"The....The Unicorn Witch? Really? You've come to see me?"

"I have! Please be patient and try to answer my questions before I explain.

"Do you remember how life was when you had a King, and only he had any magic ability?"

"Of course I do! It was you who saved us all. How could we forget?"

"I want you to bring that stone my husband Marcus is holding to your own hand. No, not yet! I'll tell you when."

"But why?"

"It's just possible that everyone in Venicia has had their powers stolen again, but if they have, I want you to be very brave, and I promise you we'll get your theurgen back and restore them!

"Now, when you're ready, Melanie here will let go of you for a moment, and we'd like you to try to bring the stone.

"This is the hard part for you. When some of the people in New America had theirs stolen, they could still do a little magic, so when you try first it's almost certain you'll think you're alright. Do you understand?"

The girl nodded, Melanie released her, and they saw her turn to face Marcus and hold her hand out to catch the stone. It came to her and Marcus called it back. They repeated this three times then on the fifth attempt it stayed in Marcus's hand and she began to sob quietly, Melanie's cue to take her in her arms and sooth her.

"Remember, Greta, Tyana promised that you'll get them back. Try to stop crying. Your father's going to be upset enough when he hears the news as it is. I want him to be proud of the way you handle it."

Tyana took over again, cashing in on the hero-worship the girl had shown, "Of all the people in Venicia he thought you were the one most likely to be able to keep in control!"

"He....(sob).... He did?"

<< Greta, my name is Karim. I'm Tyana's unicorn familiar. You've heard of me, too? >>

"Of course I have!"

<< Well, your father has a unicorn familiar himself now. His name is Kaiser, and he's going to help him speak with you. You only need to think your answers; you don't need to speak them. Try with me now, for practice. >>

<< Like this? >>

<< Exactly like that! Say Hello to Kaiser! >>

When Johann had finished his chat with Greta she wanted to know, "What happens now, Tyana? Will you wake everyone up in Venicia as you did me?"

"Do you thing that's a good idea, Greta?"

"I did at first, but Papa says it would be better to leave them asleep until you can get their theurgen back. I think he's right!"

"And what about you, do you want to stay with us?

"Or would you rather sleep again and know nothing until this is all over?"

This was a difficult question for a girl only eleven years old, but after a few minutes she answered, "I'm tempted to go back to sleep, but I'd like to stay with you if I may. I'll be able to tell my people just what you did for them when it's over.

"I don't think my friends would ever forgive me if I missed the chance to spend some time with you, Marcus, Karim, and Rebel. You've not been to see us since you sent things from the sky to break down the wall, have you?"

"Well…..no, but only because I've had my own life to lead. There was no need. The job was done. I'm sorry."

Greta was now embarrassed. "I wasn't criticising. It's just that since you haven't been back, you won't know just how the people, especially the teenagers, practically worship the name Tyana. There are more Tyanas under six years old than any other name here!"

"Fame at last, Darling!" chuckled Marcus, then spoke to the whole group.

"Everyone back in the ships, please! Karim, would you be good enough to give Greta a ride?"

As he asked he swung Tyana behind himself on Rebel.

<< *Would you like that, Greta? Remember, just think the answer.* >>

<< *Yes, please, Karim!….Oh, Yes, please!* >>

As they trotted the short distance to the ships, Tyana said,

"Greta, I'm going to ask Kresh, one of The Old Ones who's helping us to introduce the others and to tell you what's happened whilst you were asleep. Is that alright with you?"

Greta nodded and smiled at Kresh, still exhilarated from the short ride. Back in Paris, the conference called was unnecessary, as the next action was obvious to all, even to the slow thinking Godhe. As Mandrake reported to Merlin and those in New America, << *We presume they're in Moscow. Tomorrow we'll find out for sure!* >>

Chapter Eight

Kresh's ship, with Wanda, the Tyana, Marcus, and Melanie triads, and Frank left Paris after a leisurely breakfast and were able to land before the sun rose on Moscow as it was over 40° Longitude further West.

Greta, who'd been inseparable from Kresh since their introduction begged to be allowed to come, but Marcus had felt he had to be firm and refuse. "I promise you can come next time, Greta." he'd finally been driven to say to stop her crying.

Leaving the Godhe in the ship the humans first galloped on unicorn or horse, and then crept with even more caution than previously used to get within a mile of the town. Swift did a fly-over at five thousand feet.

<< If they're not here now, they've certainly been here, Marcus, Look! >>

<< Yes, Thank you, Swift. Come back, please, I don't want them getting suspicious. >>

For Frank's benefit Marcus spoke aloud, "There are six circular depressions spaced out around the town.

"Rebel, please ask Kresh if she can detect any ships here."

<< She says 'Yes' Marcus. At least six, possibly more.

<< And she warns that she has no idea whether the mirror barrier stops her detecting any inside it. Incidentally she's now completely relaxed when I talk to her. I like her! >>

<< We all do, now! >>

"Well, Frank? What do you suggest?"

"That's easy! We do what we came for. We watch and hope to learn. It's not very exciting, but until we know a lot more than we do, that's what I advise!

"Whilst we wait, tell me,

"Have you thought any more about what's going to happen to me when this is all over? I asked Merlin if I could stay and he didn't say no, but then, he didn't say yes either."

Marcus had thought, but instead of answering the question, he asked one of his own. "What would you do in our place, Frank? We have tens of thousands of people with what we call 'magic' powers, and then we get you."

"That's not fair..... Alright! I'll answer as objectively as I can.

"The obvious worry is that if I have children here it would be detrimental to the stock. Well, first, who'd want me? The only man who couldn't even go shopping for food? Second, I'm sure that the theurgen gene is dominant. Do you understand that?"

"Yes," answered Marcus and Melanie together, but "No!" said Tyana, "and that goes for the unicorns, eagles, and Cindy!"

"Cindy? You mean the horse? What's she got to do with it?"

Tyana laughed. "I'm afraid Merlin and Marcus haven't been entirely honest with you, Frank. If you're going to be able to advise us, you really will have to know all that we have on our side, as it were.

"When we take a familiar, such as Cindy with Melanie, then she acquires human intelligence, or at least shares Melanie's when near her which is almost the same. This also applies to the eagles. When I took Karim as my familiar it was the first time a unicorn had agreed to be annexed with a human. We knew that unicorns were intelligent, but only when I got to know them well did we realise that if anything they're more so than humans, so if it works in reverse then I'm probably brighter than I was before. Who knows?

"The unicorns who are annexed become as powerful as their human partners in their own right!"

She paused to let that sink in, and watched as Frank studied first the unicorns and finally the others and revised his opinion of the animals as he'd thought of them.

"That's not all! You remember when Swift took a flight over Moscow?" He nodded.

"Well Marcus could see what Swift saw just as though he was there.

"And if you think that's amazing, how about this? What Marcus could see, so could Rebel, and anything Rebel can see he can give to Karim and Victrix simultaneously, so Melanie and I could also see it. Unfortunately Caress and Cindy couldn't be included, but they got a description of it.

"Now, please tell me....What's a dominant gene?

"And make it simple!"

"Consider Julie, your daughter. She started life as a fertilised egg, and half of the things that make her what she is come from you, and half from Marcus. You know that much?"

Tyana nodded and Frank continued, "Marcus's mother has power, but as far as we know his father didn't. Right, Marcus?"

"I'm sure he didn't!"

"So when the half which came from Marcus's father competed with that from his mother, the theurgen gene from Laura won the battle, and so he has power.

"Think how many times people must have come from Earth when only one of their parents had power, yet here their own children always do!

"I'm sure, therefore, that if I'm lucky enough to find a wife here, my children will be as you are, or at least as their mother, whoever she may be, is.

"Does everyone understand?"

As he asked this, Frank turned to Tyana, Rebel, Karim, Victrix, Cindy, Swift, and Caress in turn, getting a nod from each. These nods convinced him that he was not, as he'd half suspected, having his leg pulled.

"Next question! What use could I be? And why let me stay?

"If all I could do was to develop electrical generators so that you can have lighting at home during the dark evenings, I think that would be enough to pay for my keep!

"I believe that the days of Refuge's isolation in the universe are coming to a forced ending, and a scientist will be useful to you. Frankly, several would be even better!"

"I couldn't agree more!" stated Marcus. "I know that Merlin is finally coming round to that way of thinking too.

"In fact if you think back, he actually told you that the decision on whether you stayed was to be your own. He asked me to help you decide, and the easiest way of doing that seemed to be to let you argue the case.

"Now, can we by any chance get back to dealing with Oistrach and Krast?"

"Of course, but whilst we wait and watch, will you run through all the ideas you used against them when defending your own towns?"

Frank listened with increasing wonder as Marcus listed their actions from the turning over of the first ship to try to land in Camelot to the attempts to destroy Abinger thwarted by Gabbie and Thomas and resulting in Kresh's capture and conversion. He was particularly interested in the way Tess had handled the New Salem ship, said so, and then went on, "That gives us another way of taking out those six ships. I had thought that we'd have to wait until someone came out to open them, then either destroy them or plant gas inside, but from what you say we can just bury them and recover them for our own use when convenient.

"Let's have some power limits so that I can do the math.

"Forget about what you might call 'ordinary folk', how much can a triad with unicorn/bird handle?"

"When Thomas and Jet were experimenting near Kissimmee, they found that thirty to forty tons was about their limit, but Tyana and Karim moved that when just a pair seven years ago. We could probably each handle, say fifty tons, but when we've worked together the synergy factor pushes up the limit by about half."

"And how about when it's unicorn/horse?"

"At least double! Angus's triad on its own could just about equal Tyana and me together, whilst Melanie's would be only slightly weaker.

"We haven't worked out the exact relationship yet but it's roughly in proportion to total triad body weight, then add a bit."

"Terrific! Roughly proportional to body weight and then add a bit! What a way to run a war!"

Marcus felt he had to object to this.

"What you're forgetting, Frank is that we didn't plan to become more powerful and design the ideal triad on a drawing board. Zoltan wanted to help Merlin, and so the first one was formed. First Thomas, then Tyana and I thought that having a bird as a third member, especially a fighting one like an eagle was the best possible, mainly because of the advantages of high flying and good eyesight. I don't know how well you know your birds, but birds of prey like eagles and hawks have a central area of vision that is like having a telescope to the eye. They can recognise individual people from ten thousand feet up! Sheer power isn't everything, you know. It just happened that Angus already had a very heavy horse for a familiar, and bonded with an even heavier unicorn. He didn't set out to break any records!"

Frank managed to sound contrite as he replied, "Marcus, we haven't time to start bickering. I was just thinking aloud! "When the New Salem triads buried the ship there were twelve of them?"

"That's right!"

"Back to the ships, everyone, I need to do some trials!"

Marcus looked at Tyana to see her smile, shrug her shoulders and nod, then he told Frank, "You seem to have some sort of plan, which is more than I have at the moment, so I'm now appointing you General, Field Marshall, or whatever you want to call yourself. Do you accept?"

"I'd be glad to, but I don't need a title, I'm just happy to have the chance to help!"

Back at the spaceships, Frank had one moved to the centre of an open area and had the crew leave.

"Now, Marcus, first just on your own I want you to create alongside that ship a crater as large as you can manage, putting the spoil on the side away from the ship."

<< *Well, Rebel, Tallons, you heard the man. I think I know what he has in mind, so try for a hundred feet in diameter, the same as the ship, and forty feet deep.....NOW!* >>

The ground moved slightly, but that was all.

"That time, Frank, we tried for the same sized hole they had in New Salem. Now we're going to reduce it in depth five feet at a time until something happens."

The movement of the ground increased each time until Marcus managed a hole the diameter of the ship and about ten feet deep. He then replaced the spoil in the crater, obviously resulting in a mound of earth above ground level. Frank smiled and muttered to himself, but Marcus couldn't decide whether he was pleased or not.

"Your turn, Tyana!" he said. "Please try to move what Marcus has just put back!"

This she did, and managed a little deeper.

"How do you explain that, Marcus?" asked Frank. "That wasn't in proportion to body weight, let alone the 'add a bit'."

"I can give you three suggestions. One, Tyana has been using her powers for most of her twenty-five years, whilst I've only been here just over seven. Two, I've always believed her to be more powerful than me, and this just demonstrates it; and three, she was going in cold, whereas I'd already tried several times to move more and failed."

Frank had Melanie try whilst Marcus and Tyana rested and she, as Marcus had forecast, managed about twenty feet. He then had Marcus and Tyana try together, and they produced a hole some twenty-five feet deep.

Another rest, then finally, all three triads worked together and achieved what was needed. The space ship was dropped into a crater below it and the spoil piled on top in one movement just as Magdalena had done.

"I wouldn't want to do that too often!" remarked Tyana. "I feel as though I've done a day's work and we haven't had lunch yet.

"What's so amusing?"

"Lunch is in the ship we just buried, Darling," answered Marcus, then as Tyana groaned added, "but we don't have to move it all at once this time. We'll just move the earth a few tons at a time to uncover the ship, then Kresh can fly it out."

This was done, and over a meal Frank voiced his thoughts.

"There are six ships outside the town. I presume that if there's a crew in one or more of them then they'd have food and water for at least a fortnight inside?"

Kresh and Wanda both nodded.

"So we'll need eighteen triads to deal with those six ships!

We'll do it by having the humans and unicorns stay in the trees whilst the birds and/or horses go to near where the ships are. We can then use Gabbie's technique and bury all six at once.

"It's possible that they won't even know we've done it if we can remove the extra earth so that there are still depressions there. Can you organise that, Marcus? The orders will be better coming from you!

"I also suggest that the time has come for the Council Leader of Moscow to be with us, and all his European colleagues. Please have them brought to Paris, together with every triad Merlin feels he can spare. Make sure he understands that each town must still be defended by at least six.

"Kresh, or Wanda, Can you supply Merlin with ten detectors which will warn of the approach of any of Krast's ships?"

Kresh looked at Frank with respect as she answered, "That's something we should have thought of ourselves. I'll have to visit the island, but yes, it can be done! I'll bring some for our use too."

"If you can get everyone to Paris by tomorrow morning we'll spend the day training them, then take out those six ships at dawn the following one."

"You realise that every extra day we wait represents another few dozens more people losing their theurgen?" asked Tyana.

"I do! I also know that we'll only get one chance at those six ships, and I intend it to be right first time! I also intend those within that dome to not know what's hit them when we go in!

"That brings me to the next part. Please make arrangements for us to visit Baghdad tomorrow afternoon and turn on the gas tight mirror barrier again just long enough to find out how easily, or even if, we can destroy it."

"Why Baghdad in particular?"

"It doesn't have to be, but since Hammid is part of our group, and since any town well away from here will do, why not?

"Now, back to Paris before we're noticed!"

Whilst Marcus brought the others up to date Kresh and a crew went to Camelot via their island. Wanda, Kallen, Makrill and their crews flew straight to Camelot.

Just after breakfast next morning Marcus found his army had grown to over fifty triads, so he had everyone except a guard of six of them transported near to Baghdad for a day of contests designed to develop skills and to get used to each other. Greta reminded him of his promise, so she together with Johann's triad travelled in Kresh's ship.

***

Thanks to Frank's insistence on keeping to his timetable everything worked out as he'd planned. Shortly after dawn twelve horses grazed their way slowly till there were two near each of the six depressions around Moscow. Three eagles, two falcons and a myna flew over to join them, one bird to each ship.

Six gestalts each consisting of three triads were formed within a second, such was the value of the practice of the previous day. The twelve horses and six birds looked into their allocated depression briefly and a mound of spoil appeared a hundred yards away. In case there was a camera outside the town the birds flew off and the horses continued grazing, working their way back to their partners, and finishing the final touches to the appearance of the depressions.

Frank pronounced himself well satisfied, and commented to Greta, who had appointed herself Abinger's representative and was taking notes, whilst her father chatted to Kresh, "So far, so good! We now have a numerical advantage... seven to their five!

"We'll wait till mid morning for the next stage when they'll all be busy!"

He turned to Marcus and said, "Have them all withdraw a mile or so, please, then introduce me, and we'll go over the next phase once more!"

Marcus did as ordered, and told his surprised group of allies,

"Merlin, as you know, put Tyana and myself in charge of dealing with Krast and Oistrach. You may have wondered why Frank here was always around when we were practising yesterday and now I've got his permission to tell you.

"The orders I gave were his. The plan to free Moscow is his. I believed in him all along, but rightly or wrongly he felt you should think I was running the show until he'd proved himself.

"Does anyone not feel happy about his appointment as General?"

After a suitable pause to allow anyone who wished to speak Frank got down to business, making his selection of twenty-four triads about half way through the morning.

There was a slight breeze from the South so the assault group lined up on that side of the town and two miles away. The balance was behind and to either side and started working on the wind. Soon it was just below gale force, but had increased slowly enough not to arouse suspicion if those within Moscow bothered to keep a watch.

Three ships flew in from the South at treetop height, one commanded by Kresh carrying Frank, Greta and her father's triad, Sophia, and Lotus Blossom, as observers; one by Kallen with Carlos, Javelin, and Mandrake; and one by Merco with Wanda in the weapons turret, and carrying Cantor, Vernique and Shinlu. Each dropped a twenty feet diameter lightning ball. The wind took them into the barrier that immediately went down, and Frank smiled with satisfaction, telling Greta, "Two were enough in Baghdad, yesterday but I always like a margin for error."

The ships were now two hundred feet above the centre of the town and Beethoven's Fifth Symphony was blasted downwards from speakers below Kresh's. A constantly changing pattern of lights was also directed downwards, modulated by the music.

Twenty four unicorns with ropes draped around their necks galloped the two miles at top speed, but as they did they saw Wanda fire a missile at the centre of the square, followed by one over their heads as her ship broke formation and headed South firing her third as she went out of sight. They reached the town and moved into it as quickly as safe. Eighteen horses similarly adorned with ropes and carrying the humans whose familiars they were followed only seconds behind.

Eagles Swift, Caress, and Storm; falcons Hawka, and Sweetheart; and myna Krull flew overhead, enabling Marcus, Tyana, Qamar, Shaena, Gabbie from Abinger, and Dimitri, Head of Moscow Council to work as they walked towards the town. Thus forty-eight independent attack units were in the town and working before they were noticed, though in the event only thirty-four found targets to work on.

Within the first few seconds anyone wearing headdress that looked anything like breathing apparatus, was bound and left where they fell. The male Godhe, some of whom had removed their helmets when they realised the barrier was down and the gas being blown away were recognised by their build and had no chance to even try to use the weapons they carried.

The birds overhead, especially the eagles and falcons with their acute vision were able to direct their unicorn partners to any suspicious females, and six, who could have fooled humans, were given away by their thoughts. Krull helped by enabling Dimitri to locate Moscow's two healers from those bound and to free them. They in turn identified the other eight who had been forced to help in the milking.

From the dropping of the lightning balls to the last of the Godhe being bound had taken less than two minutes but that left only eight to ten before the first of the sleepers could be expected to recover.

The twenty-four Godhe were unceremoniously dumped, still bound, just outside the town and three triads with orders not to even speak to them left on guard.

Fortunately the healers had been using a marking system so that they knew who had been 'done' and even more fortunately, eight of them had been taking only half of the theurgen before moving on to the next victim.

There was just time to move those with a red cross on their heads to the Council Chamber, the largest building in Moscow, before they started to waken. Melanie, Victrix, and the ten healers circulated amongst them as the recovered and calmed them as Dimitri explained what had happened during almost a month whilst they'd slept. Meanwhile Carlos used the outside speakers on Kallen's ship to give the same news to those lucky enough to have been left till last.

It proved possible to identify those treated by the eight healers who'd thought of only taking half as they felt fit and well. They were allowed to join the main party outside listening to Carlos but that still left thirty-seven unlucky ones with bad headaches and severe depression.

<<*Just remember,* >> said Melanie in Victrix's voice, << *We're sure they haven't moved it far, so we expect to get your theurgen, or you may know it as Essence, back where it belongs soon. Please just trust Tyana and Marcus. Have a meal now. Those whose head still aches, come to touch either me or my unicorn Victrix, and the pain will go!* >>

***

The healers had no idea what had been done with the theurgen they'd removed, except for the very last victims, into whom they had, of course, immediately replaced it.

With twenty-four Godhe and only ten of them, there had always been one available to immediately take it away. Neither did they have any idea of which of the Godhe was in charge, or whether there were six Commanders of equal rank.

Carmen, who Marcus remembered well from his first visit to Madrid explained, "They're a completely undisciplined lot. They don't seem to have a leader except for someone in an invisible ship in the square. It looked as though one of yours chased it!"

"I tried to get all the others to do as I was and pretend there wasn't much to collect, but two of them couldn't understand the signs. I'm sorry!"

Marcus reassured her, and then set about finding the answers to a few questions himself. The twenty-four prisoners suddenly found themselves with their bindings gone and entirely surrounded by riders on unicorns.

In case any of them spoke only their native language Marcus had Rebel address them, but re-broadcast by Karim so that all could hear. *<< As soon as you are able, form into a line facing the wall of the town! >>*

As they did so each found himself, or herself, facing one of the unicorns. Marcus continued, *<< First, the leader of your group take one step forward! >>*

They just looked at each other for guidance, but they had each had their thoughts read by the unicorn in front of them.

<< So, you are six crews working independently and answering here only to your own commander!

<< Trask, third from the end away from me, unless you wish to discuss the matter with Caress, the Golden Eagle my wife Tyana is holding in front of you.........Where is your store of what I believe you will call Essence? >>

Caress looked at the poor man and just as Tallons had done to intimidate Kresh, she opened her hooked beak, raised her Right leg and flexed the tallons of the foot.

Whether he would have spoken really doesn't matter, for the thought was enough for Karim to pass to Tyana the information wanted. In the same way each of the other five 'told' where his was stored, but the total was just what had been collected that morning. The main store was in the ship that was even then being chased by Merco and Wanda.

The amount collected that day was sufficient that when divided by thirty seven it proved to be adequate to replace at least half of what the worst victims had lost, and in some cases all of it. Remembering the pain caused by the sudden reinsertion of a cold viscous liquid Tyana instructed Carmen and her fellow Healers how to warm it, then insert a little at a time.

<< Rebel, this is Javelin. We've lost contact with Merco's ship. Can you spare Melanie and Victrix? >>

<< Of course! >>

<< We're leaving on the course she took. Kresh will pick up Melanie. >>

<< Wait, please! Both of you land, drop Greta and Johann's triad off, and pick up Tyana's and my triad as well! >>

As the two ships headed South Rebel, Karim, Javelin, and Lotus Blossom called in turn for their friends, noticing that they were veering East as they flew. Marcus asked why.

"As our ships travel their propulsion system leaves a trail we can follow. So far they've both gone the same way.

"Look!"

She pointed down to a wrecked ship on a hillside, and headed down towards it. She spoke into the console, "Kallen, we'll go down. You continue following, please!"

"No!" shouted Frank, flicking on the same switch he'd seen her use. "This is Frank. Forget that! Follow us down!"

The ship had obviously fallen some considerable distance and they could see a three feet diameter hole through the disc of the saucer half way to the hub. Kresh tried to open the door from her ship without success.

The whole party, led by Marcus and Tyana gathered around and the three triads went into gestalt to remove the door. Melanie was first through it to find Shinlu on her back with Vernique just recovering consciousness cradled on her lap in her arms.

Melanie touched Vernique briefly then passed her out to Marcus.

"She just needs rest.....Mother and baby will be fine!" she called.

Cantor had tried to catch Wanda as she fell from the turret and both were in a heap in the centre of the control room. Merco had stayed at the controls to the last and it looked as though his legs had been driven up through the pelvic joints. Serious though this was Melanie decided it wasn't life threatening so started with Cantor and Wanda. She gently disentangled them to find that Wanda was just knocked out and had a broken collarbone. This she reduced and fused as she'd seen Laura do then passed her out to recover.

Cantor took her longer and she needed Victrix to help rebuild his legs where they had folded under the weight of himself and Wanda. Before long though, he too was passed out of the door.

"Mandrake, what do you know of your internal organs?" she shouted through the door.

<< *Very little, I'm afraid. I do know that if she stays on her back much longer she'll die. We can't breath well in that position!* >>

"Marcus, Tyana, I need her the right way up! Can you take this ship apart so that I've room to move please?"

Working as one unit, even more closely bonded than the gestalts they'd become used to being part of, the two triads tore sections from the side until Shinlu was exposed with free space all around. Melanie and Victrix backed up by Cindy joined in and she was gently turned over. Victrix immediately broke free and started her breathing fully instead of the shallow gasps she'd been doing. Melanie felt over Mandrake to feel a normal dragon heartbeat and increased Shinlu's from the irregular faint one it was up to the same as Mandrake's.

<< *I can hear her now, Melanie.* >> said Mandrake. << *She's going to be alright! Look to Merco.* >>

Merco was no problem. After watching Laura and Megan at work and with Victrix to help, pulling the femurs back into position and fusing the pelvis back together was only a few minutes work.

"Even I can't be in two places at once, Kresh. Is there anything here that you can use to keep him unconscious till I finish dealing with the others? He'll be in terrible agony if he recovers without me there."

There was. She gave him a spray injection from the ship's med kit and Melanie was able to return to Shinlu. She took hold of the giant three fingered hand in both of her own and Victrix gently put her nose to the other.

<< *That's better! The pain… it was unbearable. My tummy still hurts, but not so much. Thank you, Melanie!*

<< *How are the others, Mandrake?* >>

<< *They'll all live, thanks to this lovely lady and her unicorn. You rest, My Love! Plenty of time to talk later!* >>

Mandrake turned to where Marcus, Tyana, Carlos, and Sophia had been waiting as anxiously as he had himself.

<< *My friends, this has suddenly become personal! Shinlu and I were only too happy to give what little help we could when you were planning, but that's no longer enough.*

<< *Carlos, I'd like to form a triad with you if you're agreeable.* >>

"I'd be honoured, Mandrake, but you do realise this would be for life? You'd no longer wish to spend your time with your pack. You'd be moving into Paris with us. It wouldn't be fair on Shinlu either. She needs you now more than ever."

<< *That's easily taken care of!*

<< *Sophia, may I join you and Lotus Blossom?* >>

"Shinlu! Is that really you? Are you alright?"

<< *Nothing that rest won't cure, Sophia. The pain's going. I'm more annoyed than hurt now!* >>

"Excuse me, Melanie," Cantor quietly said, "but was I dreaming or did I hear you say 'Mother and baby' when you passed Vernique out?"

Melanie smiled. "Me with my big mouth. I suppose she hadn't told you yet?"

"No!"

"I'm sorry I said anything then, but I'm sure you understand… the stress of what I was doing?"

"Don't apologise! I don't think Vernique knew herself, and she's sleeping now so I can't ask her. She thought she couldn't have any children! Are you really sure?"

"There are definitely two life forces there! One of them is very weak, and that usually means a new foetus… say about two months old! I bet Shinlu knew!……

"Didn't you?"

<< *That was why I grabbed her and tried to protect her from the fall.* >>

Cantor looked into the eyes in a head that was a foot larger than his whole body. "We've been friends now for twenty years, Shinlu, but I don't know the words to thank you enough!"

<< *Those words were more than adequate, Mon Ami!*

<< *Merco was brave, too. He managed to keep the ship level as it came down. If he'd failed then I don't suppose even Melanie could have saved us.*

<< *Marcus, can I suggest we all return to Paris and ask those who aren't needed in Moscow join us?* >>

"You certainly can, Shinlu. I'll have Rebel organise.."

<< *Marcus! This is Javelin. Lotus Blossom and I were telling Orchid and Bella what's happened. We've lost contact with Orchid and Bella can't reach her either.* >>

"In the ships, please everyone!" called Marcus. "We're going to Paris. It looks as though Krast and Oistrach are there!"

"Belay that last order!" contradicted Frank.

"They've got five ships. We've got two here and we're not going near Paris with less than all of the twelve we command.

"Back to Moscow!"

Chapter Nine

By the time they arrived Frank had made all his plans and was ready to give his orders. Melanie was allowed all the time she wanted to further treat the injured and had an audience of the ten healers. Even they whispered to each other in awe when they realised just what she had achieved at the crash scene. Meanwhile the twenty-four Godhe were handcuffed and given leg restraints using iron bars mentally bent and welded, then bundled aboard Kresh's ship.

"Deliver to Merlin please, Kresh, when we've finished here. He and Zoltan can advise us later what we can learn from them.

"Marcus, please have Rebel tell Merlin that they're not to be paroled. They must be kept locked in and under guard twenty-four hours a day. Stress that these are a completely different class of prisoner to the earlier ones he had.

"Tyana, please arrange for the six ships to be unearthed and made ready for battle, crewed by all except six triads to guard Moscow. If necessary make their commanders open them before they are taken to Camelot.

"Shaena, please arrange for a triad forming ceremony for Sophia and for Carlos. They're going to add Shinlu and Mandrake. I ask you as Marcus and Tyana may not have the strength left today, and as logic suggests that it will be a difficult bonding because of their mass. I'd recommend as many Whites taking part as you can arrange."

Shaena looked as surprised as Marcus himself, and asked, "What makes you think Marcus and Tyana would have trouble?"

"Kresh tells me that to tear the fabric of one of their ships requires a shear force of, in our units, about one hundred and eighty tons...They did it repeatedly when Melanie needed the room to treat Shinlu.

"Any more questions, anyone?"

Kallen's hand was first up. "Why did you stop me following Krast? If I had they might not be in Paris now!"

"Is your ship better armed than Merco's?"

"No, they're exactly the same."

"Do you know how Merco's was damaged?"

"No, I've never seen anything like it before!"

"Then trust me, Kallen. It was natural for you to want to go, but if you had then in all probability you would be down on some hillside just as Merco was, or more likely in pieces all over that hillside.

"Merco, are you well enough to tell us what happened?

"Make it easy for yourself. Just think back, and I'm sure Rebel can tell us all?"

<< I can, Frank!

<< Carry on Merco.

<< We were following the ion trail with no trouble at all when without warning the computer went dead, and a large hole appeared in the disc. The controls still responded manually so I could keep us level but with no power to speak of we just fell. >>

"That's what I thought you'd say. I looked at the hole and it was obviously caused by something punching down through it from above. There's a crater about half a mile from where you went down over two hundred yards across. I suppose your missiles have some sort of negative proximity fuse so that they only arm themselves when they're well away from the mother ship?"

<< That's right! >>

"I thought so. The one that nearly got you must have been fired from immediately above and so close that it punched a hole through your ship before it was armed, hence the large crater I told you about. I'd say you were very, very lucky!

"Agreed, Kallen?"

"Yes Sir! … Thank you, Sir!"

"I have a question!"

"Yes, Cantor? And may I say I commend your bravery trying to catch Wanda? You certainly saved her very serious injury. Now, what was your question?"

"When do we eat?"

Laughter all round followed this and conveniently Krull, Dimitri's myna, arrived and in his beautiful soprano voice directed his guests to a hastily rigged marquee and meal.

Frank turned to Kresh and said, "I hate to ask, but do you mind eating in Camelot? We're over seven hours behind them here, and I want Merlin to have time to bed down his guests safely. Then he can question them tomorrow morning. By the time you arrive he'll know what we've learned so far and he can tell us what more there is to know before we leave for Paris."

"Of course I will, Frank. Do you need me straight back here?"

"No. Enjoy your evening, as it is there, get what rest you can, and try to be back here for dawn, Moscow time!"

"Excuse me, Sir!"

"Yes, Greta?"

"Papa's going to be busy with you, so may I go with Kresh please? I've never been away from Venicia before."

Marcus looked first to Johann who just shrugged his shoulders and smiled, then to Kresh, who said, "I enjoy her company. If Jann doesn't mind, then of course she may come!

"I'd be happier if we had a unicorn along, though! You sort of get used to their easy communication across any distance.

"Any volunteers?"

Melanie almost ran forward in her eagerness. "I could do with a break after today, if that's alright. All any of my patients need now is rest, and there are ten healers here. It's just a matter of pain control for Cantor and Merco, and they can handle that. Shinlu no longer needs me. So may I?"

Smiling, Tyana nodded to her and the ship left.

After lunch Shaena had no trouble recruiting two Whites to join Qamar and herself for Carlos's and Sophia's triad forming. All four found themselves tired after the first and chose six others to perform Sophia's, and Marcus admitted to Frank, "I'm glad you insisted that Shaena handle that! I hate to think what we'd have been like tomorrow if we'd officiated."

He called over what were now the Carlos and Sophia triads then asked Frank, "Have you made any plans yet?

"We've got the twelve ships to their five. Why don't we just go in now?"

"You're the boss, Marcus. If that's what you want I can't stop you....... But I can think of half a dozen ways that I could arrange for Rosa to be in danger as a hostage and I don't advise it.

"They're not going to hurt anyone today, and I want to know why our defences didn't work.

"There was one of Kresh's detectors there to tell them if even one ship was arriving, and the way I set it up the barrier should have triggered automatically. However, from what you say that wouldn't have stopped Orchid speaking with Bella!

"I can't plan until we know more, but I suggest that just this small group of us take a look now with one of the ships!"

***

Kallen's approach was even lower and more careful than they had previously used, setting down over five miles away and they waited as Caress and Tallons went to investigate, initially from over ten thousand feet.

<< *It's not the gas tight barrier they're using,* >> Caress called, << *It's the normal transparent one. We're going lower to take a closer look.*

<< *It looks as though all five ships are here in the town, but invisible. There are two circles making a figure of eight shape with nobody near them in the square, and three circles where the buildings are flattened.*

<< *This barrier's not the same after all. Look! There's a sort of shimmer to it even though it's transparent.* >>

Rebel projected the picture as well as he was able to Frank but he still insisted, "I must see it myself. If only we had a telescope!"

"Oh… Of course!" he continued as Marcus gave him one. "Let's get within sight on foot!

"I've got an idea!" he announced after a few minutes study, "but I need to talk to Wanda, or one of the other weapons experts before I voice it. I still don't know how they got in, but I think I can explain that shimmer. … Back to Moscow!"

Wanda was called in and listened to Frank's theory.

"Suppose you had five ships, and had the barriers switching on and off in sequence and at a variable rate. Would that be a defence against the lightning balls we used here?"

"It sounds feasible. Why not try it?"

This was done, and sure enough the balls just bounced off with no generator overloading as had happened previously. Even hitting it with ten as near to simultaneously as they could manage just blew one and the other four continued unaffected.

"So, what's the answer?" Marcus wanted to know.

"Sorry, Marcus!" announced Frank. "I'm going to have to sleep on that one!

"However, please ensure that every town with more than one generator uses them like you've seen me do with these. I don't see why Krast should have all the advantages!"

***

With Victrix on board the incoming ship, Merlin had enough warning to get into Camelot and was able to have the ship settle in the square with its door facing his old apartments. The prisoners just went where he pointed and he followed them as far as the doorway. The handcuffs vanished as did the leg-irons but the latter were replaced with the same sort of ball and chain arrangement Wanda had had to endure. Looking at their anklets the hapless Godhe found that as with the handcuffs there were no seams and so no possibility of escape.

Outside Laura arranged for Melanie to take Kresh and Greta to the ranch for a late dinner. Victrix was happy to take the double load of Greta and Kresh whilst Cindy took Melanie.

<< Shall we show them how we can travel, Lace? >>

<< Why not? They're both on our side! Race? >>

<< Have you forgotten how I got my name? >>

<< No, but you're carrying double! >>

<< I'll even give you a start. Off you go! >>

Waiting just long enough to advise Kresh and Greta what they were in for Melanie galloped off and was soon half a mile ahead.

<< Hold tight to my mane, Kresh. Greta hold Kresh. Here we go! >>

It was close, but as they entered the area near the ranch house Victrix caught up and passed Cindy with twenty miles an hour to spare.

"I make that just under a minute for the five miles from Camelot! I'm pretty sure that's a record!" announced Dusty who'd been using his pulse as a timer since Victrix had told them they were coming.

"Inside all of you! I'll tend to Victrix and Cindy."

As they complied they heard him doing as he'd said.

"I suppose you'd both like a rub-down and oats? Which first?" and he called one of the hands to help.

Greta a little white-faced after the ride, found herself welcomed by Lindsey in French, introduced to Hondo, Megan, and the children, and treated as a member of the family, as was Kresh whose welcome was just as warm.

Darryl caught Melanie's arm as she entered and took her to the kitchen where, thoughtfully, Lindsey had set places for just the two of them.

"Welcome back, Lace Darling! You can't imagine how much I missed you. I'd just begun to get to know you.... and there you were, on the other side of the world.

"Can you tell me about it?

"Not straight away.... Eat first!"

Melanie did, but as soon as she'd taken the edge off her appetite she insisted on talking.

"It's not finished yet! Haven't you heard? Krast and five ships have taken over Paris, and little Rosa's there! I've never met her but I've seen Sophia's eyes and that was enough.

"I've got to be back there at dawn Moscow time tomorrow! That means leaving here just after eleven in the morning.

"I know you warned me that we'd be dealing with worse than I met in New York, and you were right. Can I be frank?"

"Everyone is, Darling, here on Refuge!"

"I took the chance to come to see you just in case I don't make it back again. I'm not sorry I volunteered to go. It's certainly no place for anyone with children, and believe me it's no fun. Greta's whole town has been stripped of their powers.

"Wanda, Merco, Cantor, Vernique, and Shinlu ..... they'd all have died if things had happened only slightly differently. If Frank hadn't made the right decisions, if Marcus and Tyana hadn't been so fast tearing the ship apart, if I hadn't been lucky. ... So many 'ifs'... I'll tell you all about it later.

"Give me a cuddle, Darryl."

He rushed to comply, and she continued, "I feel absolutely exhausted. I…"
Darryl found himself holding a limp figure.

<< *Victrix!* >>

<< *Darryl?* >>

<< *I need help! Call Megan! Tell her Lace has collapsed!* >>

<< *Darryl relax! It may be only late afternoon for her but she's done more work since dawn this morning in Paris than most people do in a week. I felt her 'go'. She's just asleep. Carry her to your room gently, undress her, put her in your bed, and give her at least five or six hours sleep. Even better if you can be patient, let her wake naturally!* >>

<< *I'll get Mum!* >>

<< *Darryl! You do it!* >>

<< *But ...* >>

<< *Do think I don't know what's best for my partner? Just why do you think she came back for a flying visit? She's never trusted a man in her life until now, yet she wanted to see you!* >>

He did as he'd been told; falling in love all over again as he gently removed her boots, shirt, and jodhpurs. As a Silver he had enough power to groom her hair magically and remove the grime of the day's work, but could not bring himself to remove any more clothing. He just covered her with a duvet and tiptoed out and into the dining room. "Sorry, Everyone, Lace is asleep. She was going to tell me what she'd been doing, but I guess it'll have to wait."

"Do you think she'd mind if I told you what I can?" asked Kresh.

Lindsey assured her that they'd all like to hear, and that judging by her reticence about her experiences on Earth, Melanie was unlikely to tell the full story herself, anyway.

"Well," began Kresh, "I've heard how Megan and Laura dealt with Juno's injuries, and I've been told of other examples of their powers, but until I saw Melanie in action today I thought the stories were exaggerated.

"One of our ships was shot down, and just fell about a hundred feet onto a hillside. Merco stood at the controls till it hit, so you can imagine the mess his legs and hips were in. Wanda had fallen from the turret and been caught by Cantor, then…"

As she catalogued the injuries and their treatment Greta never took her eyes off her, and even Megan was surprised to hear what her apprentice had managed.

"…and even when we got back to Moscow she spent another hour keeping Shinlu particularly, and the others in turn until Frank got the other healers to help, pain free.

"It's the simple truth that without her there today…

"Or of course you Megan, or Laura, ….. then Vernique and her baby, Cantor, Merco, Wanda, and Shinlu would be dead. No, perhaps Vernique would have made it as Shinlu cushioned her fall at her own expense.

"She was prepared to die, you know, to give Vernique a chance.

"I know hundreds of different races through my travels, but I've never met one who would sacrifice their own life for someone of a different species. The dragons are truly amazing!

"Now, I don't know what Merlin had in mind sending me here to the ranch, but may I be rude, and ask to hear Megan on her harp? I've heard so much about it.

"You're a legend you know, Megan, and not only for your healing!"

"Oh, Yes please, Megan," added Greta. "How about Brahms Lullaby?"

"That's one of my favourites too!" stated Laura as she and Merlin walked in.

"Just before that," interrupted Lindsey, "did you say Vernique and her baby just now?"

"That's right, she's just sufficiently gone for me to tell!"

Megan started with a few of her own favourite pieces having not played since the evening of Aristo's visit, but having proved she was a virtuosa changed smoothly to the requested lullaby.

"Is this what happened to Melanie, Darryl?" asked Hondo pointing to Kresh and Greta, both dead to the world.

"You guessed it, Dad. Victrix said to let her sleep as long as it takes, but to be there for her when she wakes. I suppose we do the same for these two. They've had quite a day, haven't they?"

Hondo scooped up Kresh and indicated that Darryl should do likewise for Greta."Who'd have thought even a fortnight ago that I'd be putting Kresh in my bed? And with your mother's approval too?"

"That's right, Hondo, Darling," said Lindsey, "but you can forget the bit about being there for her when she wakens.

"I agree you use our bed, though, as it's nearest. Put Greta with her, and we'll sleep in one of the guest rooms tonight."

Blushing profusely, Hondo complied.

***

Merlin and Laura arranged food for their prisoners without speaking. They were shown where the toilet and bathroom were, and the door closed as they went out. The prisoners failed to notice two owls sitting quietly on a beam.

<< *The only talk,* >> announced Zoltan half an hour later, << is about Oistrach's possible ancestry and I'm not going to repeat it! I think we should just leave them till morning.

<< *Bearing in mind Frank's warning, I'll have a rota of unicorns here to monitor them, with a couple of Golds to back them up if needed.*

<< *We can call in Archimedes and Guinevere and go home!* >>

The door was reopened just long enough to do this and the party returned to the ranch in time for Megan's harp recital.

***

Sometime during the night Melanie woke and froze in fear. *'I was coming to see Darryl,'* she thought. *'I'm in a strange bed, stripped, no not quite, in my underwear, and there's a shadow in that armchair!'* She conjured a small torch alight and relaxed. *'It's Darryl... but how?'* and then she remembered and relaxed.

'He managed to groom my hair and get rid of the day's dirt...

... it's a pity he didn't think to empty my bladder for me!'

She rose and tiptoed past Darryl's chair then changed her mind, conjured the contents Darryl had overlooked to the paddock and sat gently on his lap, kissing him awake.

"Wouldn't you rather share your bed, Darryl?" she whispered.

"You were giving me a hug, the last I remember. How did I get here?"

Darryl blushed as he answered, "I...I... Victrix said I should do it! Ask her in the morning. I'd never take advantage of you .... You should know that."

"If I didn't before, I certainly do now!

"Look, Darling, I don't think I could relax enough for sex yet, even with you, but I do enjoy a cuddle now, something I never thought I would.

"Come on! You'll have a terribly stiff neck in the morning the way you were sleeping. Off with those clothes and into bed with you."

Darryl turned his back and started to take off his jeans.

"I've seen a naked man or two in my time, you know...now, how did Megan say it was done? ... oh, yes!"

Darryl suddenly found himself without a stitch on and dived into bed. Melanie followed him, 'losing' the bra as she went, but found herself unwilling to go further ... '*yet*' she thought to herself.

With two totally inexperienced people it took some five minutes to find positions where they were able to cuddle and go back to sleep without having the circulation restricted somewhere, but as she thought as she drifted off, *'It was nice experimenting.*

I've got a lot of catching up to do! And Darryl's the man I'm going to do it with!'

***

With their body clocks upset by changing time zones and after such an exhausting day, Kresh, Greta, and Melanie were awake at first light and raiding the kitchen to make up for what they hadn't felt up to eating the evening before. Darryl soon joined them, but as a typical bachelor made enough noise to waken the rest of the house. Only Merlin and Laura managed to sleep through it, and Lindsey took over breakfast preparation. Watching her, Kresh marvelled again at how useful this 'magic' was.

By the time Merlin and Laura made a belated appearance she knew that if it could be arranged, she wanted to stay on Refuge to try to make up for the harm she'd done these people.

<< *I'm sorry, Kresh. This is Victrix. I didn't mean to pry, but I was just contacting you to say 'Good Morning' and I heard that. I'll see if I can help.* >>

"Thank you, Victrix."

"I beg your pardon?" asked Lindsey and Darryl together.

"I'm sorry! I haven't got used to speaking without using my mouth I'm afraid. Victrix had just wished me Good Morning."

Melanie smiled to show she wasn't annoyed as she commented,
"You seem to get on very well with her! She must like you."

"Oh I hope so, Melanie. I really do hope so. How long have you been together? All your lives?"

Melanie laughed. "I'm glad it seems like it, Kresh, but honestly I only arrived on Refuge a couple of days before Aristo was killed."

"I don't know much about our 'recruiting' operation on your Earth. Is life very different here?"

"I'm sorry, Kresh, but it would take days to list the differences. I don't mind doing it, but let's leave it for now if you don't mind.

"I'd like to spend the morning with Darryl, unless there's something you want me to do.... Anyone?"

"You enjoy the rest whilst you can, My Dear!" Merlin told her.

"Laura and I are going into Camelot to question our new guests.

"Kresh, would you like to come?"

"I certainly would. Thank you! But what about Greta?"

Merlin thought for a moment, then answered, "There's no possibility of danger, so she can come too. I understand she's been taking notes in Europe, so she may do the same here if she's willing."

"Melanie, would you ask Victrix if she'd take us. please?"

"Ask her yourself, Kresh! ...I don't mean that in a nasty way. Just think her name, visualising her, and she'll answer."

Victrix agreed, pointing out that she could pass on mentally what the prisoners were thinking just as Princess and Zoltan would be doing for Laura and Merlin.

"One condition!" insisted Merlin.

"We will not race into town!"

***

The unicorn on duty reported that the prisoners had been awake for an hour or so, but were so despondent that they had not even considered escape. They were just waiting for Oistrach to come to rescue them.

"You can all come in in a moment," Merlin told his companions, "but I think I'll let them see who's boss first, and dispel any ideas that Oistrach is coming."

He went in alone, except for Zoltan who walked behind him with Archimedes on his head just behind his horn, and looked around.

<< The even taller than usual one, he calls himself Brandt, is waiting for you to get near enough for him to attack you. >>

<< Thank you, Zoltan. Let's not disappoint the man. >>

Leaving Zoltan behind, Merlin walked across and said to the man described, "You wanted to see me, Brandt?"

"Vous voudrez parler avec Moi, Brandt?"

<< He doesn't understand either language, but has a stone behind his back to hit you on the head with. >>

Merlin continued forward until within reach and allowed Brandt to make the attempt, mentally stopping the stone dead about a quarter of an inch from his head. He then flicked Brandt with his finger and thumb on his chest, simultaneously throwing him the length of the room to smash into the wall and made sure that his head didn't hit it so that he remained conscious.

<< Your loudest mental voice now to all of them, please, Zoltan, so that they think it's in their own tongue. >>

"That didn't work out too well, for you, now did it Brandt?"

"Does anyone else feel like trying?"

"All at once, if you wish!"

<< They are thinking that if you, an old man, are that strong, what hope is there for them, even all together. I've told the others they may come in now. >>

Merlin turned again to Brandt as his friends walked in, and Zoltan resumed broadcasting mentally apparently in Standard as the Godhe knew their language, "I'm going to ask you a few questions, Brandt. Each time you fail to answer truthfully you will fly the length of the room again, but in future I'll let your head hit the wall. Understood?"

<< He doesn't believe it, but don't let that stop you! >>

"What makes you so sure that Oistrach will come for you?"

"He's never let us down before! And he needs us!"

<< The truth. >>

"How many others can Oistrach call on if he wishes?"

"Plenty! He's got another ten ships in orbit."

<< He has none! >>

"'Bye, Brandt!"

Another trip the length of the room was followed by a bone breaking smash into the wall and a crumpled heap on the floor. Merlin looked around and asked, "Who's in charge now?"

<< The female right next to you with the stone he dropped. Keep your back to her and I'll stop this one. Her name's Zelda! >>

She made her attempt, but Zoltan caused the brick to apparently bounce off which was even more effective than Merlin's effort.

He scratched his head where the brick appeared to have hit and turning, said,"You wanted something, Zelda?

"More to the point, how many others can Oistrach call on if he wishes?"

Zelda's face was as white as chalk as she answered, "On Centrallis Three a few, but here, none!

"How can you be so strong?"

"That's better!

"Laura, see to Brandt, please, but initially forget about the pain control.

"Zelda, Oistrach and Krast have five ships in Paris, and they've got the barriers running in sequence as a protection. What do you know about that defence?"

"I can guess that it's Einstein's idea, but I didn't know about it."

<< *True.* >>

"Tell me all you know about Einstein!"

"He's not of the Godhe. He looks more like a Tellus III man, in fact he may be one, and he's been with us about a year. Einstein's not his real name; it's just what he asked us to call him. He developed the gas tight barrier which made our whole plan possible."

"Has he produced any other things I should know about - - other weapons better than the Galactic Patrol have, for instance?"

"He's working on something based on information he got from Kresh in Paris, but whether it will be ready in weeks or years he can't say yet. It's supposed to duplicate what you people can do by mind alone. Frankly I didn't believe in your abilities till Brandt challenged you. Who are you, if you don't mind telling me, Sir?"

"My name is Merlin, and I have the honour to be President of this world you chose to attack."

"But Krast said she'd killed you! She saw you die."

Merlin just smiled. "One last question ... Who is in charge, Krast or Oistrach?"

"None of us know. Most of us have been with Oistrach for years, but there are times when she seems to order him, and others when she follows his instructions."

<< *That's about it, Merlin. We know from what Marcus learned that none of them know of a theurgen store. They all believe it to be with Oistrach. Let's go back to the ranch.* >>

"Thank you for cooperating, all of you!

"Laura, you may relieve Brandt's pain now, then we'll leave.

"You may, all of you, if you wish hope that Oistrach will rescue you, but I don't advise holding your breath until he does. He will have problems of his own!

"You can be provided with entertainment if you can think of anything within our powers to supply, but you may not leave this building for any reason. One last warning ... I am the weakest of the people you will see, and probably the most patient.

"Do remember that, won't you."

Halfway back to the ranch Zoltan lost contact with his duty stallion outside the temporary prison, and they turned. Descending just outside the shimmering but transparent screen that had appeared around Camelot was a cigar shaped craft over four times the size of the largest saucer shaped ones. Obviously this had triggered the defence system Kresh and Frank had designed.

By the time they reached the area the craft had landed, or at least was hovering just above the ground and one of the lightning balls was heading for the barrier.

As Camelot was used to store the surplus generators Kresh had brought from their island they had six running in sequence as Frank had requested, so it just bounced off.

The ball collapsed and a ramp extended down which six uniformed men descended carrying the now familiar assault rifles.

<< *Those black and silver uniforms fit the description Marcus gave of the Galactic Patrol ones.* >> commented Zoltan.

<< *Is that who they are, Kresh?* >>

"They're certainly dressed like it, and.. Yes, they must be.

"There's Plathe following them down the ramp and with a man who's obviously in charge. It might be prudent if he didn't see me straight away, Merlin."

"I agree! Permit me, My Dear......There! Here's a mirror, take a look."

Kresh found she now had padding to her chest, shoulders and arms and a wide brimmed hat under which her hair was concealed.

"If you don't speak until I've cleared the air they should think you're a man, especially if I introduce you as, say, Richard and your daughter Greta.

"It's obvious which is Plathe, so I'll speak with him first."

Merlin rode forward slightly ahead of the others and addressed in English the only man not in uniform. He ignored orders shouted at him in the Godhe's native tongue by the officer in charge.

<< *He's telling you to keep out of the danger zone until he has dealt with the situation. He doesn't even wonder who we are.* >>

"You are welcome, Plathe.

"Let me introduce myself. My name is Merlin, and I thank you for the help you gave our son, and our three grandchildren on your island.

"We didn't expect to hear from you for at least another week!

"This is Laura, my wife, one of my deputies, Richard, and his daughter, Greta.

"To save you asking; the children are well and will be delighted to see you again. They have much to tell you!"

"I'm happy to meet you, Sir. I guessed the children had somehow escaped when we couldn't land on the island ourselves."

"I'll tell you all about it later. Now, perhaps you would introduce your companions?"

Plathe turned to his neighbour, who was going red in the face and still shouting at Merlin to go away. Plathe interrupted him in his own language.

<< *He obviously doesn't speak either French or English, so Plathe is telling him who you are and some of what you said. When he's finished, I'll make it appear that you speak Standard, as we've done before. I don't like this man! He's arrogant, thinks this a backward planet, and wonders who you think you are, ignoring him. He's also very worried about our screen!* >>

<< *Thank you, Zoltan.* >>

Merlin turned from Plathe to the Commander, apparently addressing him in Standard.

"Well, Young Man, did they teach you no manners before giving you command of such a fine ship? Are you not used to meeting the leaders of the worlds you visit? Is it not customary where you come from to ask permission before landing?

"Please state your name and your business here!"

<< *That should annoy him. Then we can dispel his air of superiority!* >>

"I apologise, Sir!" he said as he bowed stiffly.

"Commodore Gideon, on Special duty, sixth sector Galactic Patrol, though I don't expect that to mean much to you, Sir.

"I congratulate you on your command of our language. I will be interested to learn who broke our law by teaching you!"

<< *He is thinking that you're a jumped up little prig, whatever one of those might be!* >>

"Merlin Pendragon, President of this world, which we call Refuge, but which I believe you will know as Langala IV.

"How does this 'Special Duty' involve us?"

"It doesn't, and I ask that you keep out of our way whilst I deal with it.

"Out of courtesy to your rank I will tell you a little!

"We were following the trail of about fifteen unauthorised ships heading towards this system when we answered what we call a *Mayday* from a saucer craft piloted by Plathe here.

"From their course it seems likely that the ships came here, which is prohibited, and what Plathe told us confirms the probability, though he does seem to be suffering from the effects of the sleep gas. Please ignore him if he starts talking about magic.

"We will talk later. Right now I have to work out how to breach this barrier which is around your town!"

<< *He is thinking that it is a waste of his time talking to an ignorant savage like you.* >>

"Commodore, ..."

"Yes? What is it now? Can't you see I'm busy?"

"Would you have more respect for the, how did you think of us ... ignorant savages on this world if I was able to remove the barrier for you?"

"Of course! But, but ...

<< *That's got to him! He can't think what to say!* >>

"How did you know I thought 'ignorant savage'?"

Merlin just smiled and, after making sure he had Gideon's full attention lifted the Commodore's hat and apparently produced from it a child's slate and chalk. He wrote in English,

Please turn off the screens, Merlin.

"Have one of your men hold this close to and facing the barrier, and it will have the effect you want!

"You will then please remember that you are visitors here and conduct yourself accordingly!"

<< *Sorry, Merlin, there's been no change in his attitude! He still thinks you're a jumped up little prig. Incidentally I know what that is now, but .. you don't want to know!* >>

"Young Man, I really will have to teach you some manners, or replace you with whoever is next in command!"

Merlin elevated Gideon about an inch, doing so very gently and carefully so that he was unaware of it. Laura took over the task to free him for other things.

"I have decided not to allow you to set foot on this world until you can show proper respect for its leaders.

"You may think of me personally as whatever you wish, ... but when you think of any World President, and in particular myself, in the terms you did, then you must learn the error of your ways!"

<< *He plans to ignore you and lead his small group into Camelot. It should be amusing!* >>

Gideon gave the necessary orders and Plathe walked over to Merlin whilst the men marched towards Camelot.

Their commander went through the motions of marching but found himself unable to do more than turn, and he only accomplished that because of his experience weightless in training.

Well disciplined though the troops were, laughter broke out from first one, then all of them. Plathe was the loudest and when he could, told Merlin in English, "I've had over three days of that, that.. I don't know a suitable word!"

"It was worth it though to see him now. He just doesn't believe in your magic and believes implicitly in the superiority of the Galactic Patrol. He told me so several times!

"Are you going to let him down?"

"What's the second in command like? Any better?"

"Very much so! Deanna, and she's Borl Aristo's daughter which makes her even more appropriate."

"She sounds perfect. Get her out here, please, Plathe."

Merlin apparently switched to Standard, "Gideon, you have just one chance to avoid further loss of dignity. When Deanna comes out, you will delegate your authority to her for the duration of your stay on this world. You personally may never return to it at any time in the future! Do you understand and agree?"

"I do, Sir!"

<< *He intends to give Deanna orders and have them carried out in her name!* >>

"Gideon.."

"Commodore Gideon, if you don't mind!"

"Not on this world! Here you are a civilian! You will retire to your cabin, apparently ill, and not emerge until the ship is back in space! Is that clear?"

"It is! Just let me down......At Once!"

<< *Believe it or not, he still thinks that as soon as you're not here he'll take over again and discipline Deanna for helping you ... even though she doesn't know about the plan yet.* >>

"Gideon, you give me no choice! Your intention of acting through Deanna is not acceptable to us!"

"But how?...."

"Silence!

"Laura, can you make him sleep until we can get him on one of the Godhe's sleep sets?"

"Nothing could be easier! I'll just stop the flow of blood to his brain for a few seconds, then we'll take him out to our own ranch. He can stay there as long as needed.

"On second thoughts, I've a better idea! We don't even have to keep him asleep, in fact it may do him the world of good to find out just how we live.

"Let's have him taken to Abinger. He can spend the time starting to learn one of our languages. He may even pick up a little diplomacy and some manners! I'll have Thomas come for him at once. He can sleep till he gets there!"

Deanna was as charming as had been her father and spoke both languages. She was, however, at first reluctant to assume command as she wanted no repercussions afterwards to harm her career.

"There really is no problem, Major Deanna," stated Plathe in Standard and loudly enough for Gideon's friends, if any, to overhear.

"Langala IV is under the jurisdiction of Medical Research and I, the senior representative here, support Merlin's ruling that Gideon is unacceptable to him, and appoint you in command for the duration of your stay! How's that?"

"It would seem that I have no choice!"

She turned to Merlin, "How may we be of assistance Mr President? Perhaps you can advise me of what has happened since Plathe left. Obviously much has, since you are now able to defend Camelot even against us!"

"I'll do that, but first, please put Gideon on one of your sleep-sets. He's going to spend a few days in Abinger and receive an education!"

This was quickly done then withholding only the information that Frank's presence was a mistake Merlin did as Deanna requested ending, "So you see, in less than four hours our friends are planning to try to enter Paris, capture Krast and Oistrach, and free the city, but in particular the daughter of our Paris Council Leaders."

Deanna had obviously listened carefully, for her first question was, "But what about Kresh? Plathe told us she was equally responsible! You haven't mentioned her. Is she dead?"

"Allow me, Merlin," Laura requested. "I can explain it scientifically for her.

"In a way she is dead! The Kresh Plathe knew was acting under a compulsion implanted by Oistrach using the rehabilitation equipment to obey Krast. I believe I said that right! I only know what we were told. Something like a post hypnotic suggestion.

"We believe we've restored her to the personality intended to be given to her, and she's been helping us to try to make up for the damage she did."

"And you believe her?"

"Oh, Yes! Quite simply we can't be lied to. Of course you won't believe that yet, but please tell me a few things about your life at home. Things I couldn't possible know about even from your father... like what you had for an evening meal yesterday, or how long you've served. You'll find you can't lie to us! Try! See if you can fool either of us!"

After ten attempts to fool Merlin, with truth mixed with fiction, Deanna admitted, "So! We trust Kresh!

"But that does leave me with quite a problem. Based on what Plathe had told us, our Base issued orders for us to arrest and detain her, as well of course as the others!"

Greta had been silent until then, but she screamed,

"No! I can't lose her as well! You can't take her away!"

Deanna looked closely at 'Richard' and asked, "Kresh?"

"Yes, Major, I am Kresh!

"However, you can forget any idea of arresting me. I'm far too busy doing your job to spare the time!"

Unlike her commanding officer, Deanna could think quickly and there was hardly any hesitation before she replied, "We'll worry about that at a later date. Right now I'm more interested in what you told me about Paris, and what we can do about it."

"Just a moment, Young Lady!" Merlin told her.

"I'm not sure Marcus would like the idea of this large ship arriving and threatening Oistrach. He's got too many hostages.

"Speaking of ships arriving, here comes Odel to collect your ex-commander!"

Odel greeted Deanna as an old friend, collected Gideon having already received his instructions through Jet, and left.

Watching the ship leave, Merlin said quietly to Deanna,

"I suggest you stand down your men for now. There's no danger on this continent. Leave your deputy in charge and come with us to the ranch. We'll wait until our friends in Moscow waken and then decide what we wish you to do.

"I've had a thought. Have you secure prison accommodation on board for twenty four?"

"We have!"

"Then will you please relieve us of the crews of the ships we captured in Moscow?

"I warn you, though, that I will only release them on your guarantee that they will be secure!"

This was quickly arranged, and with Princess carrying Deanna whilst Zoltan took the double load they returned to the ranch at over two hundred miles an hour just to give Deanna something to think about, where Merlin gave Kresh permission to tell the Godhe commander all that she herself knew. When asked by Deanna why Merlin had chosen her to do this Kresh smiled and replied, "They have many secrets even from me. This way you can have the information in our own language but you can only be told what they've allowed me to learn. They think of everything. Don't underestimate any of them. You saw that thirteen-year-old boy with Odel? Well he's Thomas. Remember the name.

"I'll start at the beginning and point out the things I don't understand myself as we come to them. It began seven years ago after I'd been arrested with Jove, Oistrach, and their groups for trading in what we now know as the hormone theurgen, the only known source of which is the human population of Langala IV."

"Yes! My father told me all about that!"

"He didn't tell you that Oistrach had somehow sabotaged the rehab unit and…

(Half an hour later)…so that's how we stand now! Thank you for not interrupting, Major Deanna.

"To save you asking…I have absolutely no idea how Thomas avoided the missiles we aimed at Abinger. Of course I know he turned them around to return to their ships…but…How did he know they were coming?

"Most of the other things are explained if you accept that these people can influence the random motion of molecules by will alone, but those missiles were already turned around before they came into his sight!

"Now, come and meet Melanie, the Medic I told you about, remember? The one who just put the injured crew back together like you would a doll! You've already met Laura one of the ones who rebuilt Juno. Now you can also meet Megan, the other one!"

***

Gideon was allowed to recover in one of the rooms in the house allocated to Juno and Odel. He stormed into the dining room and, as asked by Thomas, Odel greeted him in Standard with, "Good Morning, Sir. Will you join us for a mid morning snack?"

Gideon was turning a dark shade of red as he tried to keep control, and shouted, "Who are you? Where am I? How dare they?"

Thinking a female voice might be advisable Juno replied,

"Taking your questions in order:

"We are Juno and Odel, detached from Galactic Patrol for duties with Medical Research.

"You are on Langala IV in a house in Abinger, one of the oldest established towns on the planet, and I'm told will stay here until the present crisis is resolved.

"They dare because this is their world and we are, as I'm sure you are well aware, obliged to obey their local rules when here, as on any other world. Quite simply, you offended the World President and he banished you here!"

"He can't do that!"

Odel laughed, which didn't help much, as he said, "It would appear that he already has!"

"Have you a ship here?"

"There is one here, but it is not mine to command. Our orders are to carry out Thomas's wishes."

"So take me to Thomas! Who is he? Another jumped up little prig of an ignorant old fool?"

"Not exactly! Come, and we'll introduce you!"

A short walk followed to Electra's home and he was shown into the garden where a teenager was romping with what looked more like a wolf than a dog. Odel called to him saying, much to Gideon's surprise. "Thomas! .... Have you time to meet our guest Gideon?"

"Commander Gideon!" interposed Gideon indignantly.

"I wouldn't push for that if I were you, Sir." whispered Odel. "Everyone on this world knows that Merlin has decreed that here you are just a civilian!"

"That's not possible! They're savages!"

"Savages or not, I was told all about it when I received my orders to collect you. However it works, they have instant communication even between the continents ... ... and they need no equipment to do it!

"Now, take my advice and be on your best behaviour, Sir. Here he comes. He may appear a child.... But that child defeated every attempt Krast and four ships made to take over this town! She used missiles from orbit, ball lightning, and even a personal attack rocket programmed to his pattern. There was no damage to the town apart from a hole in the square where a chain melted and as you can see only too well, he's unharmed!

"I ask you...Could you have done that? ... With nothing to help you except your friends and their animals?"

Thomas walked over, followed by the wolf and a unicorn; a creature Gideon had thought a myth. Even more surprising was the landing on Thomas's arm by a Golden Eagle. This child really did have a way with animals, he had to allow him that.

Thomas spoke to Odel first in English, then switched smoothly mid-sentence to French, "Hello again, Odel. Yes I have the time to meet our guest.

"More to the point, I have a duty to do so. Merlin asked me to teach him some manners whilst he's here, but to be honest there are things I'd rather do!"

<< *They're right. He doesn't understand!*
<< *I'll give him it in Standard for you.* >>

"How do you do, Gideon?"

"Commander Gideon!"

"Oh, I see! You're still wearing the uniform and it's giving you delusions of grandeur. There, that's better!

"How do you do, Gideon?"

Odel, laughing whispered, "You'd better look down at yourself, Sir!"

Gideon did, and found that he was dressed as a clown, complete with pointed hat. He went red with rage, forgot to breath, and collapsed.

Odel rushed to help, but Jet stopped him, << *He'll be alright, Odel. As soon as he blacked out he started breathing again. Just leave him.*

<< *It looks as though we've got our work cut out, though, doesn't it. Any suggestions?* >>

"I'd say give him one more shock to think about, then ignore him until he starts to behave."

Gideon picked himself up and started to bluster, but Thomas/Jet stopped him. "I want to give you something to exercise your brain overnight, Gideon, and then I'll see you again tomorrow.

"Fallon here will not hurt you I promise."

He pointed to the wolf/dog.

"Take her well away from me, but make sure you're holding on to her with both hands so that you will know that what happens is no trick.

Intrigued, Gideon did as asked. When well away from the others he wrapped both arms around the animal and heard Thomas call,

"Fallon, please fly back to me!"

The dog became a sort of bat, slipped through his arms and flew to Thomas, wrapping her wings around him and kissing him as a lover would.

"Sleep well, Gideon. Listen to what Odel and Juno have to tell you, and be back here tomorrow afternoon when you here a voice order you to come!"

Gideon blustered in Standard for some time but was completely ignored. He turned to Odel.

"This has gone on long enough. They've obviously drugged me with a hallucinogen of some sort!

"Take me back to my ship at once!

"That's an order!"

<< *You are not allowed to give orders here!* >>

"Who said that?"

"Who said what?" asked Juno.

"It doesn't matter who spoke to you, Gideon," explained Odel.

"What matters is that you remember that this is their world, and they make the rules!

"If you think you've been drugged, then just have distilled water tonight, and stay awake! But I warn you, things will still be the same tomorrow." They took him back to his room, allowed him to lock himself in, and resumed their honeymoon.

***

Awake at dawn, Gideon found that he had his uniform back, confirming, he thought, that he'd been drugged as the room had been locked and he slept behind the door. He refused breakfast, worried about drugs again and went out into the square, just as the early risers were about. He spoke to several, but they just looked at him as though they couldn't understand. He went back to the house and asked how this was.

"It may be a coincidence," explained Odel, "or it may be a badge of office or something, but I've noticed that only those with a unicorn can speak Standard.

"We didn't realise before as, of course, we speak both of their languages. It just didn't occur to us to try our own.

"Why don't you learn one or both of theirs?"

"I won't be here long enough! Anyway the people I want to talk to understand Standard."

Odel and Juno just looked at each other and smiled. By mid-day Gideon was beginning to feel hungry and was frustrated by being unable to understand anything of what he saw. Everyone seemed to be a conjuror trying to persuade him that 'magic' was in normal everyday use. He even saw a child hold up an empty hand, produce an apple from thin air, and then smile at him.

<<Gideon!..... It's time for you to go to Thomas!

<<And this time, remember you are just a visitor! >>

Gideon looked around, but there was nobody nearer than twenty yards from him, so he started walking thinking, *'Just another mystery to solve before I leave here.'*

This time Thomas had a pretty blonde haired girl with him, and he introduced her as Fallon.

"But that was the wolf's name!"

"Gideon, I've decided it will be quicker to tell you the facts of life here, rather than have you learn them by playing games with you as I did yesterday.

"Frankly, you're not intelligent enough to work it out for yourself. Or perhaps you're just unable to accept anything new!

"Why do you think this world is off limits to your people?"

"I have no idea!"

"No, you haven't have you? And that's where you Godhe are different from the humans of Earth.

We would want to know, and wouldn't rest until we found out.

"Now, sit down and listen! Nobody drugged your food yesterday. Think, man! When Merlin lifted your feet to just above the ground you hadn't eaten or drunk anything, had you?"

"How do you know about that?"

"Merlin told me himself when he gave me the job of teaching you some manners.

"Merlin, by the way, is the most respected and one of the most powerful men on this world. He also counted Aristo as a personal friend ... . and you thought of him as a jumped up little prig. It's not surprising that he was annoyed!"

"Do you remember referring to Plathe's call for help as a 'Mayday'?"

"I do!"

"Well for your information, that's a corruption of M'aide, which is French for 'Help Me!' French is one of our languages.

"Jet tells me you haven't eaten this morning. Name what you'd like, and I will share it with you so that you need have no worries about its content."

<< *He doesn't know what to think. He's terrified. I feel a little sorry for him!* >>

"Very well! I'll decide. Three steaks with French fries and mixed salad. One uncooked, and two medium.

"Here you are, Gideon. Choose whichever you like, and I'll take the other. They really are both the same."

"But where did they come from? And why is one not cooked?"

"They came from our local meat store. I caused them to come here by simply wishing it so, and I cooked them at the same time.

"Fallon prefers her meat raw, so hers is as you see it!

"Next question!"

"Where is your pet wolf?"

Thomas was pleased to notice that he took a slice of the steak before asking this, followed by some fries.

"It's fortunate for you that Fallon here doesn't understand you. She, the wolf, and the bat are one and the same!"

"Let me give you a history lesson as we eat.

"Many thousands of your years ago your ancestors used to use my home world, Earth, as a holiday planet and...

…(half hour later)…so now do you understand why your Old Ones keep people away from here?"

<< He finally believes you, and he's decided to get Odel and Juno to teach him French and English. >>

"Yes, I do. May I leave now, Sir? You've given me a lot to think about.

"Please give my apology to Fallon. I'll be able to do so myself next time we meet."

<< Mission accomplished, Thomas. I'll advise Merlin! >>

***

When Frank was contacted just before dawn Moscow time he had no hesitation before asking Deanna to use her larger ship to accompany Kresh and Melanie on their return journey.

After introductions, and Deanna and her five Captains invited had got used to the idea that dragons and weres were intelligent people, Marcus put him in the chair for a War Cabinet meeting.

He listened as idea after idea was put forward to retake Paris, but had the same objection to each, that it was too dangerous for Rosa. An hour later he brought it to an end with, "I'm sorry, but we can't use force this time. For one thing we can't breech the force fields running in sequence, and for another we couldn't get away with what we did in Moscow. Whatever else she may be, this Krast is a fast learner.

"As I understand it, you can guarantee knocking out the power sources of the three smaller saucers if the barrier is down, Major, but the Type Sixty Nines used by Krast and Oistrach have multiple engines well protected. Right?"

Deanna nodded.

"You five Captains, I want your troopers deployed in full sight around Paris ready to take over when the barrier goes down.

"Carlos, Sophia, I want one of you on each side of the town with Mandrake and Shinlu overhead if that's possible. If either or both of the two ships in the centre make a run for it, try to stop them, but you are to ignore the others.

"Major Deanna, any of the other three ships you are welcome to, but leave the centre two alone!

"We'll need Melanie and eight of the healers along just in case. Also I'd like her permission to ride Cindy.

"Now, does everyone know their jobs?"

"Ahem!" interrupted Marcus.

"Ah yes, I knew I'd forgotten something.

"Three of us, you and Tyana and myself ride up to near either of the drawbridges before the main party arrives and attract their attention. You then tunnel in and demand to speak to Krast or Oistrach. After we've given them a chance to surrender, and probably had it refused, it will be up to you cause a distraction whilst I bring down the barrier.

"Sorry, but that's the nearest thing to a plan I could come up with!

"At least it has some chance of success. All the others didn't! Don't forget, by the way, that she probably thinks she still has the children on the island!"

"And when does all this happen?"

"Just as soon as we can get there! Have one of Deanna's people take us in Kresh's ship, drop us off over the skyline, then they can wait for the rest."

"Why not Kresh. I trust her!"

"Marcus, you have no romance in your soul, Tyana will explain on the way!"

"Come on, My Love, it seems to be down to the old team. And to save you wondering," Tyana continued, "Kresh, Johann, and Greta have been together since we returned. ... And I don't think they're planning how to retake Paris, so that will be up to us!"

***

Once sure of a good audience the two triads tunnelled under the barrier and up to be greeted as expected by half a dozen Godhe with the usual assault weapons.

<< *Standard please, Rebel!* >>

"You can put those down, Gentlemen, just take us to either Krast or Oistrach!

"I said, 'put them down!'"

As planned and taking three each they had heated the rifles rapidly to several hundred degrees on any scale so that they fell to the floor as the owners screamed in agony.

"That's better! Now, if you would be so kind, take us to your leader!"

Krast and Oistrach were each in their own ship, and requested that the animals be left outside. There was a video link so that it was just like meeting the two together.

"So!" Krast greeted them, and they were surprised to find her alone except for the holograms of Oistrach and an earthman. "We meet again. I didn't expect you for another week or so. I presume you had a purpose in coming in here? And who is this you've brought?"

"Of course we had a purpose!" answered Marcus. "By now this town is completely surrounded by over two hundred of the Galactic Patrol's best. Don't rely on me though, check for yourself! May I introduce Frank Baron? He has been to us as I believe Einstein there is to you.

"We came in to give you the chance to surrender without further loss of life. You have five ships whilst we not only have more, we have a Cruiser class vessel of the Patrol."

"There's one thing you've overlooked. Only I know where your children are!

"And this time your so called magic won't help you. You'll find that within this ship you're powerless. Just a little development based on the knowledge that you couldn't work through one of our barriers. This whole area is enclosed in a field which blocks the transmission of the same wavelengths the barriers work on. What has your Frank Baron to say about that?"

"First, Krast, I'd need to test it." answered Frank. "I'm sure you think you've already done so, but you didn't have someone with our power here, did you?"

The slight smile and air of confidence started to slip from Krast's expression.

"Allow me, Marcus and Tyana, if you will." he continued.

"Let's see, we don't want to do any serious damage, as I want to study what this Einstein has come up with. I know…

"Let me have a glass of water please, Krast."

This she produced, and watched as Frank handed it as red wine to Marcus.

"You're slipping, Frank!" he commented after sipping it. "A trifle too Nouveau. I'll adjust it slightly."

"More to the point, Krast," Frank pointed out for his companions' benefit, "your personal barrier must be off with this 'anti-magic' field running. It doesn't stop us as you've just seen, but it will certainly interfere with that."

Before she had time to think Tyana announced, "Time's up, Krast, Oistrach! …Do you surrender, or do I…What's the word, Darling?"

"Arrest!"

"Arrest you?"

"You incompetent fool, Krast!" came from Oistrach's image. "You've done it again. You've underestimated them. Well, you're on your own!"

The holographic images disappeared, and each heard from the Karim/Rebel merge, << *The barrier's down and Deanna's people are moving in! Well done!* >>

From behind her neck Krast produced a wicked looking saw toothed knife and lunged for Tyana. To Frank's surprise Marcus grabbed him and pulled him well away from the two women.

As the knife was thrust towards her navel Tyana fell backwards, her right foot

226

kicking Krast's forearm just above the wrist. The knife flew up to stick in the ceiling as Tyana continued her backward roll to end on her feet.

"Wait!" Krast called as she nursed her wrist. "What about the children?"

Tyana laughed. "The children have been safe with their grandfather Merlin for a week now, Krast.

"I gave you a lesson in unarmed combat seven years ago. Do you really want to another one?"

It appeared that she did, and Tyana noticed that from a Judo approach she had graduated to a sort of Karate, possibly taught by Einstein, or, she thought, maybe someone else from Earth. It didn't matter, as she'd been trained by Marcus. Each kick or chop was blocked then countered with the same move executed so rapidly that Krast had no time to react. Tyana restricted her power to just enough to hurt, but not to disable.

Frank now understood Marcus's lack of concern and watched with him as the cause of all their troubles was reduced to a pain racked semi-crippled wreck that finally collapsed at Tyana's feet. Frank went to what he recognised as the only new installation in the ship and turned it off just as Deanna entered with two troopers to take charge of the prisoner.

***

As soon as she observed Tyana, Marcus, and Frank ride into their new tunnel, Deanna had her force land and within five minutes Frank's orders had been carried out. The town was surrounded and the dragons were overhead as was her cruiser.

Two minutes later the barrier went down and the engines of Oistrach's ship started followed a few moments later by the three surrounding vessels.

Simultaneously each of the three received a small missile with pinpoint accuracy into its engine and the troopers moved in.

Observing through the eyes of Mandrake and Shinlu, Carlos and Sophia, already in gestalt and with the same synergy factor Tyana had referred to seized mental hold of the large saucer and held it down against every effort Oistrach made to move it. Lengths of chain were called for rapidly, welded to radiate from a circle placed over the turret, and it was tied down just as had been his previous ship seven years earlier.

They tore off the door as the troopers approached it then Mandrake and Shinlu landed near Karim, Rebel, and Cindy, to be joined quickly by Carlos and Sophia on Javelin and Lotus Blossom.

As one of the Patrol captains emerged with Oistrach and what looked like a normal human man, presumably Einstein, Deanna carried out Krast.

"Put her on Cindy if you like," suggested Frank, "I don't mind walking back. I want to study something in Krast's ship anyway."

As they walked the half-mile out of town Krast recovered consciousness and Deanna stopped to allow her to sit astride the horse. "Who..r..you?" she mumbled through her swollen lips.

"Major Deanna Aristo. Borl Aristo was my father. I have to decide whether you should stand trial for his murder, or for the attempted assassination of Merlin, the president of this world."

As she said this Deanna saw Cindy prick her ears and turn her head to look at her passenger. Afterwards she swore that there must have been a connection between that look and Krast clutching at her chest in obvious agony. "Help me! …… I'm dy …ing."

Only those privileged to read the full account of events that year would realise just how appropriate her last words were.

EPILOGUE

CAMELOT...THREE MONTHS LATER.

As expected the store of theurgen had been found in Oistrach's ship and quickly returned to its rightful place by the healers, the Patrol supplying transport as needed.

Oistrach had been taken for trial, as had his gang. This time there would be no mistake with the rehabilitation equipment. Einstein turned out to be a scientist deliberately recruited by Krast on a clandestine visit to Earth. The poor fool thought himself in love with her. On Marcus's orders he was also given the rehab. treatment to erase all memory of the last six months and taken back to Earth.

Tyana blamed herself for being too hard on Krast and causing her death but whilst the Godhe were allowed to believe this, Melanie privately admitted responsibility, and insisted that she had no regrets. Even Laura, the most gentle of the healers, when she remembered her first Princess and the imprisonment of Simeon was glad Melanie had had the strength to carry out her oath. She had settled in well to sharing the healers work with Laura and Megan and was engaged to Darryl. By mutual agreement she was still a virgin and would remain so until her wedding night.

Thomas was nursing a broken heart as Fallon had finished her studies and returned to Europe.

Gideon, a changed man, had apologised in French to Fallon, then later in English to Merlin and Laura. He was back in command with Deanna volunteering for temporary detachment to Refuge.

Frank was based in Camelot in Merlin's old quarters. On learning from Rebel of the help he had given in the fight against Krast, Scimitar went through an annexation ceremony with him and became his partner and best friend. Thus Frank had the advantages of telepathy and roughly Gold ability at his disposal.

Johann married Kresh, to Greta's delight, and Merlin forbade her extradition on the grounds that (i) she was now a Refuge citizen, and (ii) had in any case not been responsible for her actions. Learning of Frank's annexation with Scimitar, which the latter had suggested as soon as Frank returned to New America, Kaiser lost no time in having his own favourite mare joined with Kresh. The bond between her and Jann, as she called him, became even stronger as she experienced some of the power she had once thought to overcome in Tyana.

The delayed meeting of Council Heads had taken place two months after the arrest of Oistrach and death of Krast. It had been unanimously agreed that Merlin's policy of avoiding further secrecy by the Godhe be followed and as a direct result the entire Council of Old Ones was present by invitation on Refuge.

Determined to have relationships as informal as possible, Merlin insisted that the first meeting be over dinner at the Counters' ranch. All those involved were present with Carlos, Sophia, Johann, and Kresh representing Europe, Mandrake and Shinlu the dragons (their triad involvement not being known by the Godhe,) Cantor and Vernique the weres, Marcus, Tyana, Merlin, Laura, and Frank the North Americans.

In the interest of balance, and because of their respective scientific backgrounds, Deanna was seated with Frank. The twelve members of the Old Ones were equal guests of honour, and for the duration of their stay each had the services of a young unicorn of the same gender as themselves to serve as instant translator.

No business was conducted that evening, but dinner followed by live music and with everyone circulating freely set the atmosphere Merlin wanted for the next morning's discussion. He brought the Assembly to order, summarized the events of first seven years ago, and then the current year.

"Nothing like that must ever be allowed to happen again! My good friend Aristo tried to have our races mix freely after our last crisis, and I suggest that if he'd had his way then he would be alive today.

"You probably think of us as a primitive people on a backward world, but may I remind you that twice we have beaten a well armed force equipped with your most up to date weapons. We even devised a plan to retake one of our towns when your Galactic Patrol was powerless.

"I demand that in future when your recruiting team brings someone from our Earth, or Tellus III as you like to call it, they land openly either here for English, or Paris for French, and hand the new arrival over to us. You will also help by supplying a small quantity of machine tools and advice Frank Baron here requests.

"In return we propose to solve the problem which has baffled your doctors for generations. I will let Frank explain."

Frank waited until the mutterings between the Old Ones died down.

"We did not realise when Aristo referred to the Theurgen chromosome that your knowledge was so sparse in that field. We thought he was just keeping it simple for our benefit.

"On Earth we have the ability to identify which gene, the small parts of which the chromosomes are made up is responsible for each characteristic or defect. I am sure we can, if allowed to, recruit a geneticist from Earth who will quickly devise a treatment. He or she may or may not be able to cure this generation, but I am certain that within a few years no more sufferers will be born.

"I would appreciate permission to recruit a few scientists as well, but that I don't insist on."

<< *They won't admit it yet, Frank, but you'll get your wish. They can't resist the promise of a cure.* >>

<< *Thanks, Scimitar!* >>

Thus began a new phase in Refuge's history.

Coming soon:

Unicorn Witch III:
Return to Earth

Printed in the United Kingdom
by Lightning Source UK Ltd.
105686UKS00001B/250-267